NOTES ON A THESIS

TIPHAINE RIVIÈRE

NOTES ON A THESIS

TRANSLATED BY FRANCESCA BARRIE

JONATHAN CAPE
LONDON

1 3 5 7 9 10 8 6 4 2

Jonathan Cape, an imprint of Vintage,
20 Vauxhall Bridge Road,
London SW1V 2SA

Jonathan Cape is part of the Penguin Random House group of companies
whose addresses can be found at global.penguinrandomhouse.com

Penguin Random House UK

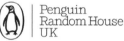

First published as *Carnets de thèse* by Éditions du Seuil, Paris in 2015
First published in the United Kingdom by Jonathan Cape in 2016

penguin.co.uk/vintage

A CIP catalogue record for this book is available from the British Library

ISBN 9781910702499

Printed and bound in India by Replika Press Pvt Ltd

Penguin Random House is committed to a sustainable future for our business, our readers and our planet. This book is made from Forest Stewardship Council® certified paper.

MIX
Paper from responsible sources
FSC www.fsc.org FSC® C018179

INSTITUT FRANÇAIS
ROYAUME-UNI

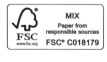

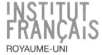

This book is supported by the Institut français (Royaume-Uni) as part of the Burgess programme

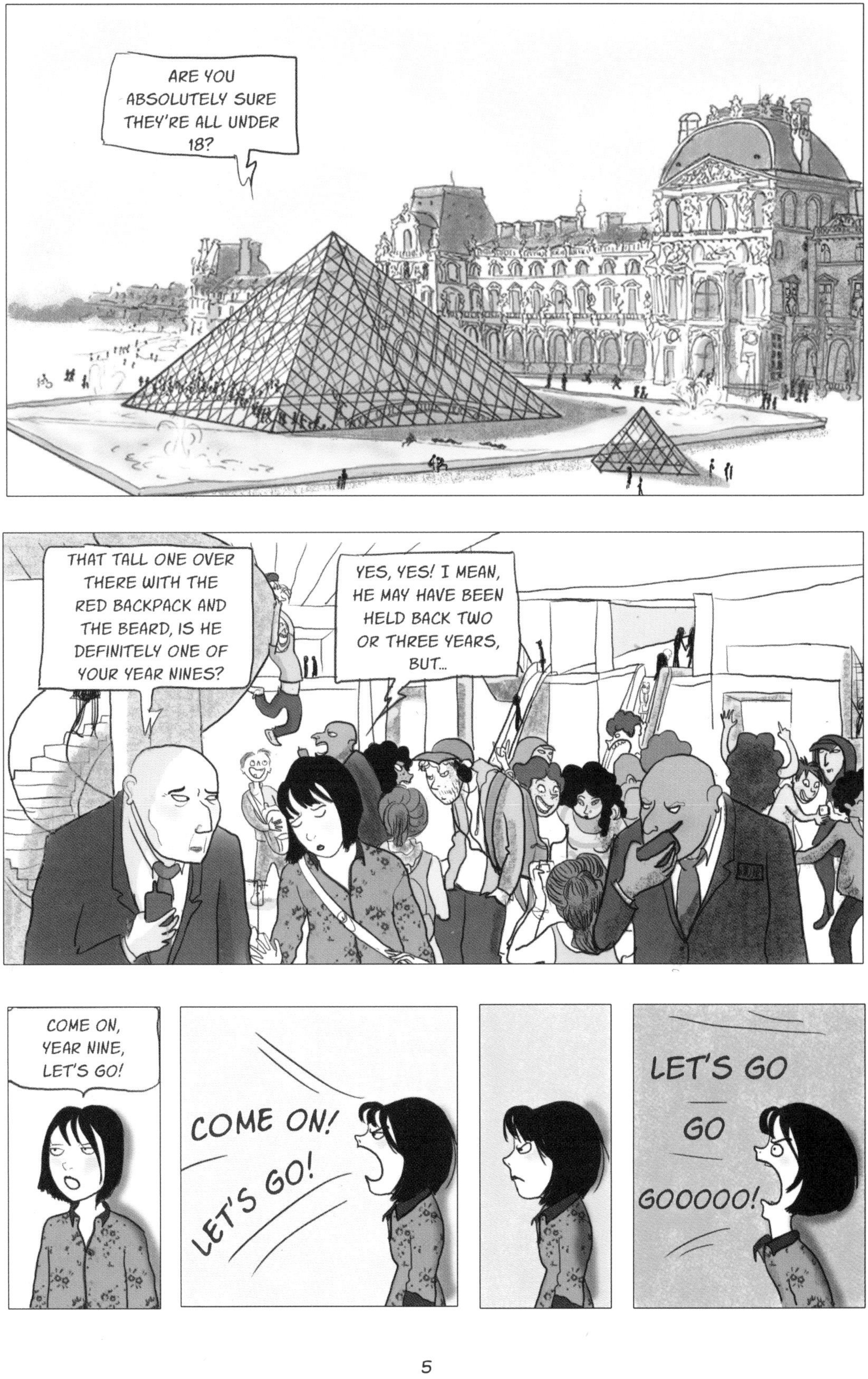
ARE YOU ABSOLUTELY SURE THEY'RE ALL UNDER 18?
THAT TALL ONE OVER THERE WITH THE RED BACKPACK AND THE BEARD, IS HE DEFINITELY ONE OF YOUR YEAR NINES?
YES, YES! I MEAN, HE MAY HAVE BEEN HELD BACK TWO OR THREE YEARS, BUT...
COME ON, YEAR NINE, LET'S GO!
COME ON!
LET'S GO!
LET'S GO
GO
GOOOOO!

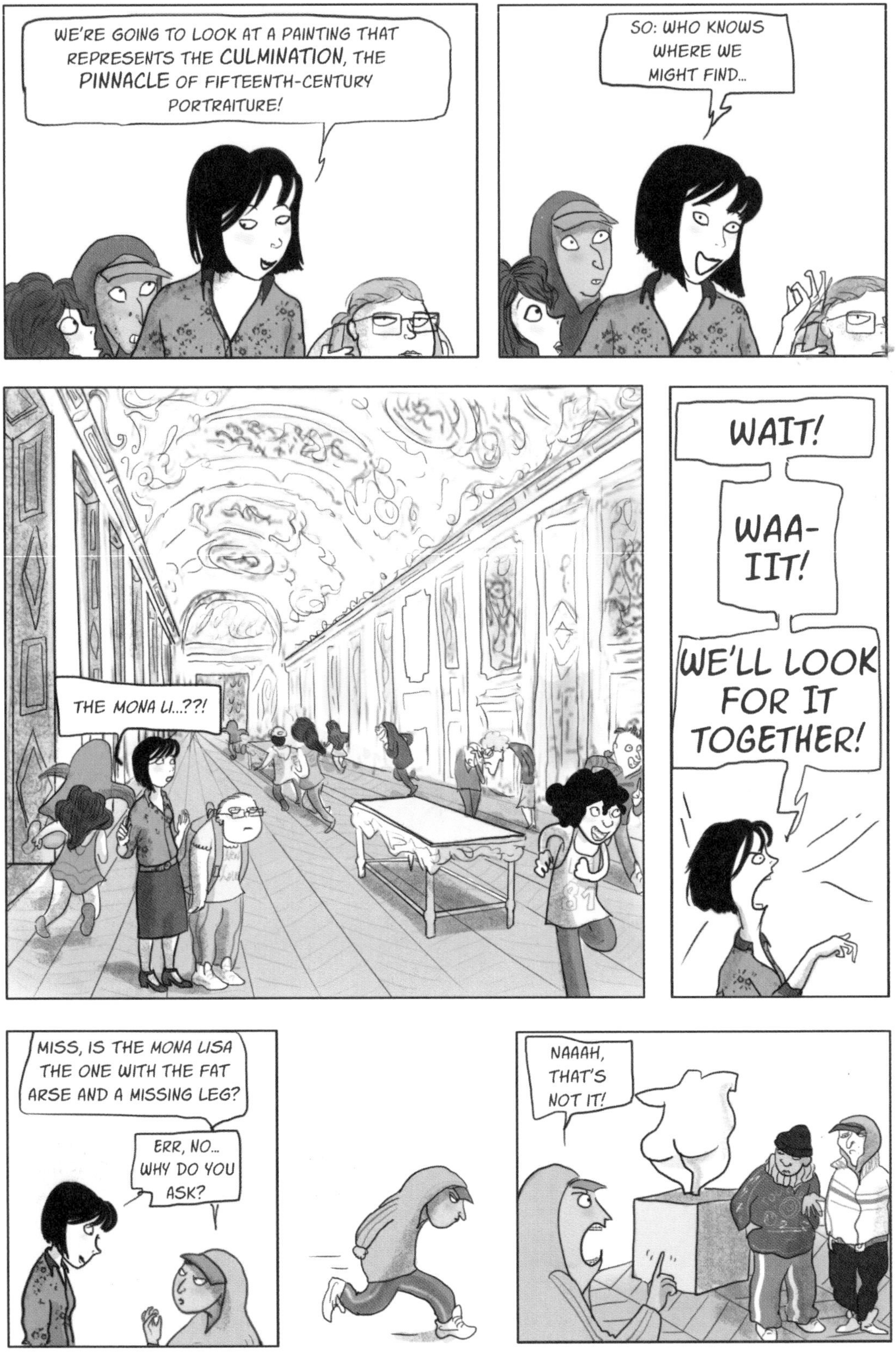

WE'RE GOING TO LOOK AT A PAINTING THAT REPRESENTS THE CULMINATION, THE PINNACLE OF FIFTEENTH-CENTURY PORTRAITURE!
SO: WHO KNOWS WHERE WE MIGHT FIND...
THE MONA LI...??!
WAIT!
WAA-IIT!
WE'LL LOOK FOR IT TOGETHER!
MISS, IS THE MONA LISA THE ONE WITH THE FAT ARSE AND A MISSING LEG?
ERR, NO... WHY DO YOU ASK?
NAAAH, THAT'S NOT IT!

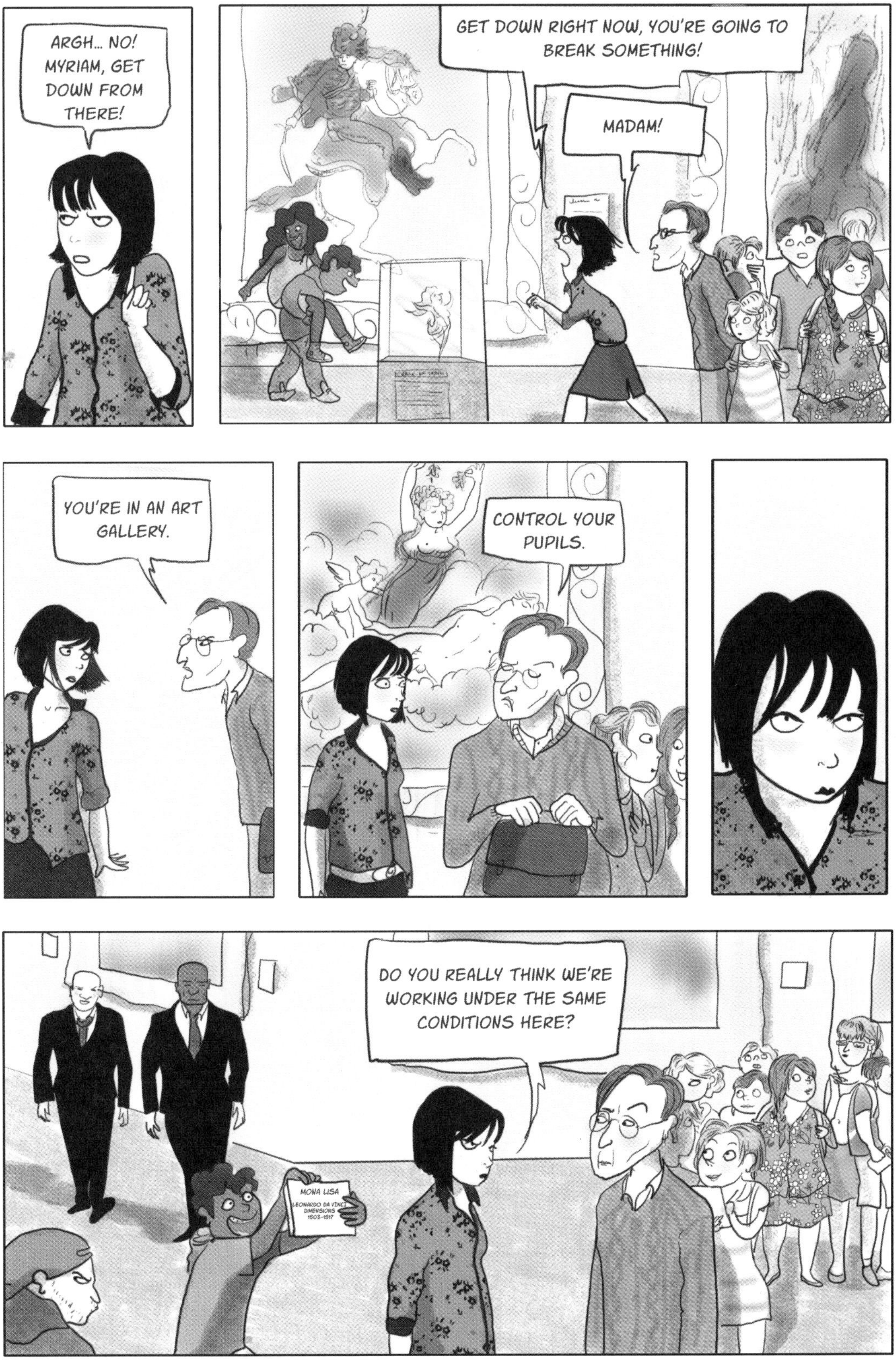
ARGH... NO! MYRIAM, GET DOWN FROM THERE!
GET DOWN RIGHT NOW, YOU'RE GOING TO BREAK SOMETHING!
MADAM!
YOU'RE IN AN ART GALLERY.
CONTROL YOUR PUPILS.
DO YOU REALLY THINK WE'RE WORKING UNDER THE SAME CONDITIONS HERE?
MONA LISA
LEONARDO DA VINCI
DIMENSIONS
1503-1517

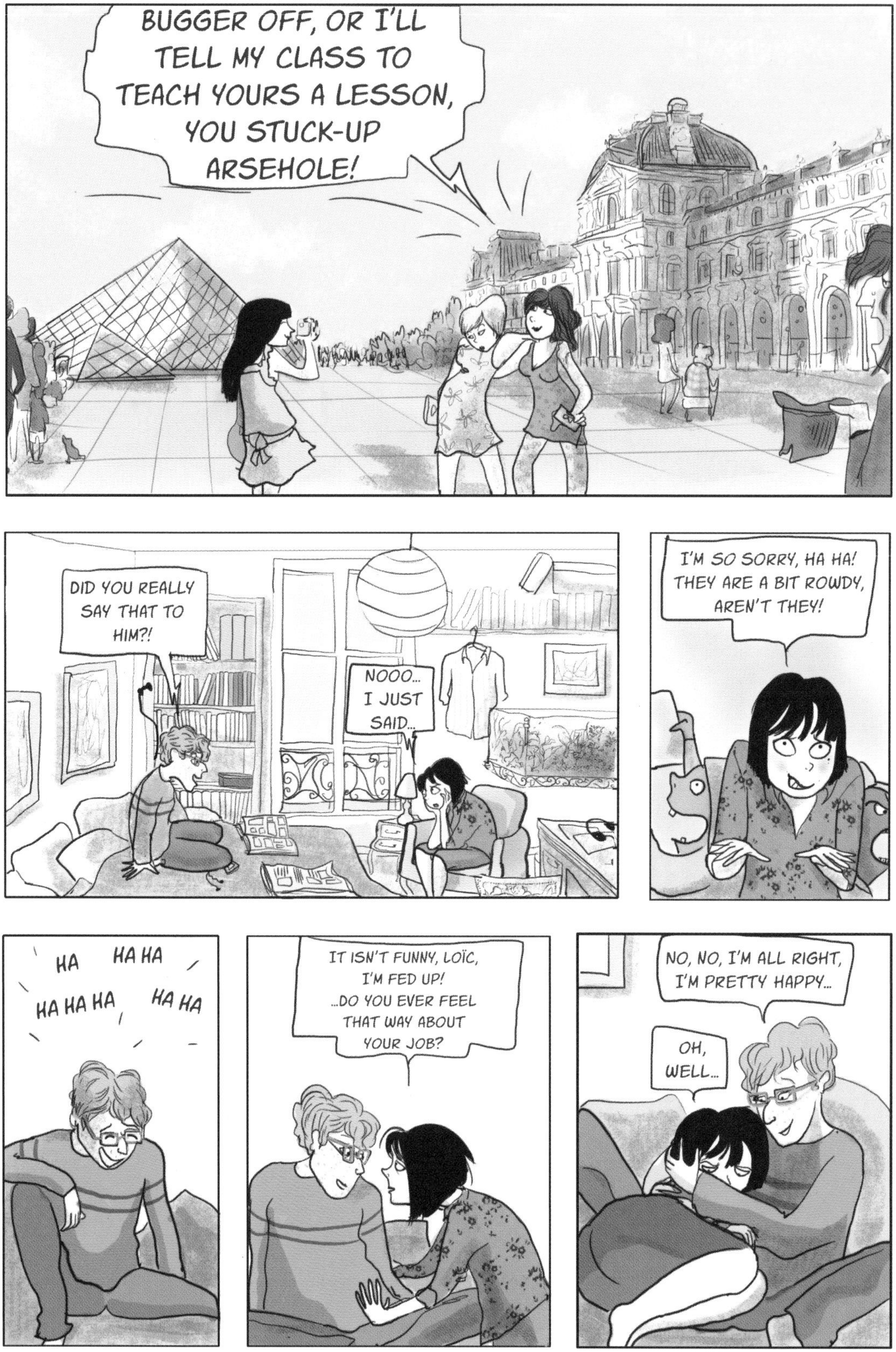
BUGGER OFF, OR I'LL TELL MY CLASS TO TEACH YOURS A LESSON, YOU STUCK-UP ARSEHOLE!
DID YOU REALLY SAY THAT TO HIM?!
NOOO... I JUST SAID...
I'M SO SORRY, HA HA! THEY ARE A BIT ROWDY, AREN'T THEY!
HA HA HA
HA HA HA HA HA
IT ISN'T FUNNY, LOÏC, I'M FED UP! ...DO YOU EVER FEEL THAT WAY ABOUT YOUR JOB?
NO, NO, I'M ALL RIGHT, I'M PRETTY HAPPY...
OH, WELL...

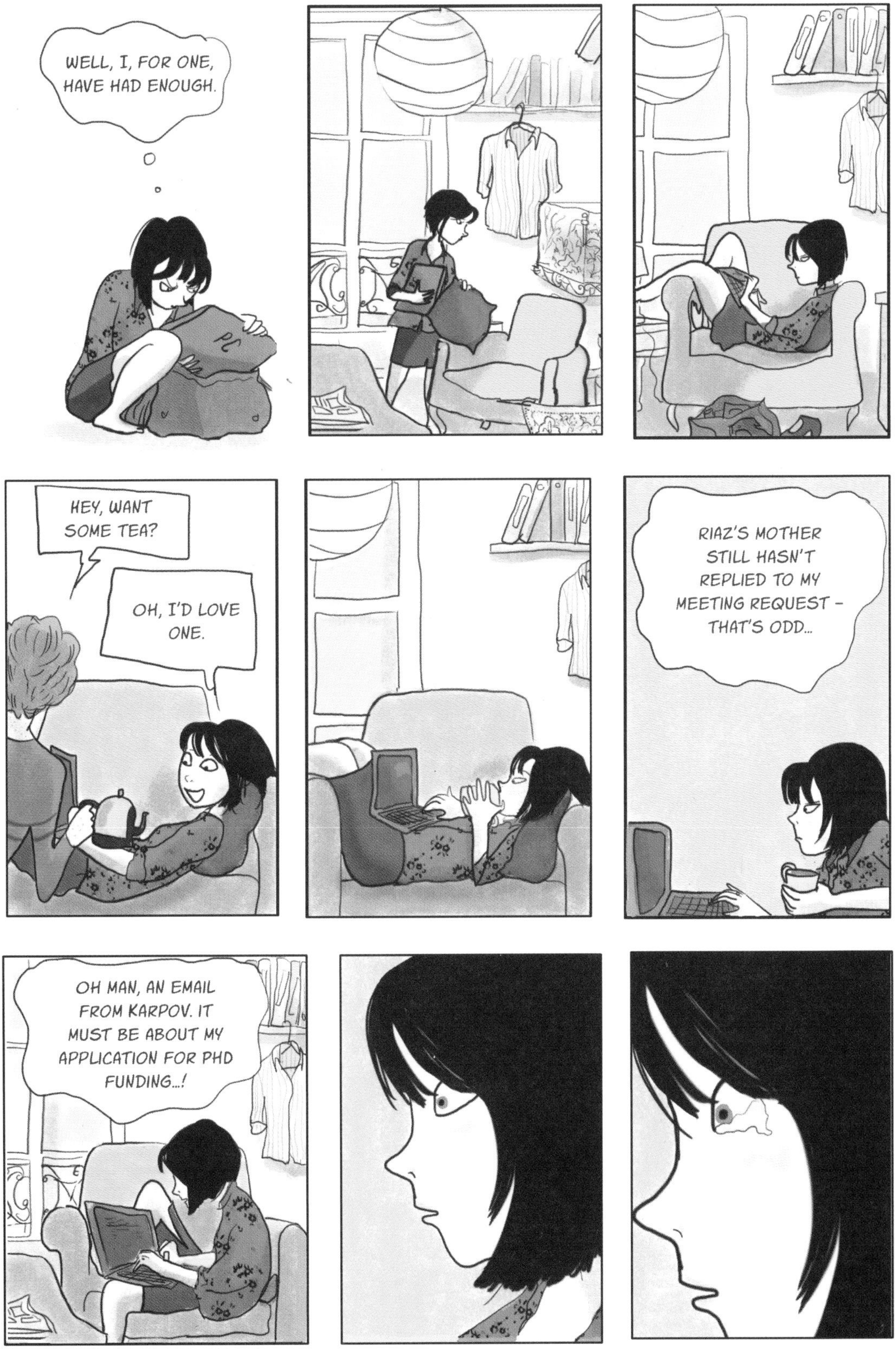
WELL, I, FOR ONE, HAVE HAD ENOUGH.
PC
HEY, WANT SOME TEA?
OH, I'D LOVE ONE.
RIAZ'S MOTHER STILL HASN'T REPLIED TO MY MEETING REQUEST – THAT'S ODD...
OH MAN, AN EMAIL FROM KARPOV. IT MUST BE ABOUT MY APPLICATION FOR PHD FUNDING...!

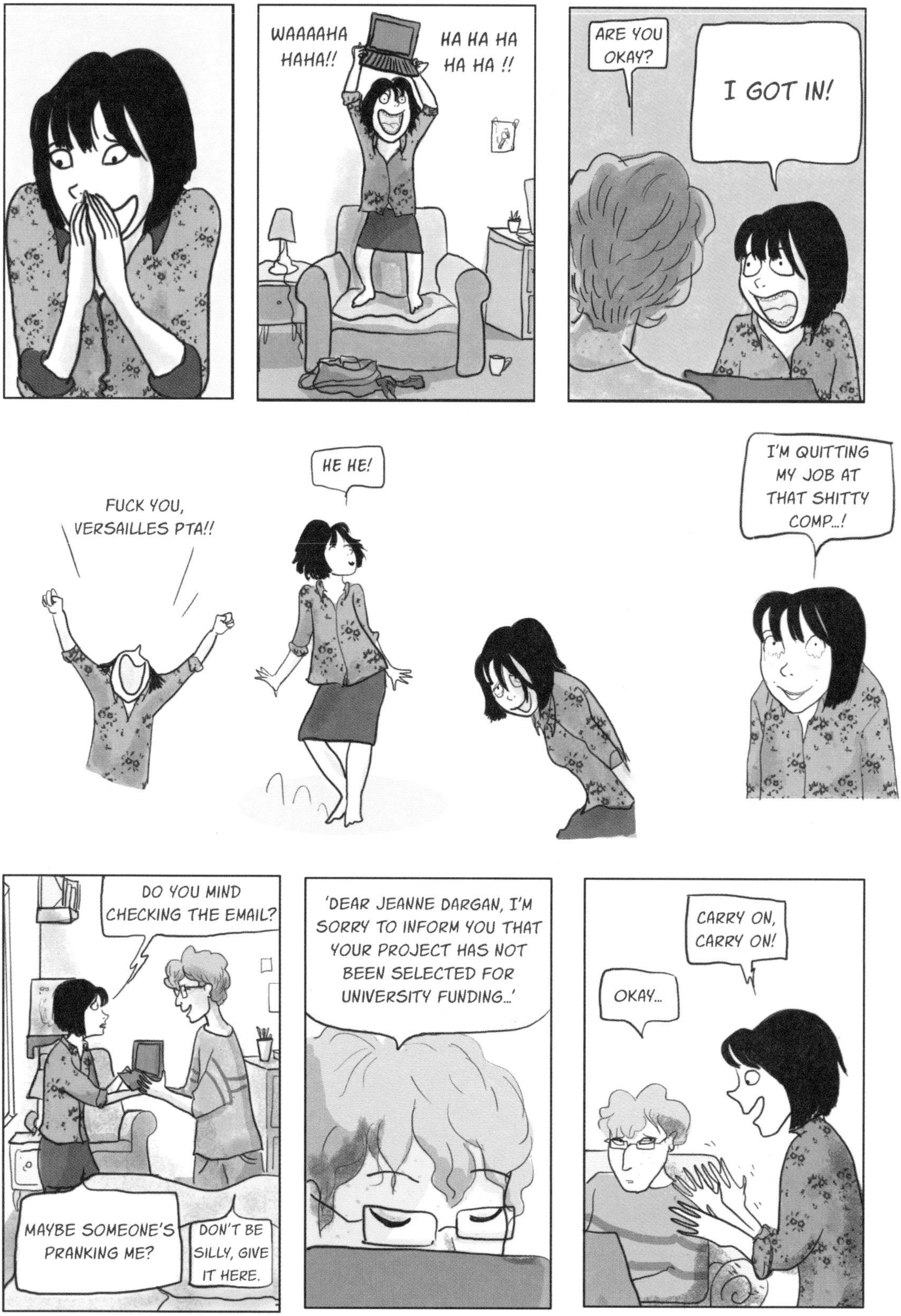

WAAAAHA HAHA!!
HA HA HA HA HA !!
ARE YOU OKAY?
I GOT IN!
FUCK YOU, VERSAILLES PTA!!
HE HE!
I'M QUITTING MY JOB AT THAT SHITTY COMP...!
DO YOU MIND CHECKING THE EMAIL?
MAYBE SOMEONE'S PRANKING ME?
DON'T BE SILLY, GIVE IT HERE.
'DEAR JEANNE DARGAN, I'M SORRY TO INFORM YOU THAT YOUR PROJECT HAS NOT BEEN SELECTED FOR UNIVERSITY FUNDING...'
CARRY ON, CARRY ON!
OKAY...

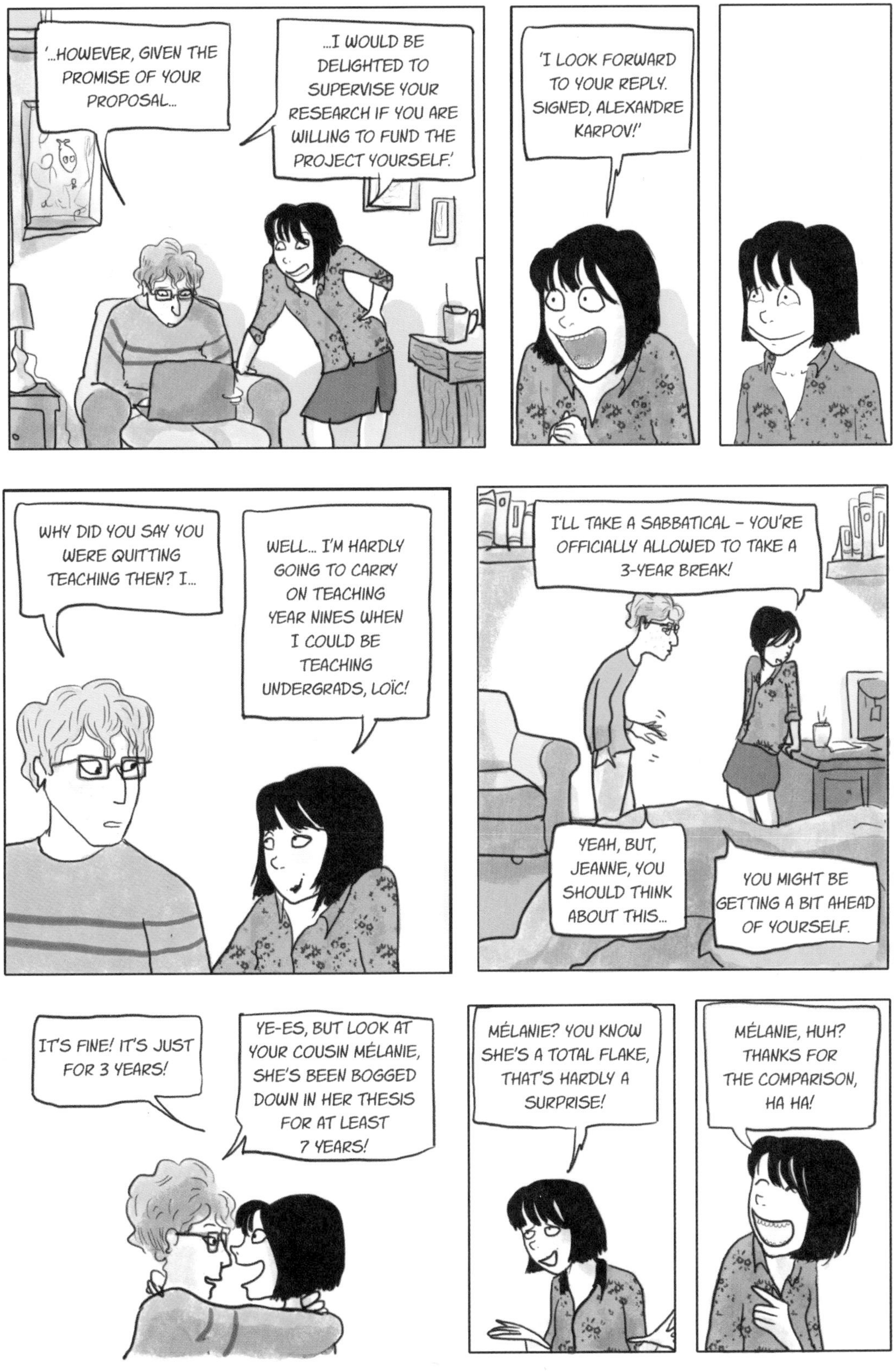
'...HOWEVER, GIVEN THE PROMISE OF YOUR PROPOSAL...
...I WOULD BE DELIGHTED TO SUPERVISE YOUR RESEARCH IF YOU ARE WILLING TO FUND THE PROJECT YOURSELF.'
'I LOOK FORWARD TO YOUR REPLY. SIGNED, ALEXANDRE KARPOV!'
WHY DID YOU SAY YOU WERE QUITTING TEACHING THEN? I...
WELL... I'M HARDLY GOING TO CARRY ON TEACHING YEAR NINES WHEN I COULD BE TEACHING UNDERGRADS, LOÏC!
I'LL TAKE A SABBATICAL – YOU'RE OFFICIALLY ALLOWED TO TAKE A 3-YEAR BREAK!
YEAH, BUT, JEANNE, YOU SHOULD THINK ABOUT THIS...
YOU MIGHT BE GETTING A BIT AHEAD OF YOURSELF.
IT'S FINE! IT'S JUST FOR 3 YEARS!
YE-ES, BUT LOOK AT YOUR COUSIN MÉLANIE, SHE'S BEEN BOGGED DOWN IN HER THESIS FOR AT LEAST 7 YEARS!
MÉLANIE? YOU KNOW SHE'S A TOTAL FLAKE, THAT'S HARDLY A SURPRISE!
MÉLANIE, HUH? THANKS FOR THE COMPARISON, HA HA!

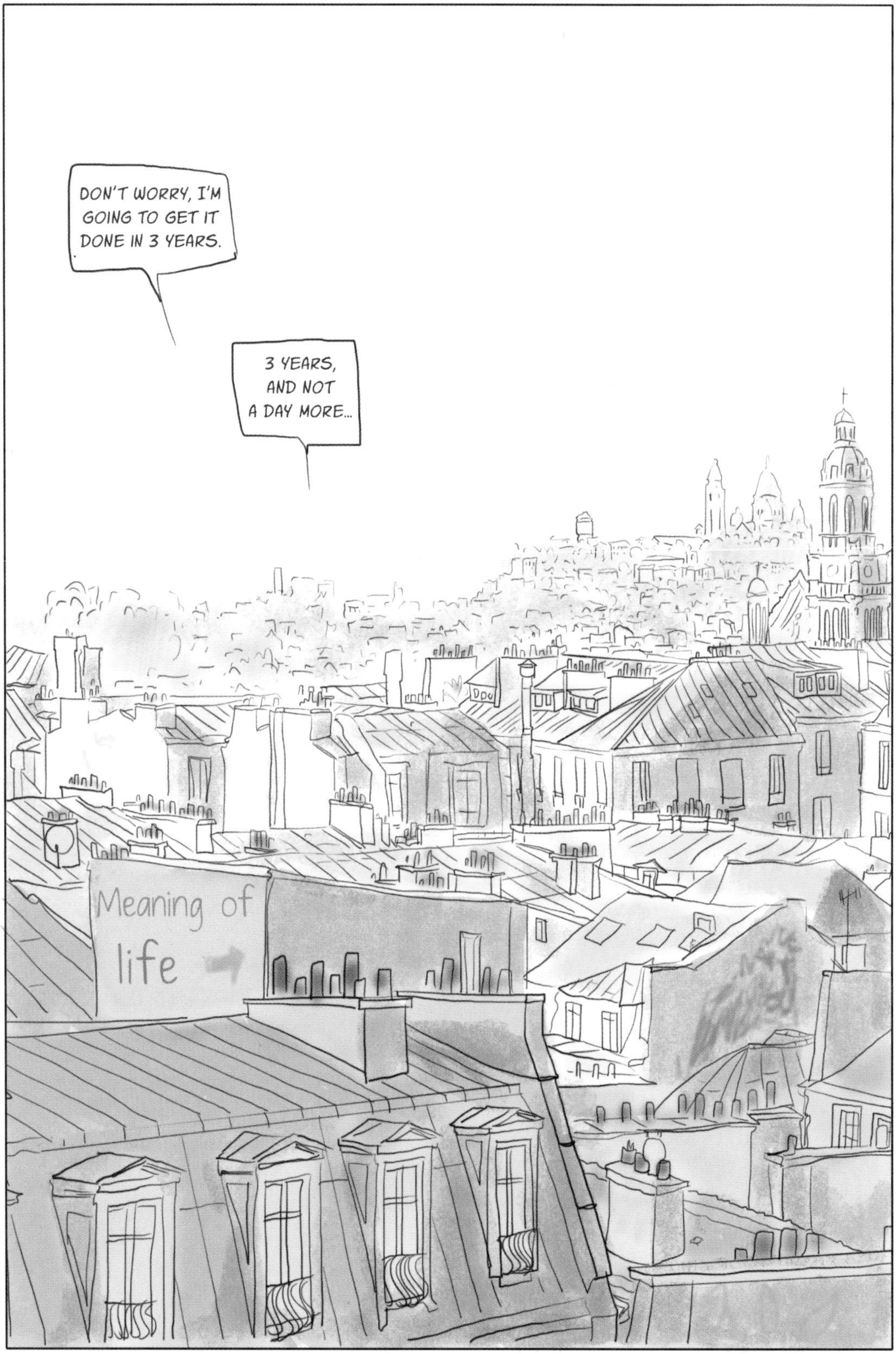
DON'T WORRY, I'M GOING TO GET IT DONE IN 3 YEARS.
3 YEARS, AND NOT A DAY MORE...
Meaning of life

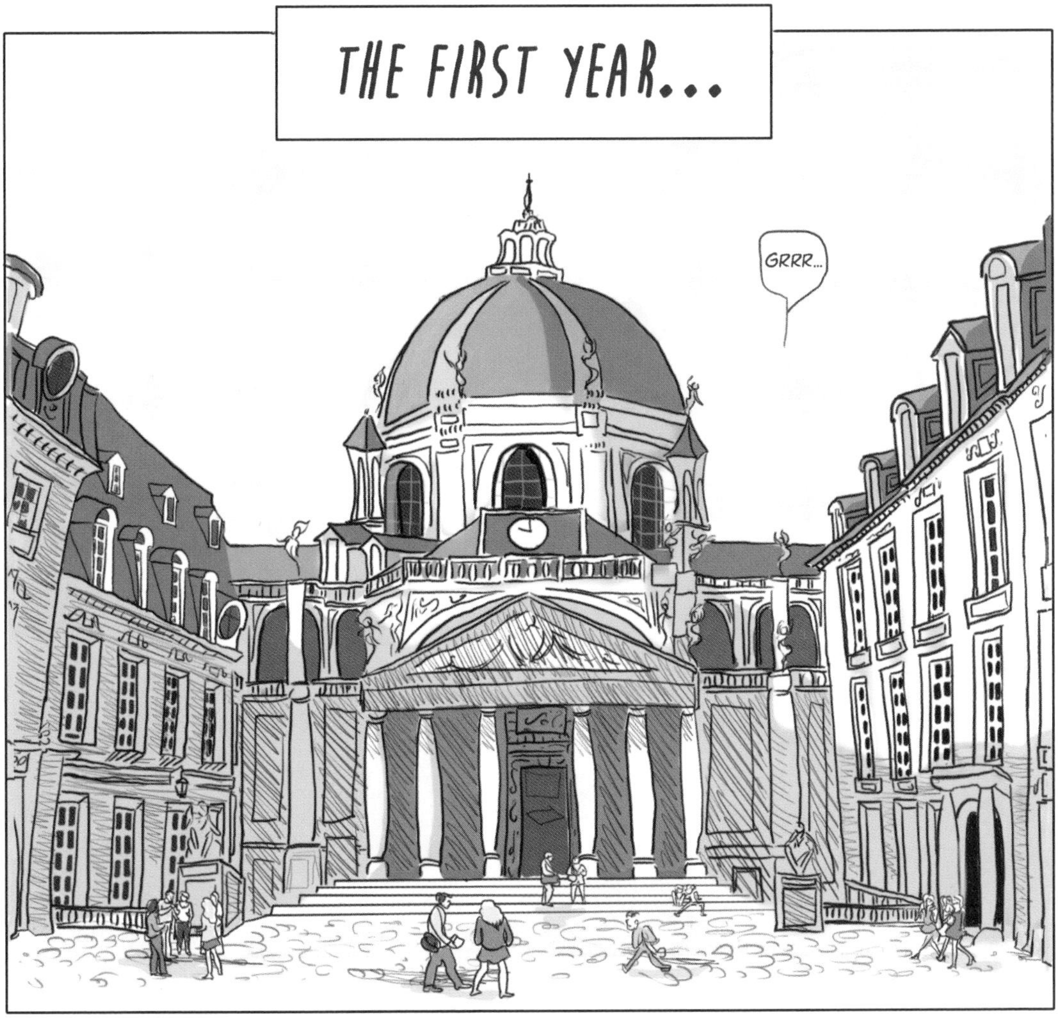
THE FIRST YEAR...
GRRR...

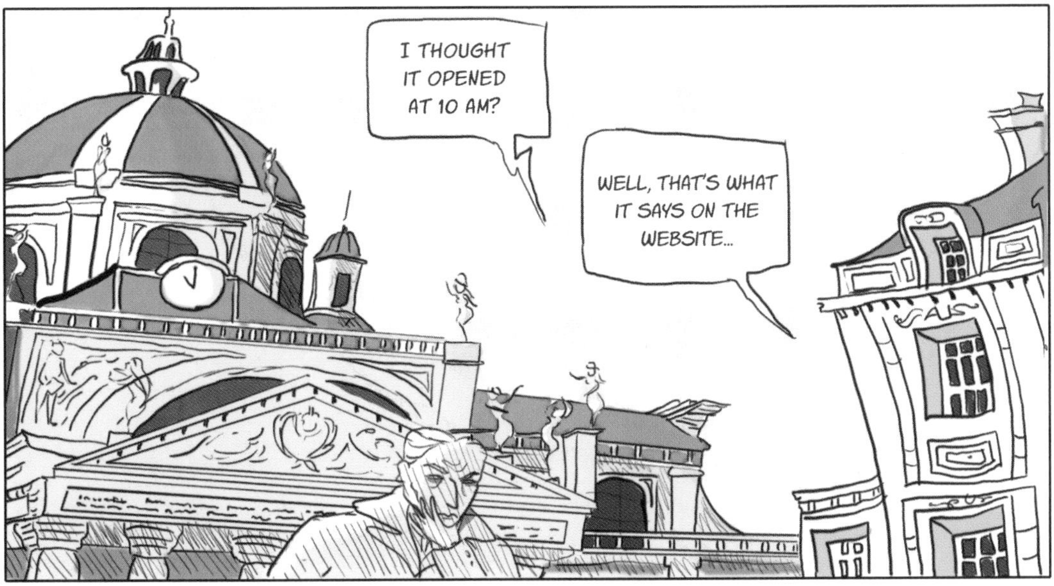
I THOUGHT IT OPENED AT 10 AM?
WELL, THAT'S WHAT IT SAYS ON THE WEBSITE...

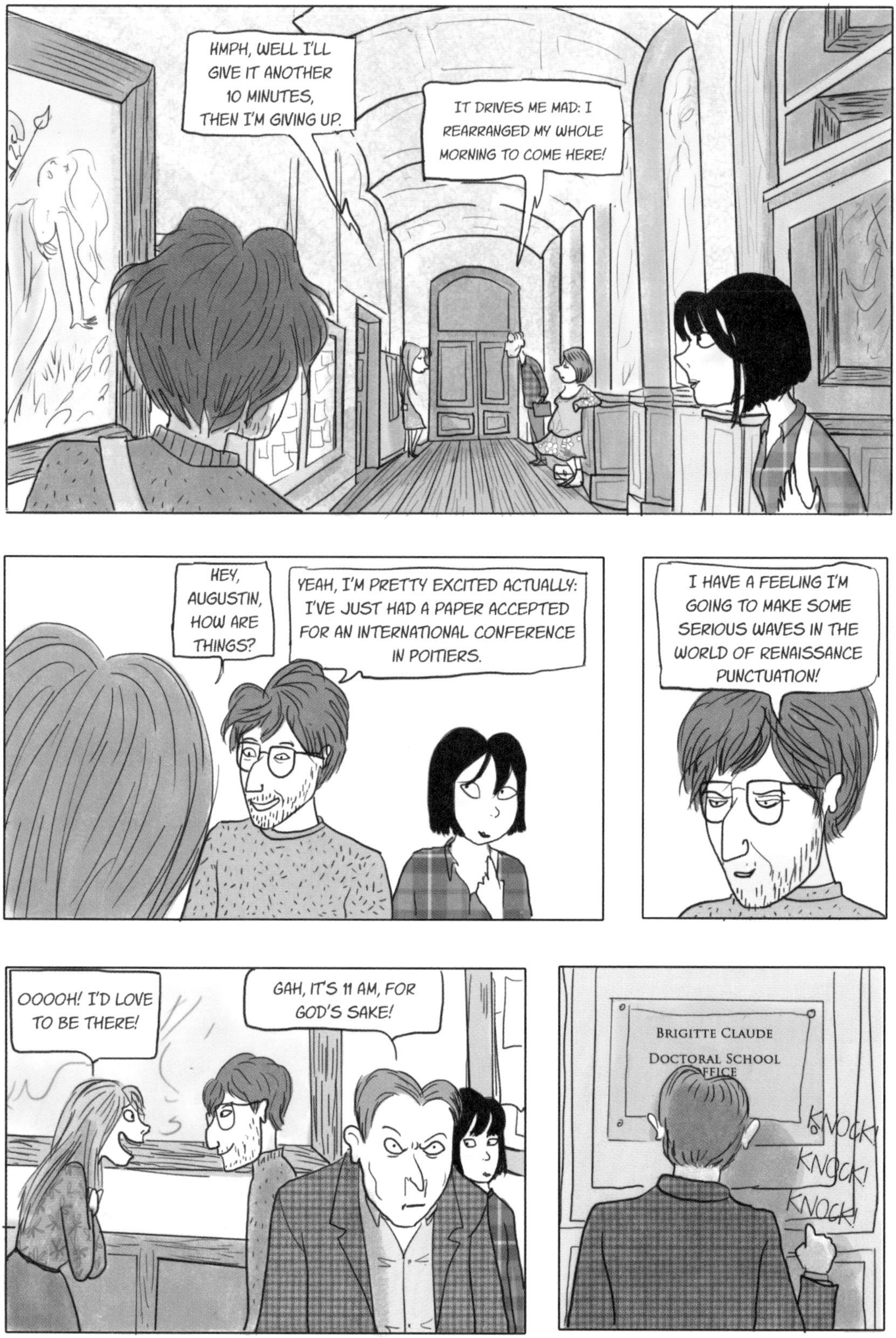
HMPH, WELL I'LL GIVE IT ANOTHER 10 MINUTES, THEN I'M GIVING UP.
IT DRIVES ME MAD: I REARRANGED MY WHOLE MORNING TO COME HERE!
HEY, AUGUSTIN, HOW ARE THINGS?
YEAH, I'M PRETTY EXCITED ACTUALLY: I'VE JUST HAD A PAPER ACCEPTED FOR AN INTERNATIONAL CONFERENCE IN POITIERS.
I HAVE A FEELING I'M GOING TO MAKE SOME SERIOUS WAVES IN THE WORLD OF RENAISSANCE PUNCTUATION!
OOOOH! I'D LOVE TO BE THERE!
GAH, IT'S 11 AM, FOR GOD'S SAKE!
BRIGITTE CLAUDE
DOCTORAL SCHOOL
KNOCK! KNOCK! KNOCK!

BRIGITTE CLAUDE HAS BEEN THE SECRETARY FOR THE DOCTORAL SCHOOL SINCE 1987.

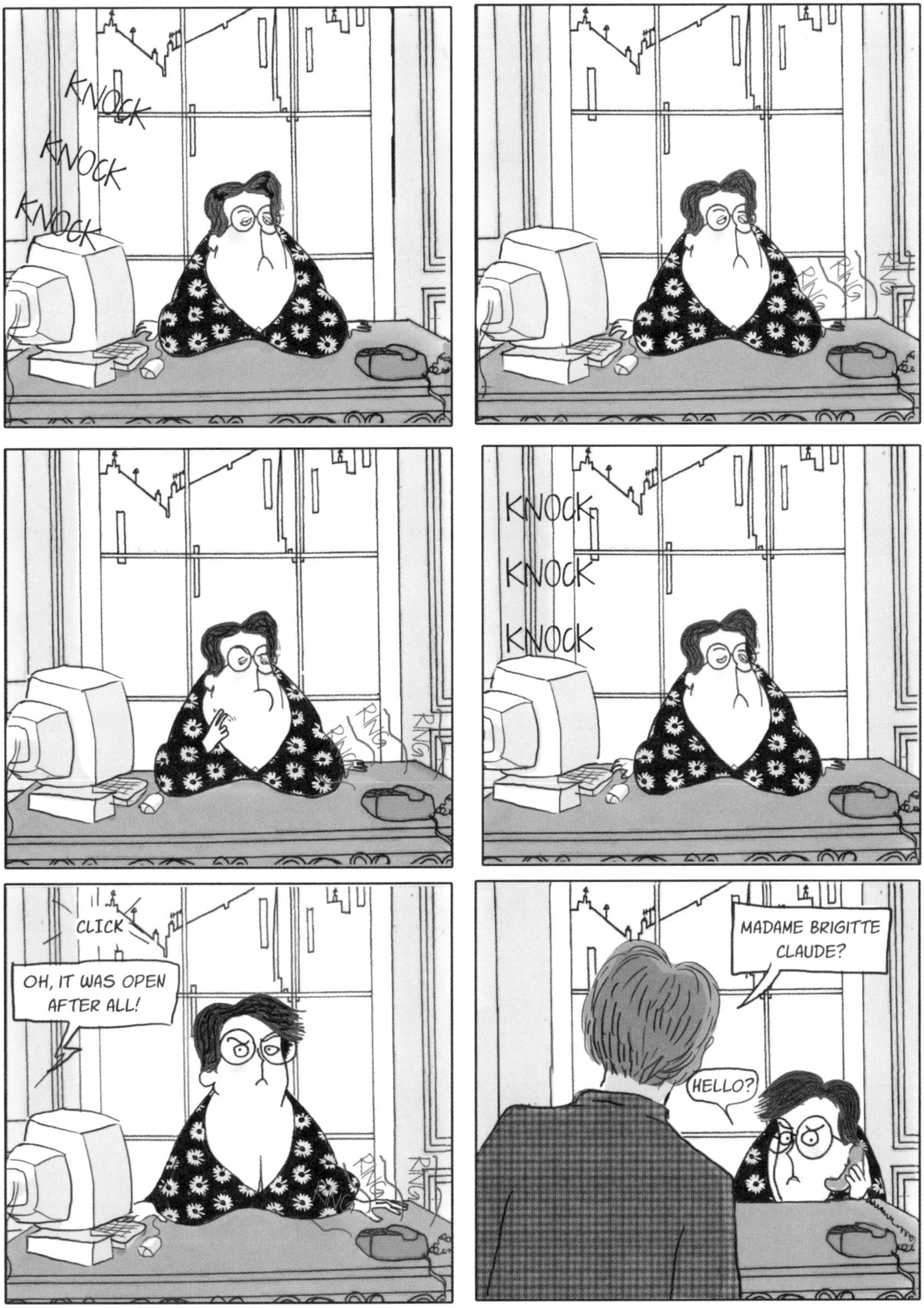
KNOCK
KNOCK
KNOCK
RING
RING
RING
RING
RING
RING
KNOCK
KNOCK
KNOCK
CLICK
OH, IT WAS OPEN AFTER ALL!
RING
RING
RING
MADAME BRIGITTE CLAUDE?
HELLO?

BRIGITTE CLAUDE HAS A SECRET TACTIC: FEIGNING GROSS INCOMPETENCE TO WEAR DOWN HER ADVERSARIES, UNTIL THEY EVENTUALLY STOP ASKING HER TO DO ANYTHING AT ALL.

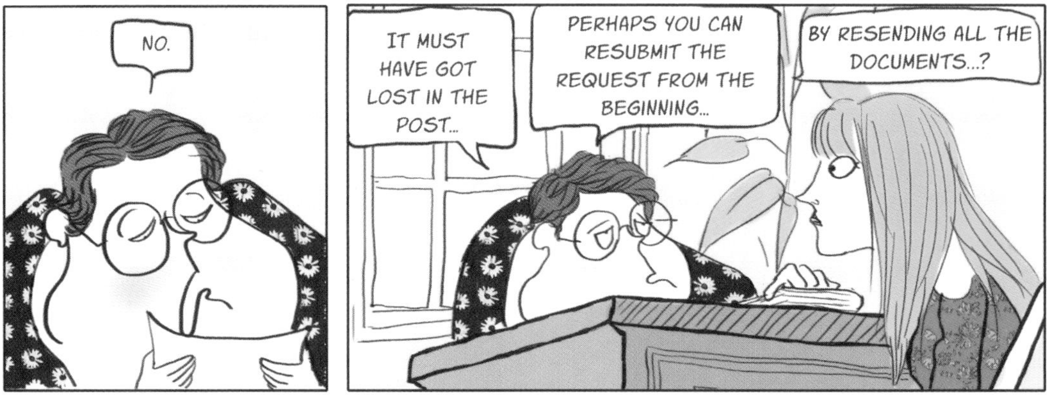
NO.
IT MUST HAVE GOT LOST IN THE POST...
PERHAPS YOU CAN RESUBMIT THE REQUEST FROM THE BEGINNING...
BY RESENDING ALL THE DOCUMENTS...?

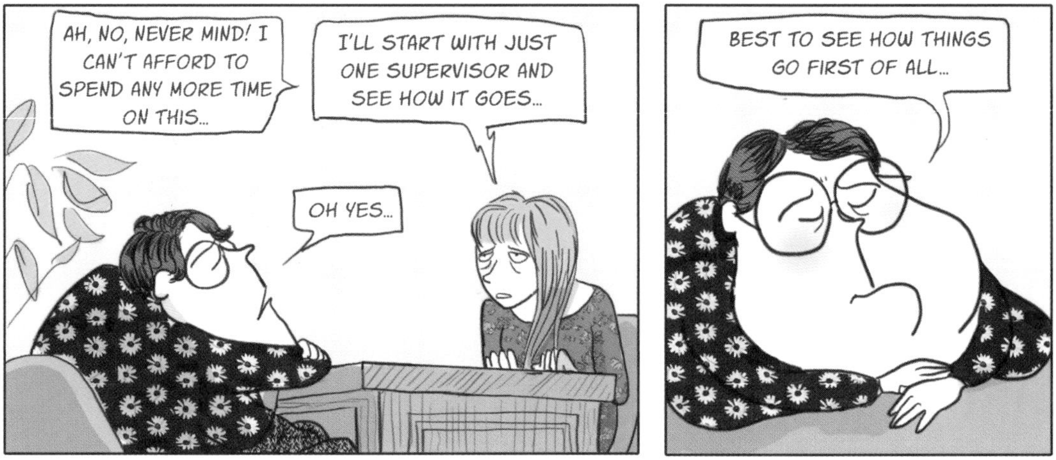
AH, NO, NEVER MIND! I CAN'T AFFORD TO SPEND ANY MORE TIME ON THIS...
I'LL START WITH JUST ONE SUPERVISOR AND SEE HOW IT GOES...
OH YES...
BEST TO SEE HOW THINGS GO FIRST OF ALL...

ANOTHER VERY EFFECTIVE STRATEGY IS TO FEIGN THE EXACT OPPOSITE.

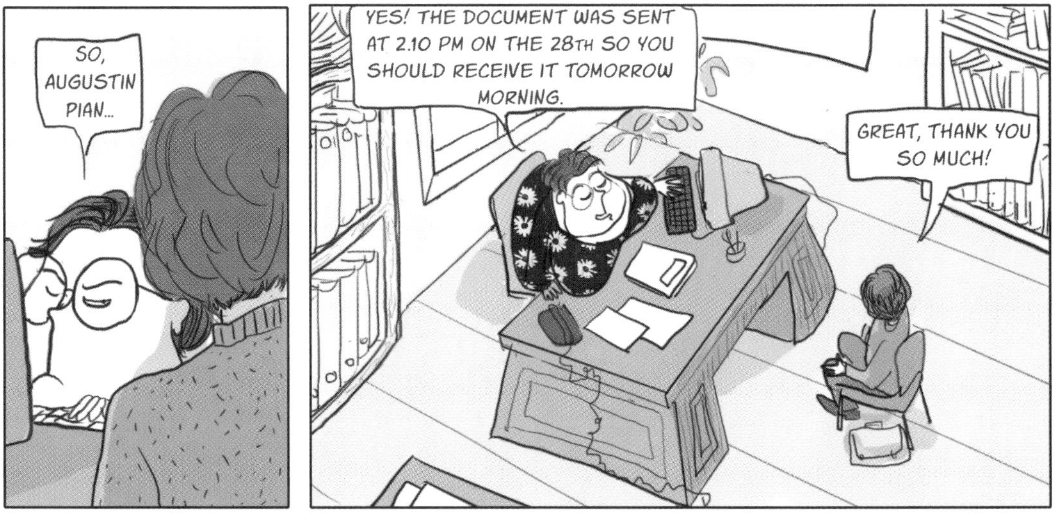
SO, AUGUSTIN PIAN...
YES! THE DOCUMENT WAS SENT AT 2.10 PM ON THE 28TH SO YOU SHOULD RECEIVE IT TOMORROW MORNING.
GREAT, THANK YOU SO MUCH!

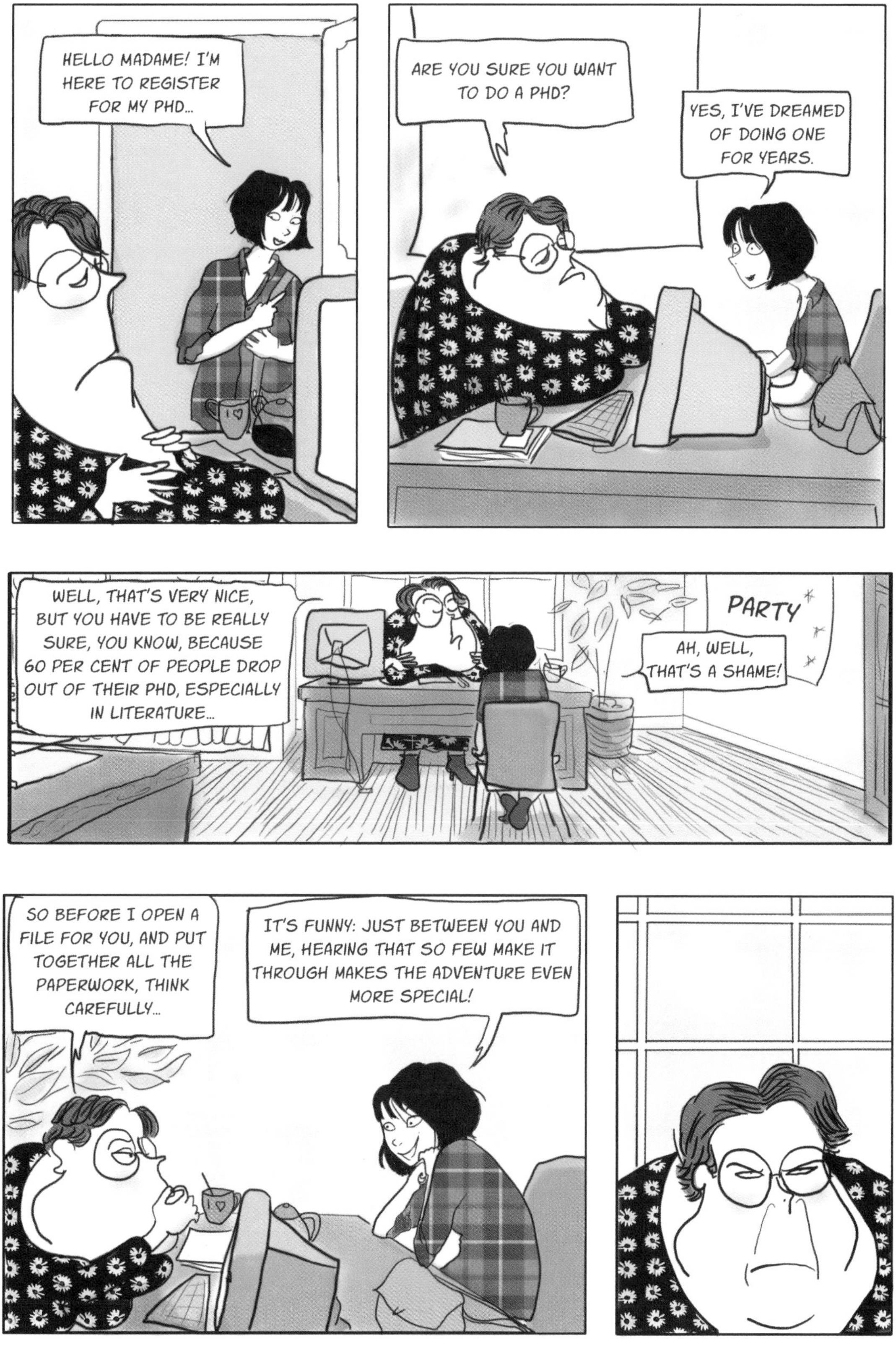
HELLO MADAME! I'M HERE TO REGISTER FOR MY PHD...
ARE YOU SURE YOU WANT TO DO A PHD?
YES, I'VE DREAMED OF DOING ONE FOR YEARS.
WELL, THAT'S VERY NICE, BUT YOU HAVE TO BE REALLY SURE, YOU KNOW, BECAUSE 60 PER CENT OF PEOPLE DROP OUT OF THEIR PHD, ESPECIALLY IN LITERATURE...
PARTY
AH, WELL, THAT'S A SHAME!
SO BEFORE I OPEN A FILE FOR YOU, AND PUT TOGETHER ALL THE PAPERWORK, THINK CAREFULLY...
IT'S FUNNY: JUST BETWEEN YOU AND ME, HEARING THAT SO FEW MAKE IT THROUGH MAKES THE ADVENTURE EVEN MORE SPECIAL!

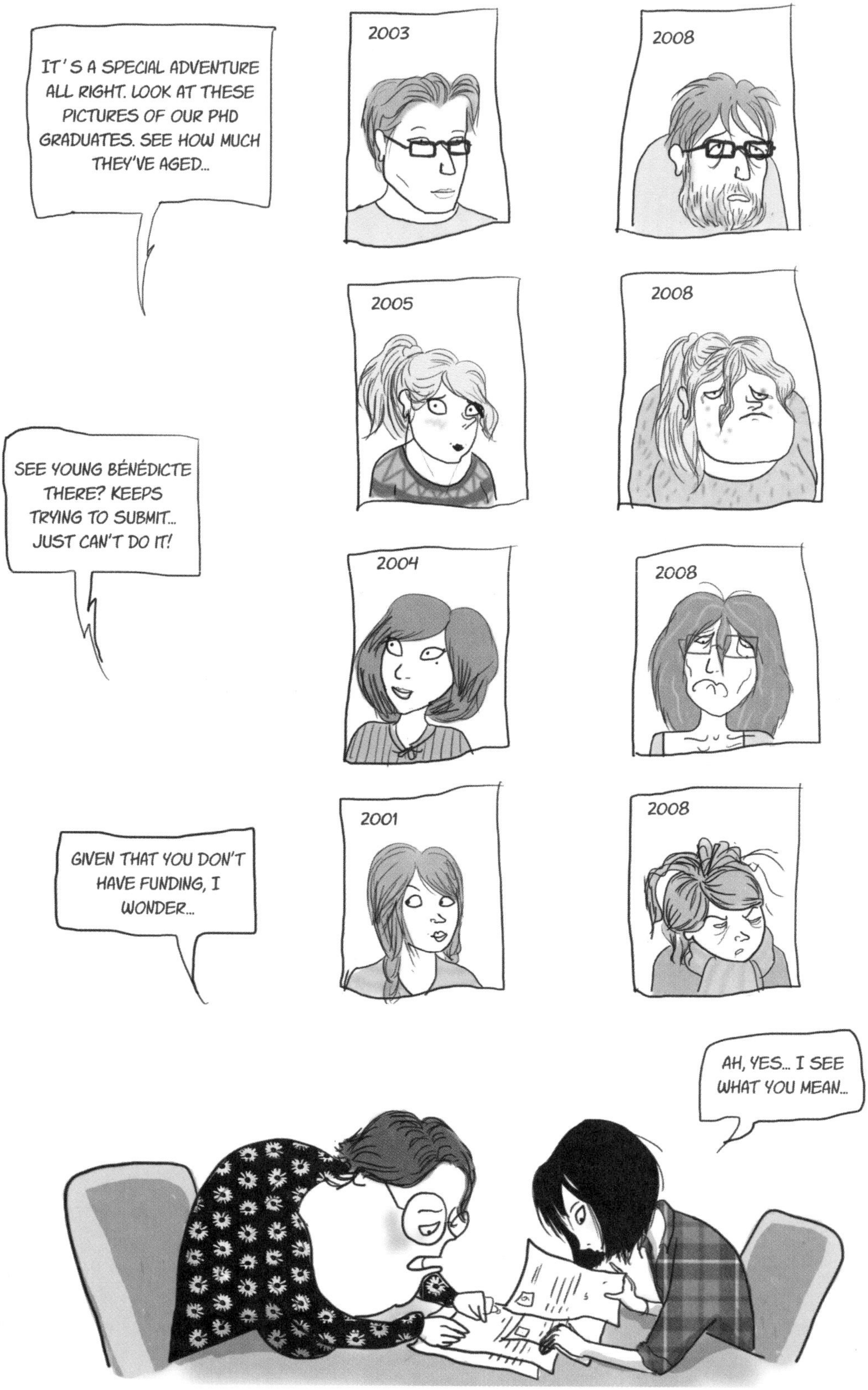
IT'S A SPECIAL ADVENTURE ALL RIGHT. LOOK AT THESE PICTURES OF OUR PHD GRADUATES. SEE HOW MUCH THEY'VE AGED...
2003
2008
2005
2008
SEE YOUNG BÉNÉDICTE THERE? KEEPS TRYING TO SUBMIT... JUST CAN'T DO IT!
2004
2008
2001
2008
GIVEN THAT YOU DON'T HAVE FUNDING, I WONDER...
AH, YES... I SEE WHAT YOU MEAN...

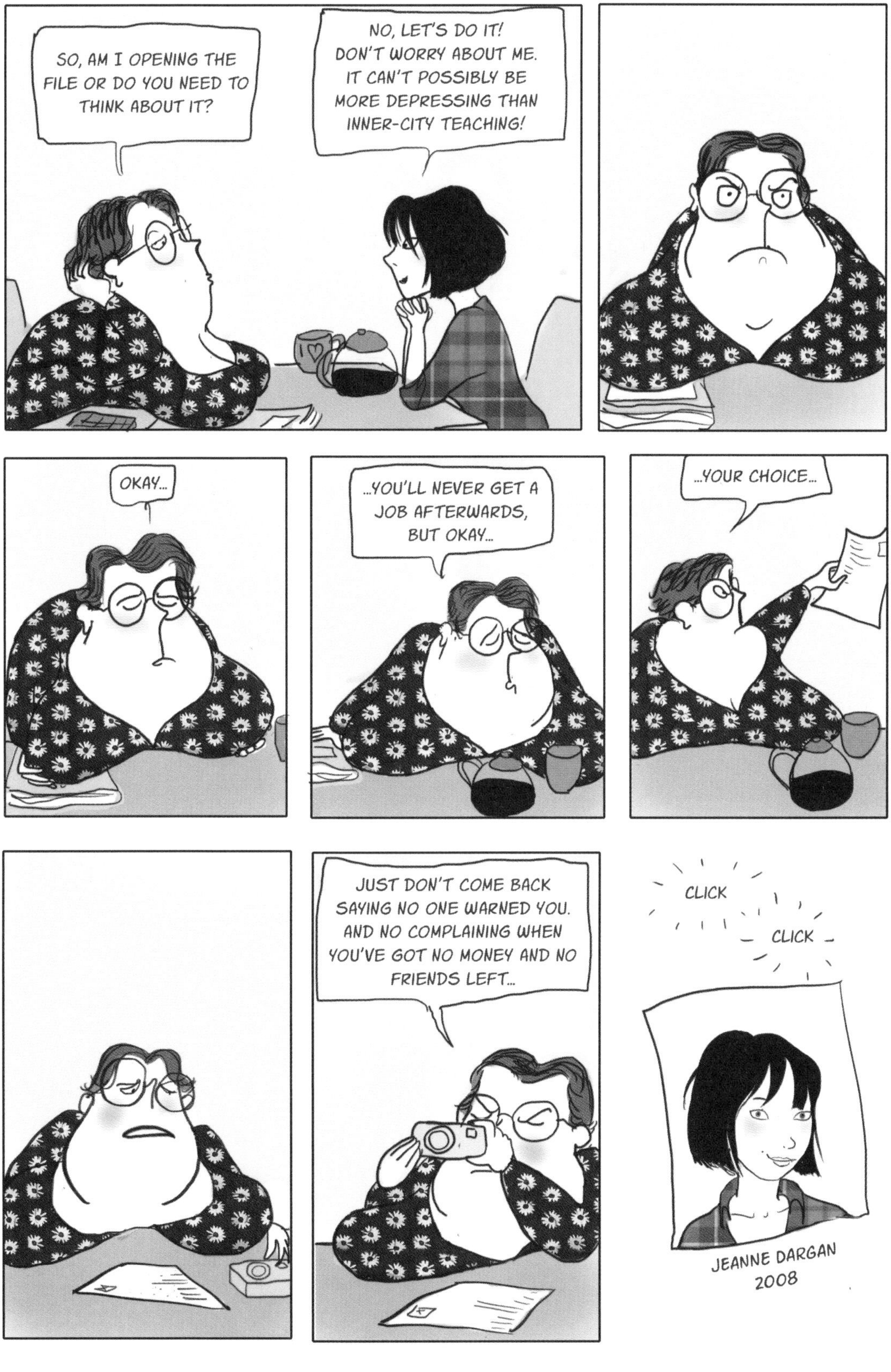
SO, AM I OPENING THE FILE OR DO YOU NEED TO THINK ABOUT IT?
NO, LET'S DO IT! DON'T WORRY ABOUT ME. IT CAN'T POSSIBLY BE MORE DEPRESSING THAN INNER-CITY TEACHING!
OKAY...
...YOU'LL NEVER GET A JOB AFTERWARDS, BUT OKAY...
...YOUR CHOICE...
JUST DON'T COME BACK SAYING NO ONE WARNED YOU. AND NO COMPLAINING WHEN YOU'VE GOT NO MONEY AND NO FRIENDS LEFT...
CLICK
CLICK
JEANNE DARGAN 2008

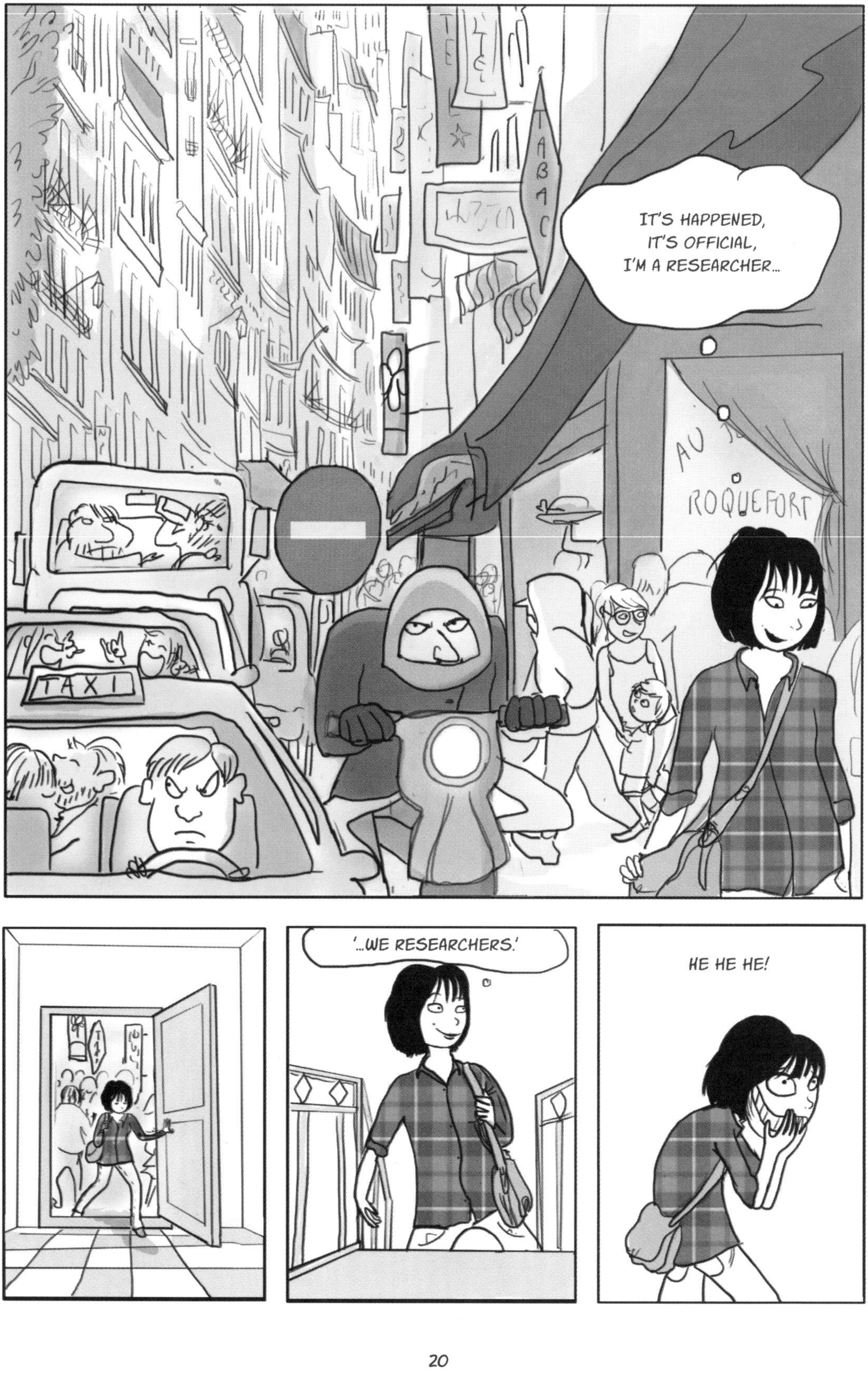
TABAC
IT'S HAPPENED,
IT'S OFFICIAL,
I'M A RESEARCHER...
ROQUEFORT
TAXI
'...WE RESEARCHERS.'
HE HE HE!

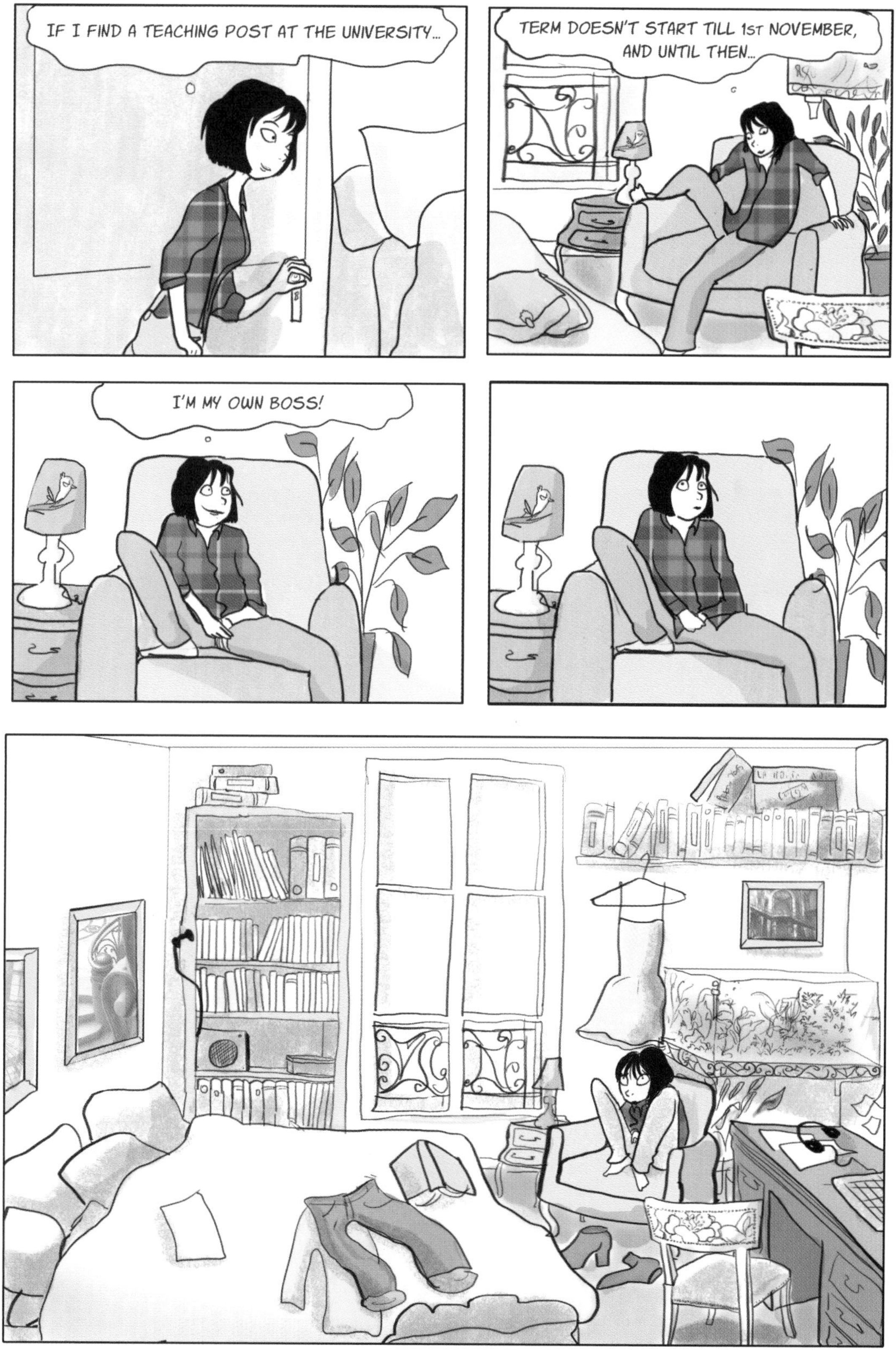
IF I FIND A TEACHING POST AT THE UNIVERSITY...
TERM DOESN'T START TILL 1ST NOVEMBER, AND UNTIL THEN...
I'M MY OWN BOSS!

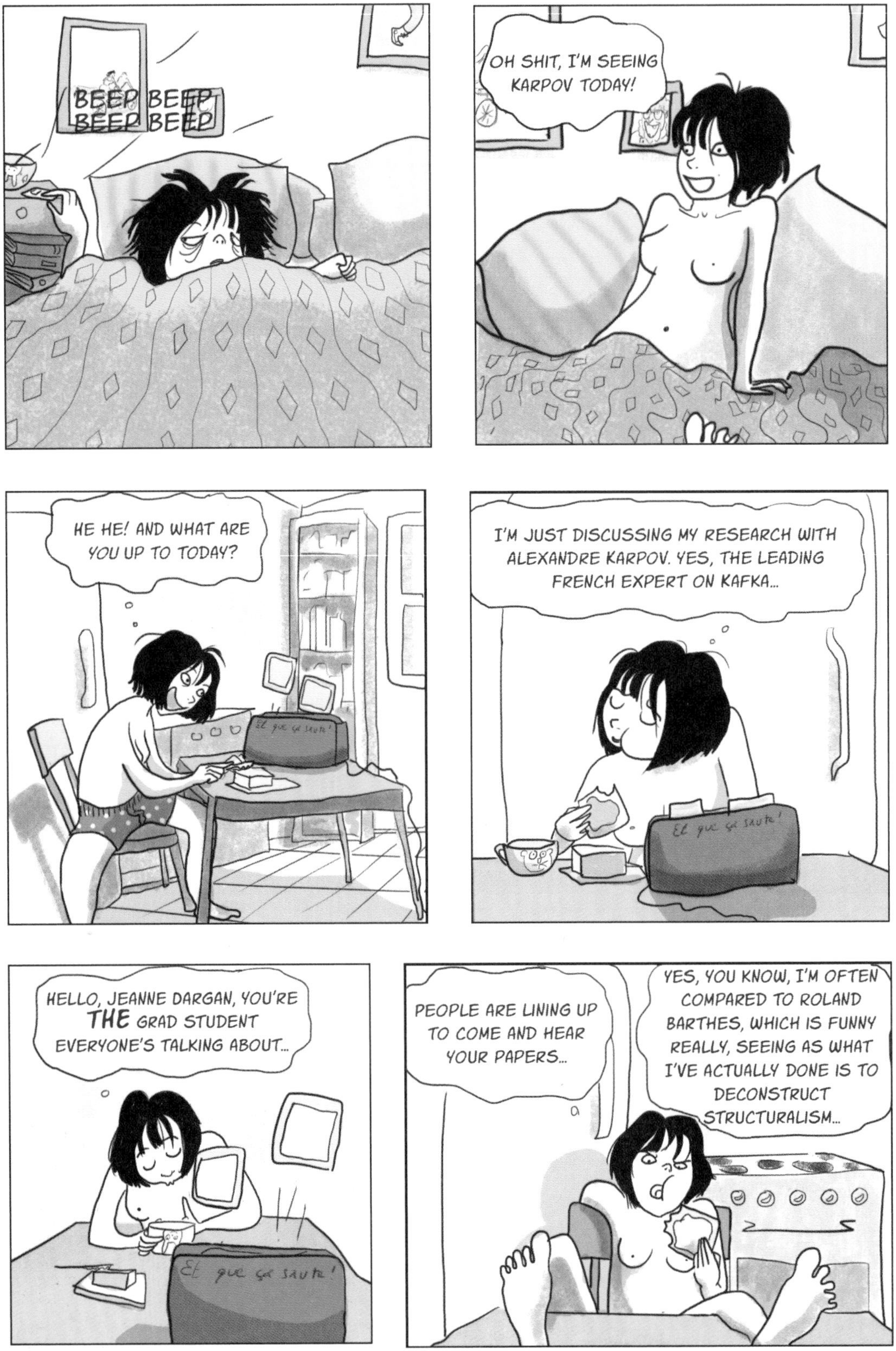
BEEP BEEP BEEP BEEP
OH SHIT, I'M SEEING KARPOV TODAY!
HE HE! AND WHAT ARE YOU UP TO TODAY?
Et que ça saute!
I'M JUST DISCUSSING MY RESEARCH WITH ALEXANDRE KARPOV. YES, THE LEADING FRENCH EXPERT ON KAFKA...
Et que ça saute!
HELLO, JEANNE DARGAN, YOU'RE THE GRAD STUDENT EVERYONE'S TALKING ABOUT...
Et que ça saute!
PEOPLE ARE LINING UP TO COME AND HEAR YOUR PAPERS...
YES, YOU KNOW, I'M OFTEN COMPARED TO ROLAND BARTHES, WHICH IS FUNNY REALLY, SEEING AS WHAT I'VE ACTUALLY DONE IS TO DECONSTRUCT STRUCTURALISM...

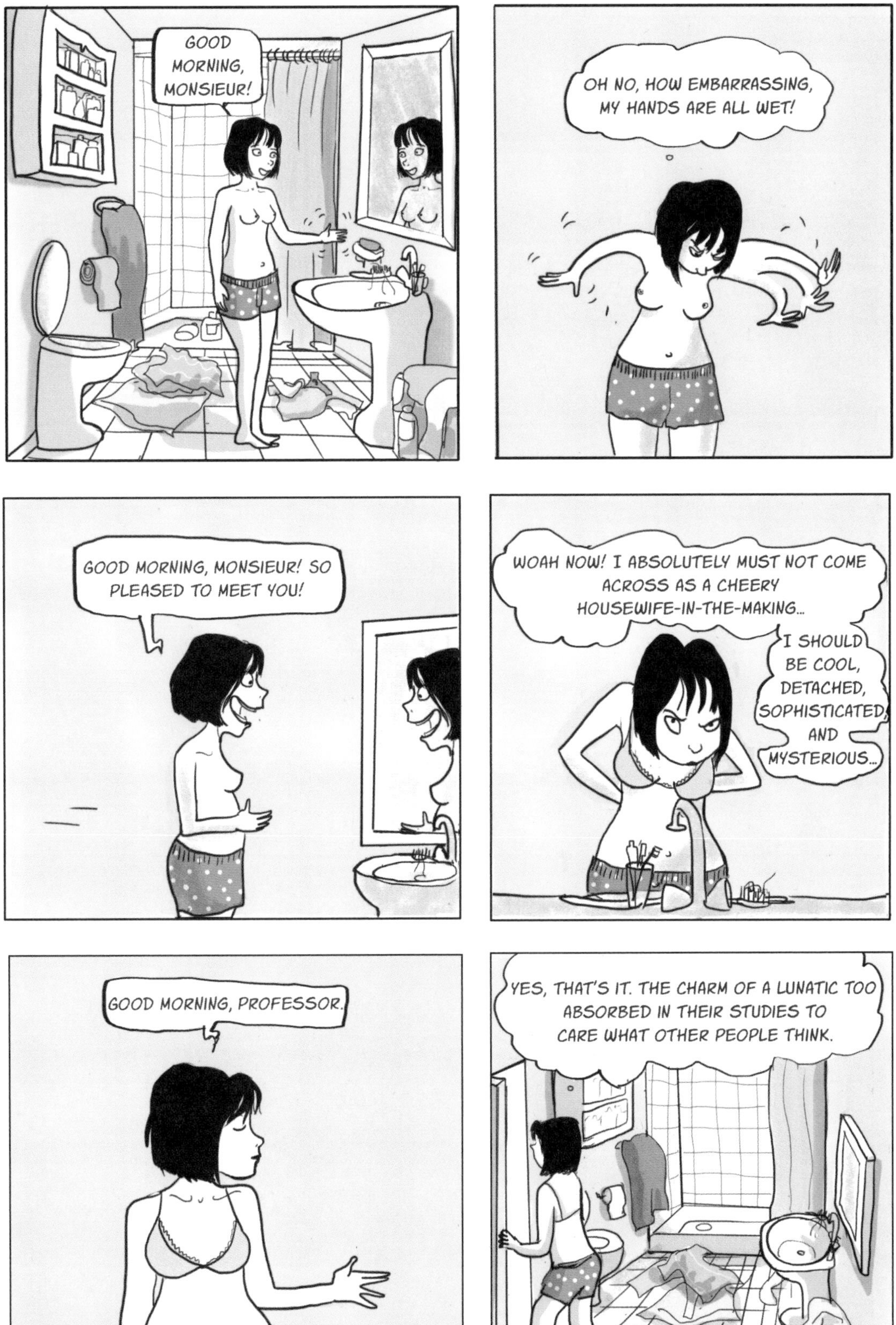
GOOD MORNING, MONSIEUR!
OH NO, HOW EMBARRASSING, MY HANDS ARE ALL WET!
GOOD MORNING, MONSIEUR! SO PLEASED TO MEET YOU!
WOAH NOW! I ABSOLUTELY MUST NOT COME ACROSS AS A CHEERY HOUSEWIFE-IN-THE-MAKING...
I SHOULD BE COOL, DETACHED, SOPHISTICATED, AND MYSTERIOUS...
GOOD MORNING, PROFESSOR.
YES, THAT'S IT. THE CHARM OF A LUNATIC TOO ABSORBED IN THEIR STUDIES TO CARE WHAT OTHER PEOPLE THINK.

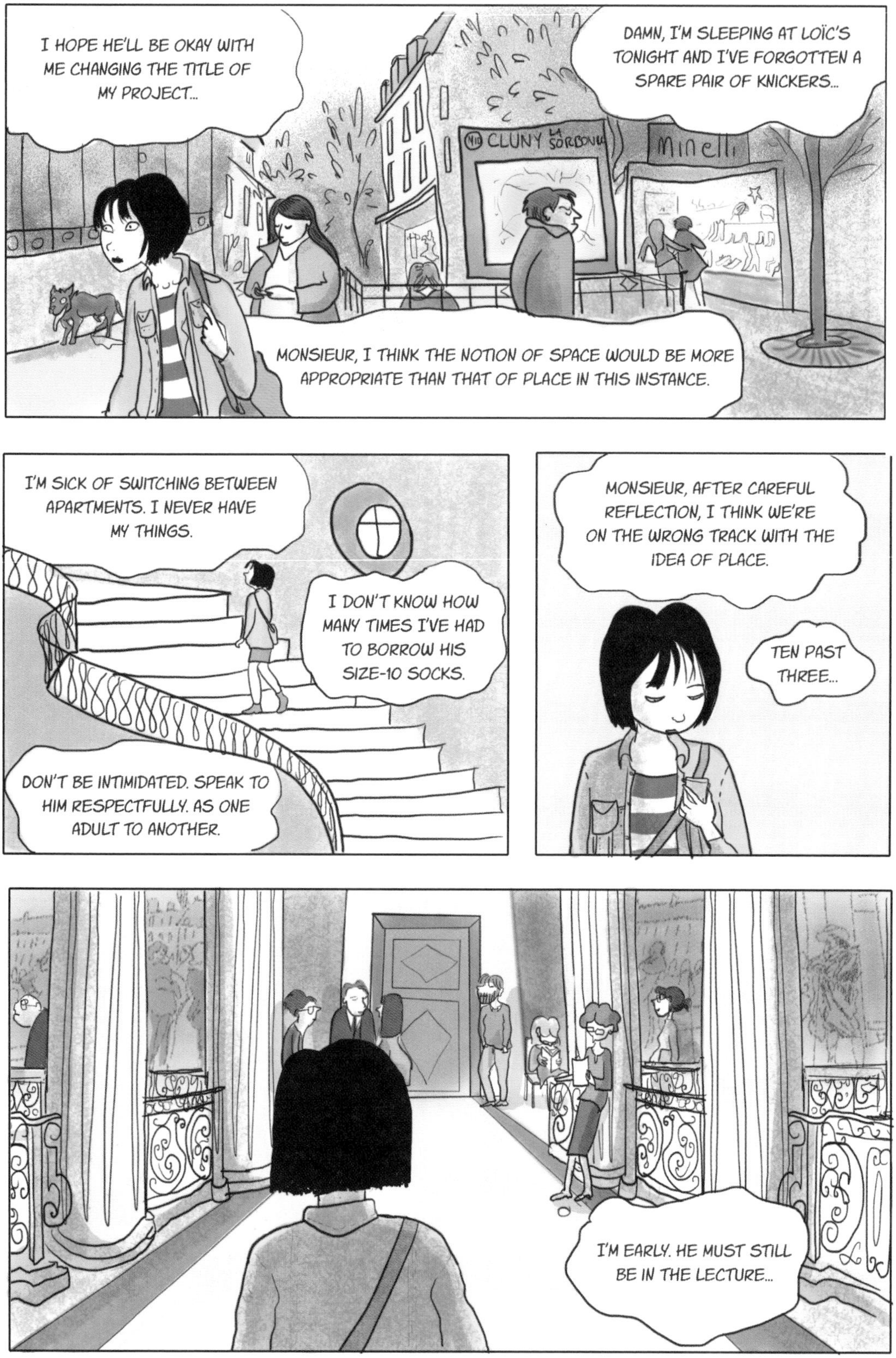
I HOPE HE'LL BE OKAY WITH ME CHANGING THE TITLE OF MY PROJECT...
DAMN, I'M SLEEPING AT LOÏC'S TONIGHT AND I'VE FORGOTTEN A SPARE PAIR OF KNICKERS...
CLUNY
Minelli
MONSIEUR, I THINK THE NOTION OF SPACE WOULD BE MORE APPROPRIATE THAN THAT OF PLACE IN THIS INSTANCE.
I'M SICK OF SWITCHING BETWEEN APARTMENTS. I NEVER HAVE MY THINGS.
I DON'T KNOW HOW MANY TIMES I'VE HAD TO BORROW HIS SIZE-10 SOCKS.
DON'T BE INTIMIDATED. SPEAK TO HIM RESPECTFULLY. AS ONE ADULT TO ANOTHER.
MONSIEUR, AFTER CAREFUL REFLECTION, I THINK WE'RE ON THE WRONG TRACK WITH THE IDEA OF PLACE.
TEN PAST THREE...
I'M EARLY. HE MUST STILL BE IN THE LECTURE...

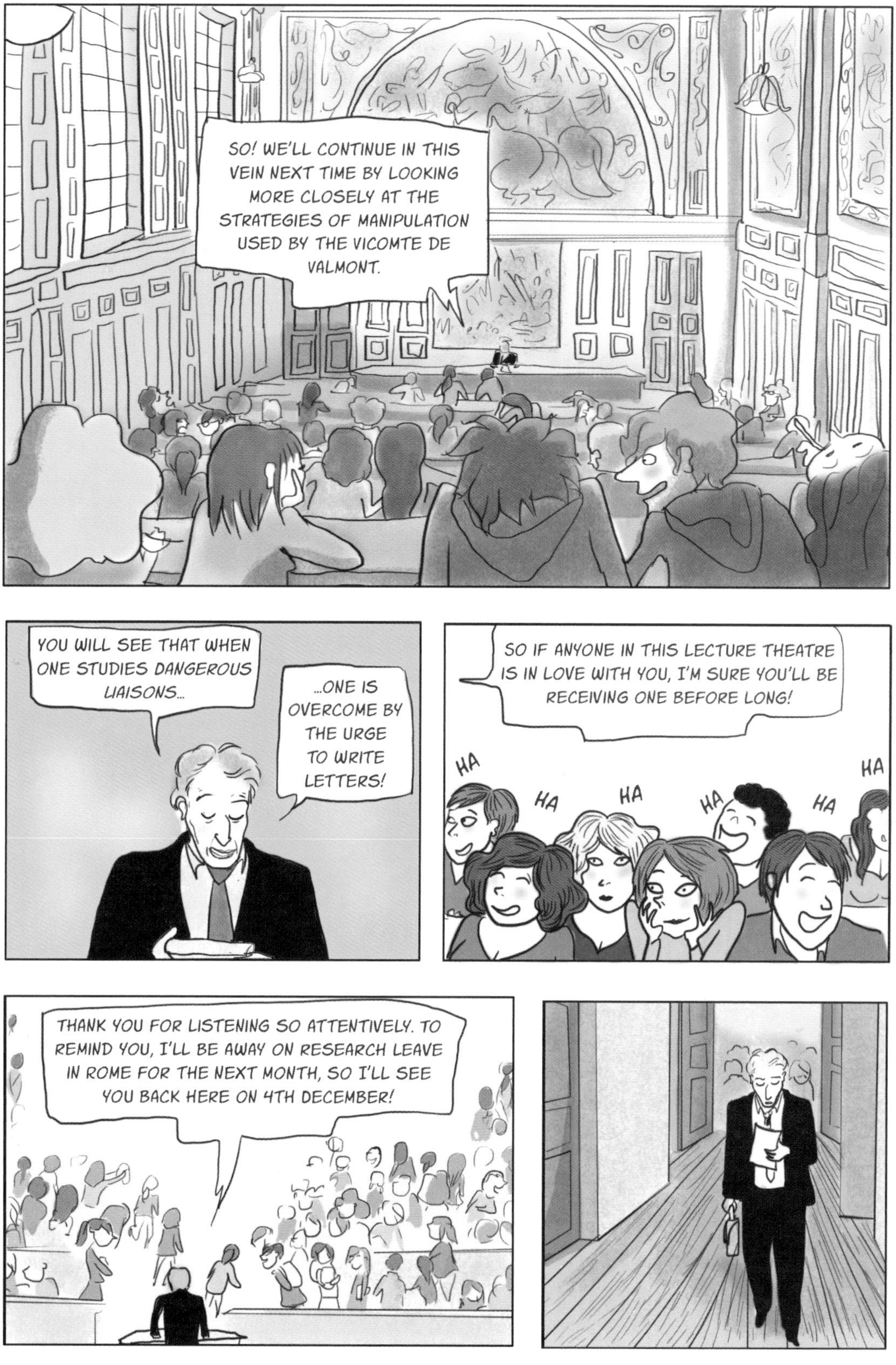
SO! WE'LL CONTINUE IN THIS VEIN NEXT TIME BY LOOKING MORE CLOSELY AT THE STRATEGIES OF MANIPULATION USED BY THE VICOMTE DE VALMONT.
YOU WILL SEE THAT WHEN ONE STUDIES DANGEROUS LIAISONS...
...ONE IS OVERCOME BY THE URGE TO WRITE LETTERS!
SO IF ANYONE IN THIS LECTURE THEATRE IS IN LOVE WITH YOU, I'M SURE YOU'LL BE RECEIVING ONE BEFORE LONG!
HA
HA
HA
HA
HA
HA
THANK YOU FOR LISTENING SO ATTENTIVELY. TO REMIND YOU, I'LL BE AWAY ON RESEARCH LEAVE IN ROME FOR THE NEXT MONTH, SO I'LL SEE YOU BACK HERE ON 4TH DECEMBER!

THE ONLY TIME OF THE WEEK HIS STUDENTS CAN BE SURE TO FIND ALEXANDRE KARPOV ON CAMPUS IS ON TUESDAYS, AFTER HIS LECTURES.

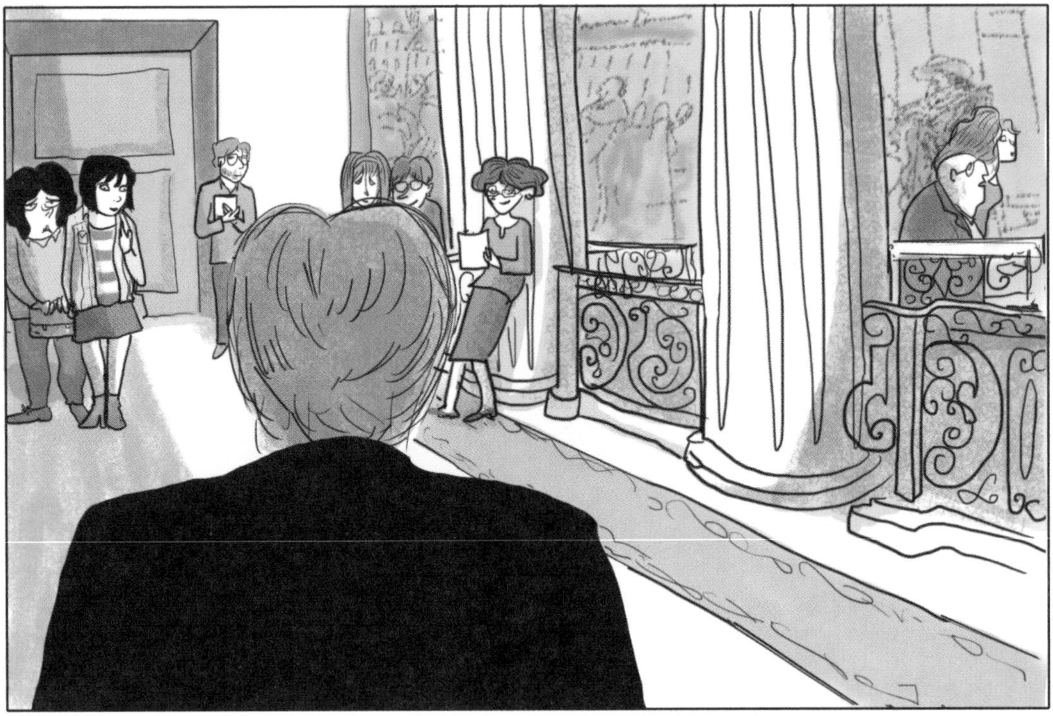

IT'S A NIGHTMARE OF A DAY FOR KARPOV.
EVERY SINGLE PHD STUDENT WHO HAS SENT HIM THEIR WORK COMES TO SEE IF HE'S READ THEIR PILE OF CRAP YET.

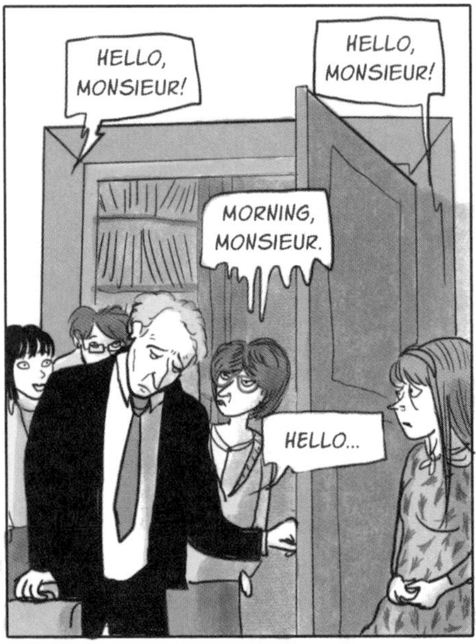
HELLO, MONSIEUR!
HELLO, MONSIEUR!
MORNING, MONSIEUR.
HELLO...

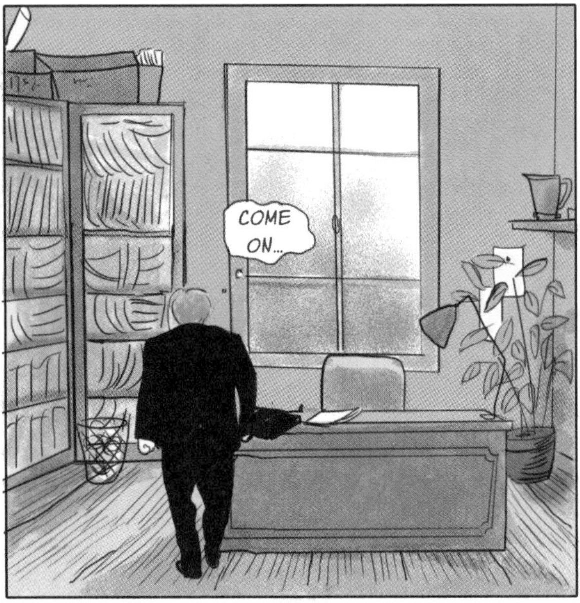
COME ON...

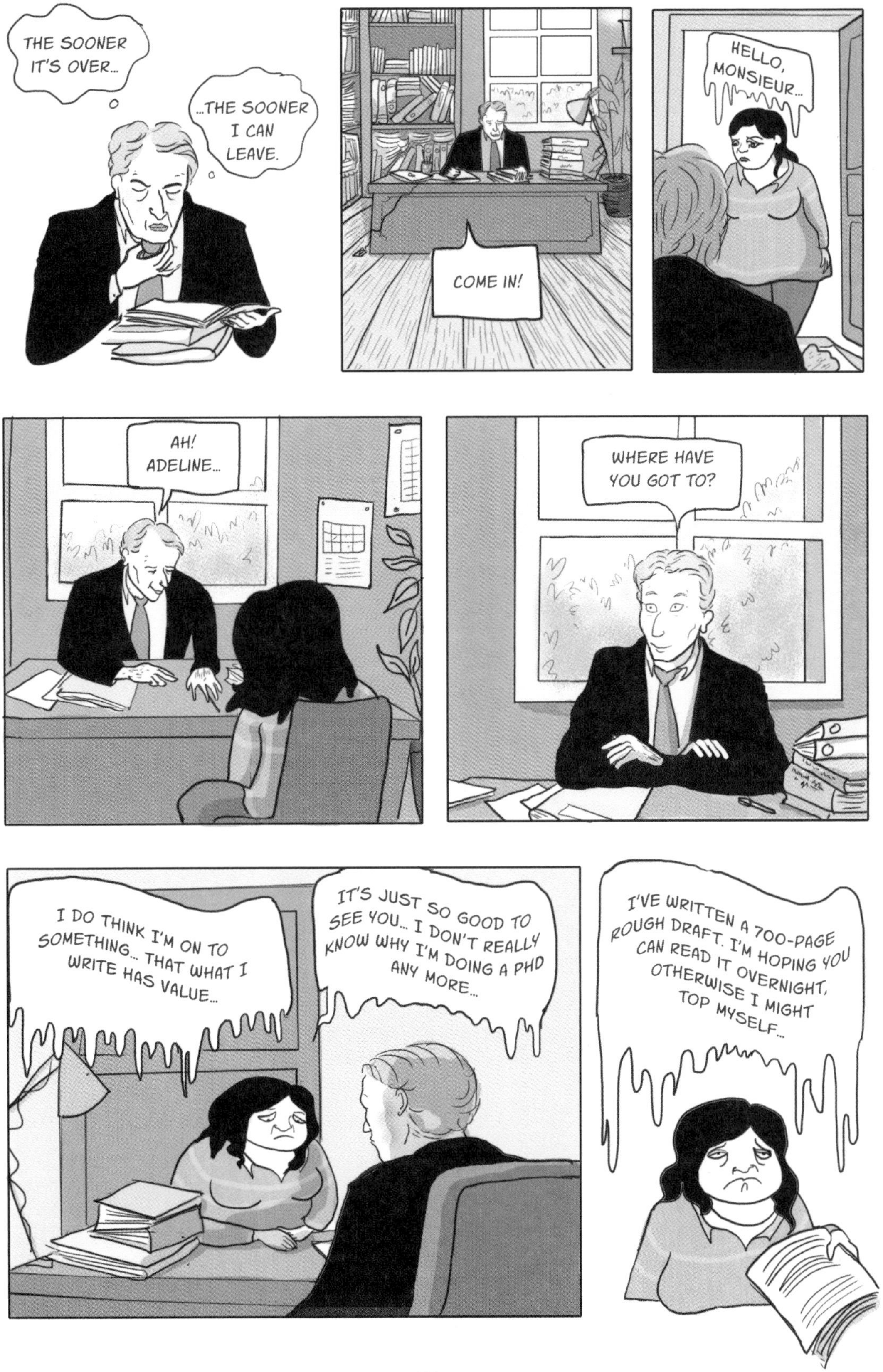
THE SOONER IT'S OVER...
...THE SOONER I CAN LEAVE.
COME IN!
HELLO, MONSIEUR...
AH! ADELINE...
WHERE HAVE YOU GOT TO?
I DO THINK I'M ON TO SOMETHING... THAT WHAT I WRITE HAS VALUE...
IT'S JUST SO GOOD TO SEE YOU... I DON'T REALLY KNOW WHY I'M DOING A PHD ANY MORE...
I'VE WRITTEN A 700-PAGE ROUGH DRAFT. I'M HOPING YOU CAN READ IT OVERNIGHT, OTHERWISE I MIGHT TOP MYSELF...

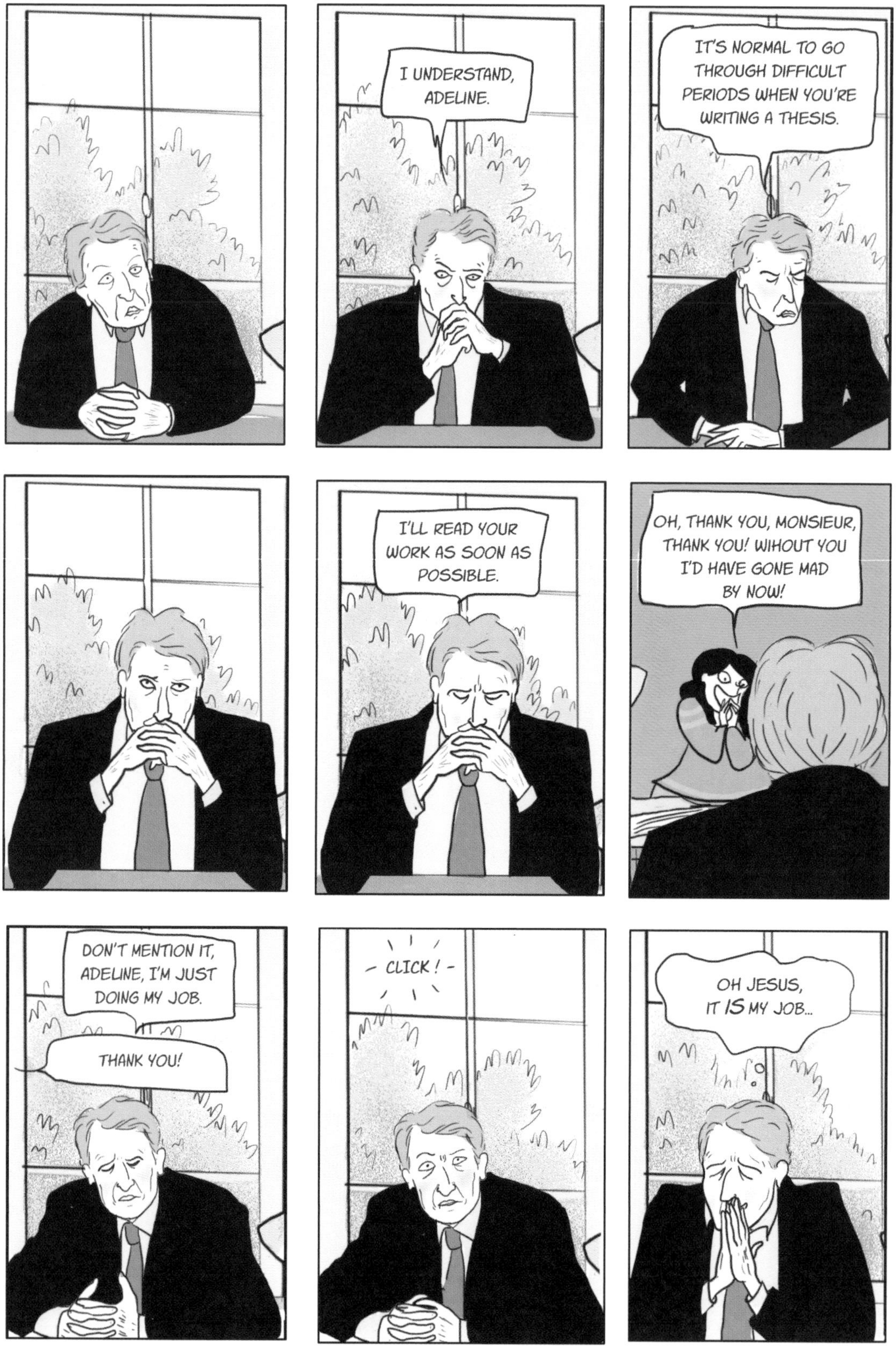
I UNDERSTAND, ADELINE.
IT'S NORMAL TO GO THROUGH DIFFICULT PERIODS WHEN YOU'RE WRITING A THESIS.
I'LL READ YOUR WORK AS SOON AS POSSIBLE.
OH, THANK YOU, MONSIEUR, THANK YOU! WIHOUT YOU I'D HAVE GONE MAD BY NOW!
DON'T MENTION IT, ADELINE, I'M JUST DOING MY JOB.
THANK YOU!
CLICK!
OH JESUS, IT IS MY JOB...

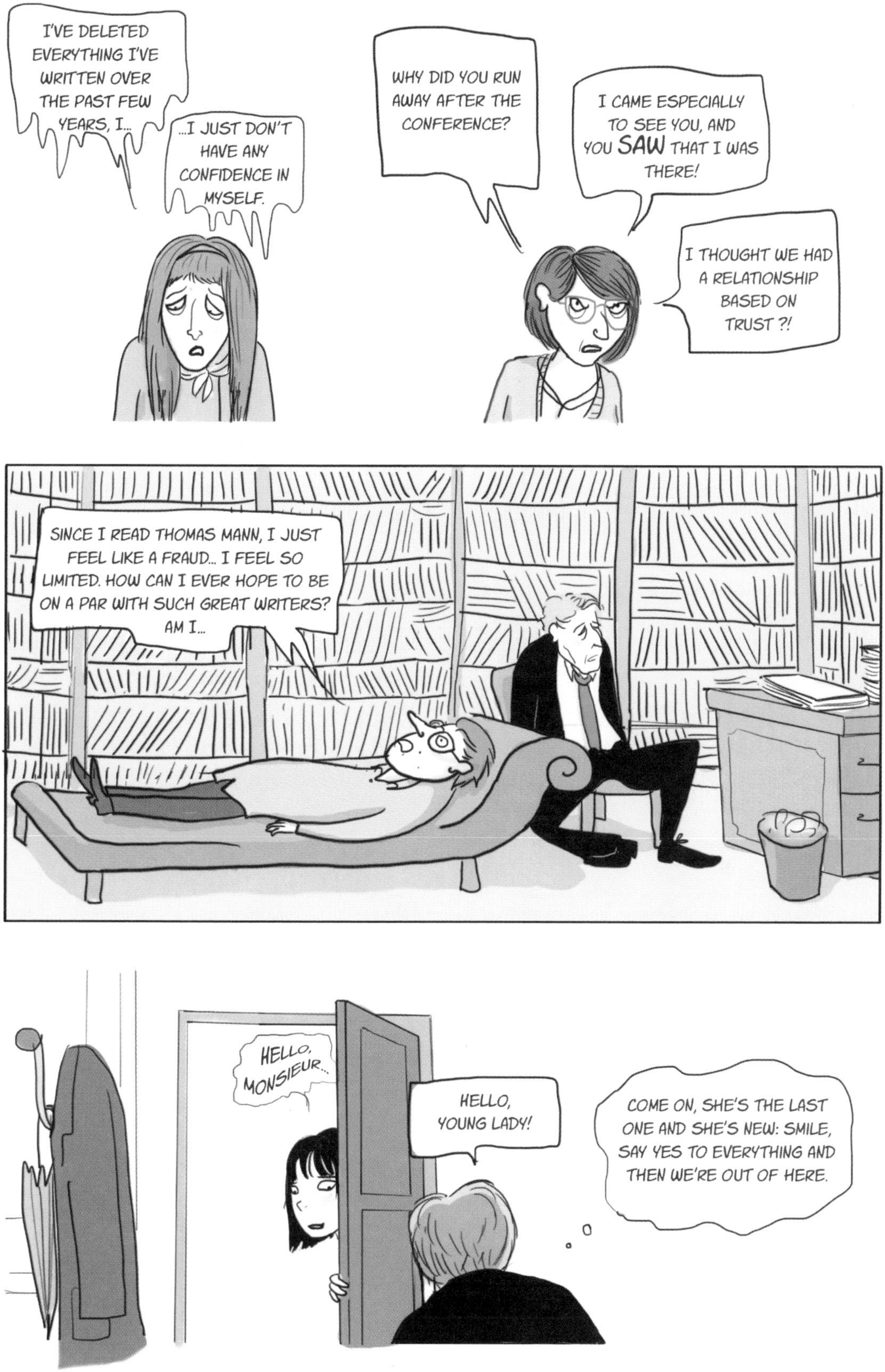
I'VE DELETED EVERYTHING I'VE WRITTEN OVER THE PAST FEW YEARS, I...
...I JUST DON'T HAVE ANY CONFIDENCE IN MYSELF.
WHY DID YOU RUN AWAY AFTER THE CONFERENCE?
I CAME ESPECIALLY TO SEE YOU, AND YOU SAW THAT I WAS THERE!
I THOUGHT WE HAD A RELATIONSHIP BASED ON TRUST ?!
SINCE I READ THOMAS MANN, I JUST FEEL LIKE A FRAUD... I FEEL SO LIMITED. HOW CAN I EVER HOPE TO BE ON A PAR WITH SUCH GREAT WRITERS? AM I...
HELLO, MONSIEUR...
HELLO, YOUNG LADY!
COME ON, SHE'S THE LAST ONE AND SHE'S NEW: SMILE, SAY YES TO EVERYTHING AND THEN WE'RE OUT OF HERE.

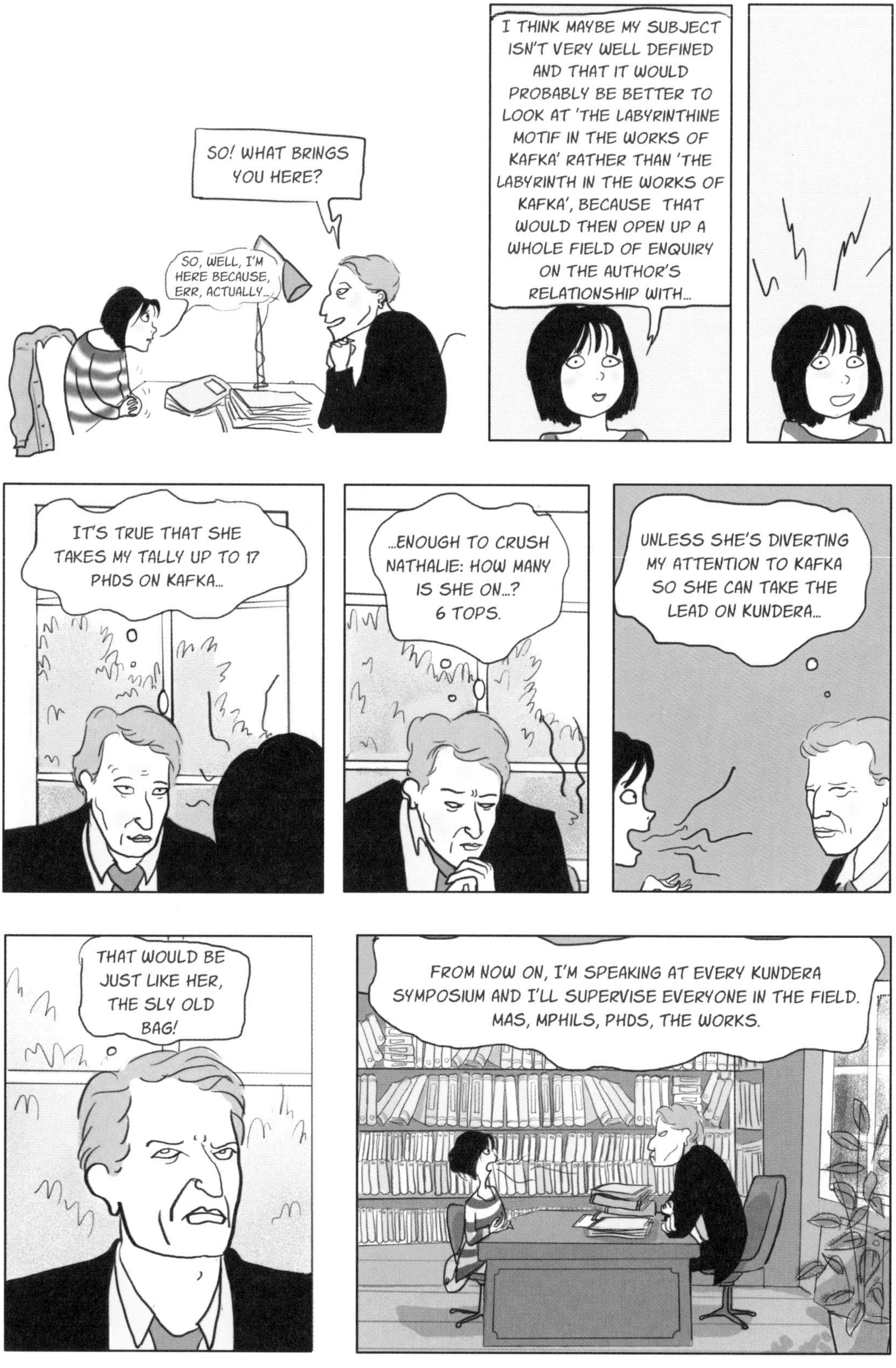
SO! WHAT BRINGS YOU HERE?
SO, WELL, I'M HERE BECAUSE, ERR, ACTUALLY...
I THINK MAYBE MY SUBJECT ISN'T VERY WELL DEFINED AND THAT IT WOULD PROBABLY BE BETTER TO LOOK AT 'THE LABYRINTHINE MOTIF IN THE WORKS OF KAFKA' RATHER THAN 'THE LABYRINTH IN THE WORKS OF KAFKA', BECAUSE THAT WOULD THEN OPEN UP A WHOLE FIELD OF ENQUIRY ON THE AUTHOR'S RELATIONSHIP WITH...
IT'S TRUE THAT SHE TAKES MY TALLY UP TO 17 PHDS ON KAFKA...
...ENOUGH TO CRUSH NATHALIE: HOW MANY IS SHE ON...? 6 TOPS.
UNLESS SHE'S DIVERTING MY ATTENTION TO KAFKA SO SHE CAN TAKE THE LEAD ON KUNDERA...
THAT WOULD BE JUST LIKE HER, THE SLY OLD BAG!
FROM NOW ON, I'M SPEAKING AT EVERY KUNDERA SYMPOSIUM AND I'LL SUPERVISE EVERYONE IN THE FIELD. MAS, MPHILS, PHDS, THE WORKS.

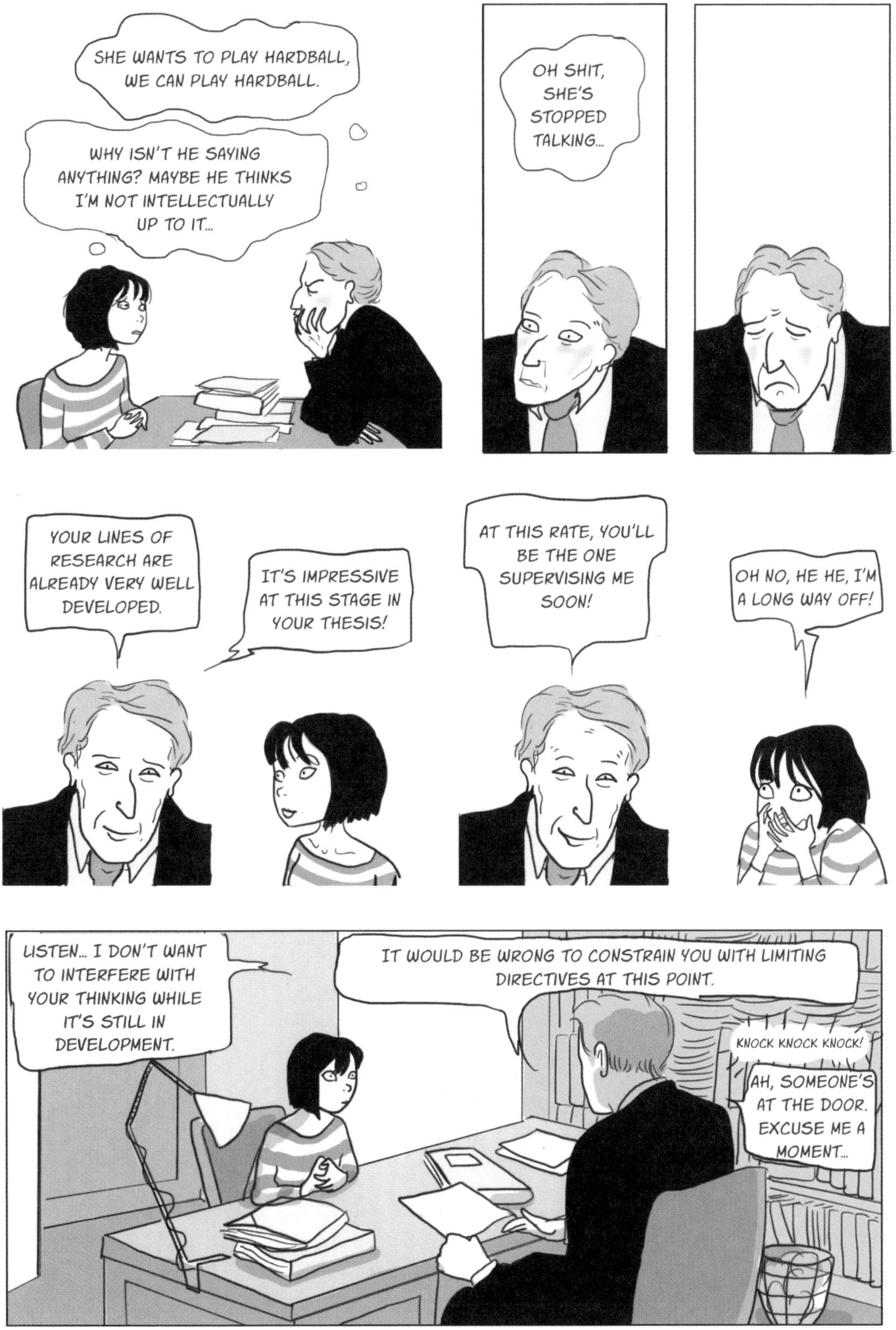
SHE WANTS TO PLAY HARDBALL, WE CAN PLAY HARDBALL.
WHY ISN'T HE SAYING ANYTHING? MAYBE HE THINKS I'M NOT INTELLECTUALLY UP TO IT...
OH SHIT, SHE'S STOPPED TALKING...
YOUR LINES OF RESEARCH ARE ALREADY VERY WELL DEVELOPED.
IT'S IMPRESSIVE AT THIS STAGE IN YOUR THESIS!
AT THIS RATE, YOU'LL BE THE ONE SUPERVISING ME SOON!
OH NO, HE HE, I'M A LONG WAY OFF!
LISTEN... I DON'T WANT TO INTERFERE WITH YOUR THINKING WHILE IT'S STILL IN DEVELOPMENT.
IT WOULD BE WRONG TO CONSTRAIN YOU WITH LIMITING DIRECTIVES AT THIS POINT.
KNOCK KNOCK KNOCK!
AH, SOMEONE'S AT THE DOOR. EXCUSE ME A MOMENT...

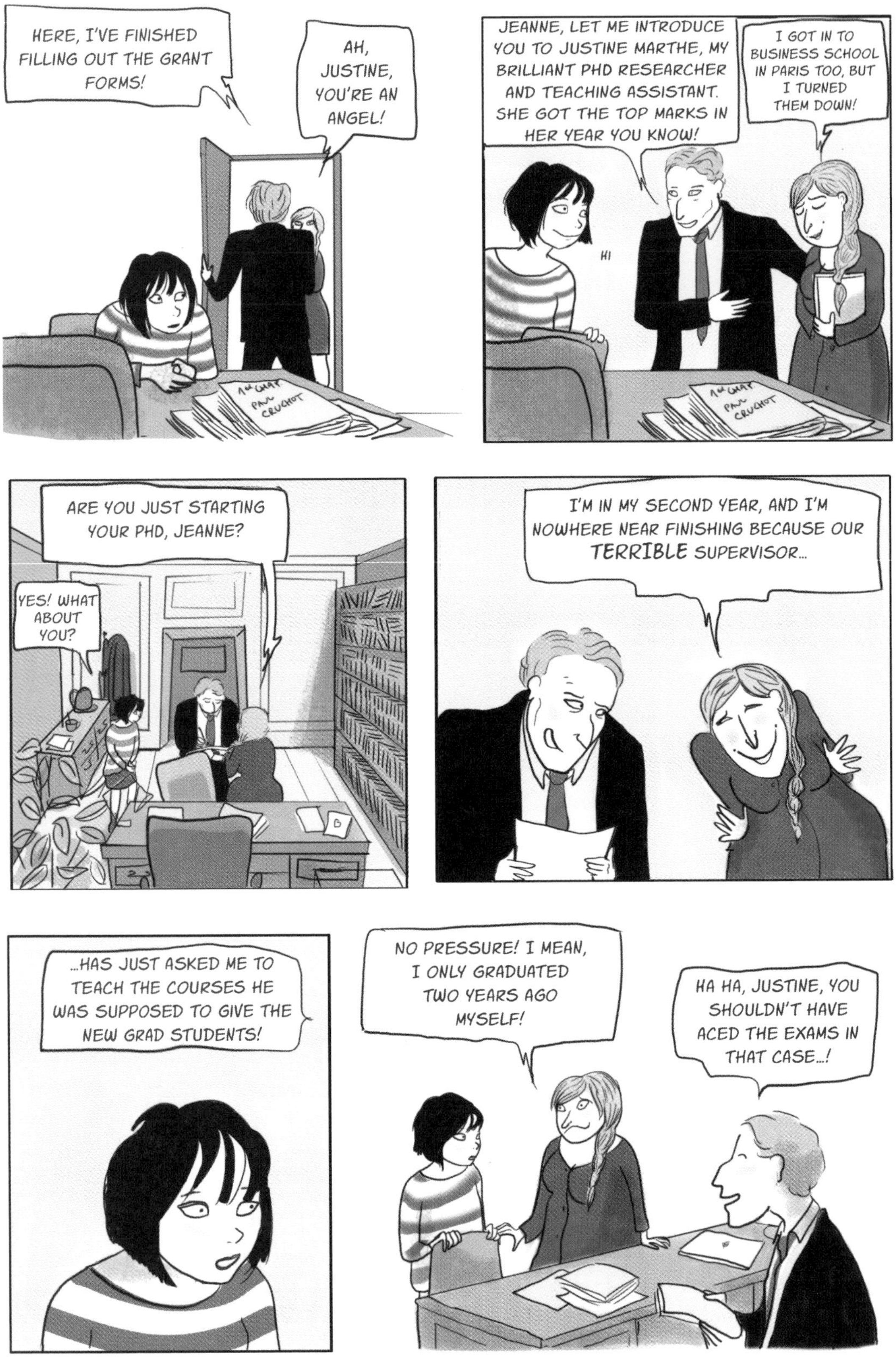
HERE, I'VE FINISHED FILLING OUT THE GRANT FORMS!
AH, JUSTINE, YOU'RE AN ANGEL!
JEANNE, LET ME INTRODUCE YOU TO JUSTINE MARTHE, MY BRILLIANT PHD RESEARCHER AND TEACHING ASSISTANT. SHE GOT THE TOP MARKS IN HER YEAR YOU KNOW!
I GOT IN TO BUSINESS SCHOOL IN PARIS TOO, BUT I TURNED THEM DOWN!
HI
ARE YOU JUST STARTING YOUR PHD, JEANNE?
YES! WHAT ABOUT YOU?
I'M IN MY SECOND YEAR, AND I'M NOWHERE NEAR FINISHING BECAUSE OUR TERRIBLE SUPERVISOR...
...HAS JUST ASKED ME TO TEACH THE COURSES HE WAS SUPPOSED TO GIVE THE NEW GRAD STUDENTS!
NO PRESSURE! I MEAN, I ONLY GRADUATED TWO YEARS AGO MYSELF!
HA HA, JUSTINE, YOU SHOULDN'T HAVE ACED THE EXAMS IN THAT CASE...!

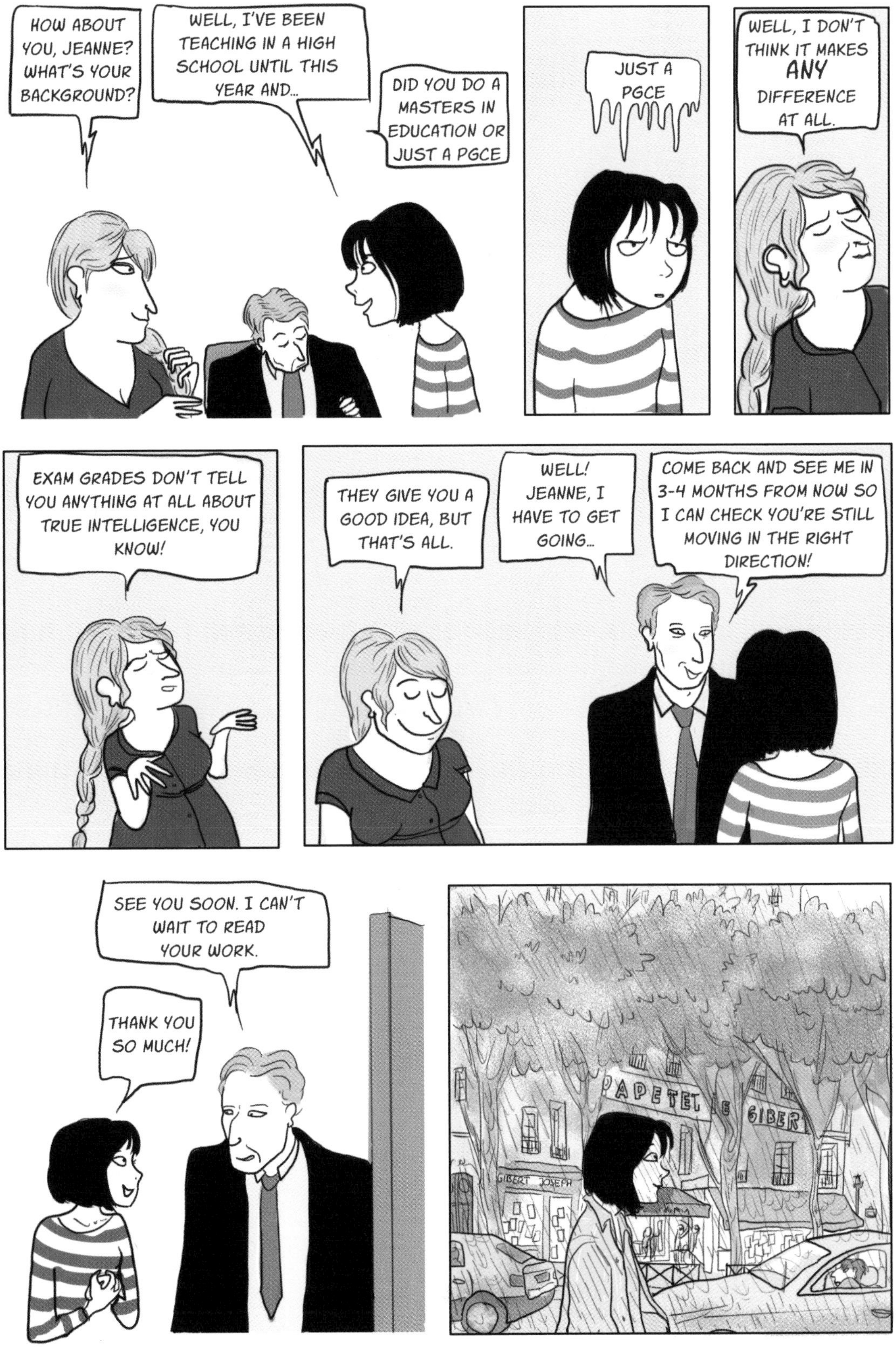
HOW ABOUT YOU, JEANNE? WHAT'S YOUR BACKGROUND?
WELL, I'VE BEEN TEACHING IN A HIGH SCHOOL UNTIL THIS YEAR AND...
DID YOU DO A MASTERS IN EDUCATION OR JUST A PGCE
JUST A PGCE
WELL, I DON'T THINK IT MAKES ANY DIFFERENCE AT ALL.
EXAM GRADES DON'T TELL YOU ANYTHING AT ALL ABOUT TRUE INTELLIGENCE, YOU KNOW!
THEY GIVE YOU A GOOD IDEA, BUT THAT'S ALL.
WELL! JEANNE, I HAVE TO GET GOING...
COME BACK AND SEE ME IN 3-4 MONTHS FROM NOW SO I CAN CHECK YOU'RE STILL MOVING IN THE RIGHT DIRECTION!
SEE YOU SOON. I CAN'T WAIT TO READ YOUR WORK.
THANK YOU SO MUCH!
GIBERT JOSEPH

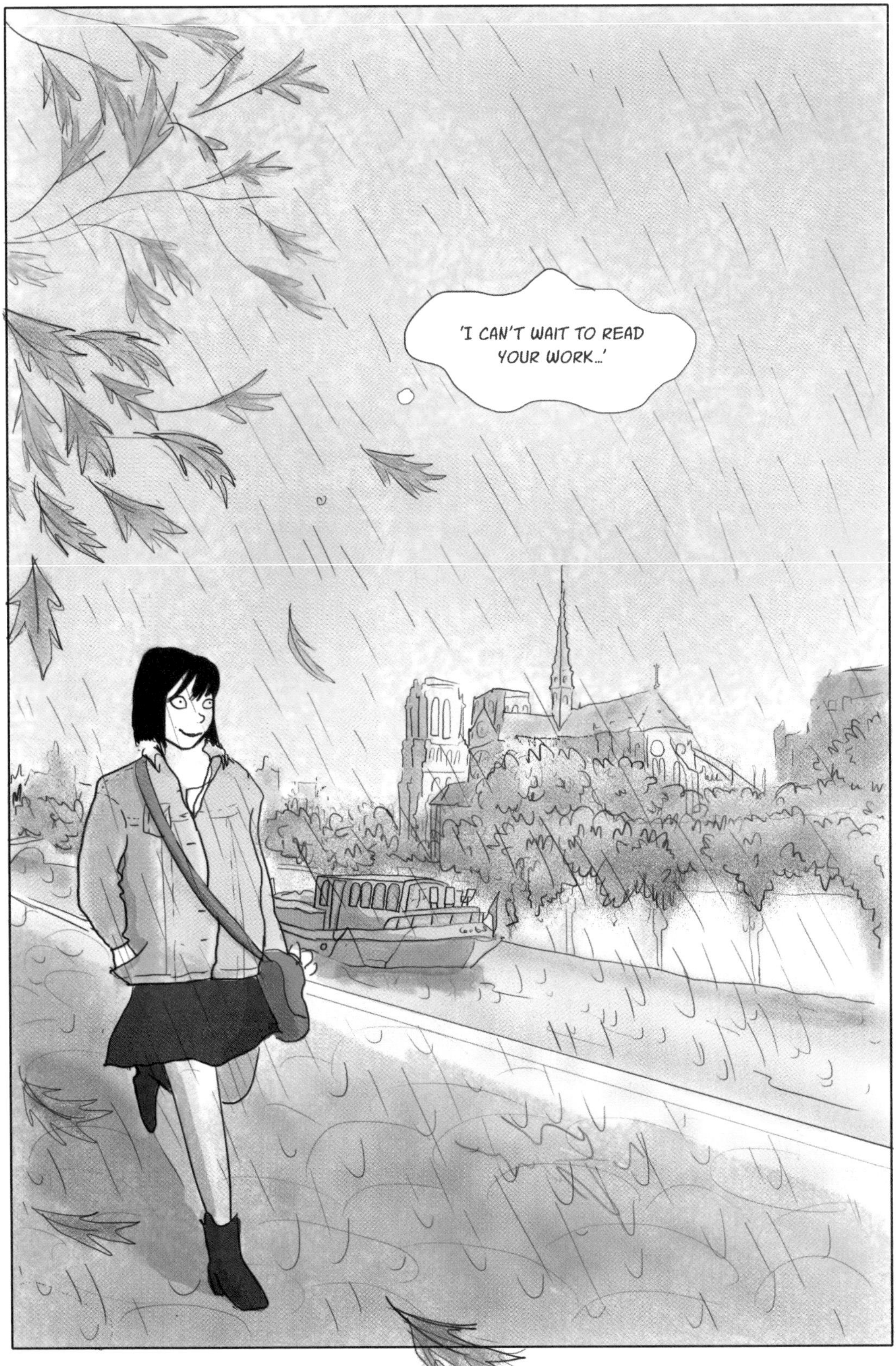
'I CAN'T WAIT TO READ YOUR WORK...'

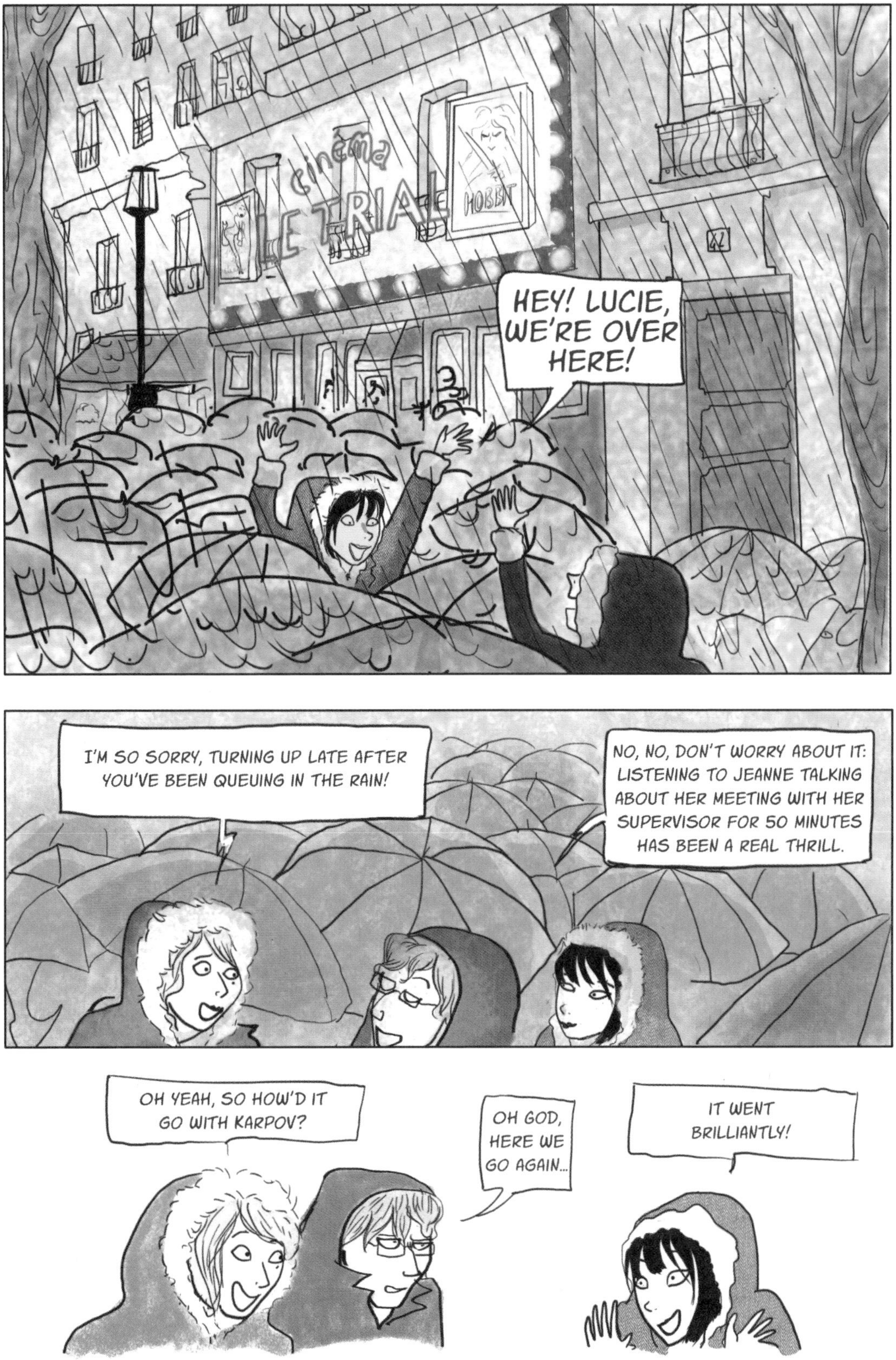
cinéma
LE TRIAL
HOBBIT
HEY! LUCIE, WE'RE OVER HERE!
I'M SO SORRY, TURNING UP LATE AFTER YOU'VE BEEN QUEUING IN THE RAIN!
NO, NO, DON'T WORRY ABOUT IT: LISTENING TO JEANNE TALKING ABOUT HER MEETING WITH HER SUPERVISOR FOR 50 MINUTES HAS BEEN A REAL THRILL.
OH YEAH, SO HOW'D IT GO WITH KARPOV?
OH GOD, HERE WE GO AGAIN...
IT WENT BRILLIANTLY!

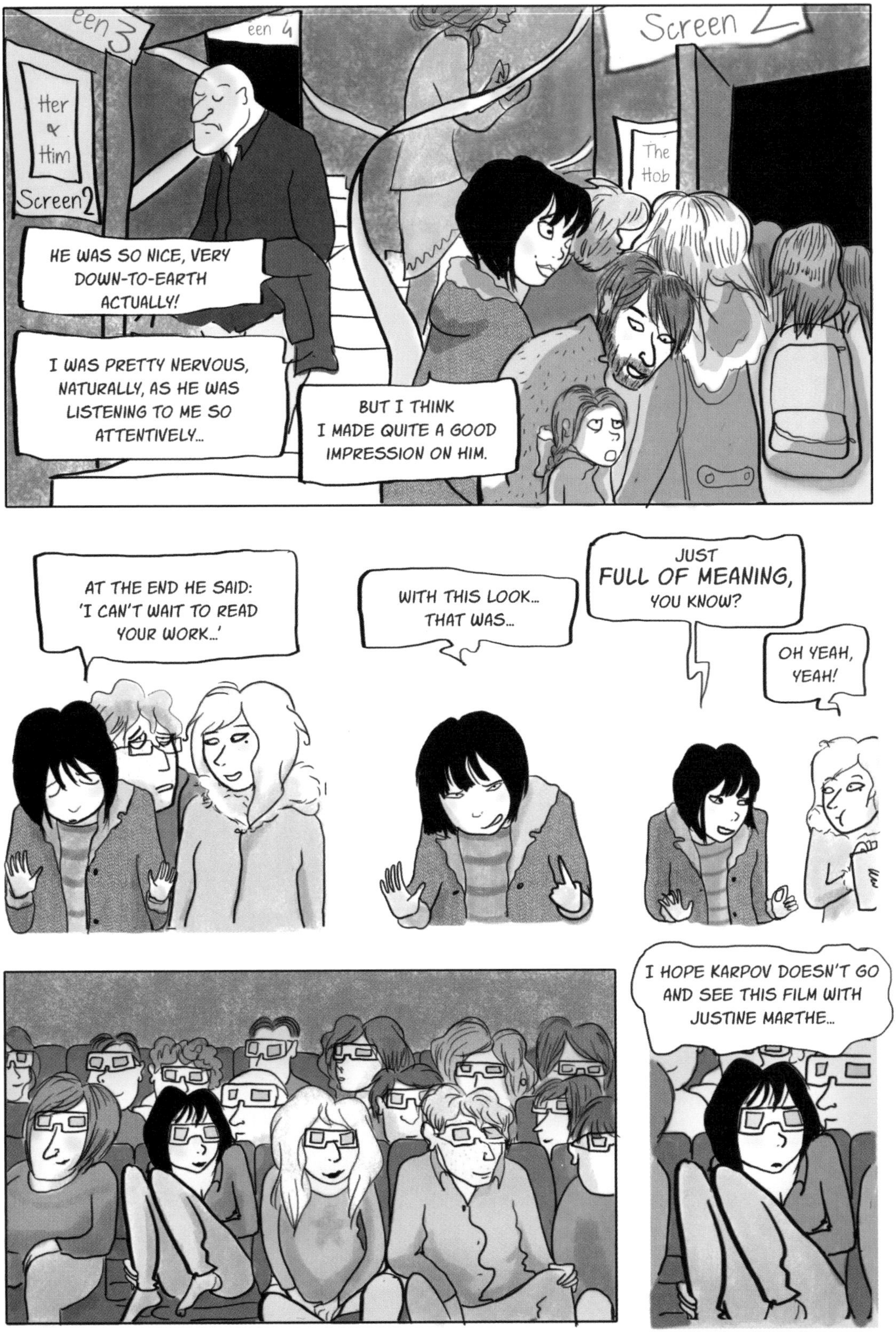
een 3
een 4
Screen 2
Her & Him
Screen 2
The Hob
HE WAS SO NICE, VERY DOWN-TO-EARTH ACTUALLY!
I WAS PRETTY NERVOUS, NATURALLY, AS HE WAS LISTENING TO ME SO ATTENTIVELY...
BUT I THINK I MADE QUITE A GOOD IMPRESSION ON HIM.
AT THE END HE SAID: 'I CAN'T WAIT TO READ YOUR WORK...'
WITH THIS LOOK... THAT WAS...
JUST FULL OF MEANING, YOU KNOW?
OH YEAH, YEAH!
I HOPE KARPOV DOESN'T GO AND SEE THIS FILM WITH JUSTINE MARTHE...

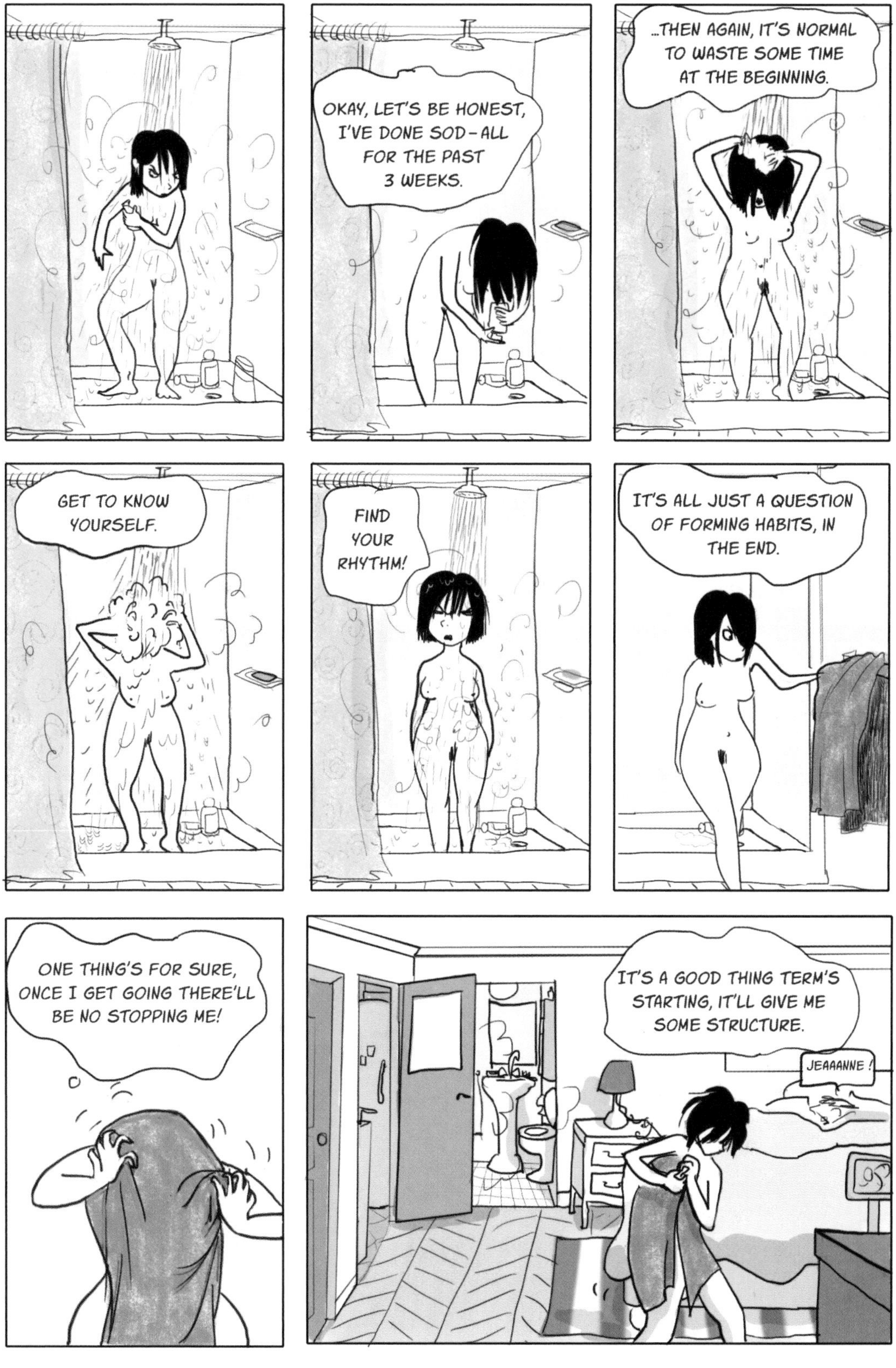
OKAY, LET'S BE HONEST, I'VE DONE SOD-ALL FOR THE PAST 3 WEEKS.
...THEN AGAIN, IT'S NORMAL TO WASTE SOME TIME AT THE BEGINNING.
GET TO KNOW YOURSELF.
FIND YOUR RHYTHM!
IT'S ALL JUST A QUESTION OF FORMING HABITS, IN THE END.
ONE THING'S FOR SURE, ONCE I GET GOING THERE'LL BE NO STOPPING ME!
IT'S A GOOD THING TERM'S STARTING, IT'LL GIVE ME SOME STRUCTURE.
JEAAANNE!

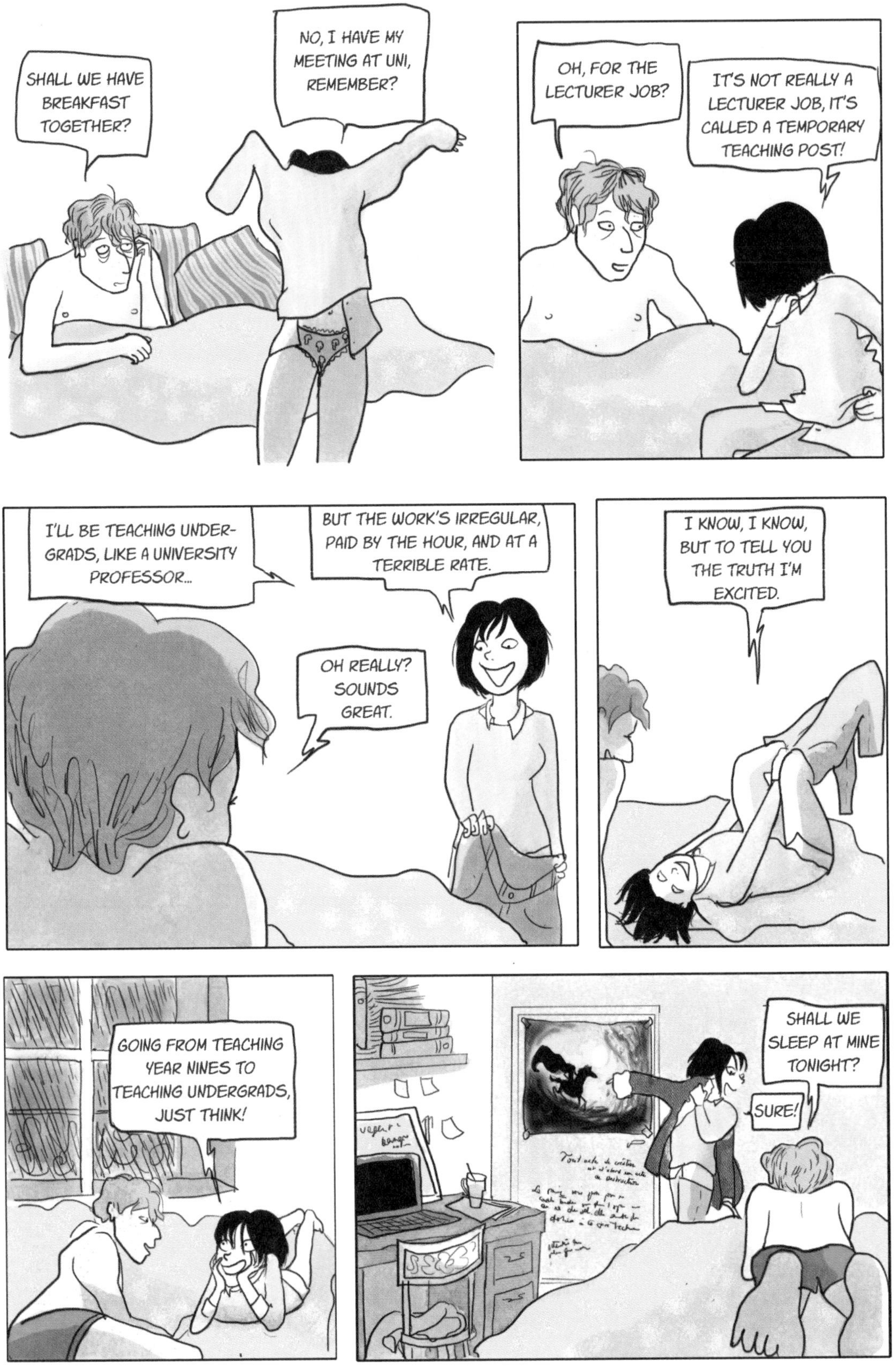
SHALL WE HAVE BREAKFAST TOGETHER?
NO, I HAVE MY MEETING AT UNI, REMEMBER?
OH, FOR THE LECTURER JOB?
IT'S NOT REALLY A LECTURER JOB, IT'S CALLED A TEMPORARY TEACHING POST!
I'LL BE TEACHING UNDER-GRADS, LIKE A UNIVERSITY PROFESSOR...
BUT THE WORK'S IRREGULAR, PAID BY THE HOUR, AND AT A TERRIBLE RATE.
OH REALLY? SOUNDS GREAT.
I KNOW, I KNOW, BUT TO TELL YOU THE TRUTH I'M EXCITED.
GOING FROM TEACHING YEAR NINES TO TEACHING UNDERGRADS, JUST THINK!
SHALL WE SLEEP AT MINE TONIGHT?
SURE!

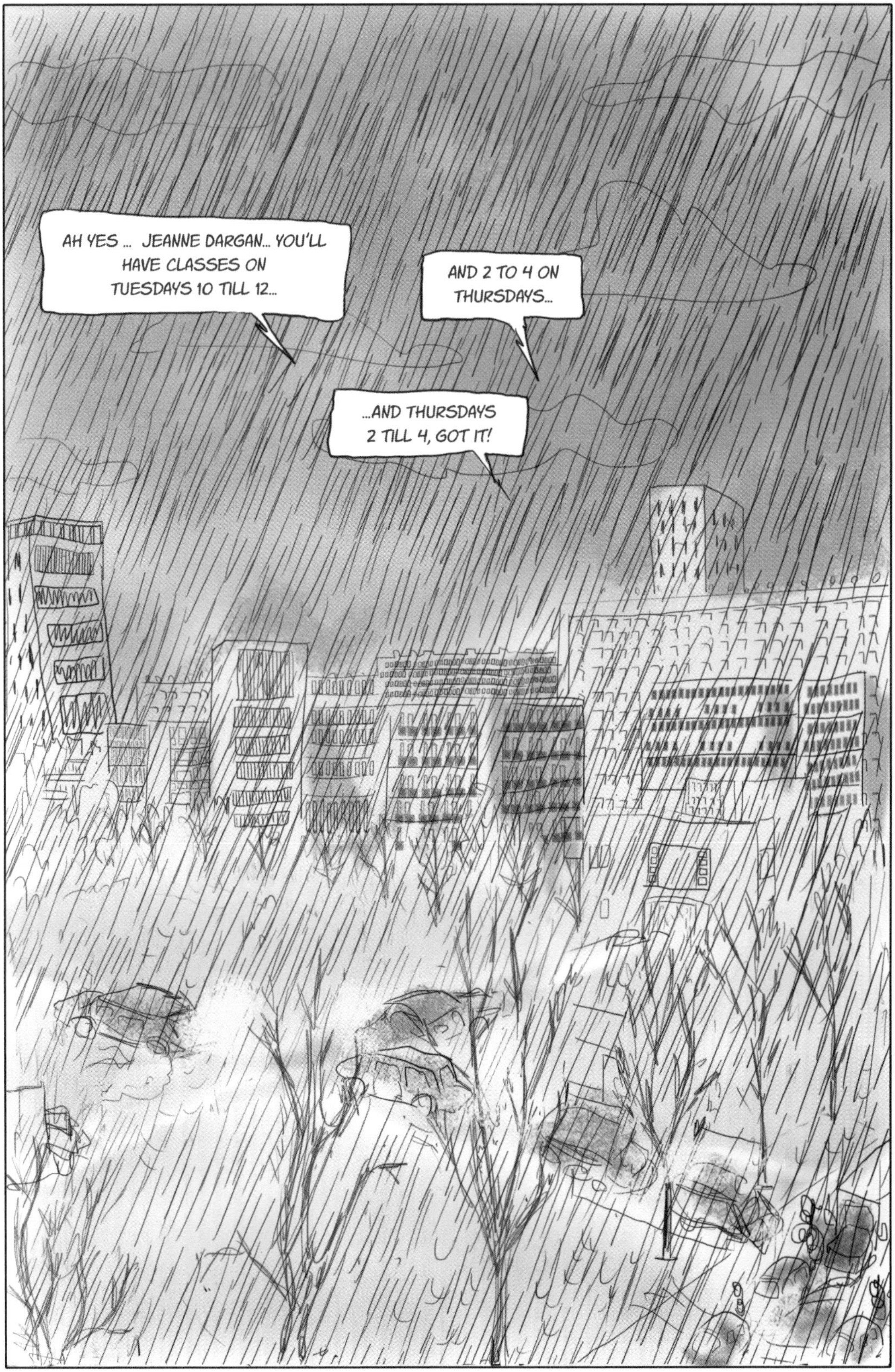
AH YES ... JEANNE DARGAN... YOU'LL HAVE CLASSES ON TUESDAYS 10 TILL 12...
AND 2 TO 4 ON THURSDAYS...
...AND THURSDAYS 2 TILL 4, GOT IT!

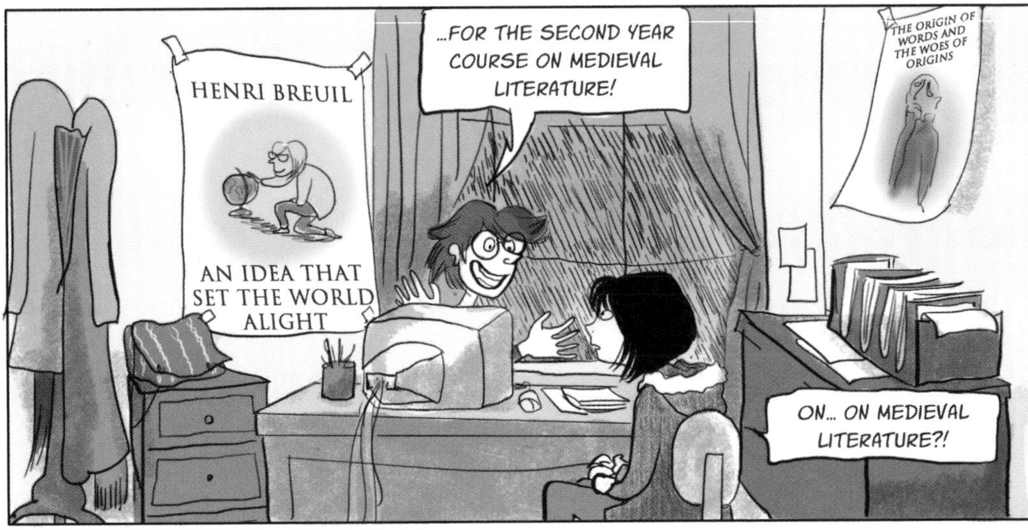
HENRI BREUIL
AN IDEA THAT SET THE WORLD ALIGHT
…FOR THE SECOND YEAR COURSE ON MEDIEVAL LITERATURE!
THE ORIGIN OF WORDS AND THE WOES OF ORIGINS
ON… ON MEDIEVAL LITERATURE?!

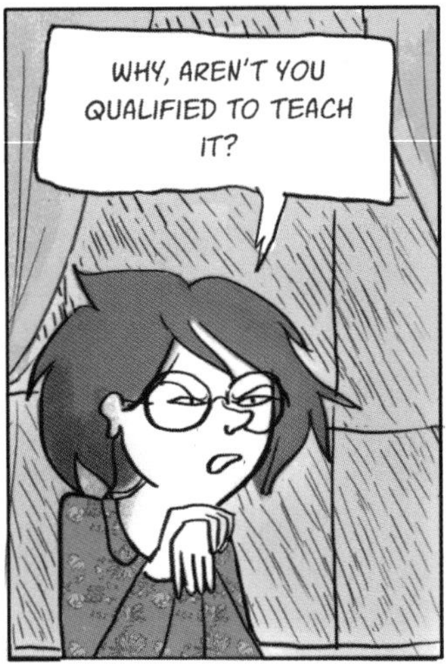
WHY, AREN'T YOU QUALIFIED TO TEACH IT?

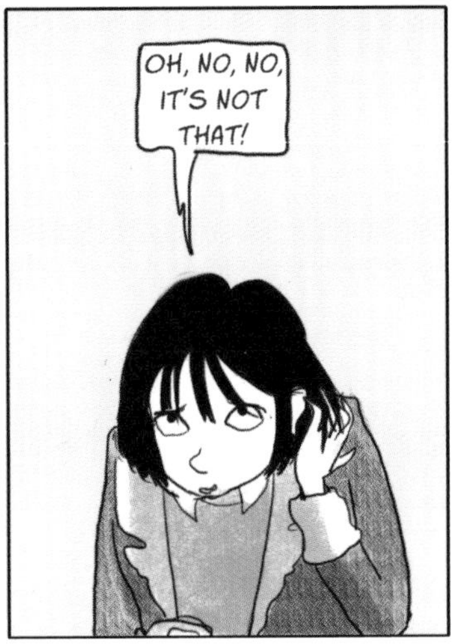
OH, NO, NO, IT'S NOT THAT!

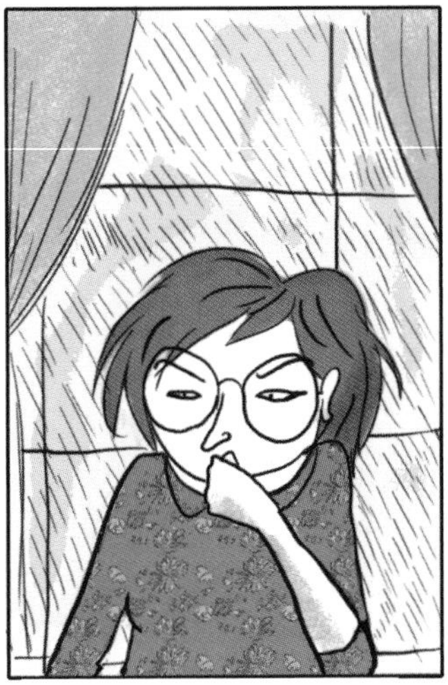

SYLVIE LALUSSE, ADMINISTRATOR FOR THE LITERATURE DEPARTMENT AT PARIS XXII, IS CONVINCED THAT SHE HAS A REAL SIXTH SENSE FOR GAUGING NEW TEACHERS.

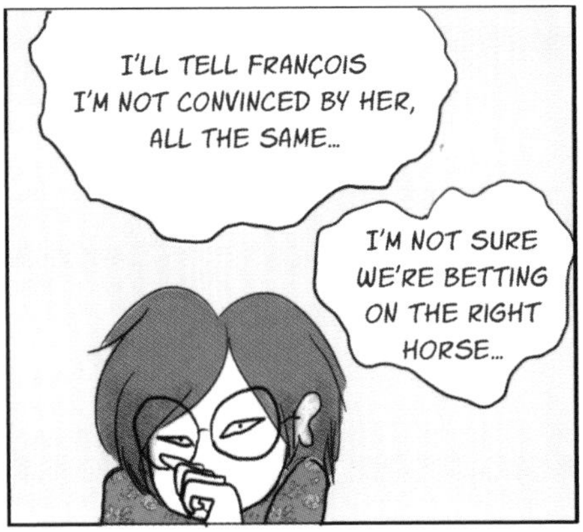
I'LL TELL FRANÇOIS I'M NOT CONVINCED BY HER, ALL THE SAME…
I'M NOT SURE WE'RE BETTING ON THE RIGHT HORSE…

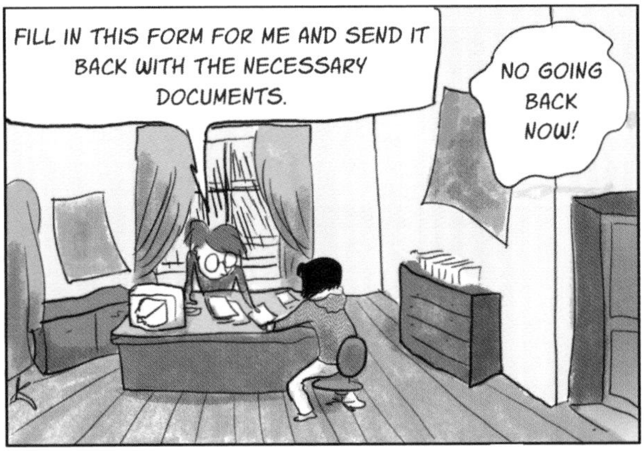
FILL IN THIS FORM FOR ME AND SEND IT BACK WITH THE NECESSARY DOCUMENTS.
NO GOING BACK NOW!

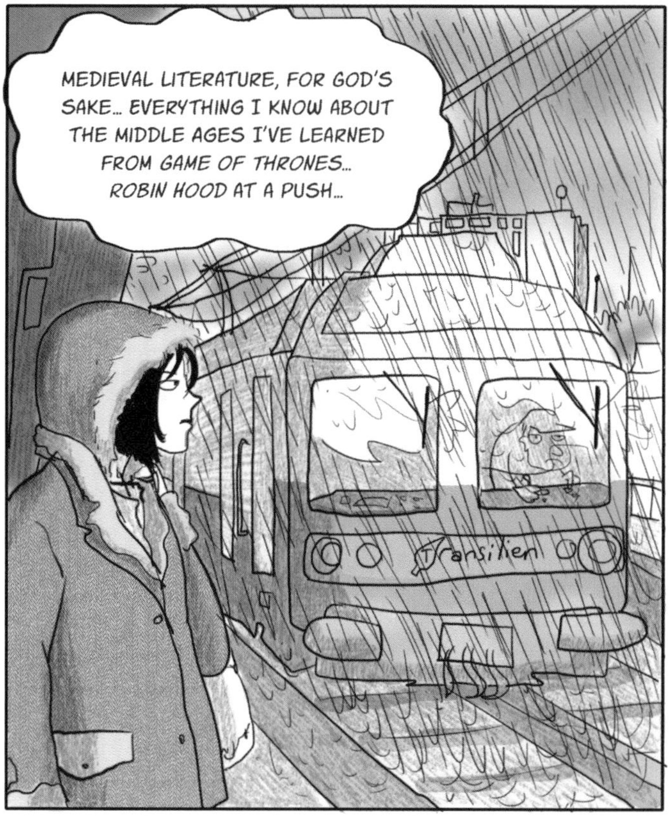
MEDIEVAL LITERATURE, FOR GOD'S SAKE... EVERYTHING I KNOW ABOUT THE MIDDLE AGES I'VE LEARNED FROM GAME OF THRONES... ROBIN HOOD AT A PUSH...
Transilien

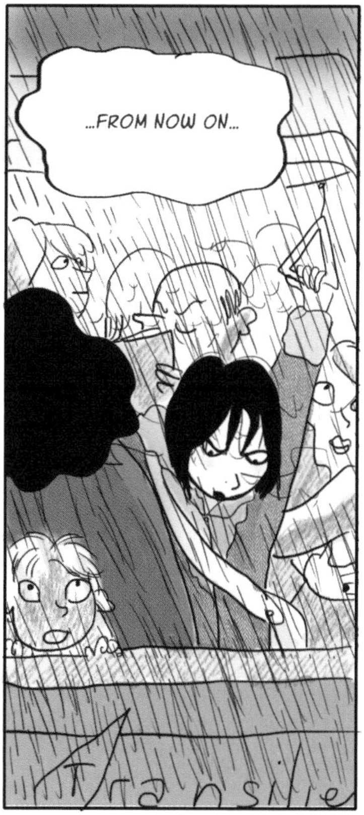
...FROM NOW ON...

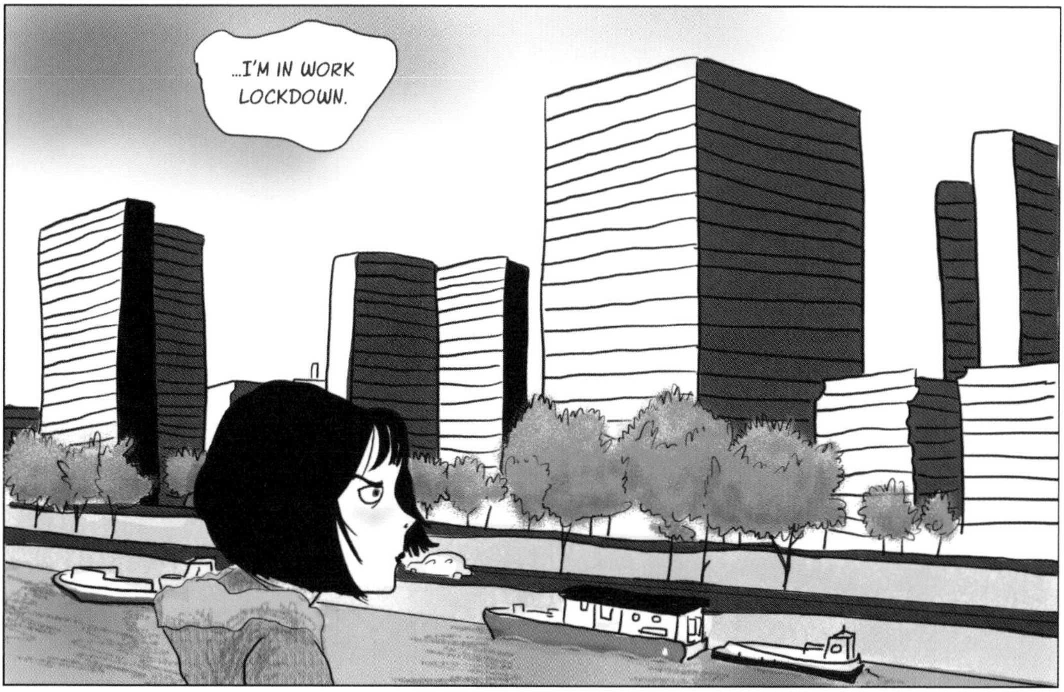
...I'M IN WORK LOCKDOWN.

THE BNF, NATIONAL LIBRARY OF FRANCE, IS A SECOND HOME FOR ALL PARISIAN PHD STUDENTS.

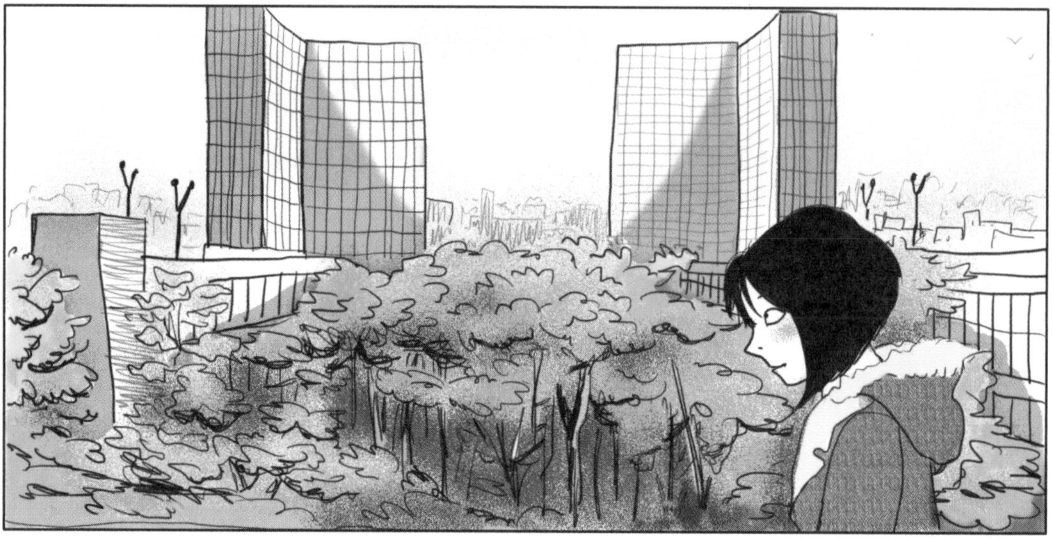

PARTLY BECAUSE IT HOLDS MORE THAN 14 MILLION BOOKS, BUT, ABOVE ALL, BECAUSE THERE'S A SPACE ON THE 'LOWER GROUND' FLOOR RESERVED FOR RESEARCHERS.

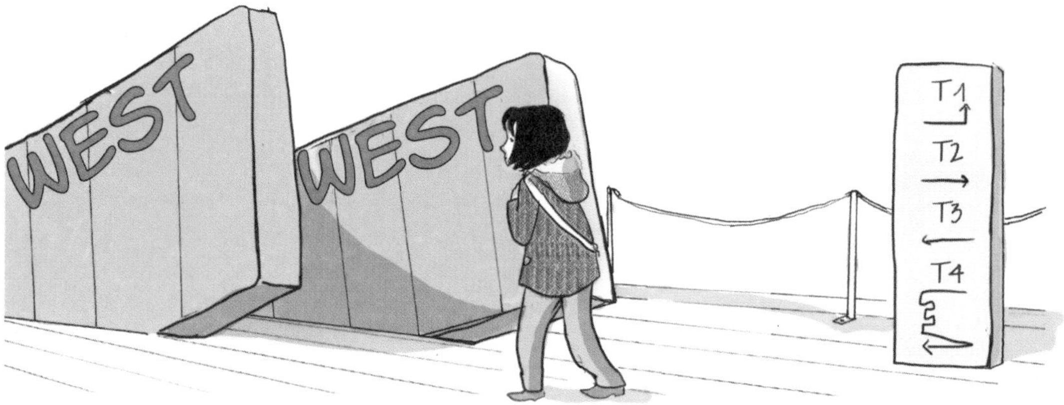
WEST
WEST
T1
T2
T3
T4

ALTHOUGH, IF YOU'RE TRYING TO REACH IT, IT'S BEST NOT TO BE OF A NERVOUS DISPOSITION...

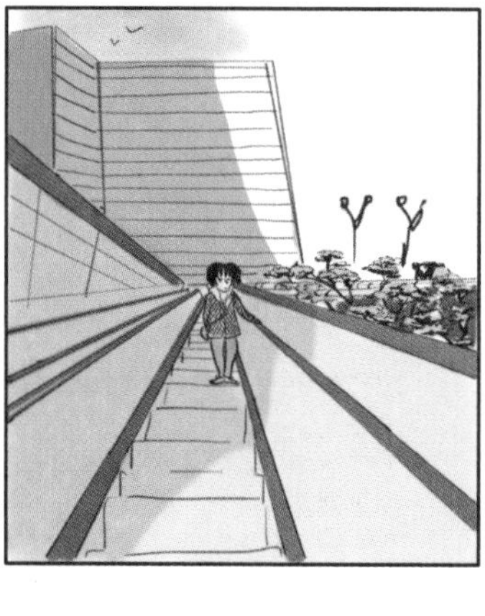

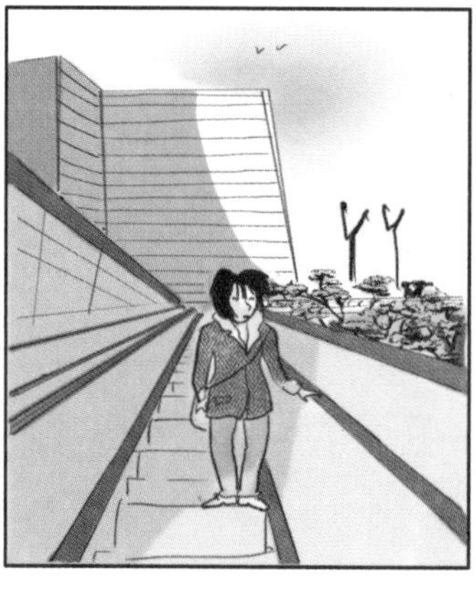

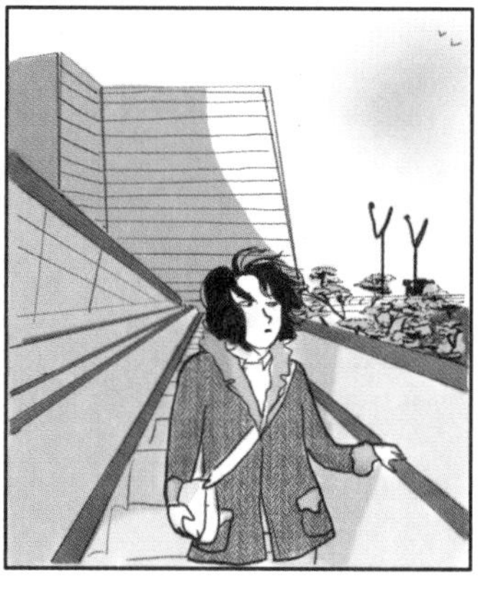

WHEN YOU ARRIVE, YOU HAVE TO EMPTY YOUR BAG, PLACE THE CONTENTS IN A TRANSPARENT FOLDER AND LEAVE YOUR COAT IN THE CLOAKROOM...

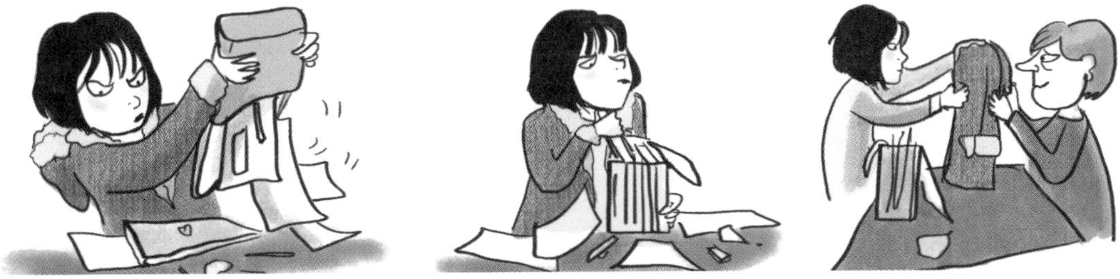

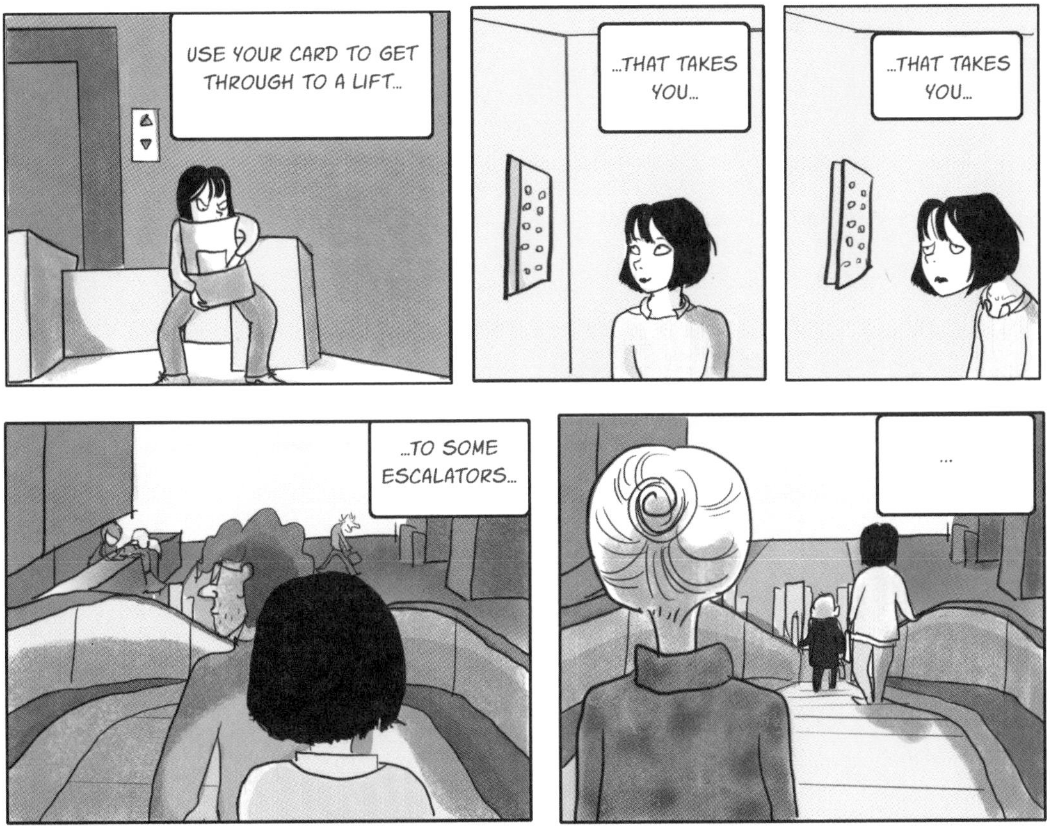
USE YOUR CARD TO GET THROUGH TO A LIFT...
...THAT TAKES YOU...
...THAT TAKES YOU...
...TO SOME ESCALATORS...
...

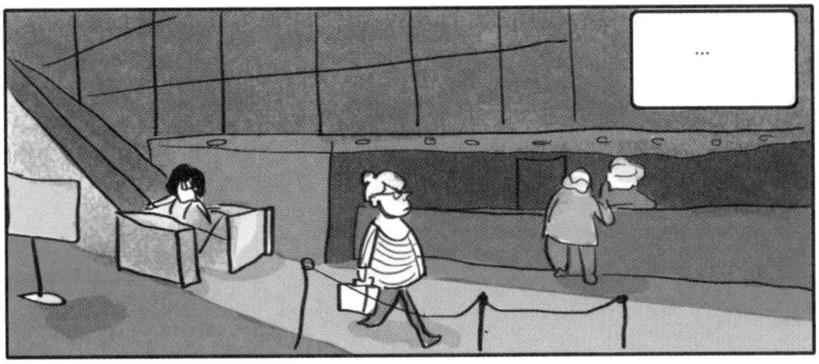
...

THEN TO SOME COMPUTERS WHERE YOU HAVE TO CONFIRM THE NUMBER OF THE DESK YOU RESERVED THE NIGHT BEFORE.

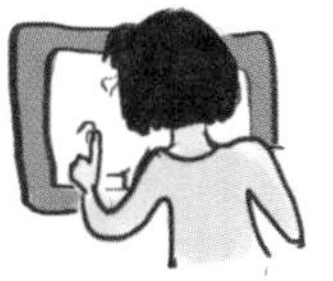

THE FINAL HURDLE IS TO SUBTLY APPROPRIATE ONE OF THE ELECTRIC SOCKETS ON THE TABLE, TO PLUG IN YOUR LAPTOP BEFORE ORDERING UP YOUR BOOKS.

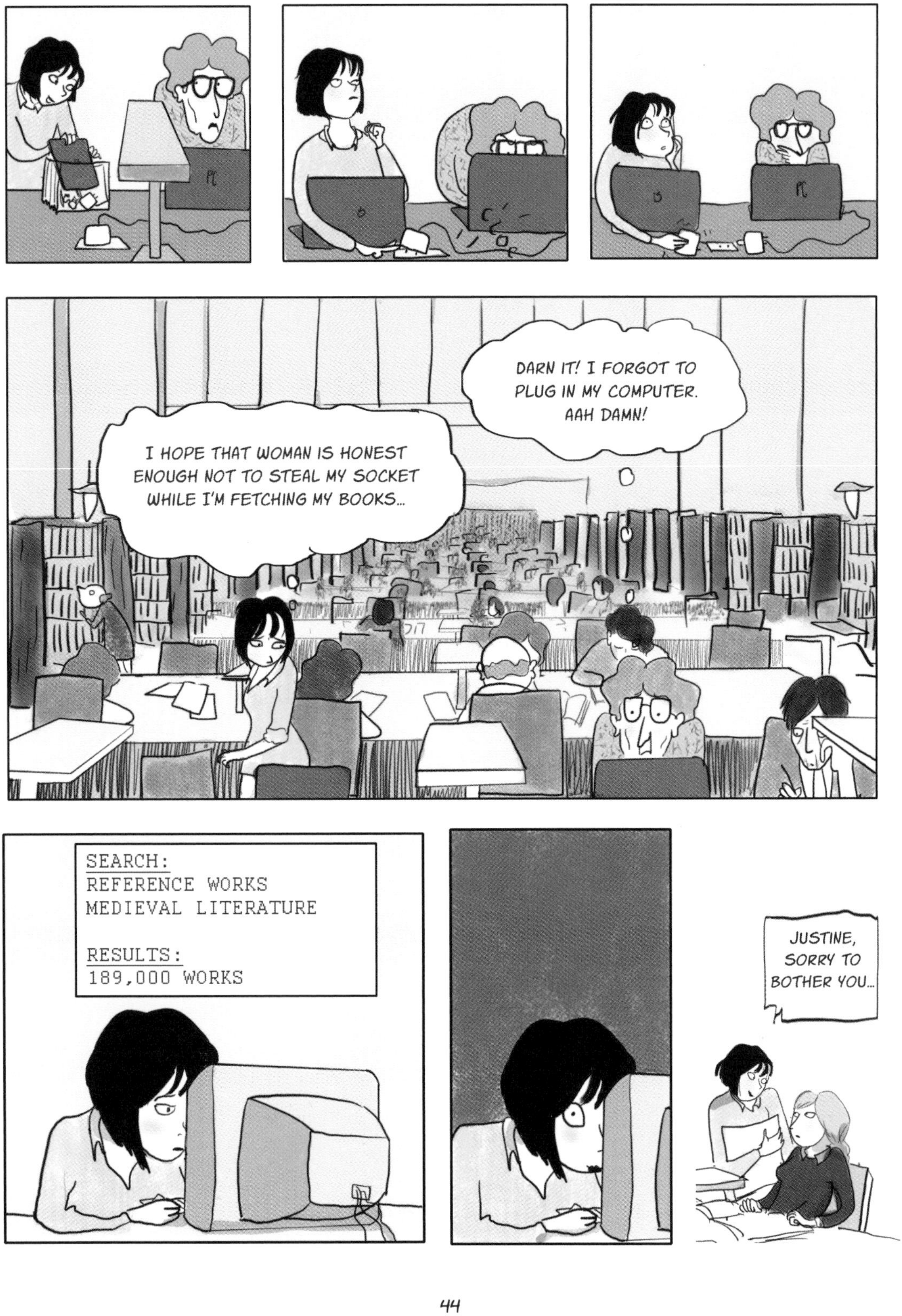

PC
PC
PC
I HOPE THAT WOMAN IS HONEST ENOUGH NOT TO STEAL MY SOCKET WHILE I'M FETCHING MY BOOKS...
DARN IT! I FORGOT TO PLUG IN MY COMPUTER. AAH DAMN!
SEARCH:
REFERENCE WORKS
MEDIEVAL LITERATURE
RESULTS:
189,000 WORKS
JUSTINE, SORRY TO BOTHER YOU...

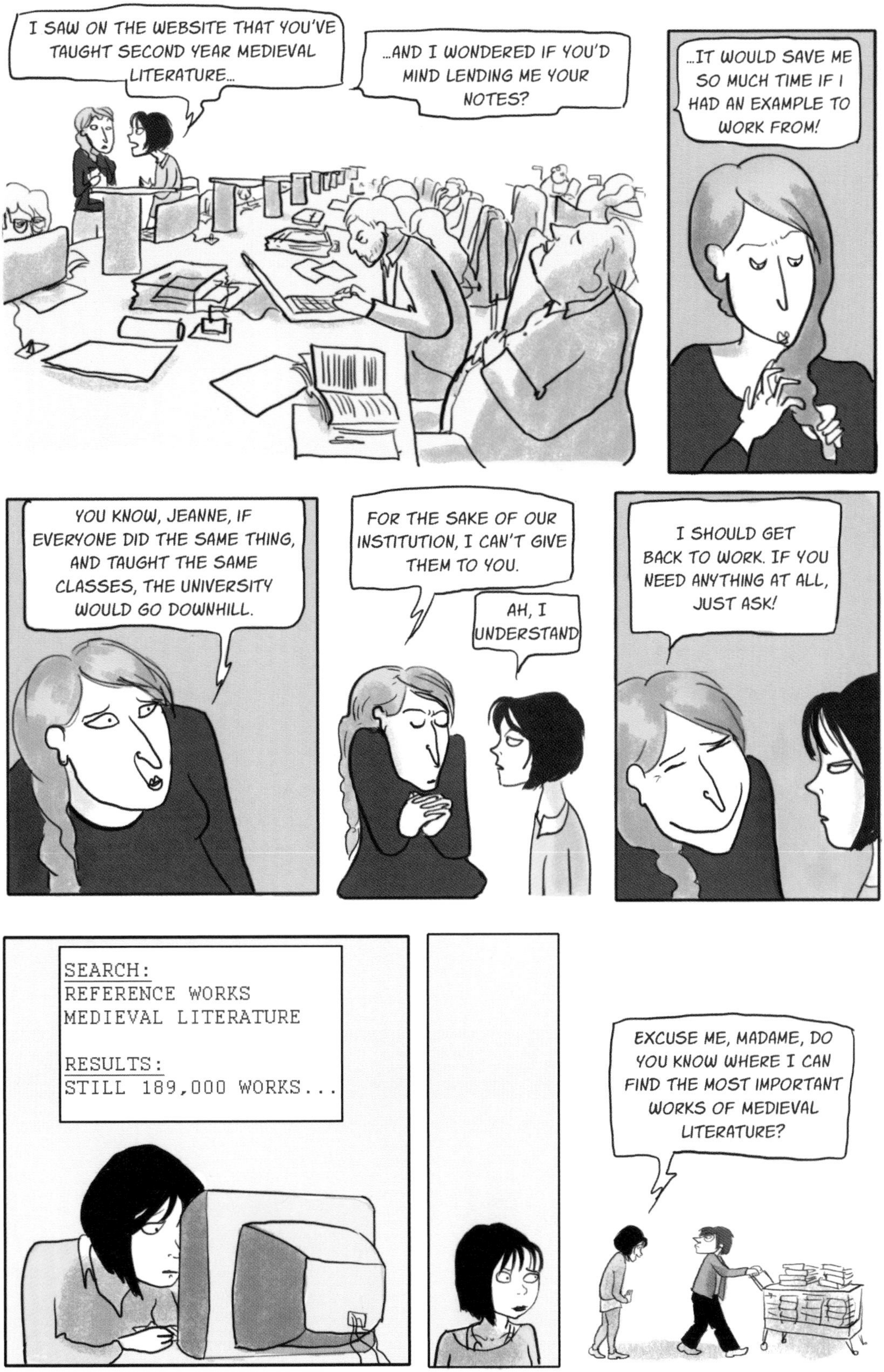
I SAW ON THE WEBSITE THAT YOU'VE TAUGHT SECOND YEAR MEDIEVAL LITERATURE...
...AND I WONDERED IF YOU'D MIND LENDING ME YOUR NOTES?
...IT WOULD SAVE ME SO MUCH TIME IF I HAD AN EXAMPLE TO WORK FROM!
YOU KNOW, JEANNE, IF EVERYONE DID THE SAME THING, AND TAUGHT THE SAME CLASSES, THE UNIVERSITY WOULD GO DOWNHILL.
FOR THE SAKE OF OUR INSTITUTION, I CAN'T GIVE THEM TO YOU.
AH, I UNDERSTAND
I SHOULD GET BACK TO WORK. IF YOU NEED ANYTHING AT ALL, JUST ASK!
SEARCH:
REFERENCE WORKS
MEDIEVAL LITERATURE
RESULTS:
STILL 189,000 WORKS...
EXCUSE ME, MADAME, DO YOU KNOW WHERE I CAN FIND THE MOST IMPORTANT WORKS OF MEDIEVAL LITERATURE?

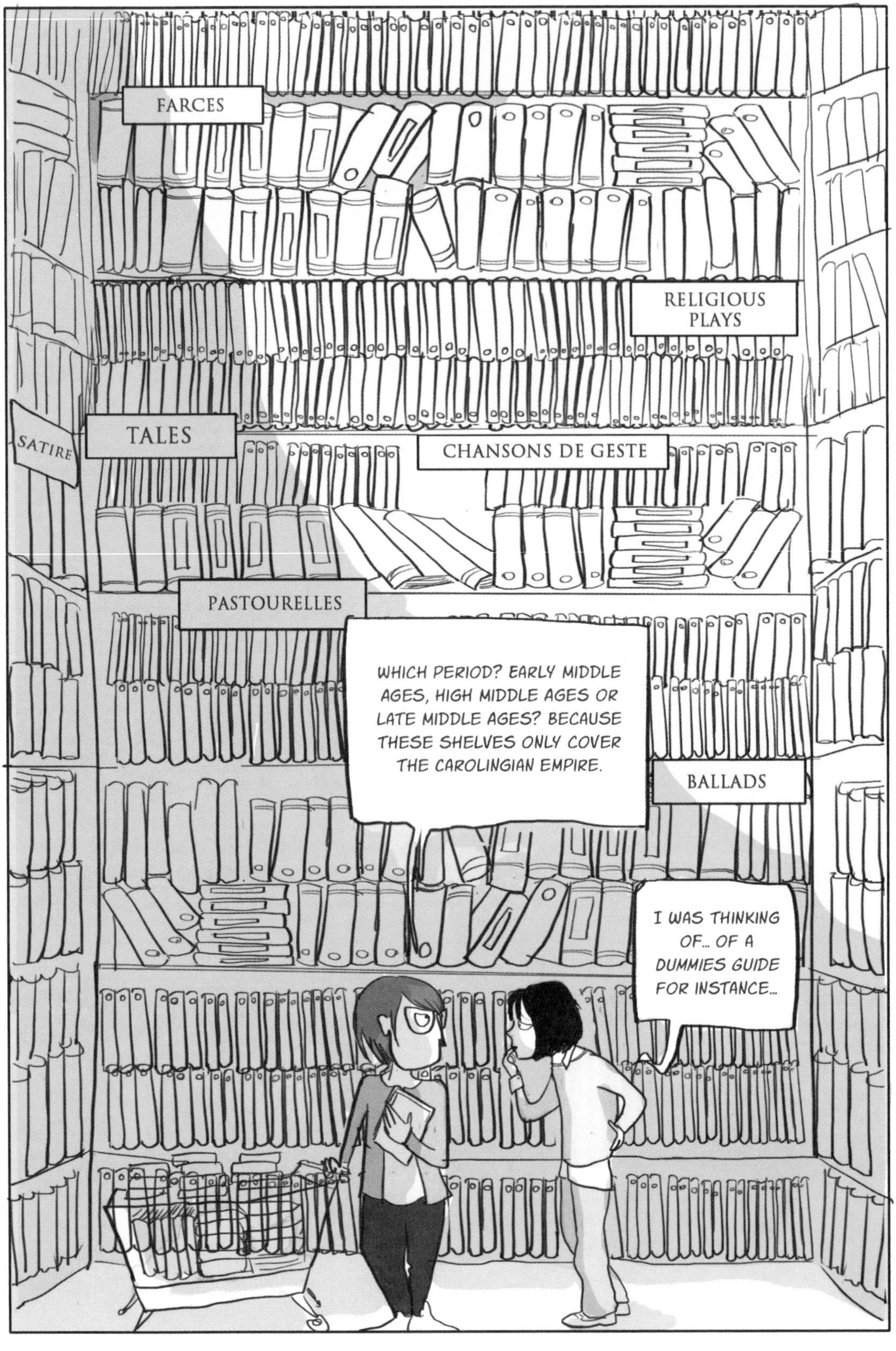
FARCES
RELIGIOUS PLAYS
SATIRE
TALES
CHANSONS DE GESTE
PASTOURELLES
BALLADS
WHICH PERIOD? EARLY MIDDLE AGES, HIGH MIDDLE AGES OR LATE MIDDLE AGES? BECAUSE THESE SHELVES ONLY COVER THE CAROLINGIAN EMPIRE.
I WAS THINKING OF... OF A DUMMIES GUIDE FOR INSTANCE...

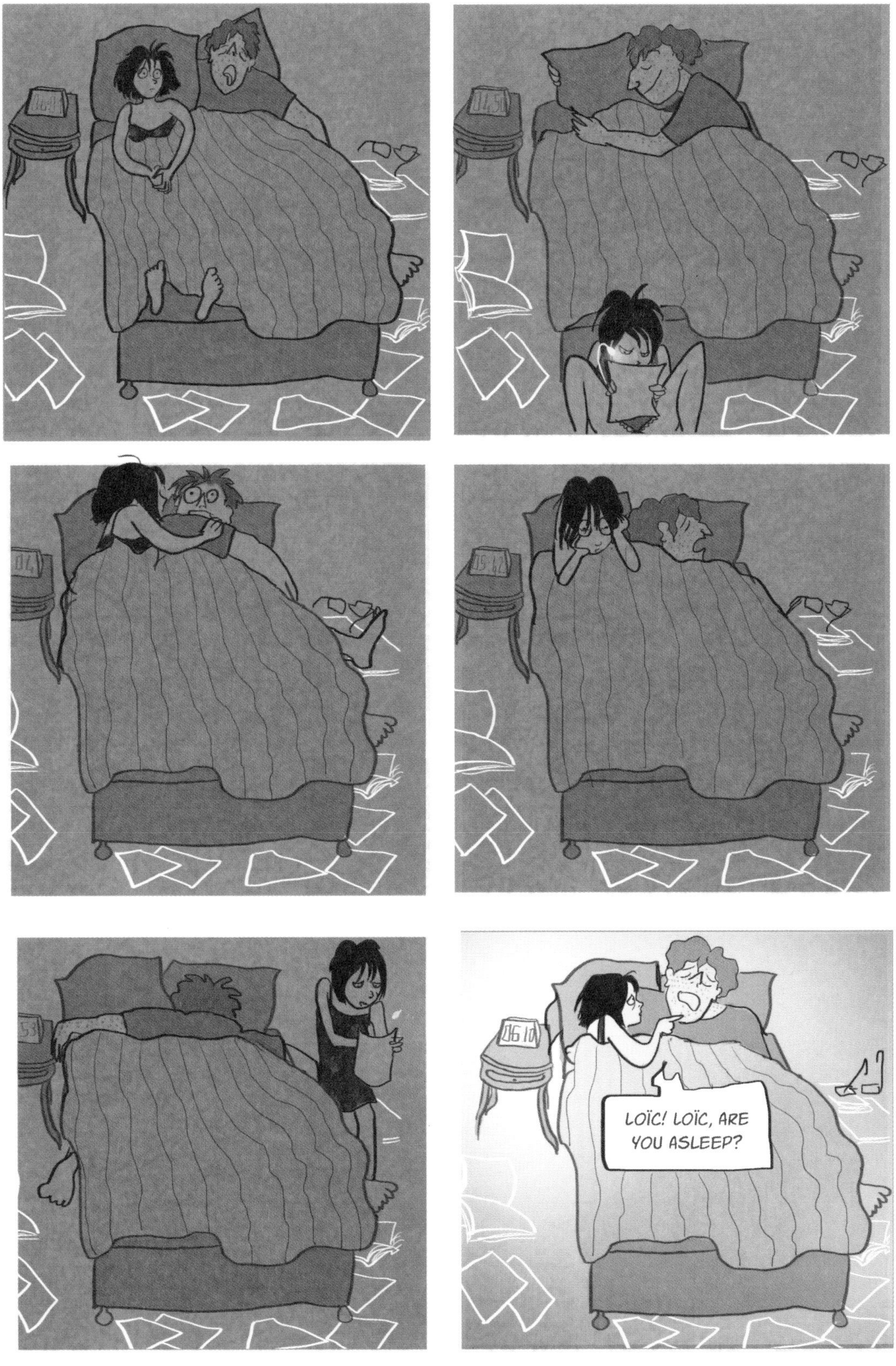
LOÏC! LOÏC, ARE
YOU ASLEEP?

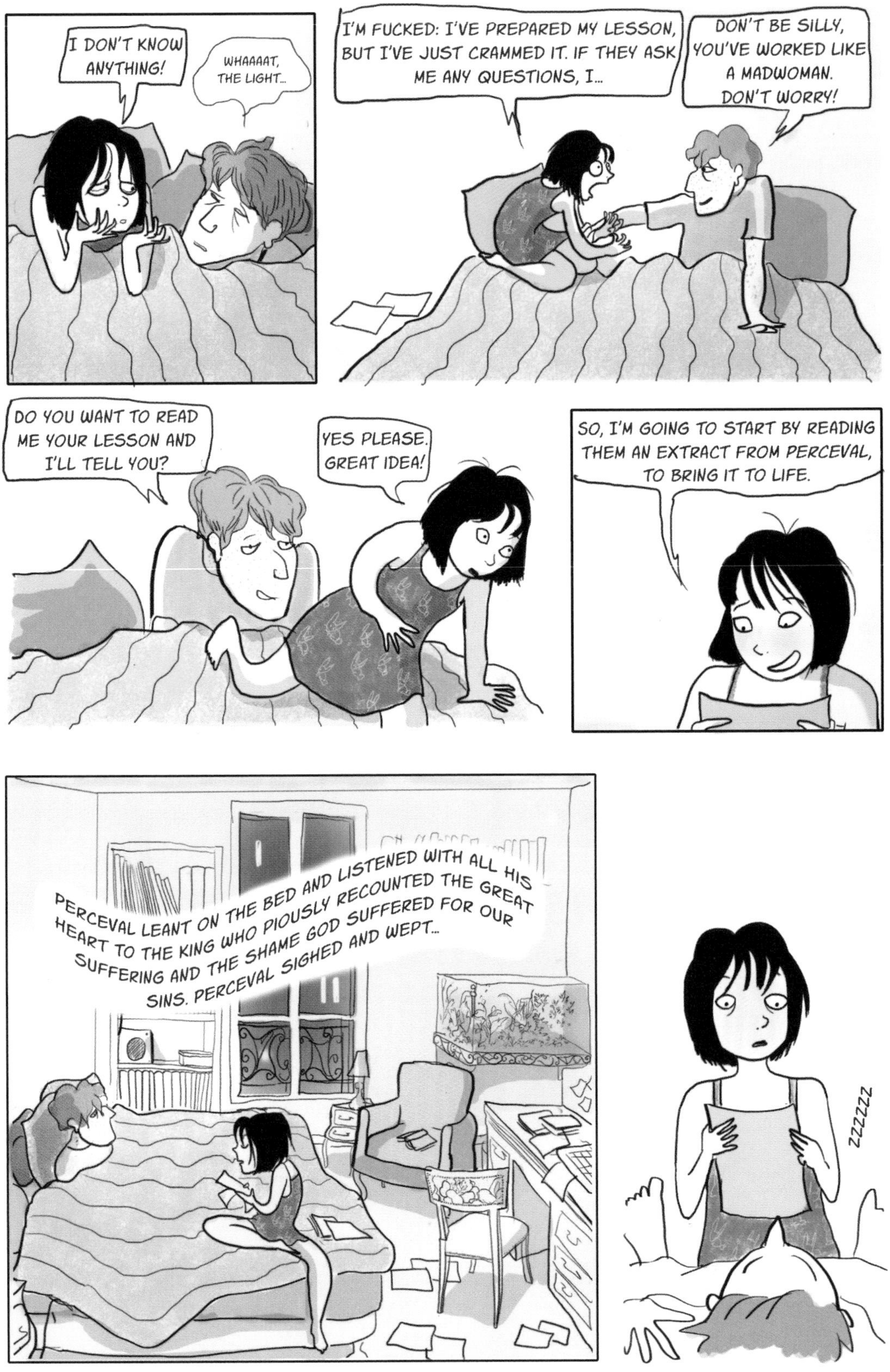
I DON'T KNOW ANYTHING!
WHAAAAT, THE LIGHT...
I'M FUCKED: I'VE PREPARED MY LESSON, BUT I'VE JUST CRAMMED IT. IF THEY ASK ME ANY QUESTIONS, I...
DON'T BE SILLY, YOU'VE WORKED LIKE A MADWOMAN. DON'T WORRY!
DO YOU WANT TO READ ME YOUR LESSON AND I'LL TELL YOU?
YES PLEASE. GREAT IDEA!
SO, I'M GOING TO START BY READING THEM AN EXTRACT FROM PERCEVAL, TO BRING IT TO LIFE.
PERCEVAL LEANT ON THE BED AND LISTENED WITH ALL HIS HEART TO THE KING WHO PIOUSLY RECOUNTED THE GREAT SUFFERING AND THE SHAME GOD SUFFERED FOR OUR SINS. PERCEVAL SIGHED AND WEPT...
ZZZZZZ

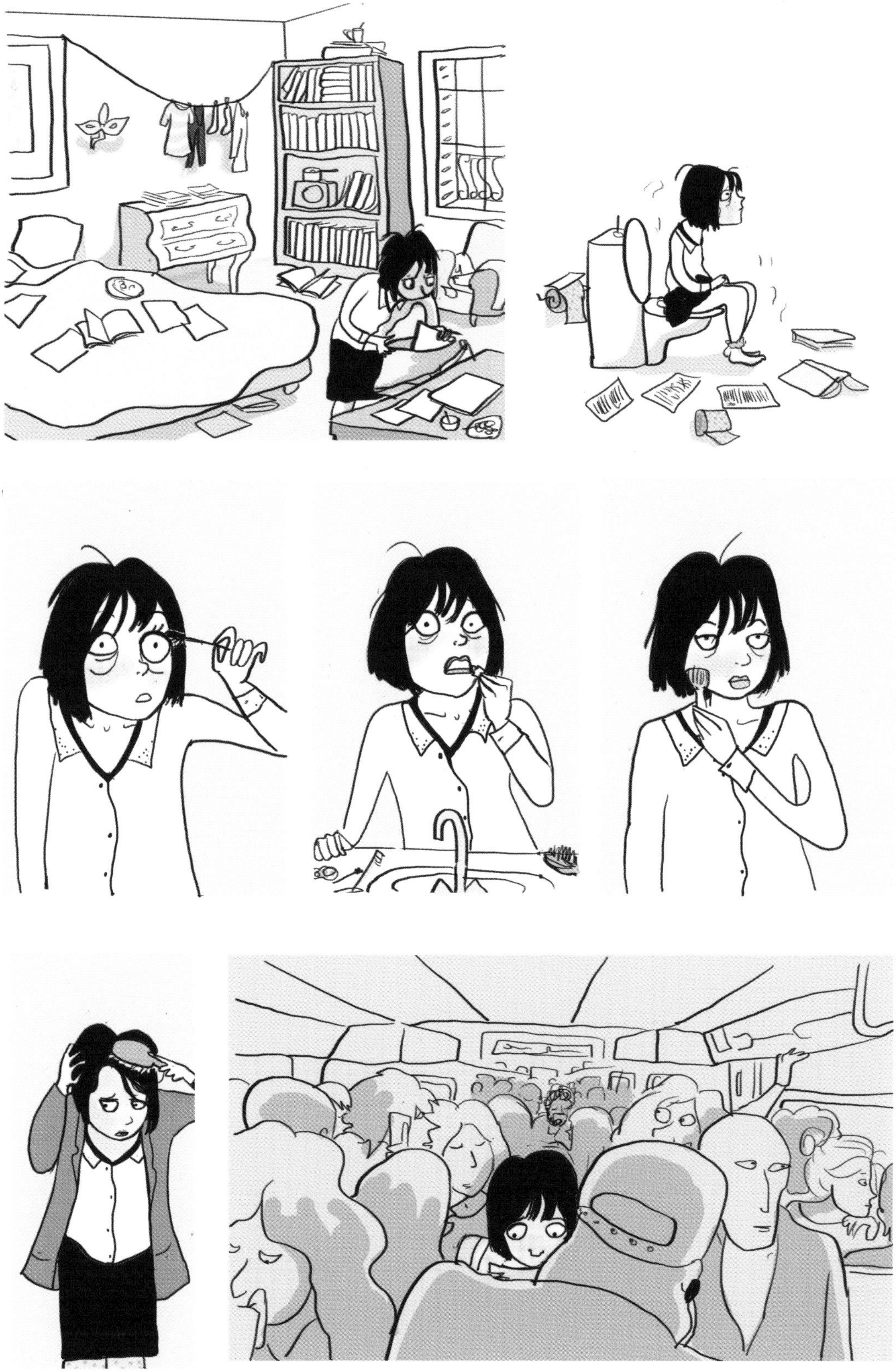

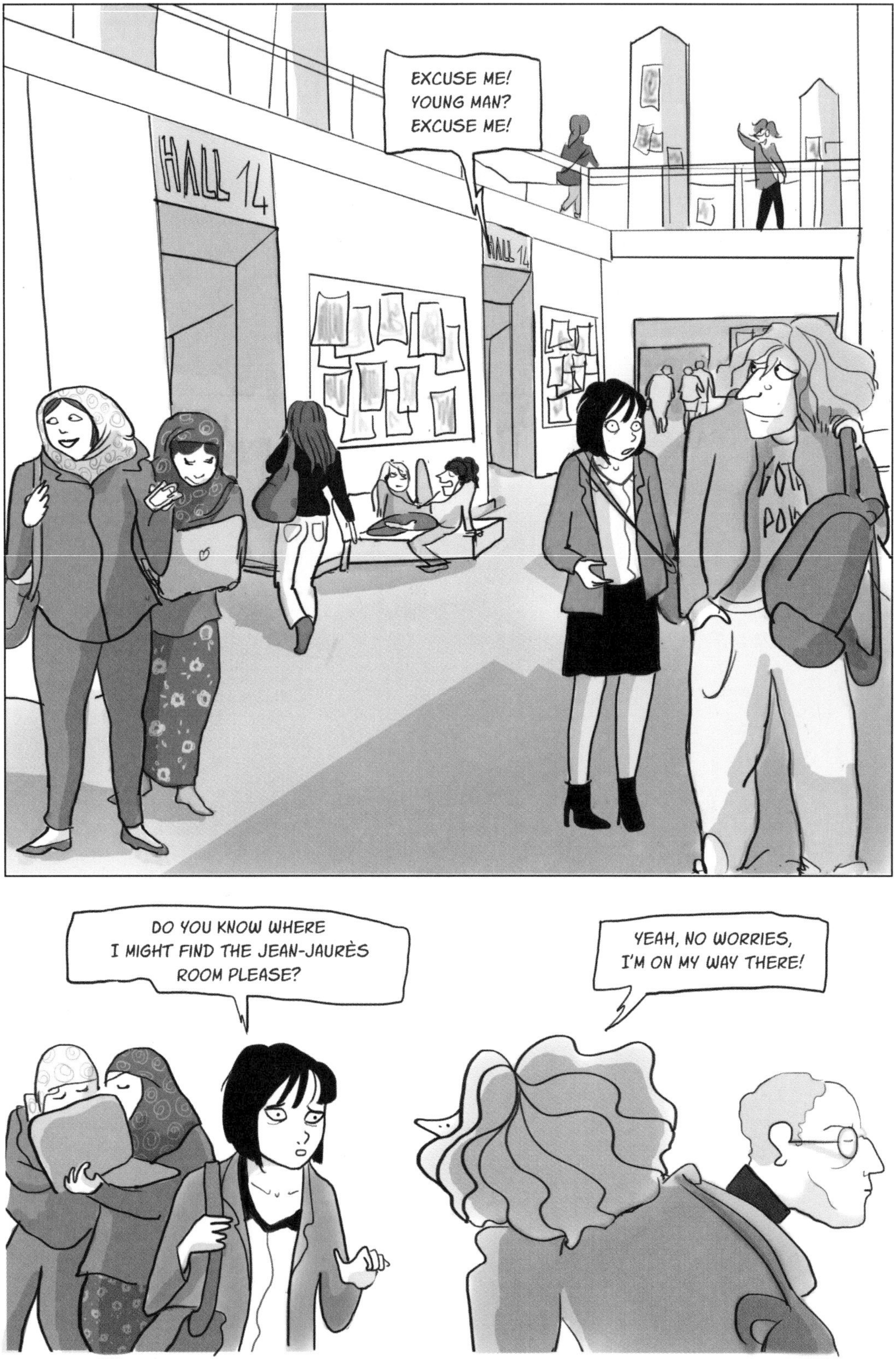
HALL 14
EXCUSE ME! YOUNG MAN? EXCUSE ME!
HALL 14
DO YOU KNOW WHERE I MIGHT FIND THE JEAN-JAURÈS ROOM PLEASE?
YEAH, NO WORRIES, I'M ON MY WAY THERE!

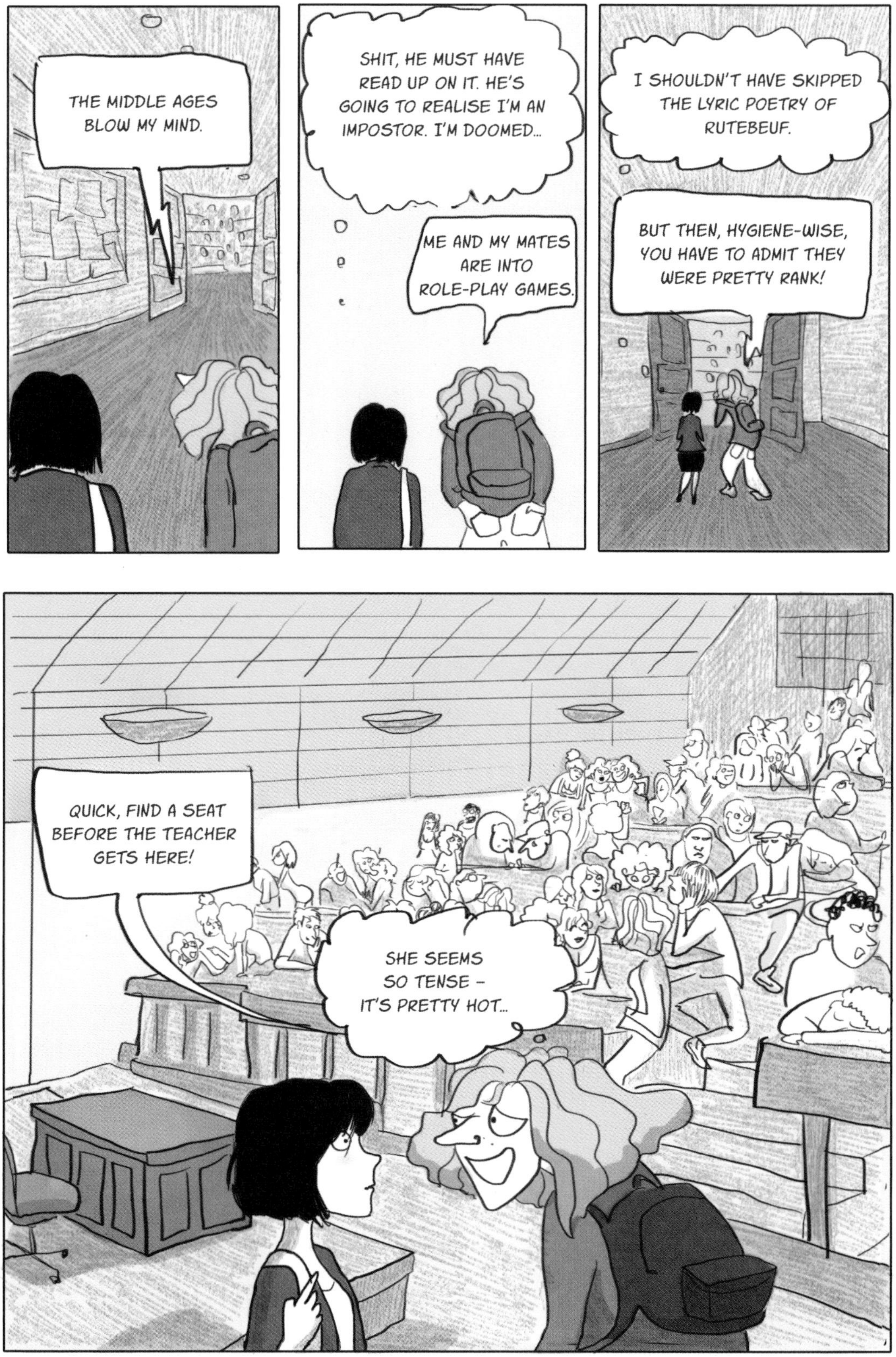
THE MIDDLE AGES BLOW MY MIND.
SHIT, HE MUST HAVE READ UP ON IT. HE'S GOING TO REALISE I'M AN IMPOSTOR. I'M DOOMED...
ME AND MY MATES ARE INTO ROLE-PLAY GAMES.
I SHOULDN'T HAVE SKIPPED THE LYRIC POETRY OF RUTEBEUF.
BUT THEN, HYGIENE-WISE, YOU HAVE TO ADMIT THEY WERE PRETTY RANK!
QUICK, FIND A SEAT BEFORE THE TEACHER GETS HERE!
SHE SEEMS SO TENSE – IT'S PRETTY HOT...

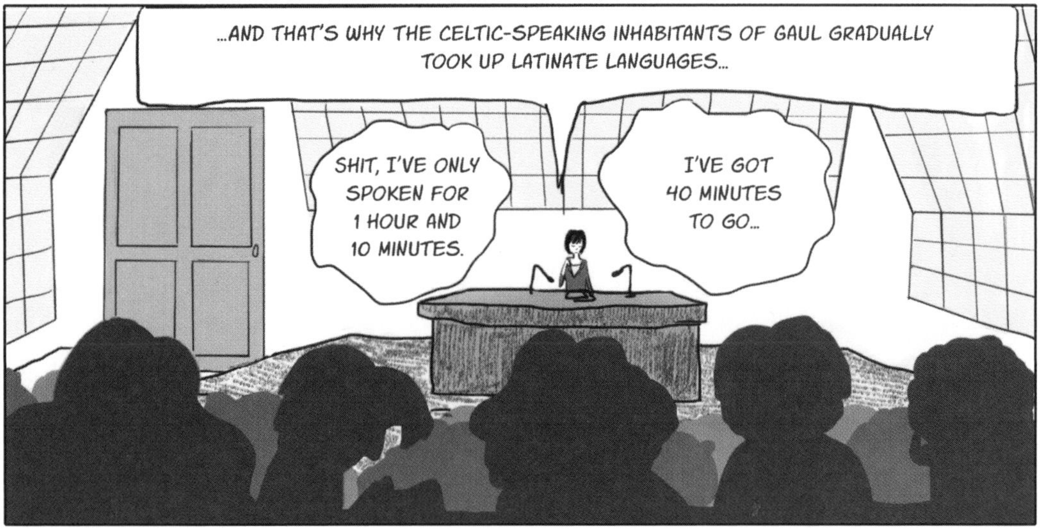
...AND THAT'S WHY THE CELTIC-SPEAKING INHABITANTS OF GAUL GRADUALLY TOOK UP LATINATE LANGUAGES...
SHIT, I'VE ONLY SPOKEN FOR 1 HOUR AND 10 MINUTES.
I'VE GOT 40 MINUTES TO GO...

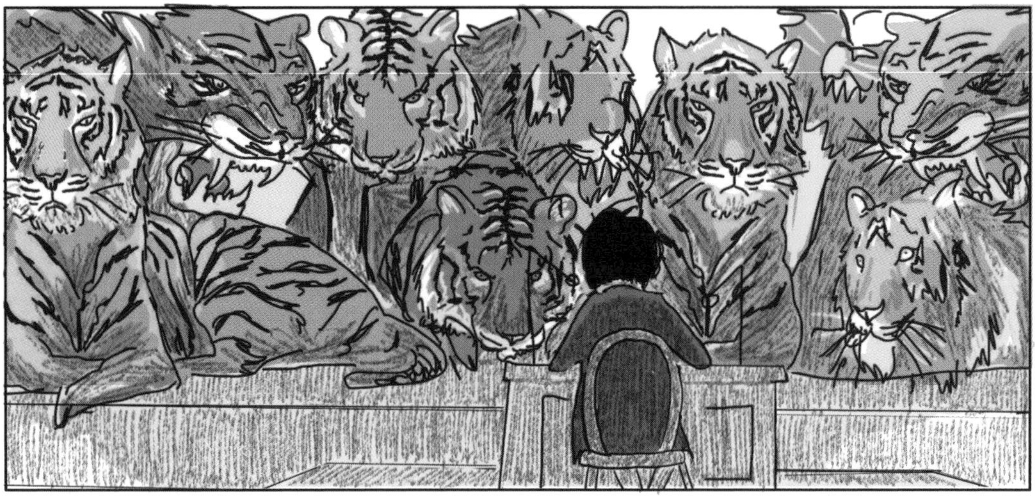

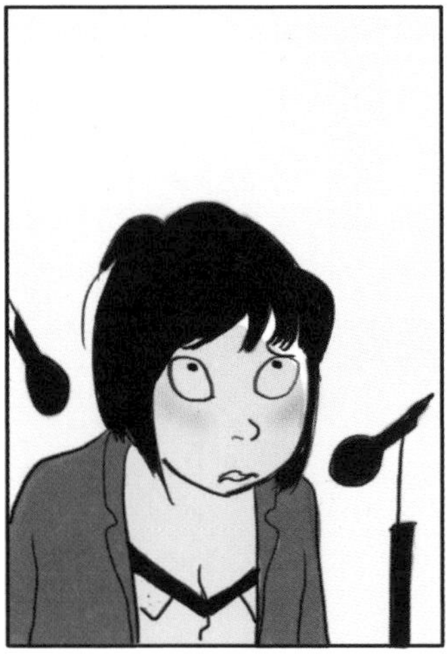

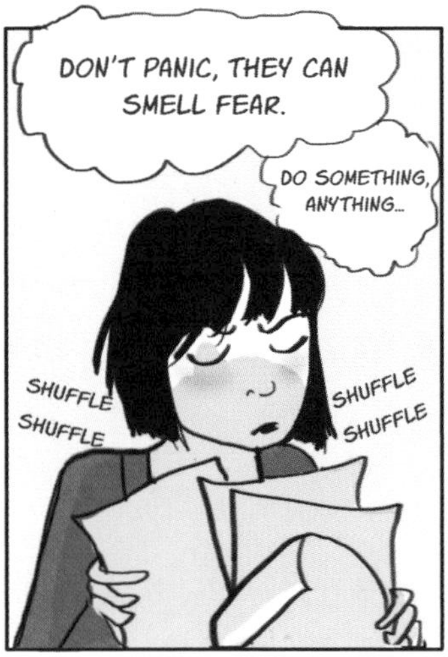
DON'T PANIC, THEY CAN SMELL FEAR.
DO SOMETHING, ANYTHING...
SHUFFLE SHUFFLE
SHUFFLE SHUFFLE

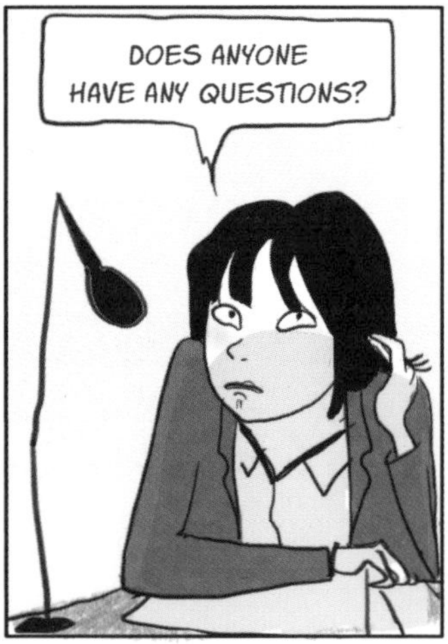
DOES ANYONE HAVE ANY QUESTIONS?

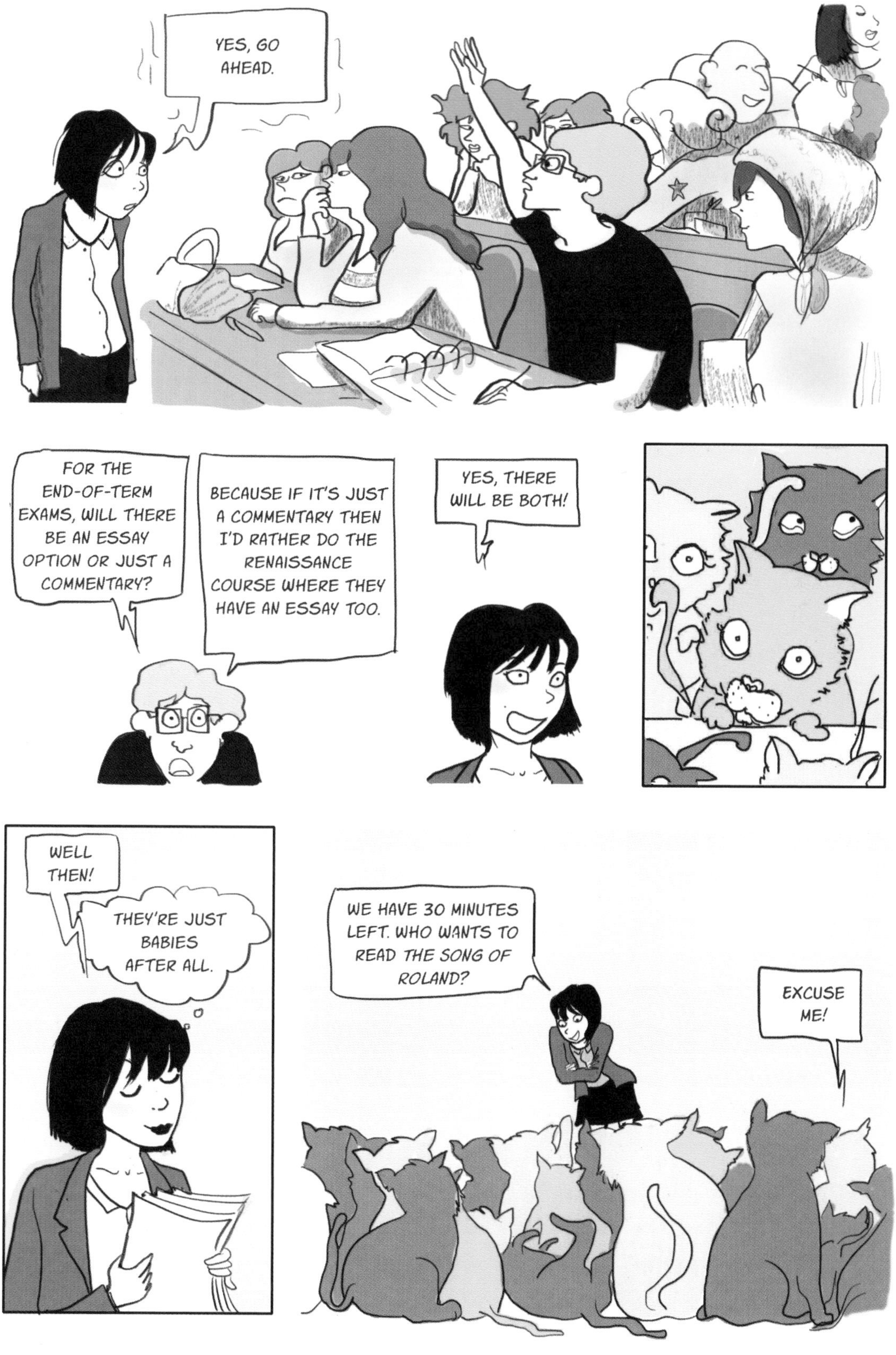
YES, GO AHEAD.
FOR THE END-OF-TERM EXAMS, WILL THERE BE AN ESSAY OPTION OR JUST A COMMENTARY?
BECAUSE IF IT'S JUST A COMMENTARY THEN I'D RATHER DO THE RENAISSANCE COURSE WHERE THEY HAVE AN ESSAY TOO.
YES, THERE WILL BE BOTH!
WELL THEN!
THEY'RE JUST BABIES AFTER ALL.
WE HAVE 30 MINUTES LEFT. WHO WANTS TO READ THE SONG OF ROLAND?
EXCUSE ME!

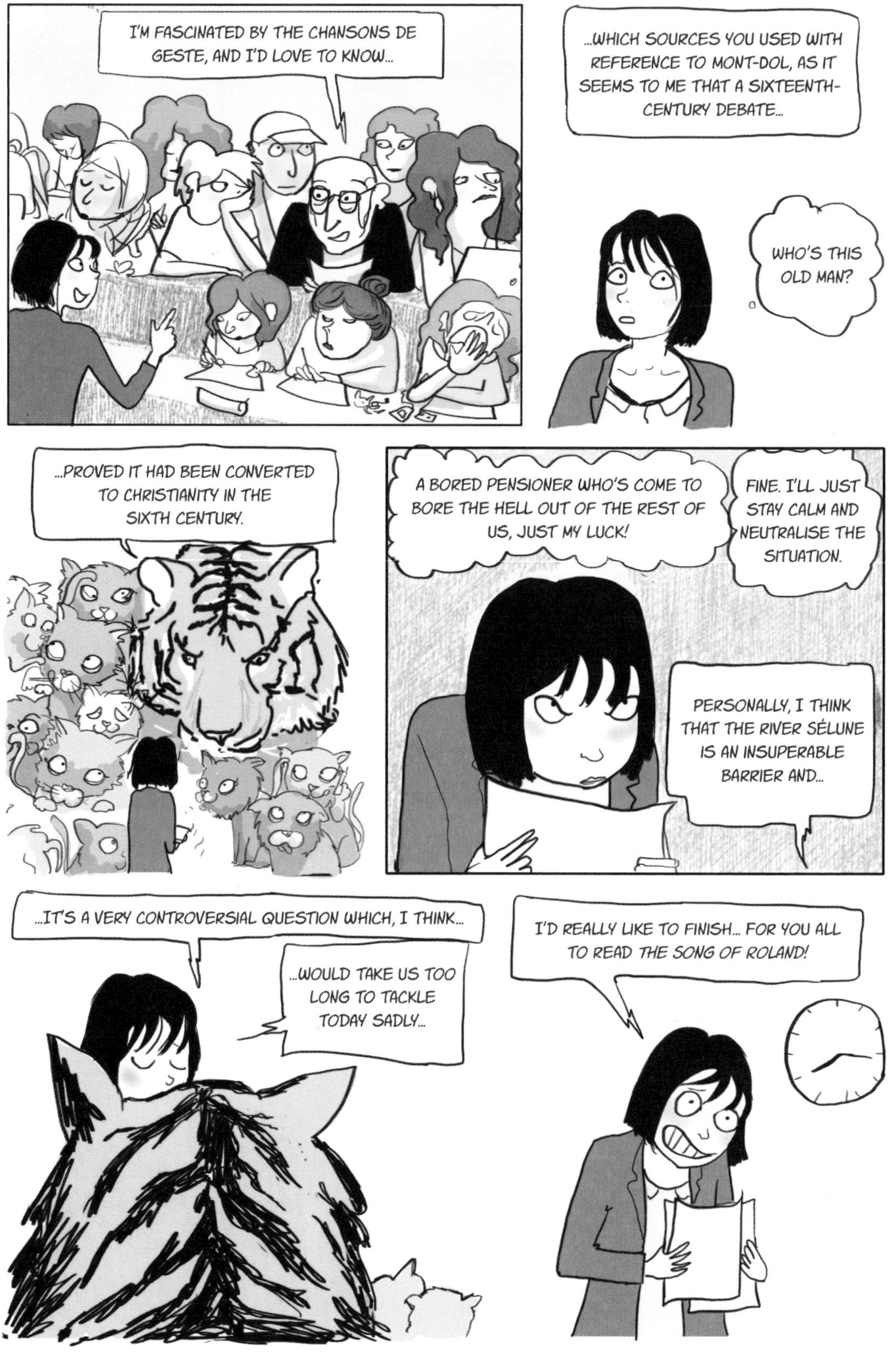

I'M FASCINATED BY THE CHANSONS DE GESTE, AND I'D LOVE TO KNOW...
...WHICH SOURCES YOU USED WITH REFERENCE TO MONT-DOL, AS IT SEEMS TO ME THAT A SIXTEENTH-CENTURY DEBATE...
WHO'S THIS OLD MAN?
...PROVED IT HAD BEEN CONVERTED TO CHRISTIANITY IN THE SIXTH CENTURY.
A BORED PENSIONER WHO'S COME TO BORE THE HELL OUT OF THE REST OF US, JUST MY LUCK!
FINE. I'LL JUST STAY CALM AND NEUTRALISE THE SITUATION.
PERSONALLY, I THINK THAT THE RIVER SÉLUNE IS AN INSUPERABLE BARRIER AND...
...IT'S A VERY CONTROVERSIAL QUESTION WHICH, I THINK...
...WOULD TAKE US TOO LONG TO TACKLE TODAY SADLY...
I'D REALLY LIKE TO FINISH... FOR YOU ALL TO READ THE SONG OF ROLAND!

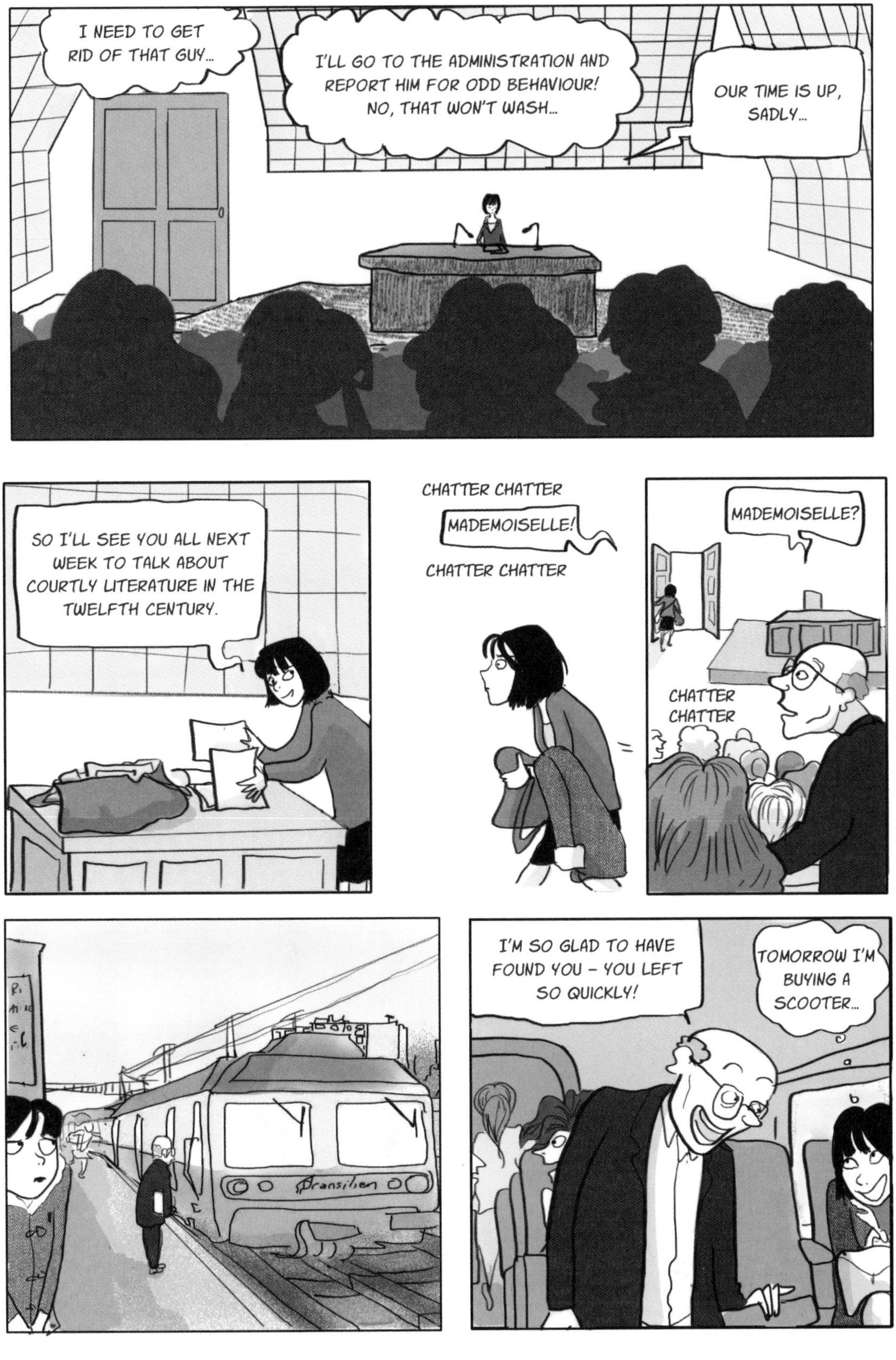
I NEED TO GET RID OF THAT GUY...
I'LL GO TO THE ADMINISTRATION AND REPORT HIM FOR ODD BEHAVIOUR! NO, THAT WON'T WASH...
OUR TIME IS UP, SADLY...
SO I'LL SEE YOU ALL NEXT WEEK TO TALK ABOUT COURTLY LITERATURE IN THE TWELFTH CENTURY.
CHATTER CHATTER
MADEMOISELLE!
CHATTER CHATTER
MADEMOISELLE?
CHATTER CHATTER
I'M SO GLAD TO HAVE FOUND YOU – YOU LEFT SO QUICKLY!
TOMORROW I'M BUYING A SCOOTER...

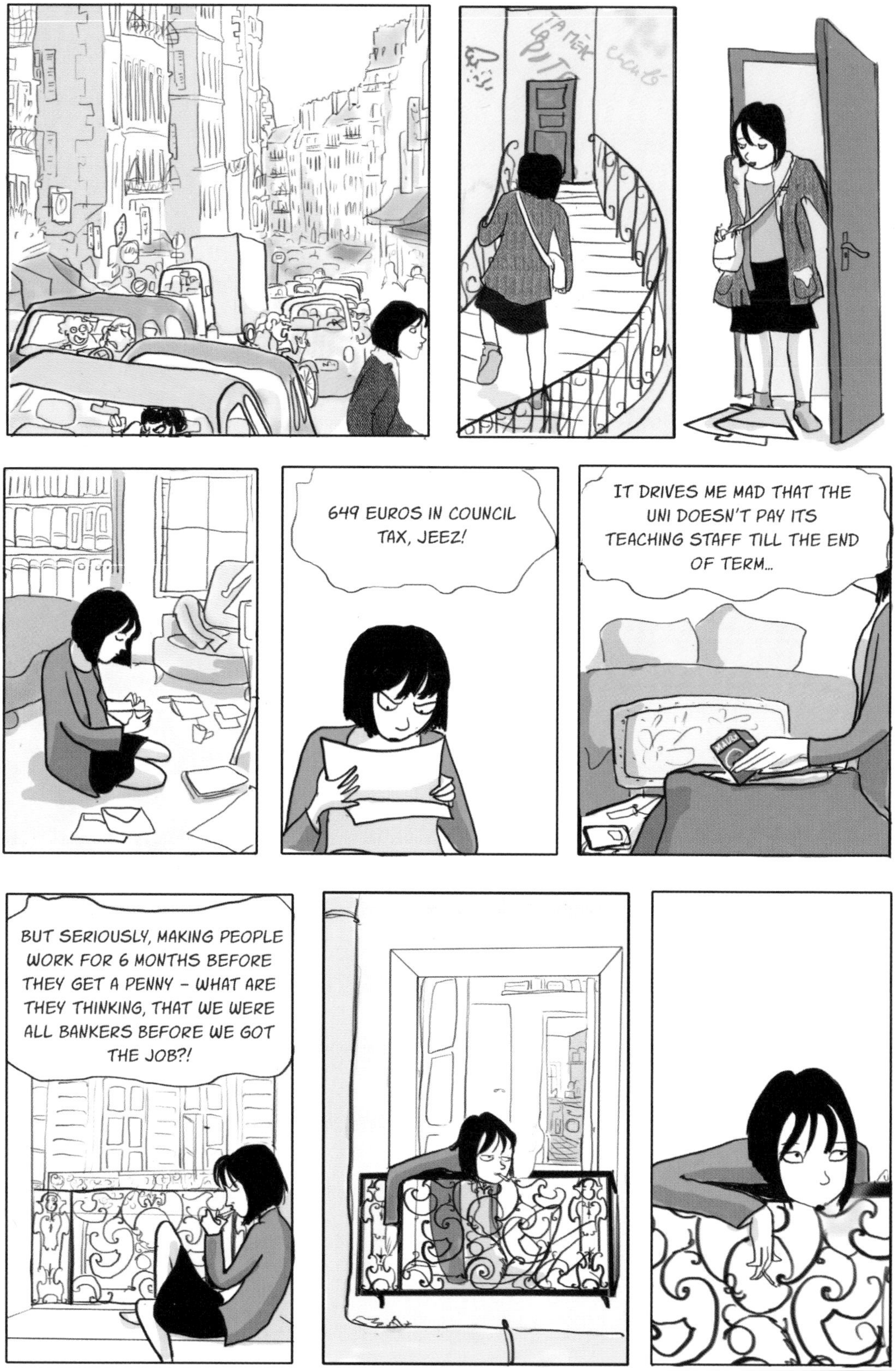
649 EUROS IN COUNCIL TAX, JEEZ!
IT DRIVES ME MAD THAT THE UNI DOESN'T PAY ITS TEACHING STAFF TILL THE END OF TERM...
BUT SERIOUSLY, MAKING PEOPLE WORK FOR 6 MONTHS BEFORE THEY GET A PENNY – WHAT ARE THEY THINKING, THAT WE WERE ALL BANKERS BEFORE WE GOT THE JOB?!

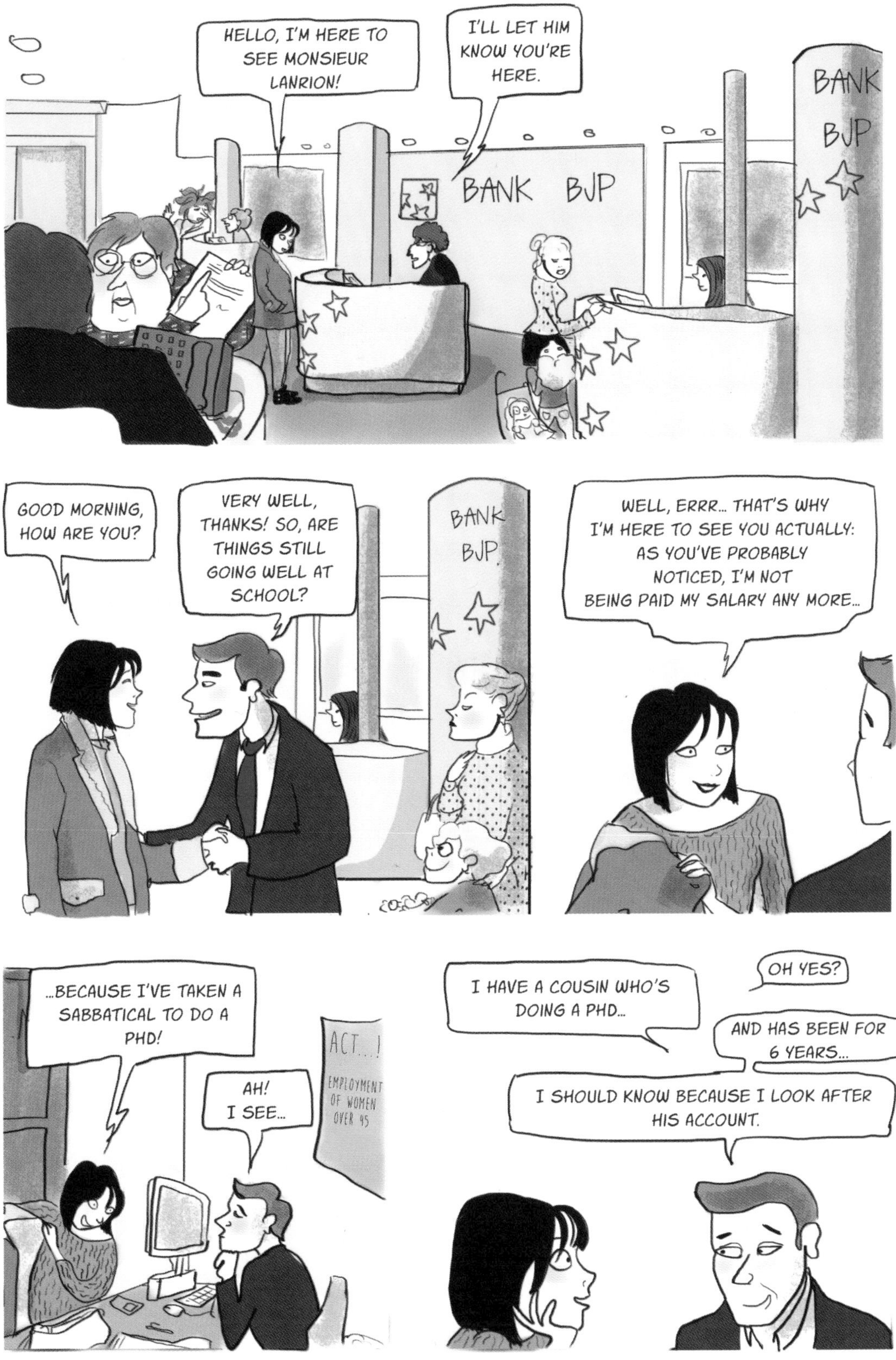
HELLO, I'M HERE TO SEE MONSIEUR LANRION!
I'LL LET HIM KNOW YOU'RE HERE.
BANK BJP
BANK BJP
GOOD MORNING, HOW ARE YOU?
VERY WELL, THANKS! SO, ARE THINGS STILL GOING WELL AT SCHOOL?
BANK BJP
WELL, ERRR... THAT'S WHY I'M HERE TO SEE YOU ACTUALLY: AS YOU'VE PROBABLY NOTICED, I'M NOT BEING PAID MY SALARY ANY MORE...
...BECAUSE I'VE TAKEN A SABBATICAL TO DO A PHD!
ACT...!
EMPLOYMENT OF WOMEN OVER 45
AH! I SEE...
I HAVE A COUSIN WHO'S DOING A PHD...
OH YES?
AND HAS BEEN FOR 6 YEARS...
I SHOULD KNOW BECAUSE I LOOK AFTER HIS ACCOUNT.

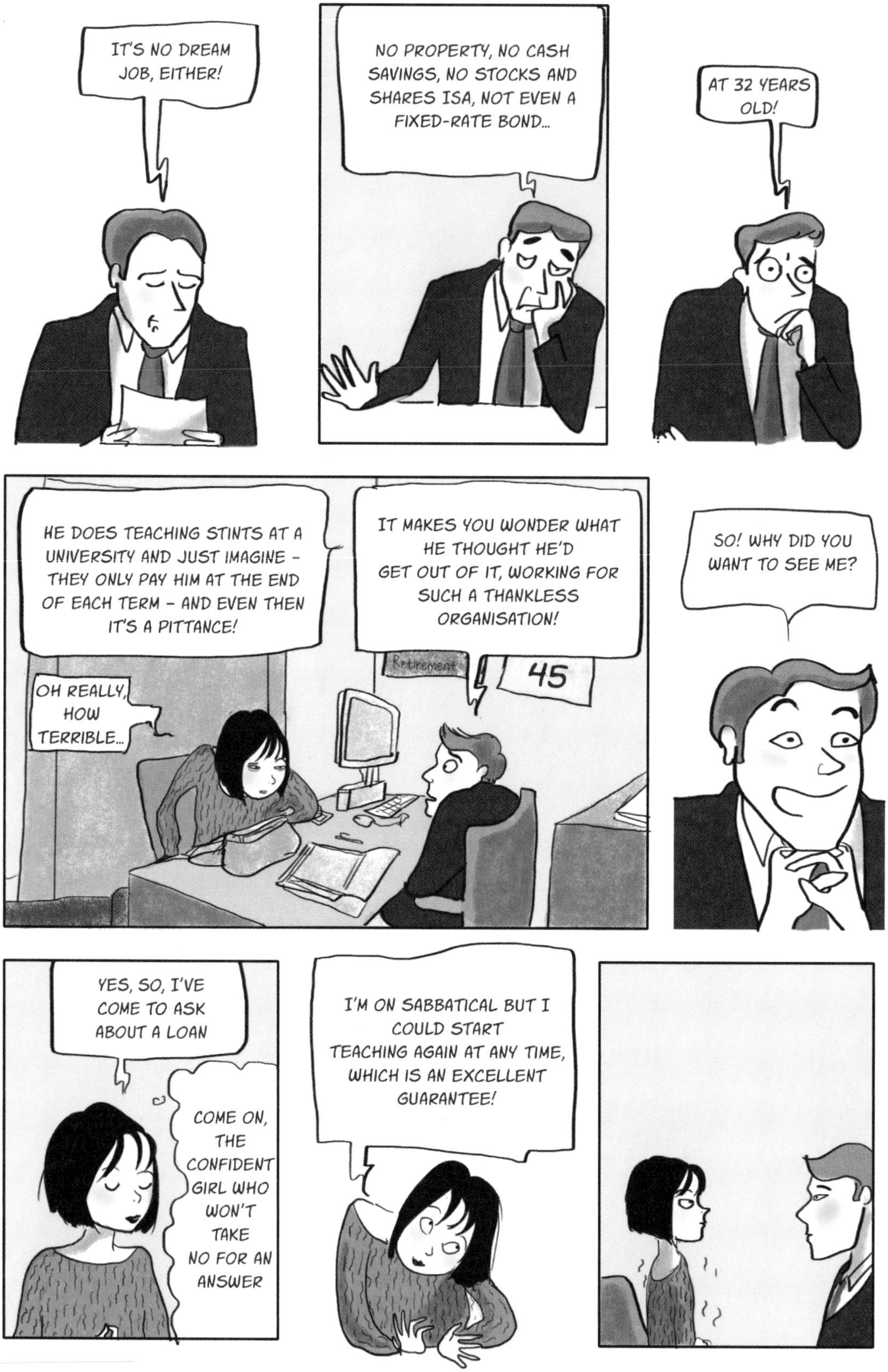
IT'S NO DREAM JOB, EITHER!
NO PROPERTY, NO CASH SAVINGS, NO STOCKS AND SHARES ISA, NOT EVEN A FIXED-RATE BOND...
AT 32 YEARS OLD!
HE DOES TEACHING STINTS AT A UNIVERSITY AND JUST IMAGINE - THEY ONLY PAY HIM AT THE END OF EACH TERM - AND EVEN THEN IT'S A PITTANCE!
IT MAKES YOU WONDER WHAT HE THOUGHT HE'D GET OUT OF IT, WORKING FOR SUCH A THANKLESS ORGANISATION!
Retirement
45
OH REALLY, HOW TERRIBLE...
SO! WHY DID YOU WANT TO SEE ME?
YES, SO, I'VE COME TO ASK ABOUT A LOAN
COME ON, THE CONFIDENT GIRL WHO WON'T TAKE NO FOR AN ANSWER
I'M ON SABBATICAL BUT I COULD START TEACHING AGAIN AT ANY TIME, WHICH IS AN EXCELLENT GUARANTEE!

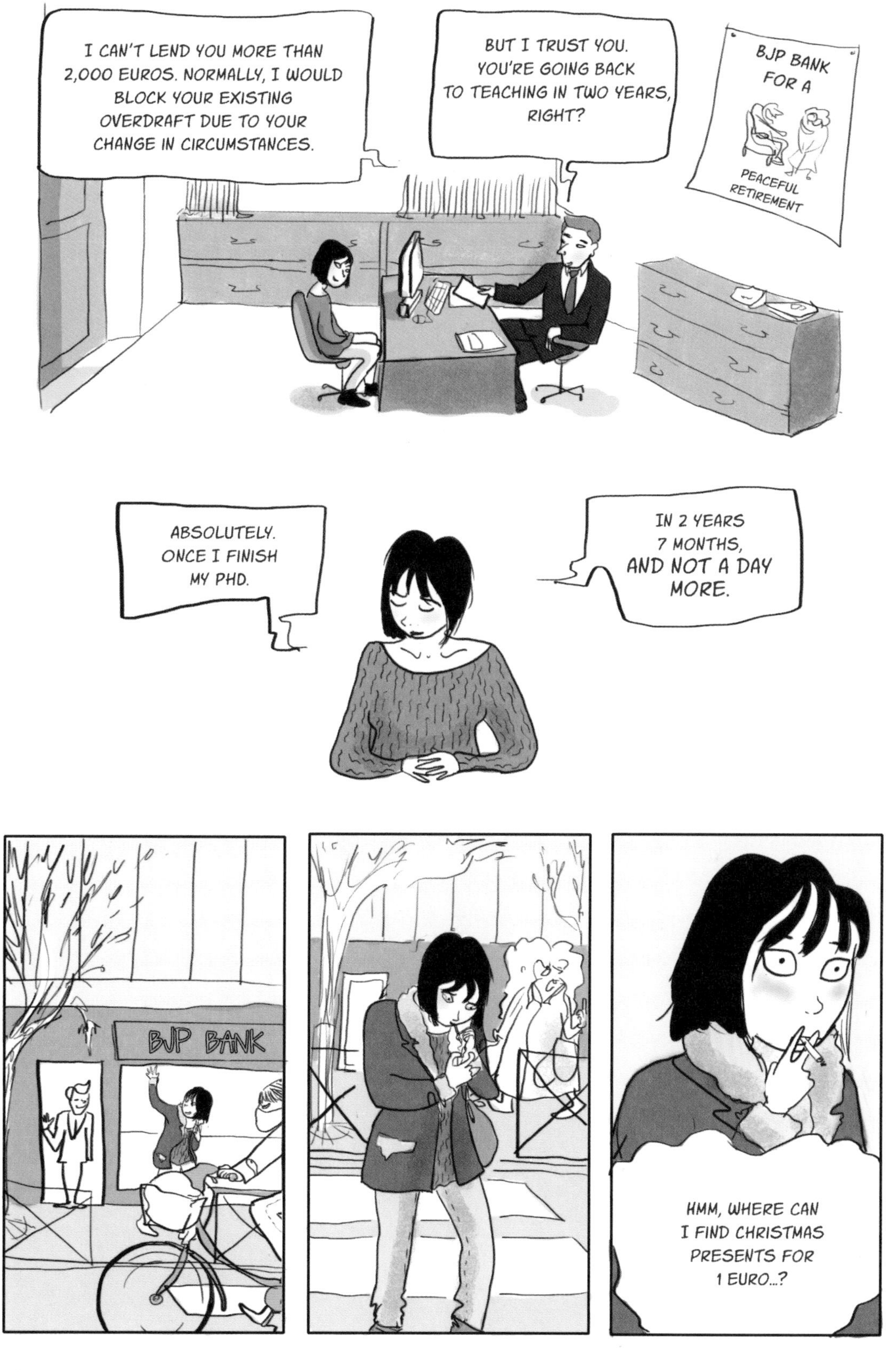
I CAN'T LEND YOU MORE THAN 2,000 EUROS. NORMALLY, I WOULD BLOCK YOUR EXISTING OVERDRAFT DUE TO YOUR CHANGE IN CIRCUMSTANCES.
BUT I TRUST YOU. YOU'RE GOING BACK TO TEACHING IN TWO YEARS, RIGHT?
BJP BANK FOR A PEACEFUL RETIREMENT
ABSOLUTELY. ONCE I FINISH MY PHD.
IN 2 YEARS 7 MONTHS, AND NOT A DAY MORE.
BJP BANK
HMM, WHERE CAN I FIND CHRISTMAS PRESENTS FOR 1 EURO...?

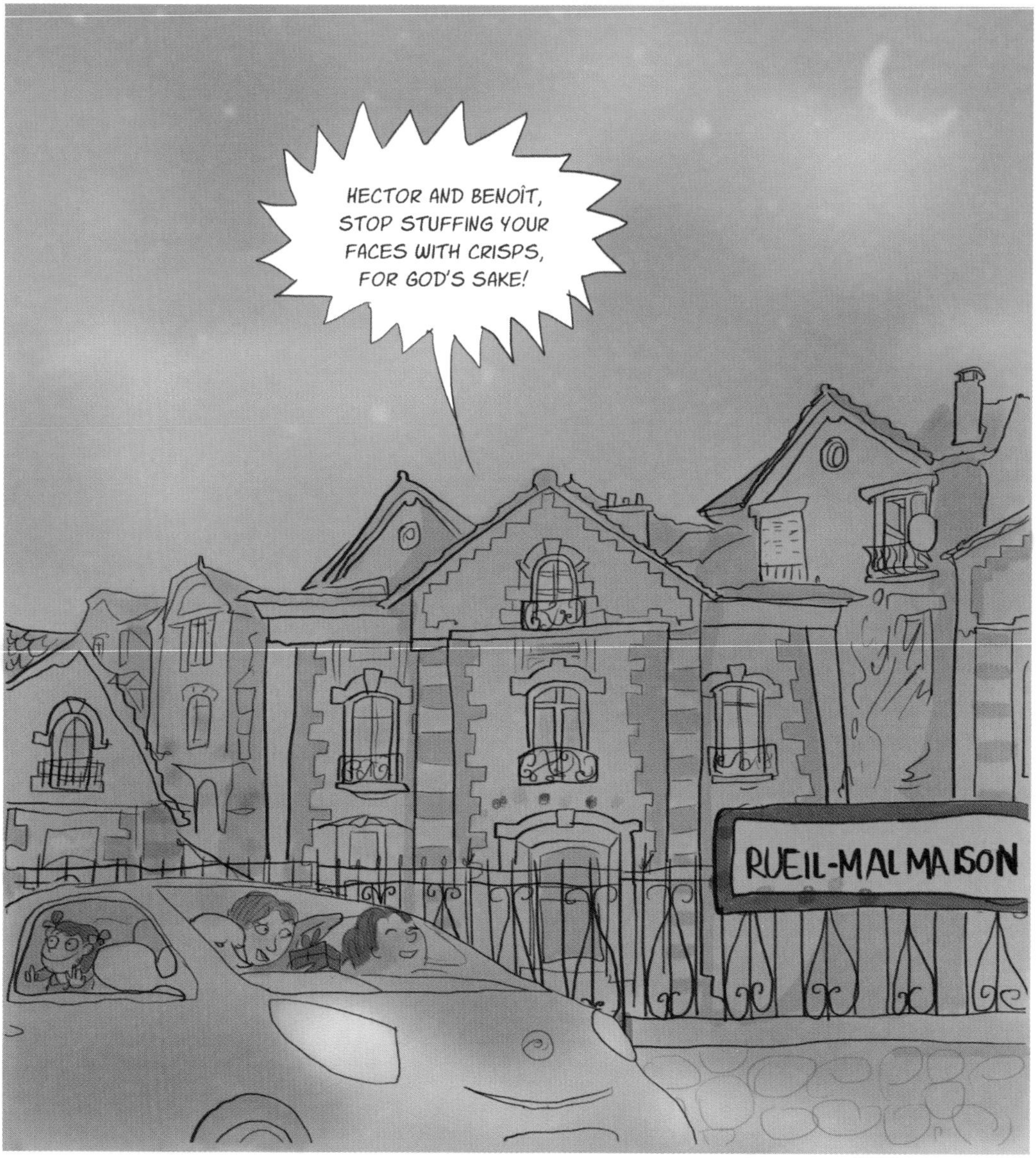
HECTOR AND BENOÎT, STOP STUFFING YOUR FACES WITH CRISPS, FOR GOD'S SAKE!
RUEIL-MALMAISON

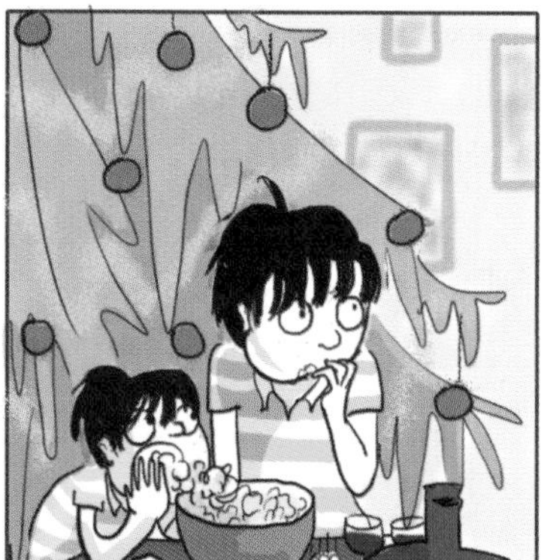

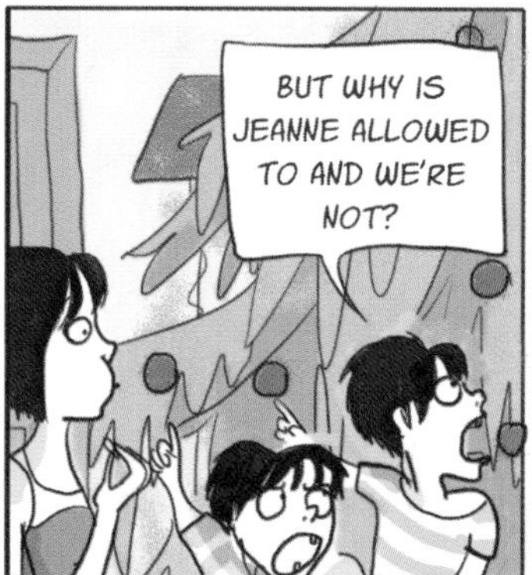
BUT WHY IS JEANNE ALLOWED TO AND WE'RE NOT?

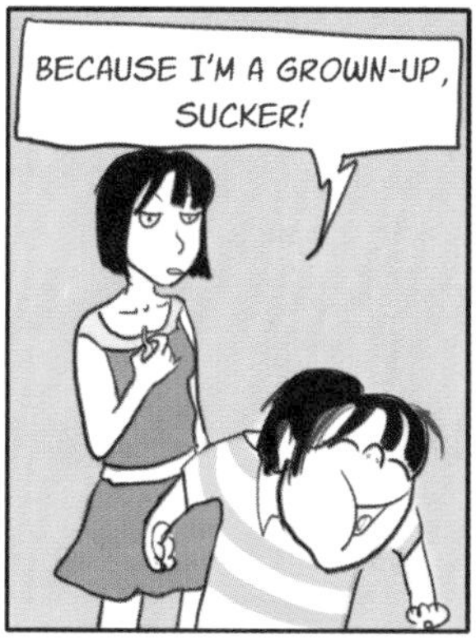
BECAUSE I'M A GROWN-UP, SUCKER!

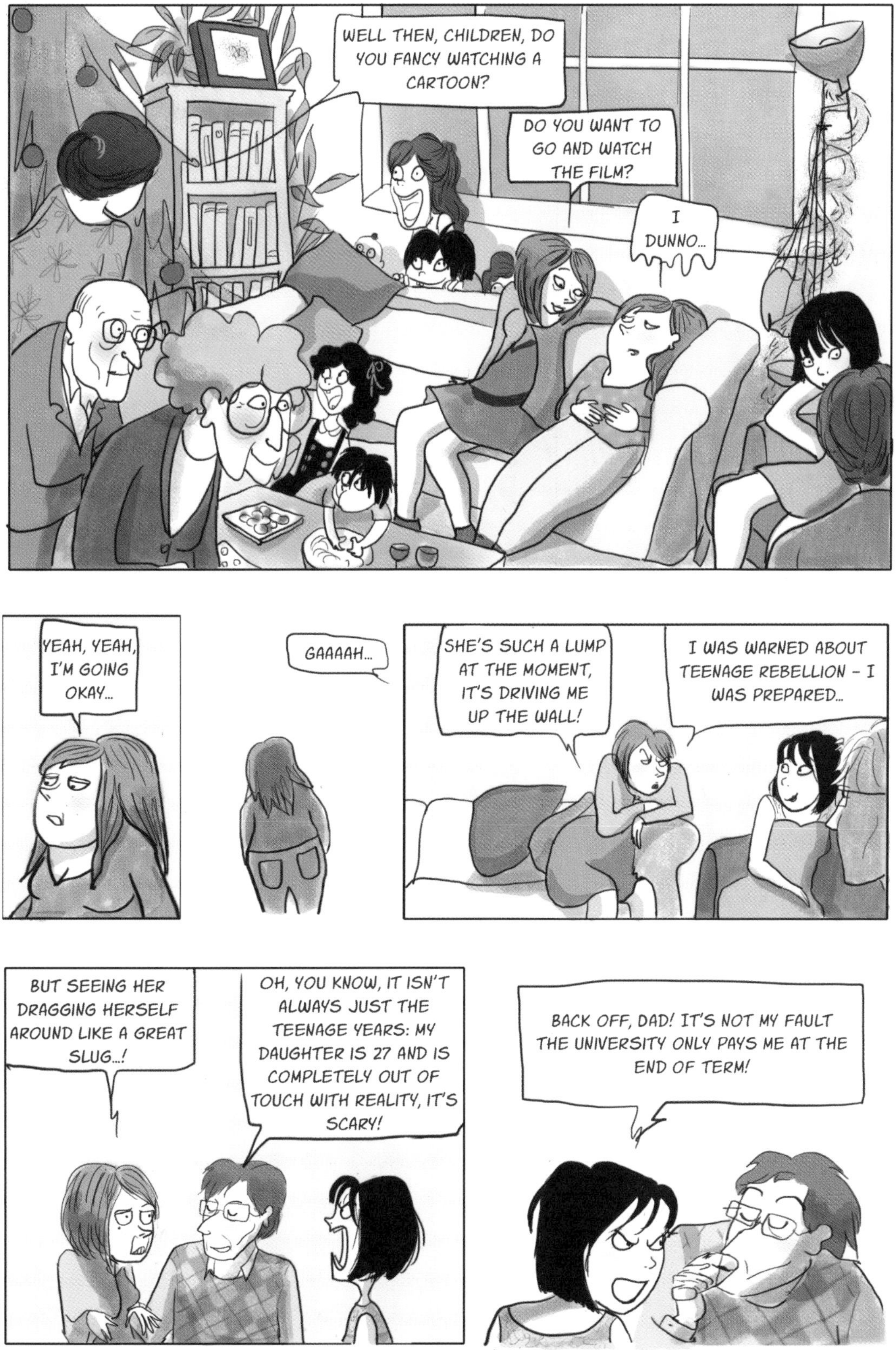
WELL THEN, CHILDREN, DO YOU FANCY WATCHING A CARTOON?
DO YOU WANT TO GO AND WATCH THE FILM?
I DUNNO...
YEAH, YEAH, I'M GOING OKAY...
GAAAAH...
SHE'S SUCH A LUMP AT THE MOMENT, IT'S DRIVING ME UP THE WALL!
I WAS WARNED ABOUT TEENAGE REBELLION – I WAS PREPARED...
BUT SEEING HER DRAGGING HERSELF AROUND LIKE A GREAT SLUG...!
OH, YOU KNOW, IT ISN'T ALWAYS JUST THE TEENAGE YEARS: MY DAUGHTER IS 27 AND IS COMPLETELY OUT OF TOUCH WITH REALITY, IT'S SCARY!
BACK OFF, DAD! IT'S NOT MY FAULT THE UNIVERSITY ONLY PAYS ME AT THE END OF TERM!

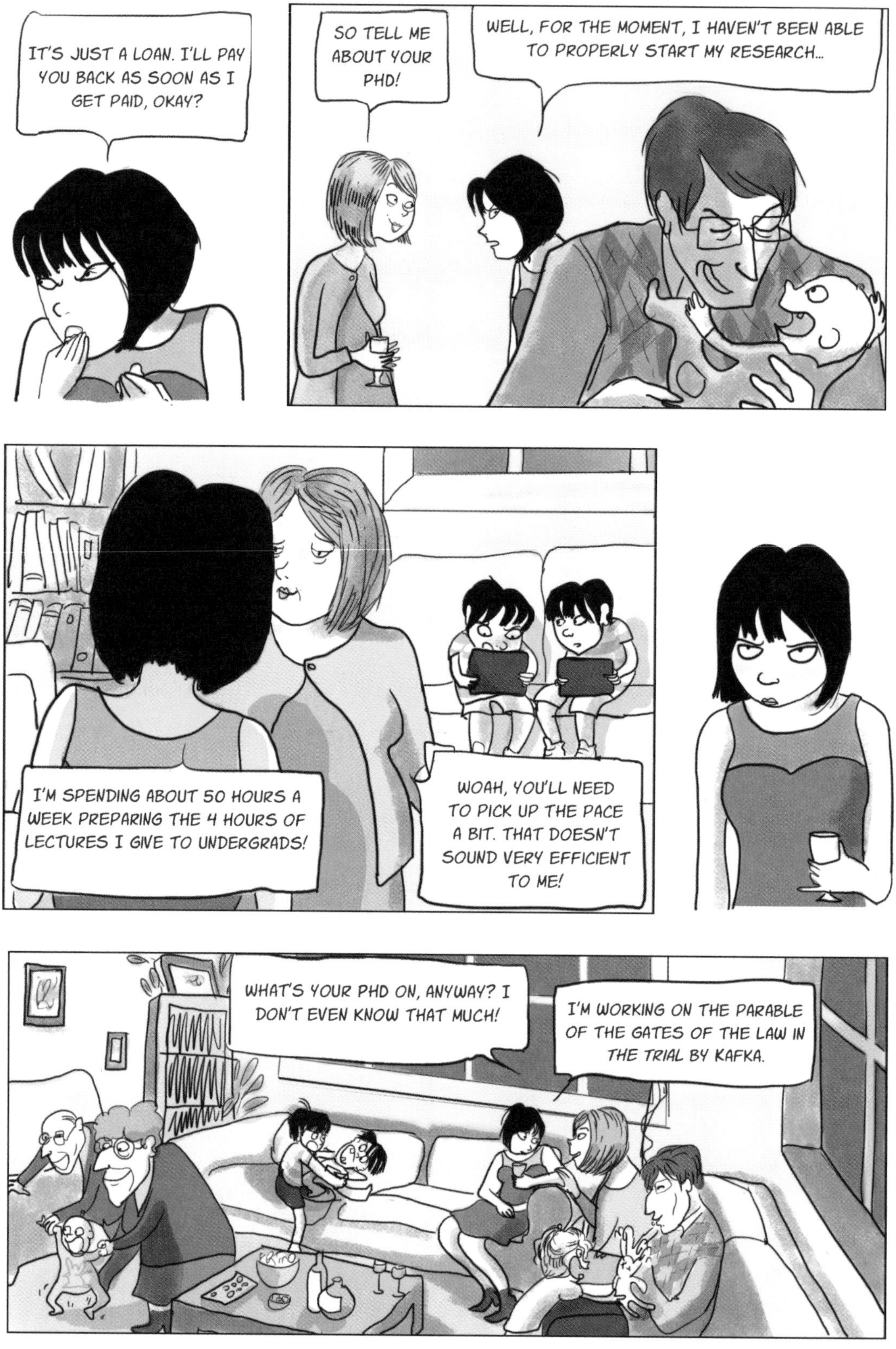

IT'S JUST A LOAN. I'LL PAY YOU BACK AS SOON AS I GET PAID, OKAY?
SO TELL ME ABOUT YOUR PHD!
WELL, FOR THE MOMENT, I HAVEN'T BEEN ABLE TO PROPERLY START MY RESEARCH...
I'M SPENDING ABOUT 50 HOURS A WEEK PREPARING THE 4 HOURS OF LECTURES I GIVE TO UNDERGRADS!
WOAH, YOU'LL NEED TO PICK UP THE PACE A BIT. THAT DOESN'T SOUND VERY EFFICIENT TO ME!
WHAT'S YOUR PHD ON, ANYWAY? I DON'T EVEN KNOW THAT MUCH!
I'M WORKING ON THE PARABLE OF THE GATES OF THE LAW IN THE TRIAL BY KAFKA.

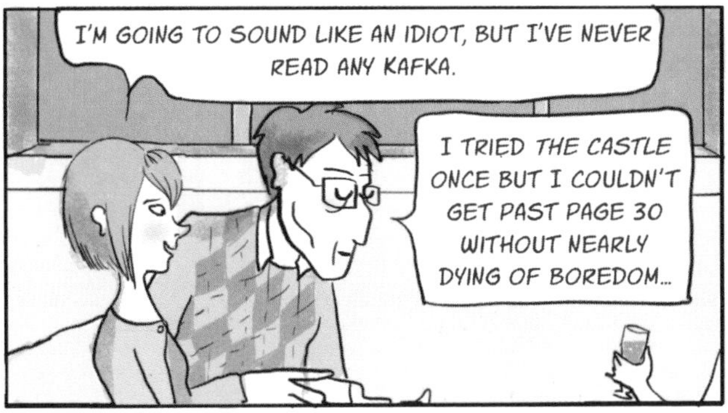
I'M GOING TO SOUND LIKE AN IDIOT, BUT I'VE NEVER READ ANY KAFKA.
I TRIED *THE CASTLE* ONCE BUT I COULDN'T GET PAST PAGE 30 WITHOUT NEARLY DYING OF BOREDOM...

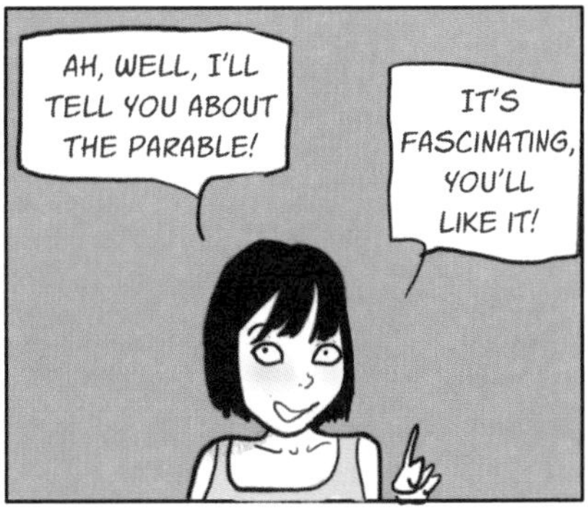
AH, WELL, I'LL TELL YOU ABOUT THE PARABLE!
IT'S FASCINATING, YOU'LL LIKE IT!

IT'S THE STORY OF A MAN WHO COMES TO THE GATES
WISHING TO GAIN ENTRY INTO THE LAW...

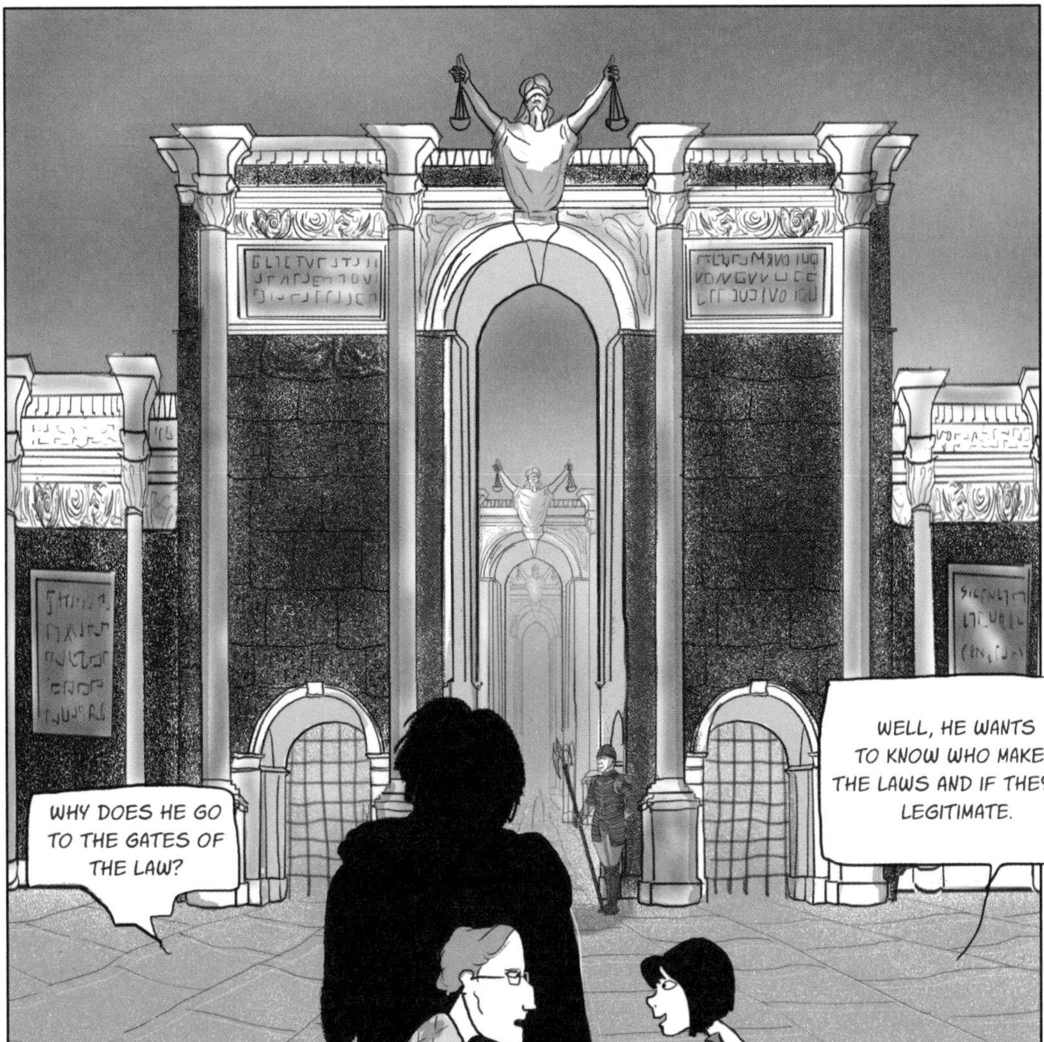
WHY DOES HE GO TO THE GATES OF THE LAW?
WELL, HE WANTS TO KNOW WHO MAKES THE LAWS AND IF THEY'RE LEGITIMATE.

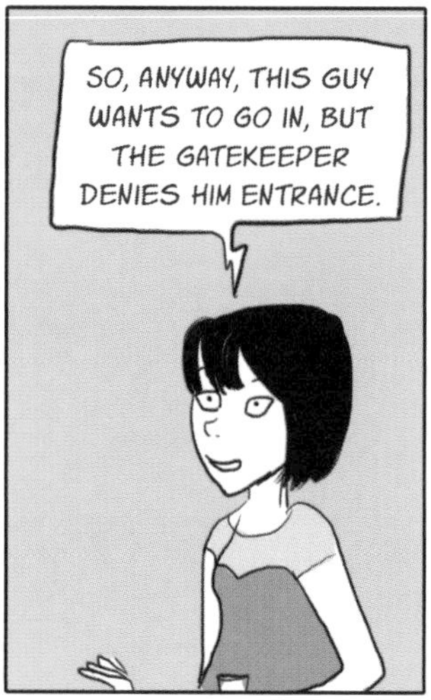
SO, ANYWAY, THIS GUY WANTS TO GO IN, BUT THE GATEKEEPER DENIES HIM ENTRANCE.

HE TELLS HIM THAT BEHIND HIM THERE ARE 7 MORE GATEKEEPERS, WHO ARE EVEN MORE POWERFUL, AND THEY'RE SO STRONG THAT EVEN HE IS AFRAID OF THEM!

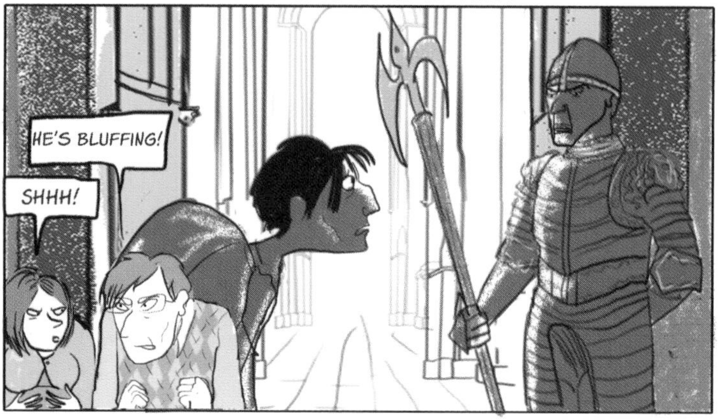
HE'S BLUFFING!
SHHH!

THE MAN IS HESITANT TO FORCE HIS WAY IN. HE ASKS THE GATEKEEPER IF HE MIGHT COME BACK LATER AND HE REPLIES: 'LATER, MAYBE.'

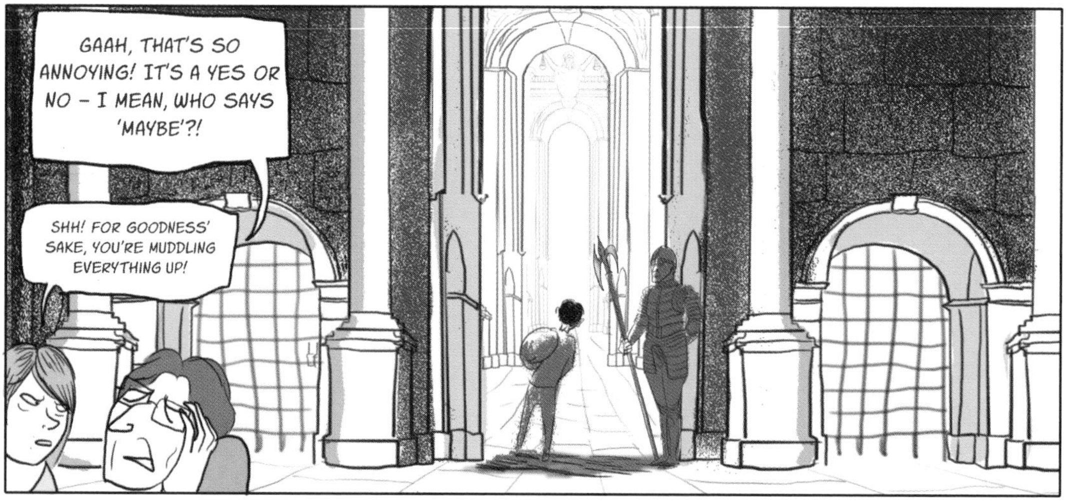
GAAH, THAT'S SO ANNOYING! IT'S A YES OR NO – I MEAN, WHO SAYS 'MAYBE'?!
SHH! FOR GOODNESS' SAKE, YOU'RE MUDDLING EVERYTHING UP!

SO THE MAN DECIDES TO WAIT.

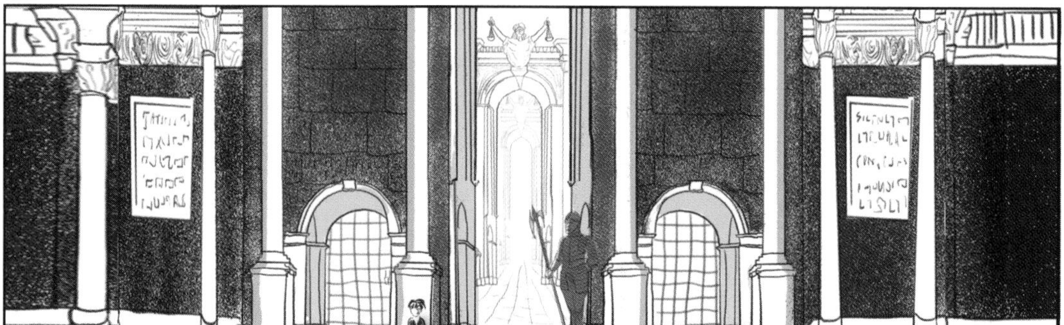

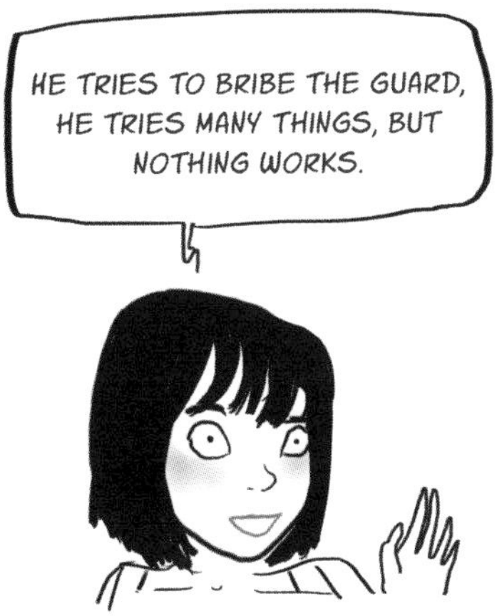
HE TRIES TO BRIBE THE GUARD, HE TRIES MANY THINGS, BUT NOTHING WORKS.

SEASONS PASS...

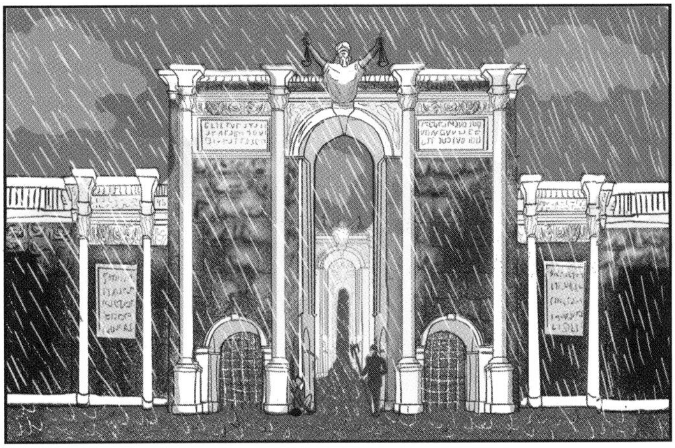

IN A BLUR...

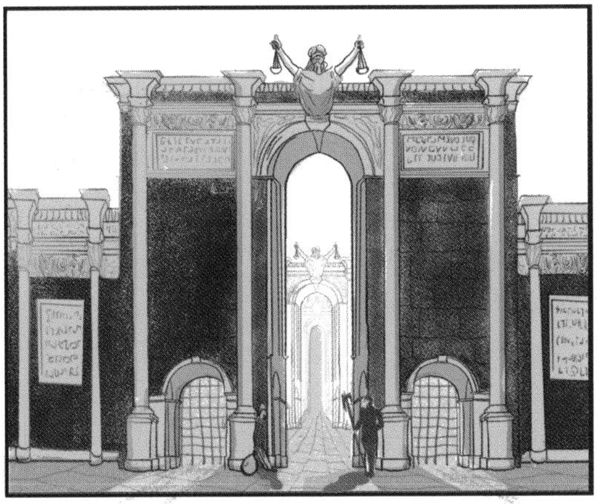

THE MAN GETS OLDER AND OLDER...

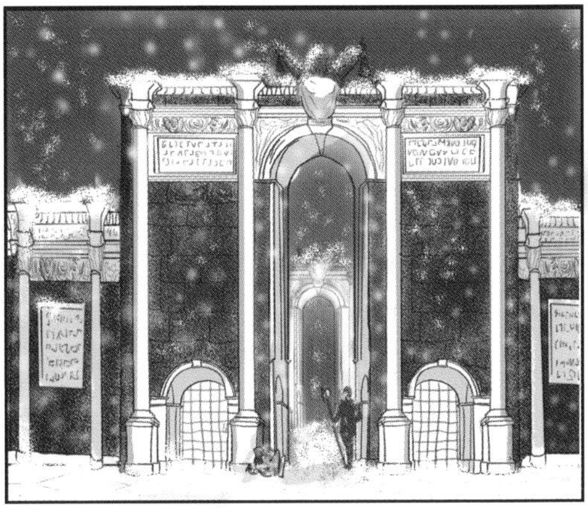

HE SENSES HE WILL DIE SOON, SO HE ASKS THE GATEKEEPER:

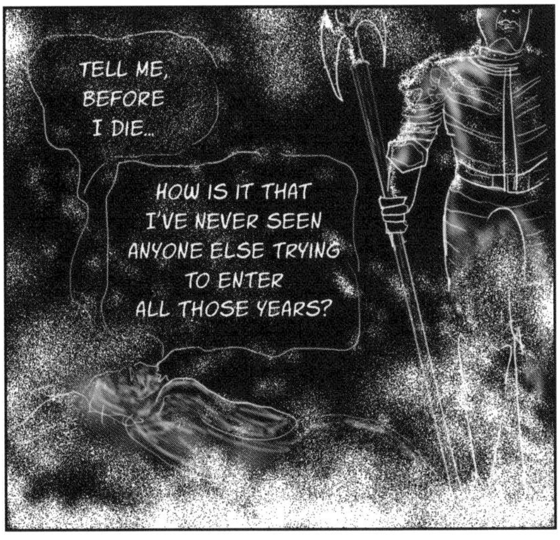
TELL ME, BEFORE I DIE...
HOW IS IT THAT I'VE NEVER SEEN ANYONE ELSE TRYING TO ENTER ALL THOSE YEARS?

AND THE GATEKEEPER REPLIES:

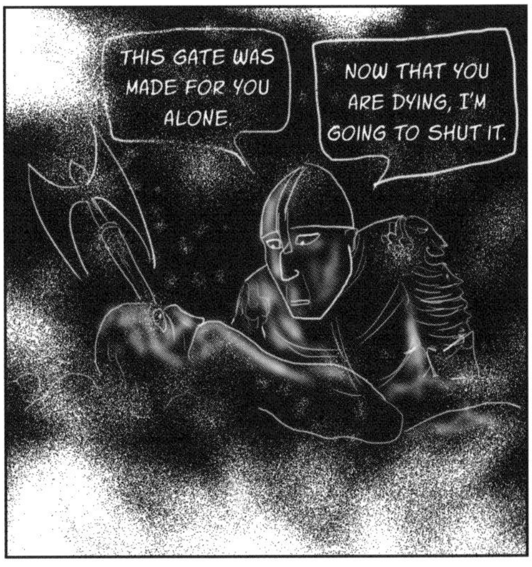
THIS GATE WAS MADE FOR YOU ALONE.
NOW THAT YOU ARE DYING, I'M GOING TO SHUT IT.

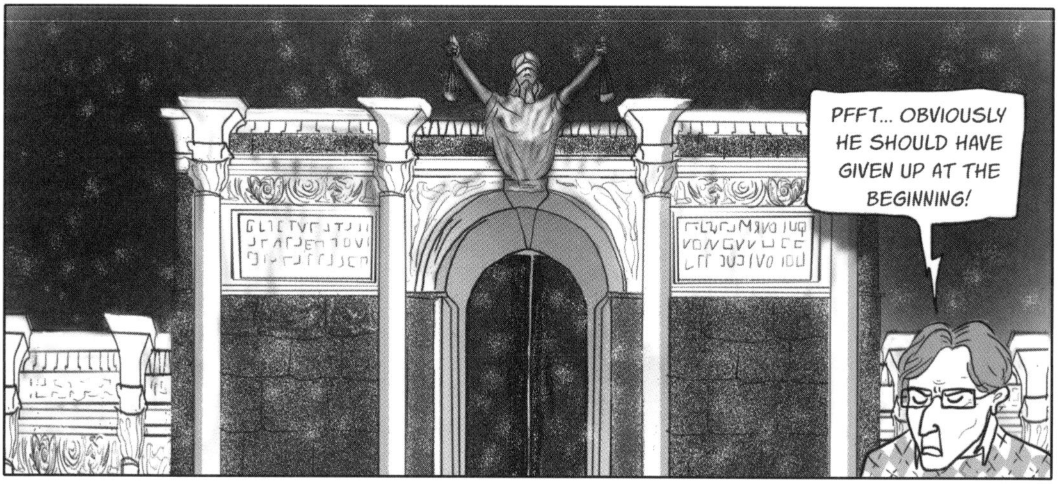
PFFT... OBVIOUSLY HE SHOULD HAVE GIVEN UP AT THE BEGINNING!

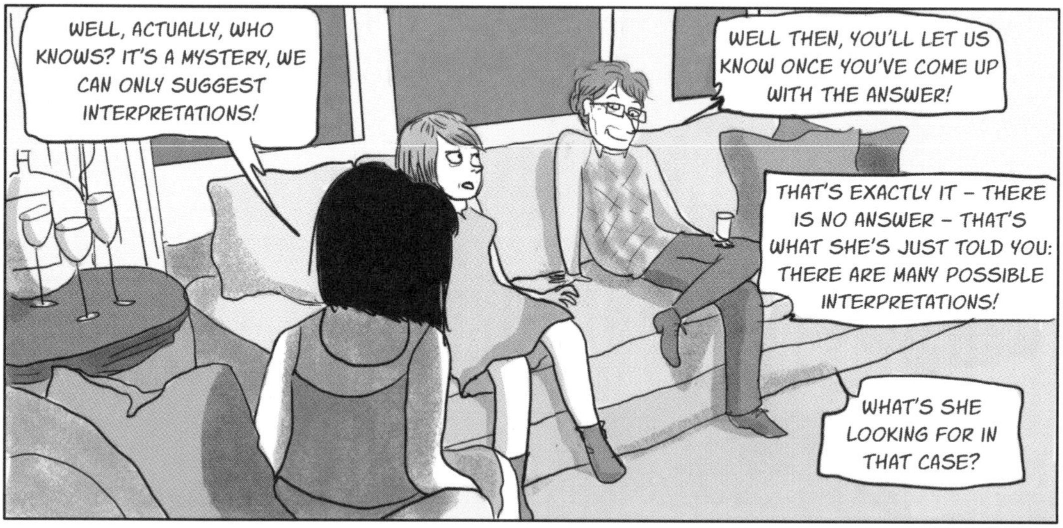
WELL, ACTUALLY, WHO KNOWS? IT'S A MYSTERY, WE CAN ONLY SUGGEST INTERPRETATIONS!
WELL THEN, YOU'LL LET US KNOW ONCE YOU'VE COME UP WITH THE ANSWER!
THAT'S EXACTLY IT – THERE IS NO ANSWER – THAT'S WHAT SHE'S JUST TOLD YOU: THERE ARE MANY POSSIBLE INTERPRETATIONS!
WHAT'S SHE LOOKING FOR IN THAT CASE?

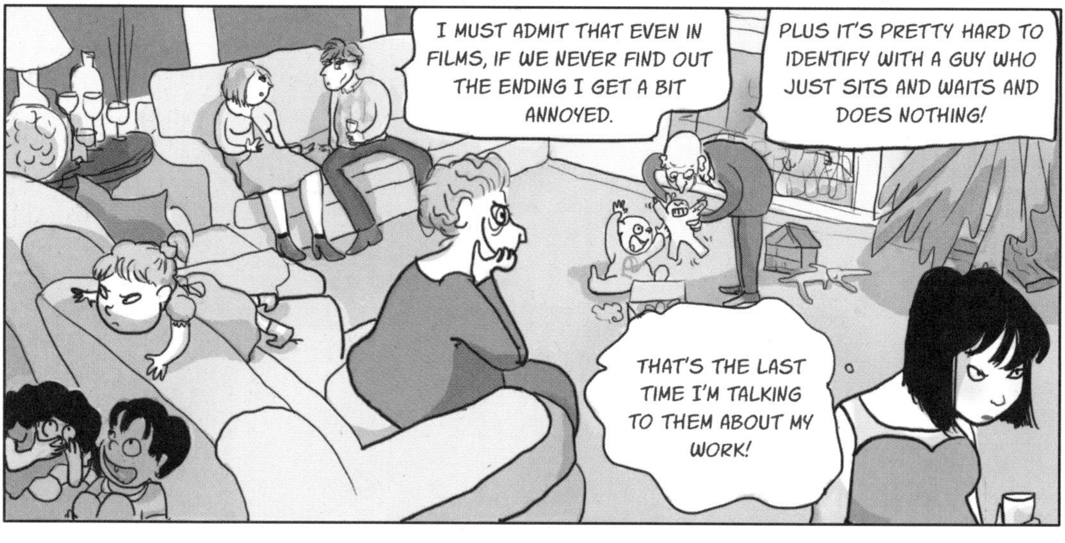
I MUST ADMIT THAT EVEN IN FILMS, IF WE NEVER FIND OUT THE ENDING I GET A BIT ANNOYED.
PLUS IT'S PRETTY HARD TO IDENTIFY WITH A GUY WHO JUST SITS AND WAITS AND DOES NOTHING!
THAT'S THE LAST TIME I'M TALKING TO THEM ABOUT MY WORK!

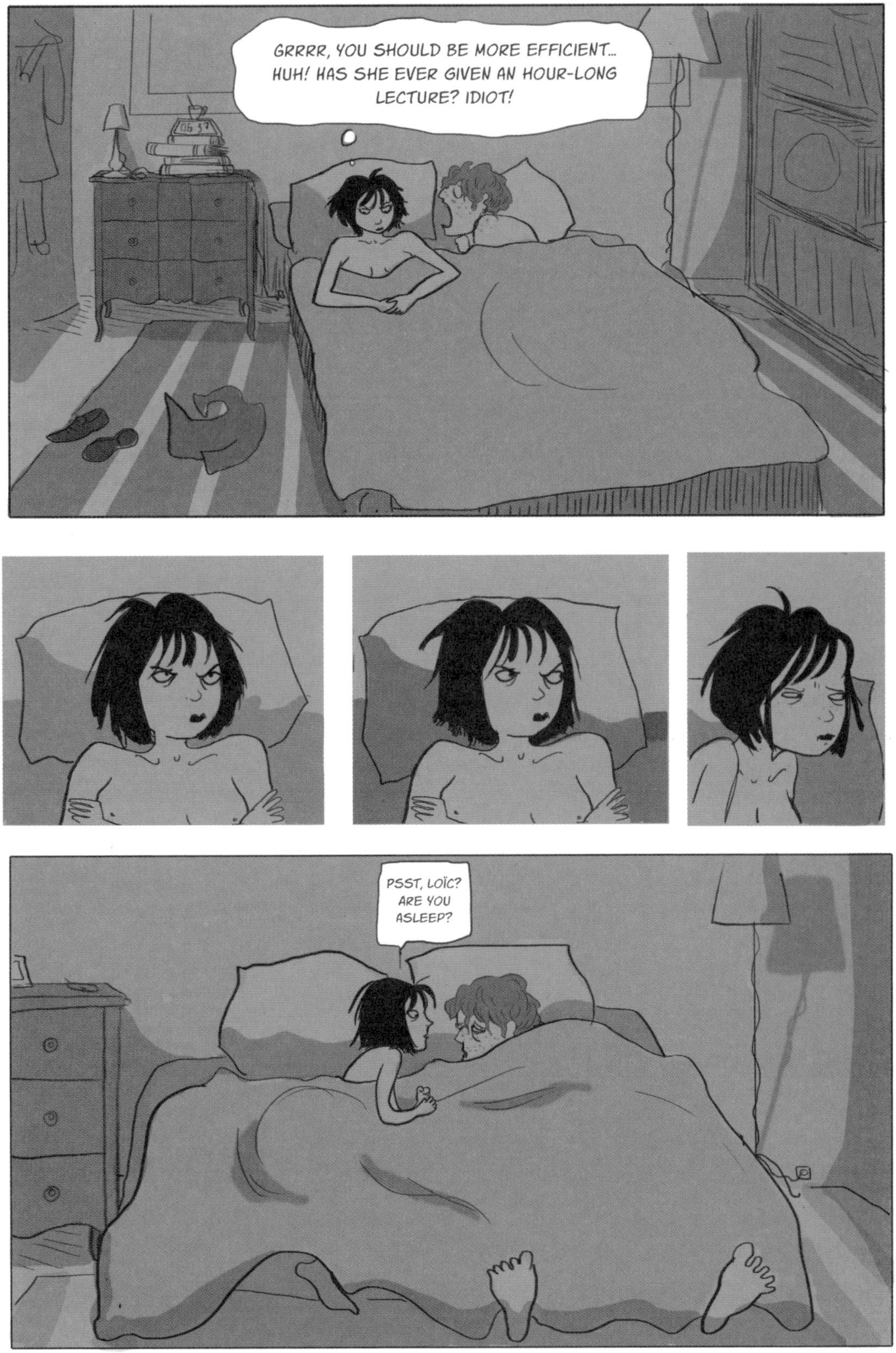
GRRRR, YOU SHOULD BE MORE EFFICIENT... HUH! HAS SHE EVER GIVEN AN HOUR-LONG LECTURE? IDIOT!
PSST, LOÏC? ARE YOU ASLEEP?

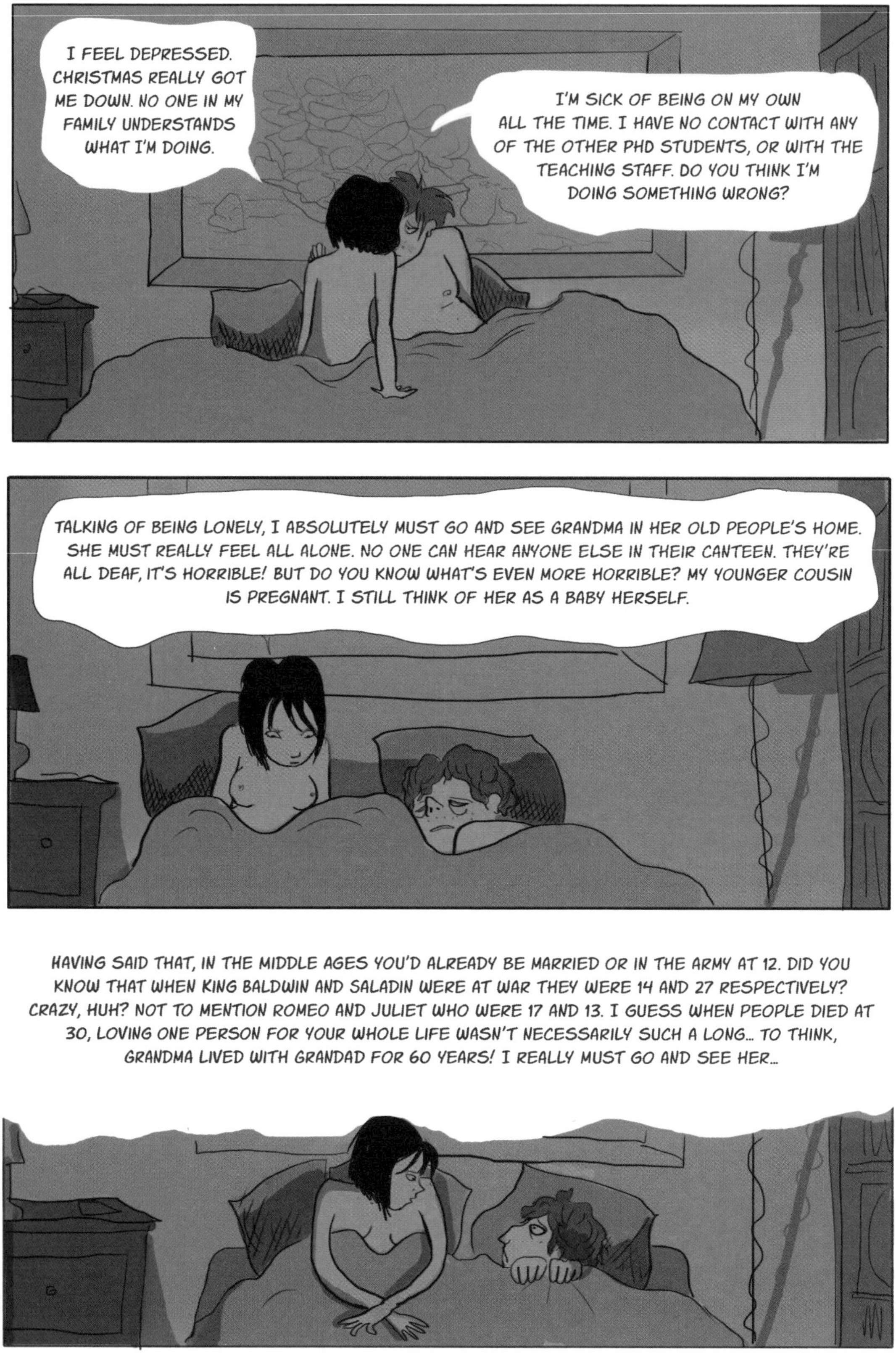
I FEEL DEPRESSED. CHRISTMAS REALLY GOT ME DOWN. NO ONE IN MY FAMILY UNDERSTANDS WHAT I'M DOING.
I'M SICK OF BEING ON MY OWN ALL THE TIME. I HAVE NO CONTACT WITH ANY OF THE OTHER PHD STUDENTS, OR WITH THE TEACHING STAFF. DO YOU THINK I'M DOING SOMETHING WRONG?
TALKING OF BEING LONELY, I ABSOLUTELY MUST GO AND SEE GRANDMA IN HER OLD PEOPLE'S HOME. SHE MUST REALLY FEEL ALL ALONE. NO ONE CAN HEAR ANYONE ELSE IN THEIR CANTEEN. THEY'RE ALL DEAF, IT'S HORRIBLE! BUT DO YOU KNOW WHAT'S EVEN MORE HORRIBLE? MY YOUNGER COUSIN IS PREGNANT. I STILL THINK OF HER AS A BABY HERSELF.
HAVING SAID THAT, IN THE MIDDLE AGES YOU'D ALREADY BE MARRIED OR IN THE ARMY AT 12. DID YOU KNOW THAT WHEN KING BALDWIN AND SALADIN WERE AT WAR THEY WERE 14 AND 27 RESPECTIVELY? CRAZY, HUH? NOT TO MENTION ROMEO AND JULIET WHO WERE 17 AND 13. I GUESS WHEN PEOPLE DIED AT 30, LOVING ONE PERSON FOR YOUR WHOLE LIFE WASN'T NECESSARILY SUCH A LONG... TO THINK, GRANDMA LIVED WITH GRANDAD FOR 60 YEARS! I REALLY MUST GO AND SEE HER...

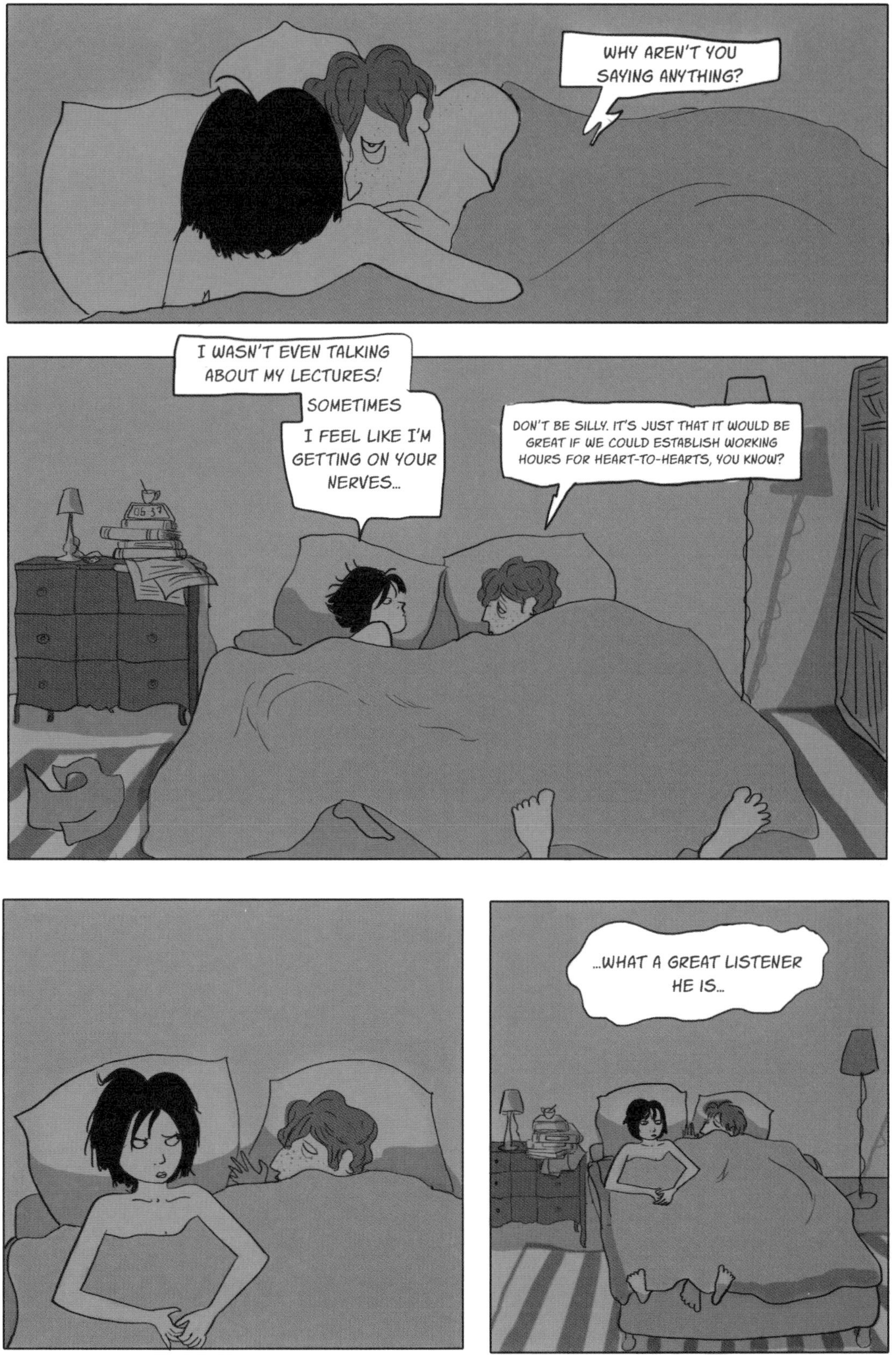
WHY AREN'T YOU SAYING ANYTHING?
I WASN'T EVEN TALKING ABOUT MY LECTURES!
SOMETIMES I FEEL LIKE I'M GETTING ON YOUR NERVES...
DON'T BE SILLY. IT'S JUST THAT IT WOULD BE GREAT IF WE COULD ESTABLISH WORKING HOURS FOR HEART-TO-HEARTS, YOU KNOW?
...WHAT A GREAT LISTENER HE IS...

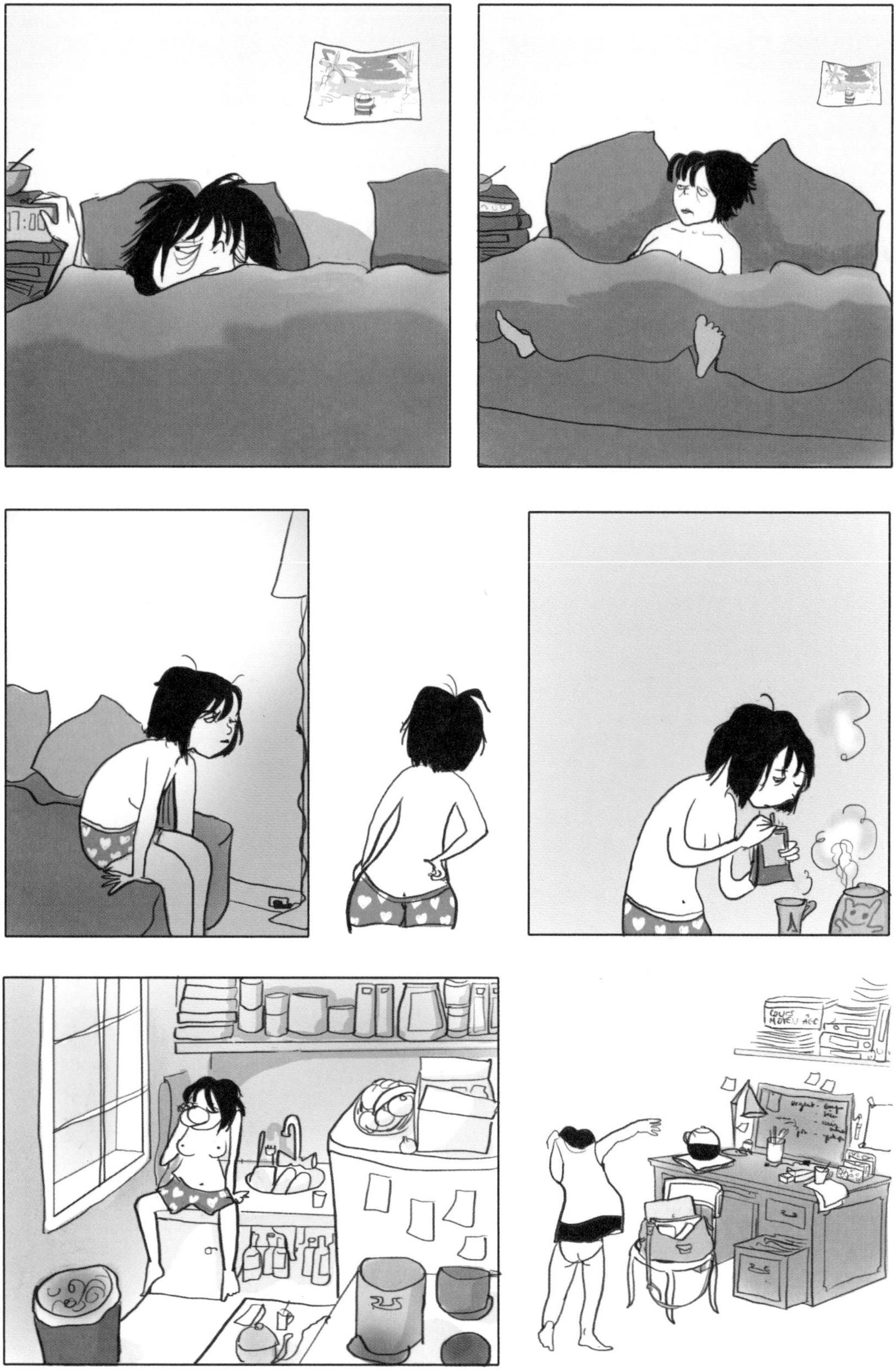
COURS MOYEN ÂGE

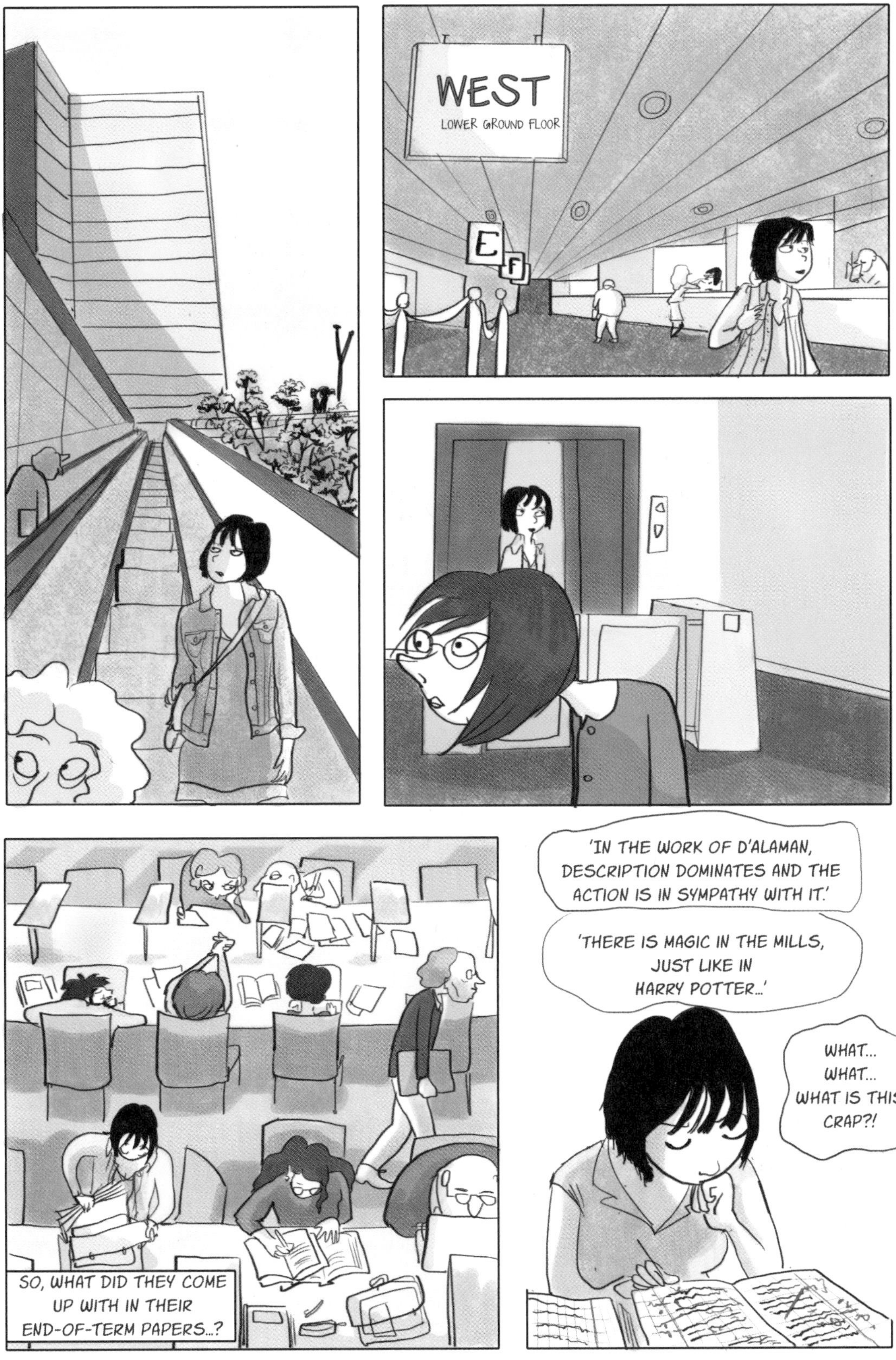
WEST
LOWER GROUND FLOOR
E
F
SO, WHAT DID THEY COME UP WITH IN THEIR END-OF-TERM PAPERS...?
'IN THE WORK OF D'ALAMAN, DESCRIPTION DOMINATES AND THE ACTION IS IN SYMPATHY WITH IT.'
'THERE IS MAGIC IN THE MILLS, JUST LIKE IN HARRY POTTER...'
WHAT... WHAT... WHAT IS THIS CRAP?!

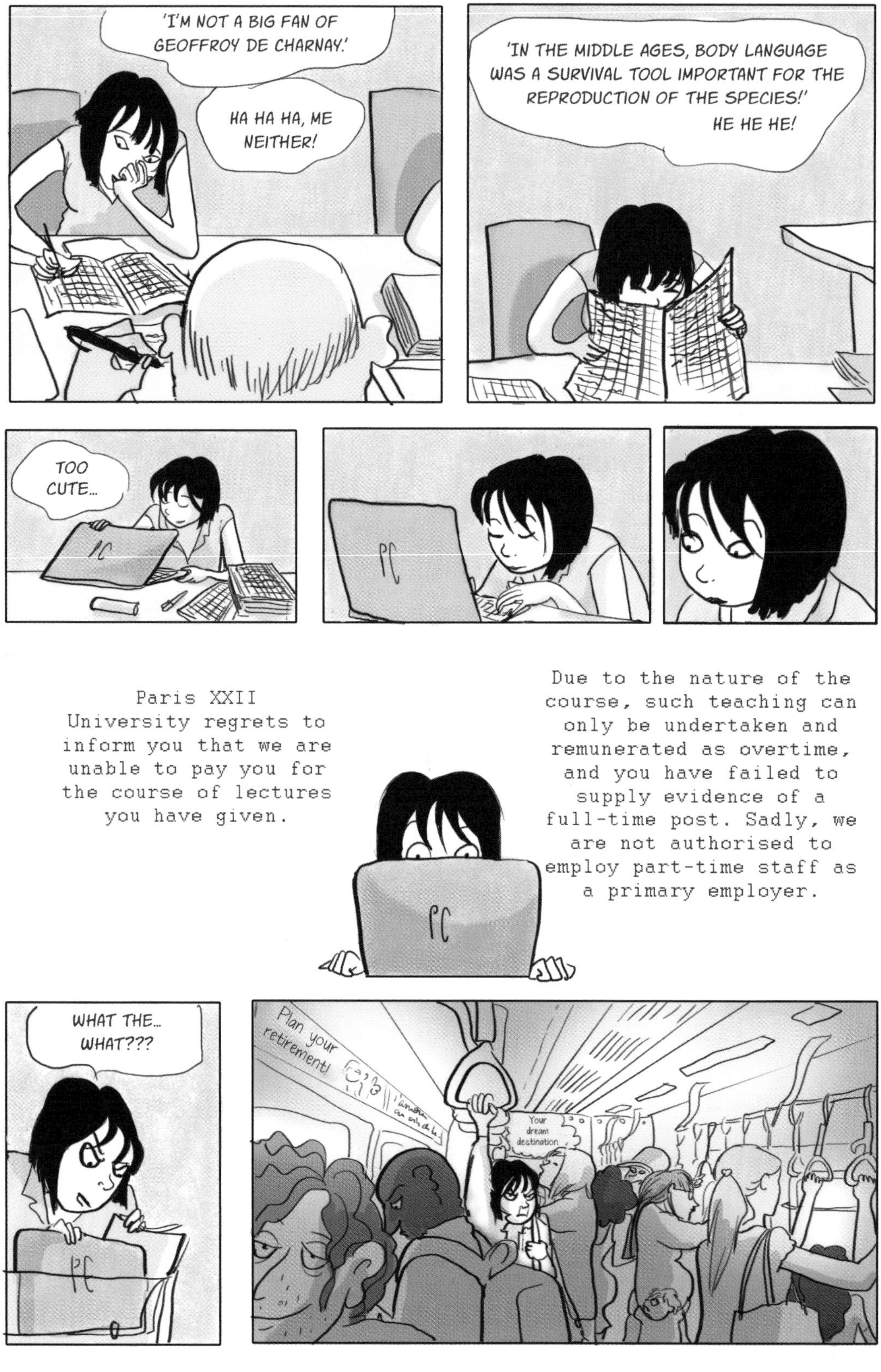
'I'M NOT A BIG FAN OF GEOFFROY DE CHARNAY.'
HA HA HA, ME NEITHER!
'IN THE MIDDLE AGES, BODY LANGUAGE WAS A SURVIVAL TOOL IMPORTANT FOR THE REPRODUCTION OF THE SPECIES!'
HE HE HE!
TOO CUTE...
PC
PC
Paris XXII University regrets to inform you that we are unable to pay you for the course of lectures you have given.
Due to the nature of the course, such teaching can only be undertaken and remunerated as overtime, and you have failed to supply evidence of a full-time post. Sadly, we are not authorised to employ part-time staff as a primary employer.
PC
WHAT THE... WHAT???
PC
Plan your retirement!
Your dream destination

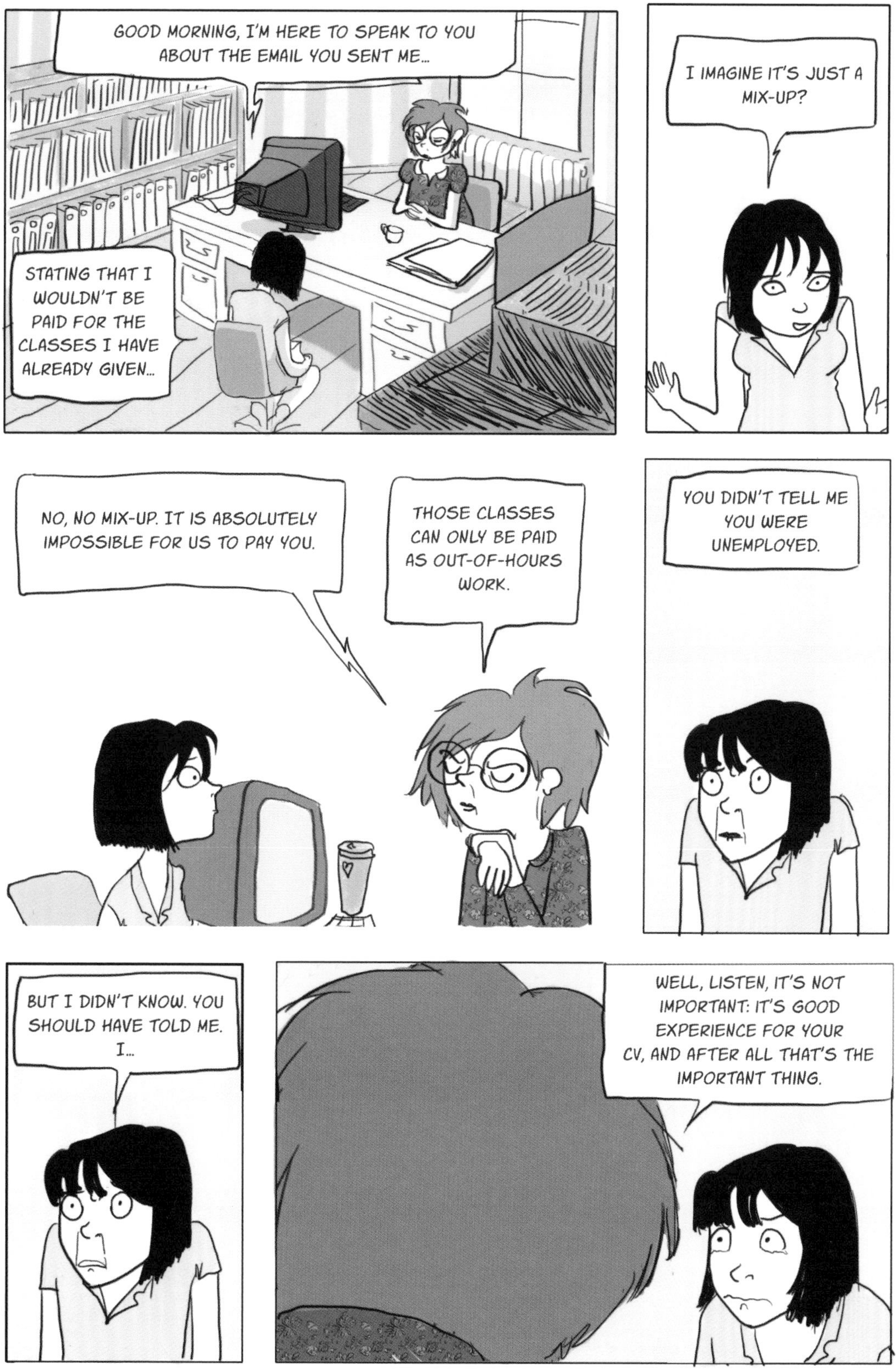
GOOD MORNING, I'M HERE TO SPEAK TO YOU ABOUT THE EMAIL YOU SENT ME...
STATING THAT I WOULDN'T BE PAID FOR THE CLASSES I HAVE ALREADY GIVEN...
I IMAGINE IT'S JUST A MIX-UP?
NO, NO MIX-UP. IT IS ABSOLUTELY IMPOSSIBLE FOR US TO PAY YOU.
THOSE CLASSES CAN ONLY BE PAID AS OUT-OF-HOURS WORK.
YOU DIDN'T TELL ME YOU WERE UNEMPLOYED.
BUT I DIDN'T KNOW. YOU SHOULD HAVE TOLD ME. I...
WELL, LISTEN, IT'S NOT IMPORTANT: IT'S GOOD EXPERIENCE FOR YOUR CV, AND AFTER ALL THAT'S THE IMPORTANT THING.

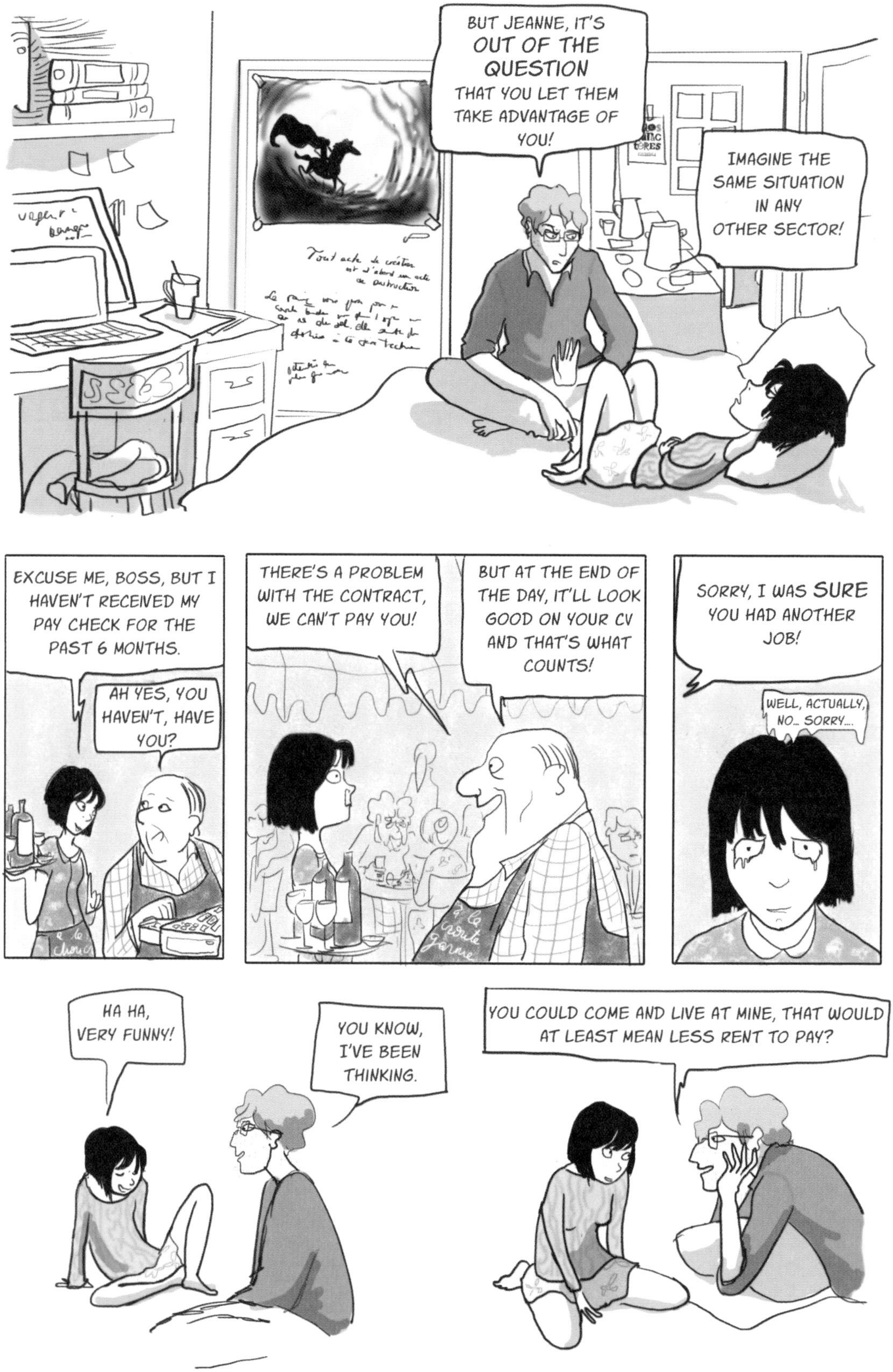
BUT JEANNE, IT'S OUT OF THE QUESTION THAT YOU LET THEM TAKE ADVANTAGE OF YOU!
IMAGINE THE SAME SITUATION IN ANY OTHER SECTOR!
EXCUSE ME, BOSS, BUT I HAVEN'T RECEIVED MY PAY CHECK FOR THE PAST 6 MONTHS.
AH YES, YOU HAVEN'T, HAVE YOU?
THERE'S A PROBLEM WITH THE CONTRACT, WE CAN'T PAY YOU!
BUT AT THE END OF THE DAY, IT'LL LOOK GOOD ON YOUR CV AND THAT'S WHAT COUNTS!
SORRY, I WAS SURE YOU HAD ANOTHER JOB!
WELL, ACTUALLY, NO... SORRY....
HA HA, VERY FUNNY!
YOU KNOW, I'VE BEEN THINKING.
YOU COULD COME AND LIVE AT MINE, THAT WOULD AT LEAST MEAN LESS RENT TO PAY?

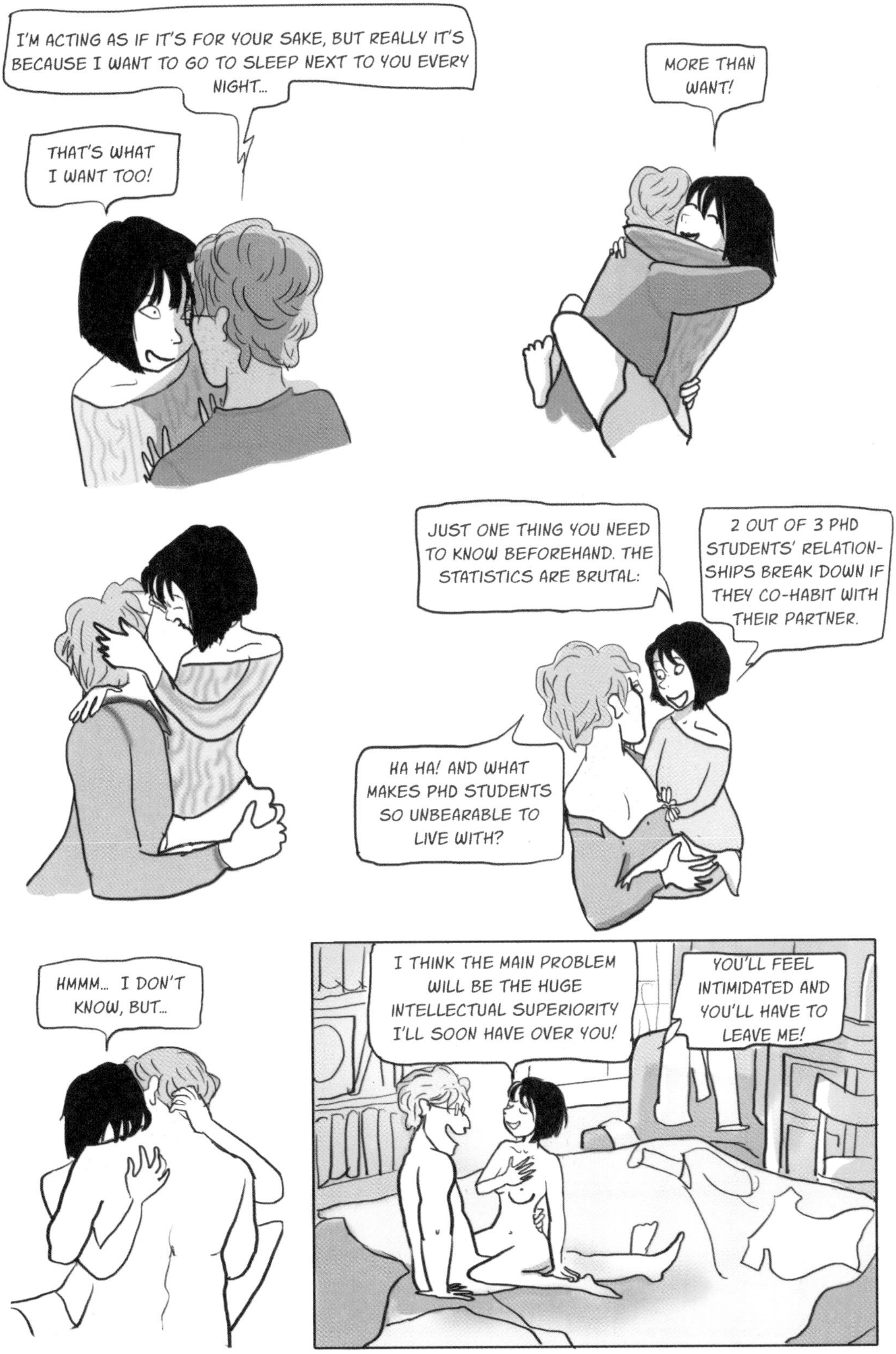
I'M ACTING AS IF IT'S FOR YOUR SAKE, BUT REALLY IT'S BECAUSE I WANT TO GO TO SLEEP NEXT TO YOU EVERY NIGHT...
THAT'S WHAT I WANT TOO!
MORE THAN WANT!
JUST ONE THING YOU NEED TO KNOW BEFOREHAND. THE STATISTICS ARE BRUTAL:
2 OUT OF 3 PHD STUDENTS' RELATIONSHIPS BREAK DOWN IF THEY CO-HABIT WITH THEIR PARTNER.
HA HA! AND WHAT MAKES PHD STUDENTS SO UNBEARABLE TO LIVE WITH?
HMMM... I DON'T KNOW, BUT...
I THINK THE MAIN PROBLEM WILL BE THE HUGE INTELLECTUAL SUPERIORITY I'LL SOON HAVE OVER YOU!
YOU'LL FEEL INTIMIDATED AND YOU'LL HAVE TO LEAVE ME!

COVER LETTER FOR THE ROLE OF MUSEUM GUARD AT THE MUSÉE D'ORSAY

Having cultivated a passion for painting, and the world of art in general, from a young age, I have always dreamed of spending my days surrounded by masterpieces.

Thanks to my excellent powers of concentration, I would be able to monitor the coming and going of visitors with faultless vigilance. With me in the room, you can be sure that no one will get away with touching the paintings or talking loudly.

COVER LETTER FOR THE ROLE OF AUTOCUE TECHNICIAN AT FRANCE 2

Having cultivated a passion for television, and the world of production in general, from a young age, I have always dreamed of spending my days surrounded by TV presenters.

I have a natural talent for ensuring text scrolls smoothly and I have always had a way with a spanner. It would be a real thrill to hear a news bulletin and to ensure the text runs speedily, without breaking a sweat.

COVER LETTER FOR THE ROLE OF BALL-GIRL AT ROLAND-GARROS

Having cultivated a passion for tennis, and the world of sport in general, from a young age...

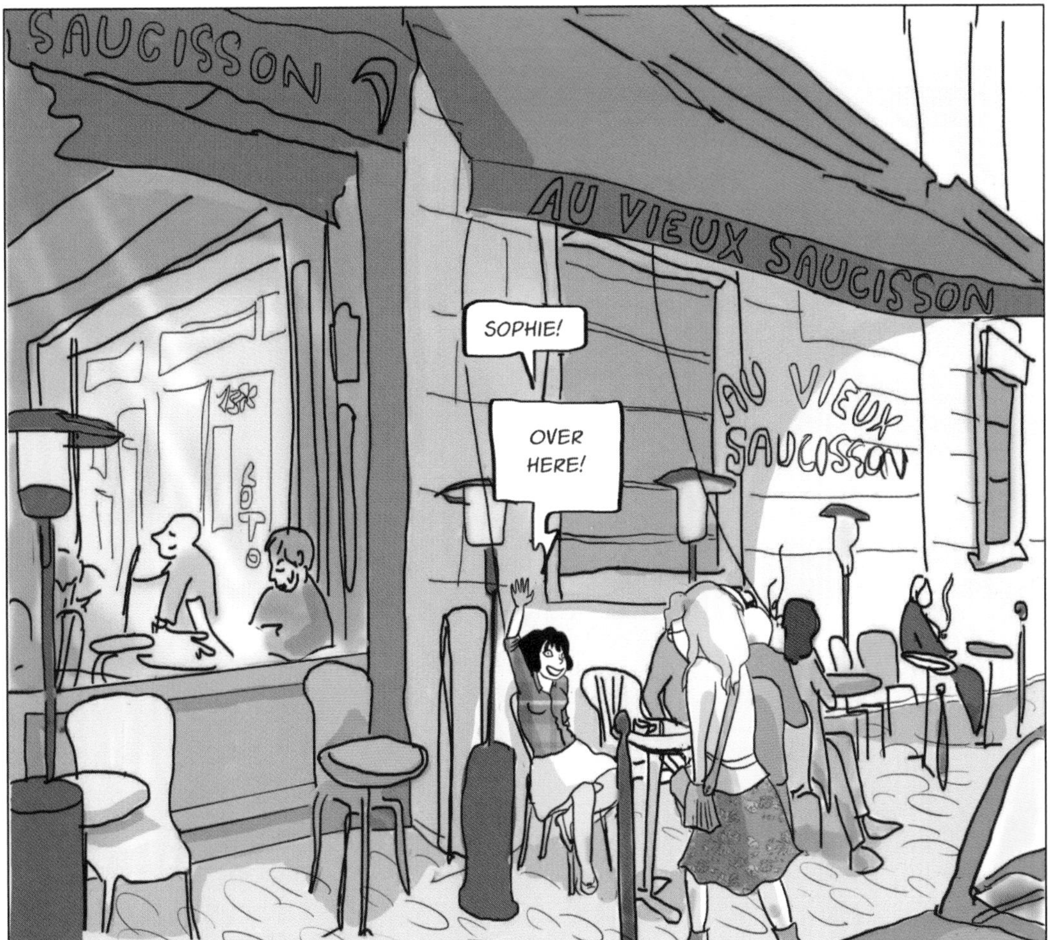
SAUCISSON
AU VIEUX SAUCISSON
SOPHIE!
OVER HERE!
AU VIEUX SAUCISSON

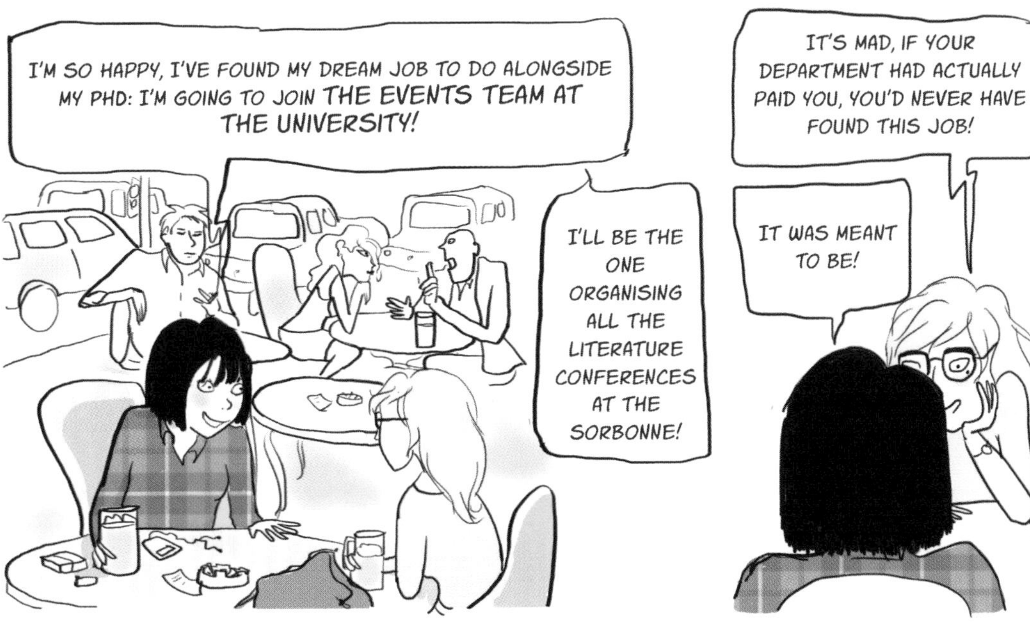
I'M SO HAPPY, I'VE FOUND MY DREAM JOB TO DO ALONGSIDE MY PHD: I'M GOING TO JOIN THE EVENTS TEAM AT THE UNIVERSITY!
I'LL BE THE ONE ORGANISING ALL THE LITERATURE CONFERENCES AT THE SORBONNE!
IT'S MAD, IF YOUR DEPARTMENT HAD ACTUALLY PAID YOU, YOU'D NEVER HAVE FOUND THIS JOB!
IT WAS MEANT TO BE!

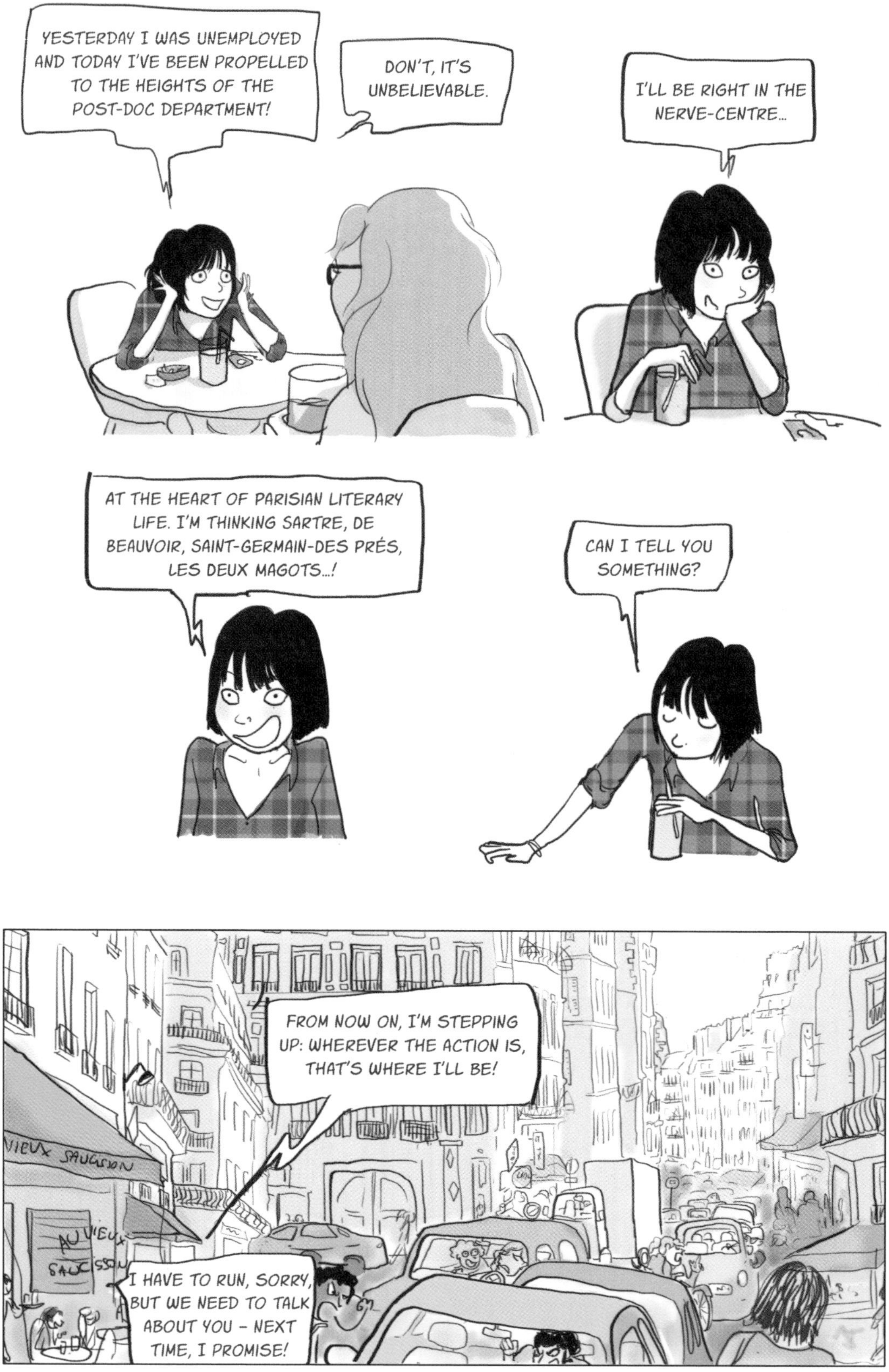
YESTERDAY I WAS UNEMPLOYED AND TODAY I'VE BEEN PROPELLED TO THE HEIGHTS OF THE POST-DOC DEPARTMENT!
DON'T, IT'S UNBELIEVABLE.
I'LL BE RIGHT IN THE NERVE-CENTRE...
AT THE HEART OF PARISIAN LITERARY LIFE. I'M THINKING SARTRE, DE BEAUVOIR, SAINT-GERMAIN-DES PRÉS, LES DEUX MAGOTS...!
CAN I TELL YOU SOMETHING?
FROM NOW ON, I'M STEPPING UP: WHEREVER THE ACTION IS, THAT'S WHERE I'LL BE!
VIEUX SAUCISSON
AU VIEUX SAUCISSON
I HAVE TO RUN, SORRY, BUT WE NEED TO TALK ABOUT YOU – NEXT TIME, I PROMISE!

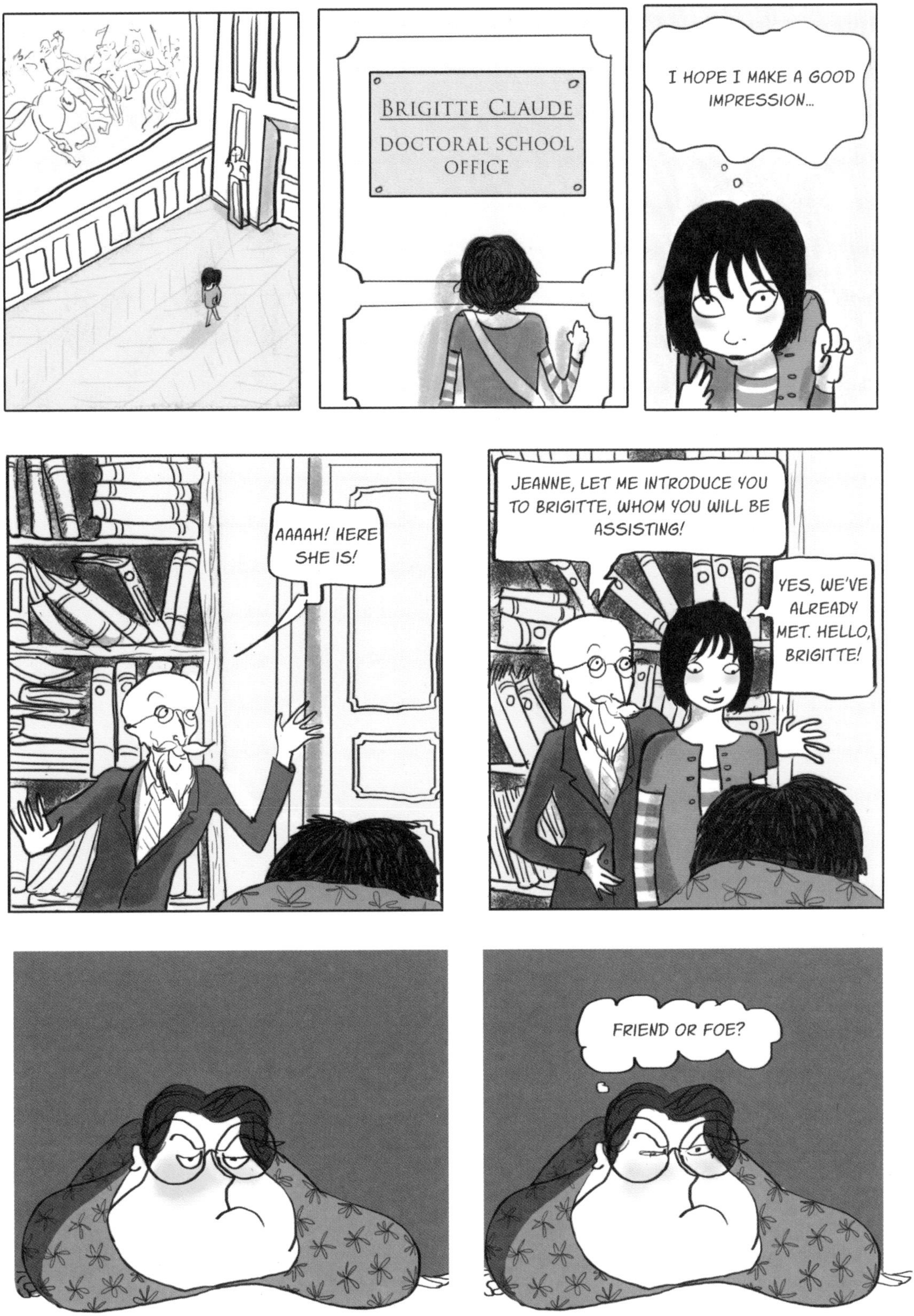
BRIGITTE CLAUDE
DOCTORAL SCHOOL OFFICE
I HOPE I MAKE A GOOD IMPRESSION...
AAAAH! HERE SHE IS!
JEANNE, LET ME INTRODUCE YOU TO BRIGITTE, WHOM YOU WILL BE ASSISTING!
YES, WE'VE ALREADY MET. HELLO, BRIGITTE!
FRIEND OR FOE?

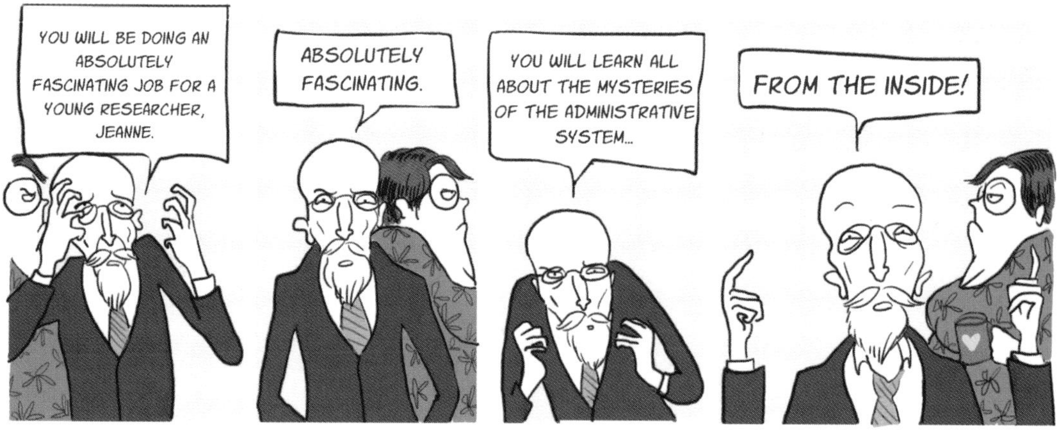
YOU WILL BE DOING AN ABSOLUTELY FASCINATING JOB FOR A YOUNG RESEARCHER, JEANNE.
ABSOLUTELY FASCINATING.
YOU WILL LEARN ALL ABOUT THE MYSTERIES OF THE ADMINISTRATIVE SYSTEM...
FROM THE INSIDE!

WHILE BRIGITTE IS ENROLLING PHD STUDENTS, YOU WILL BE HELPING OUR RESEARCHERS AND TEACHING STAFF TO ORGANISE MAJOR INTERNATIONAL CONFERENCES!

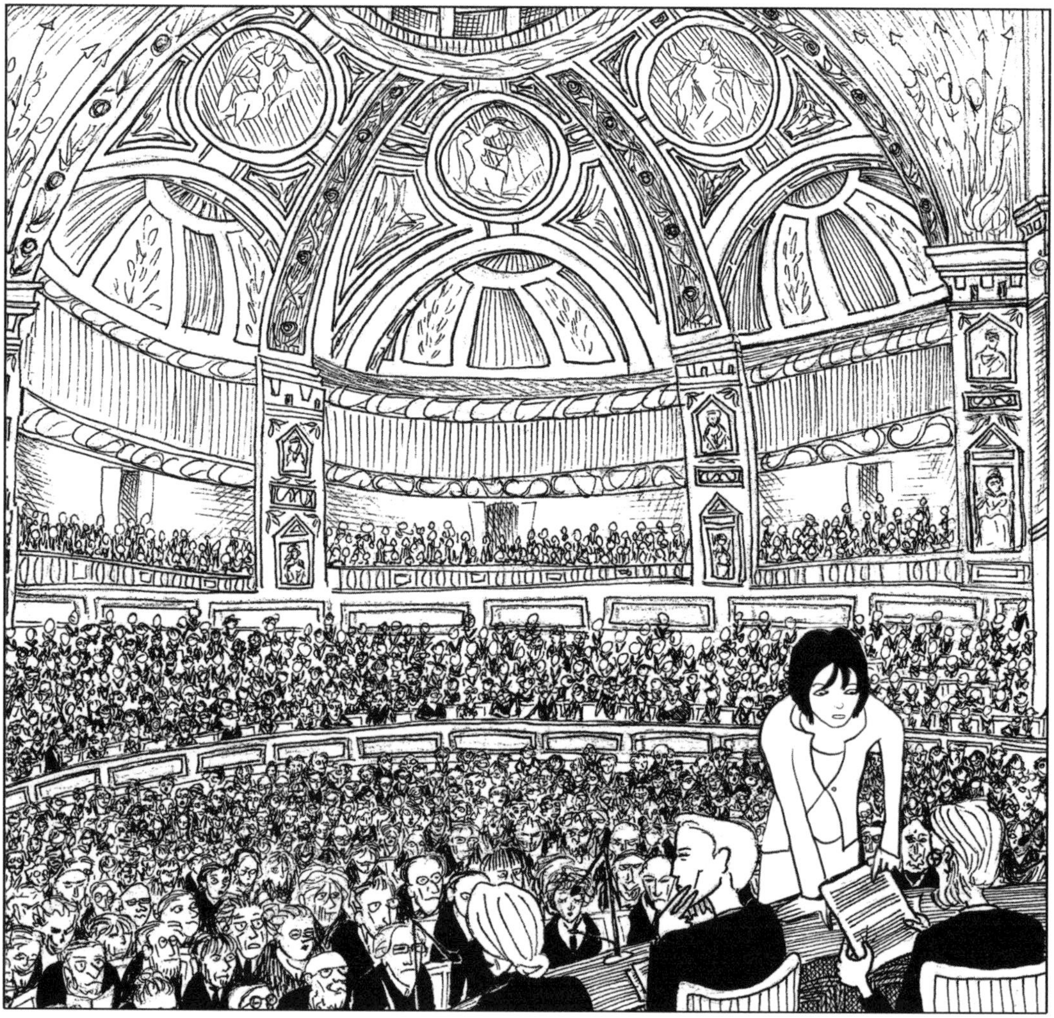

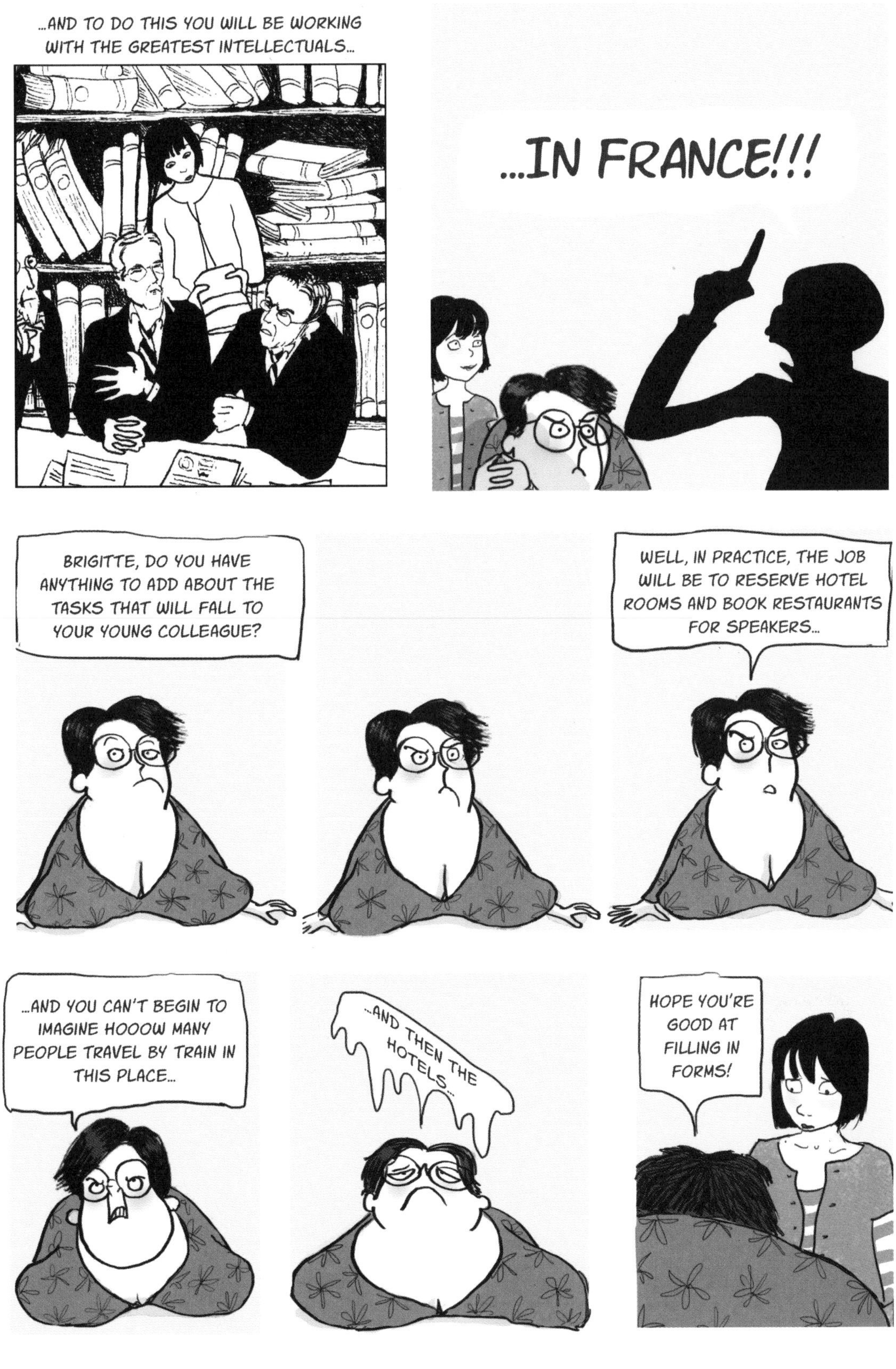
...AND TO DO THIS YOU WILL BE WORKING WITH THE GREATEST INTELLECTUALS...
...IN FRANCE!!!
BRIGITTE, DO YOU HAVE ANYTHING TO ADD ABOUT THE TASKS THAT WILL FALL TO YOUR YOUNG COLLEAGUE?
WELL, IN PRACTICE, THE JOB WILL BE TO RESERVE HOTEL ROOMS AND BOOK RESTAURANTS FOR SPEAKERS...
...AND YOU CAN'T BEGIN TO IMAGINE HOOOW MANY PEOPLE TRAVEL BY TRAIN IN THIS PLACE...
...AND THEN THE HOTELS...
HOPE YOU'RE GOOD AT FILLING IN FORMS!

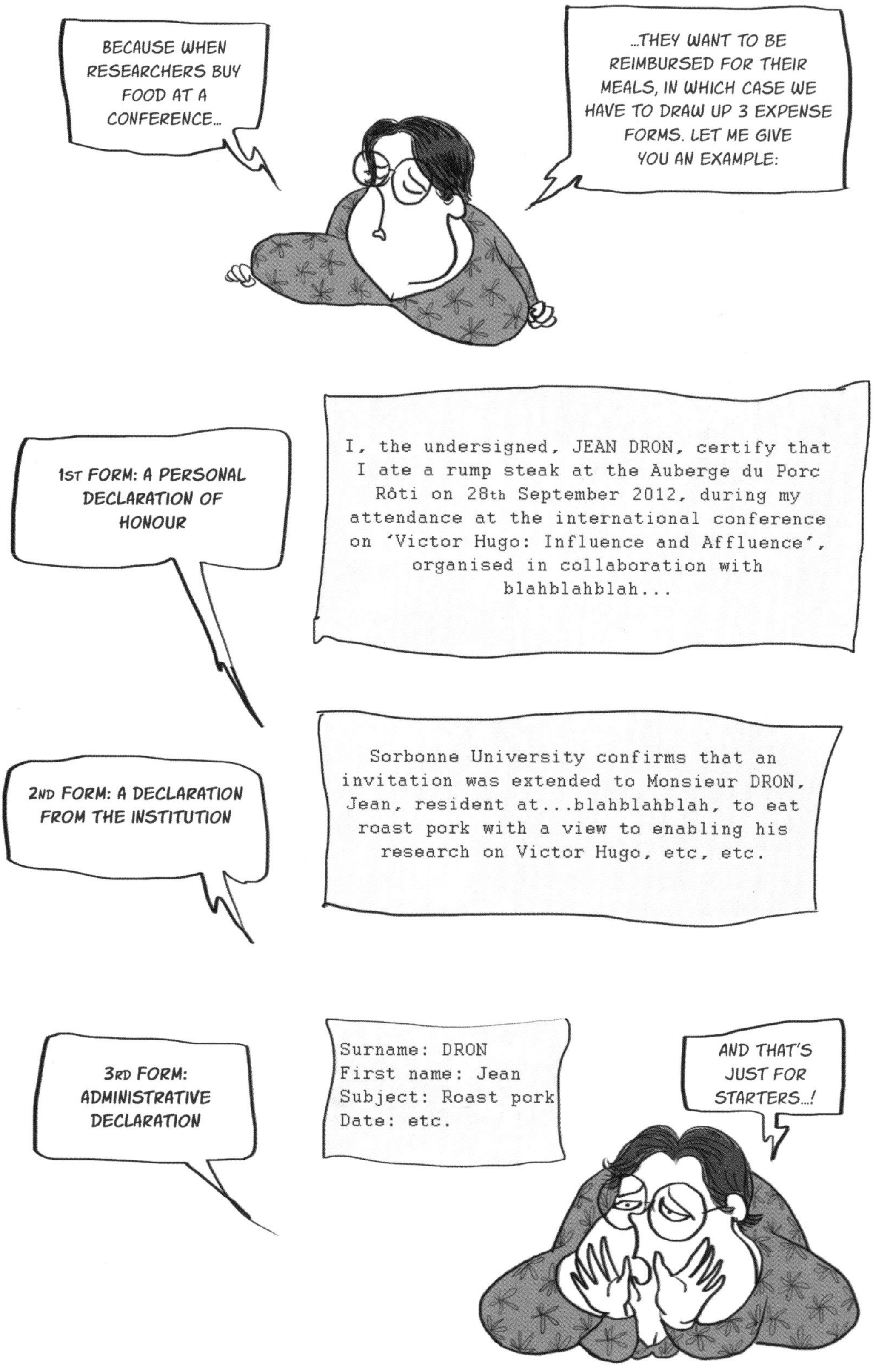
BECAUSE WHEN RESEARCHERS BUY FOOD AT A CONFERENCE...
...THEY WANT TO BE REIMBURSED FOR THEIR MEALS, IN WHICH CASE WE HAVE TO DRAW UP 3 EXPENSE FORMS. LET ME GIVE YOU AN EXAMPLE:
1ST FORM: A PERSONAL DECLARATION OF HONOUR
I, the undersigned, JEAN DRON, certify that I ate a rump steak at the Auberge du Porc Rôti on 28th September 2012, during my attendance at the international conference on 'Victor Hugo: Influence and Affluence', organised in collaboration with blahblahblah...
2ND FORM: A DECLARATION FROM THE INSTITUTION
Sorbonne University confirms that an invitation was extended to Monsieur DRON, Jean, resident at...blahblahblah, to eat roast pork with a view to enabling his research on Victor Hugo, etc, etc.
3RD FORM: ADMINISTRATIVE DECLARATION
Surname: DRON
First name: Jean
Subject: Roast pork
Date: etc.
AND THAT'S JUST FOR STARTERS...!

AFTER ALL THAT, YOU HAVE TO PLACE THE FORMS IN AN ENVELOPE AND CIRCULATE THEM TO ALL THE SIGNATORIES TO BE STAMPED BY THE 8 OBLIGATORY STAMPS REQUIRED FOR REIMBURSEMENT.

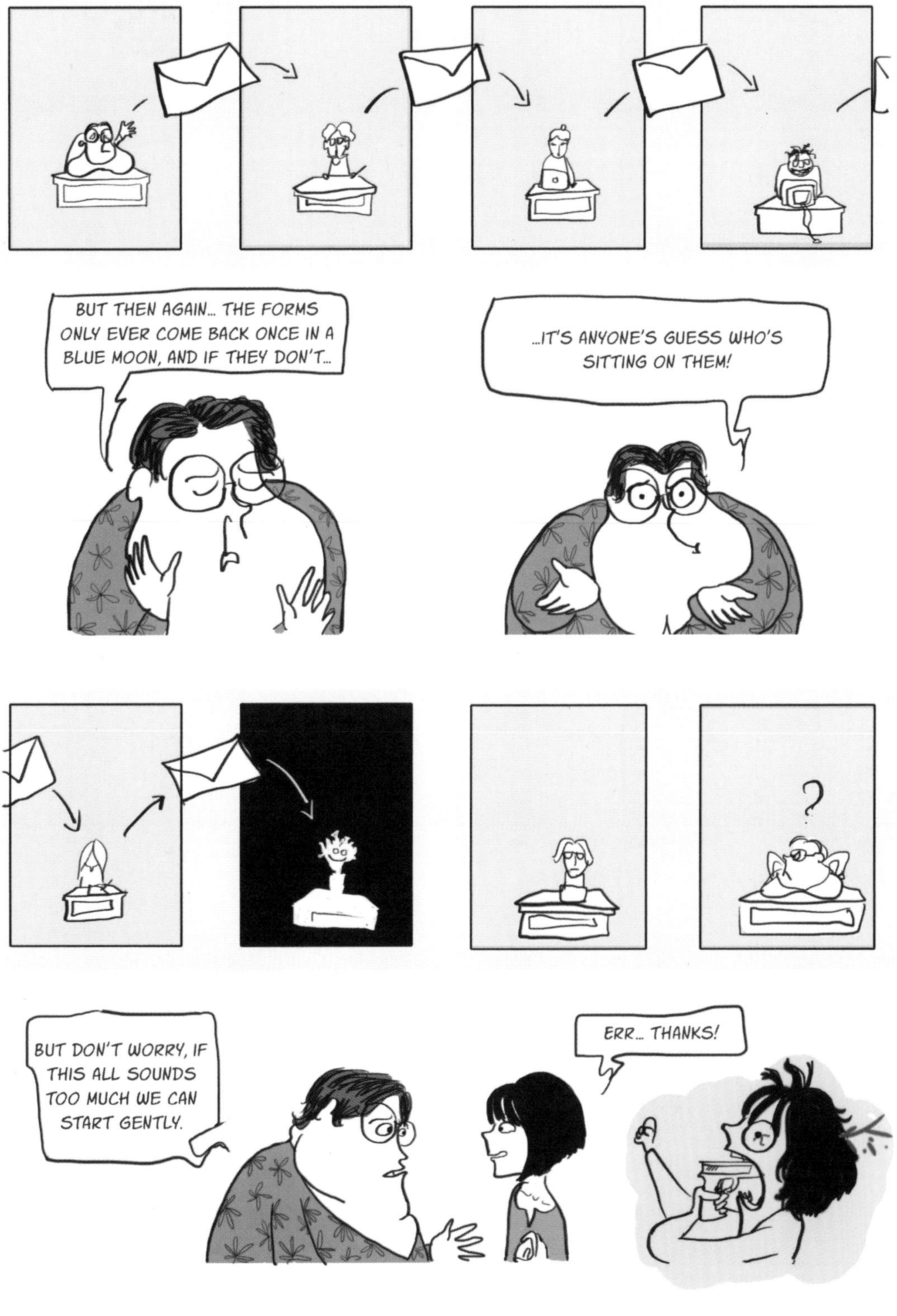
BUT THEN AGAIN... THE FORMS ONLY EVER COME BACK ONCE IN A BLUE MOON, AND IF THEY DON'T...
...IT'S ANYONE'S GUESS WHO'S SITTING ON THEM!
?
BUT DON'T WORRY, IF THIS ALL SOUNDS TOO MUCH WE CAN START GENTLY.
ERR... THANKS!

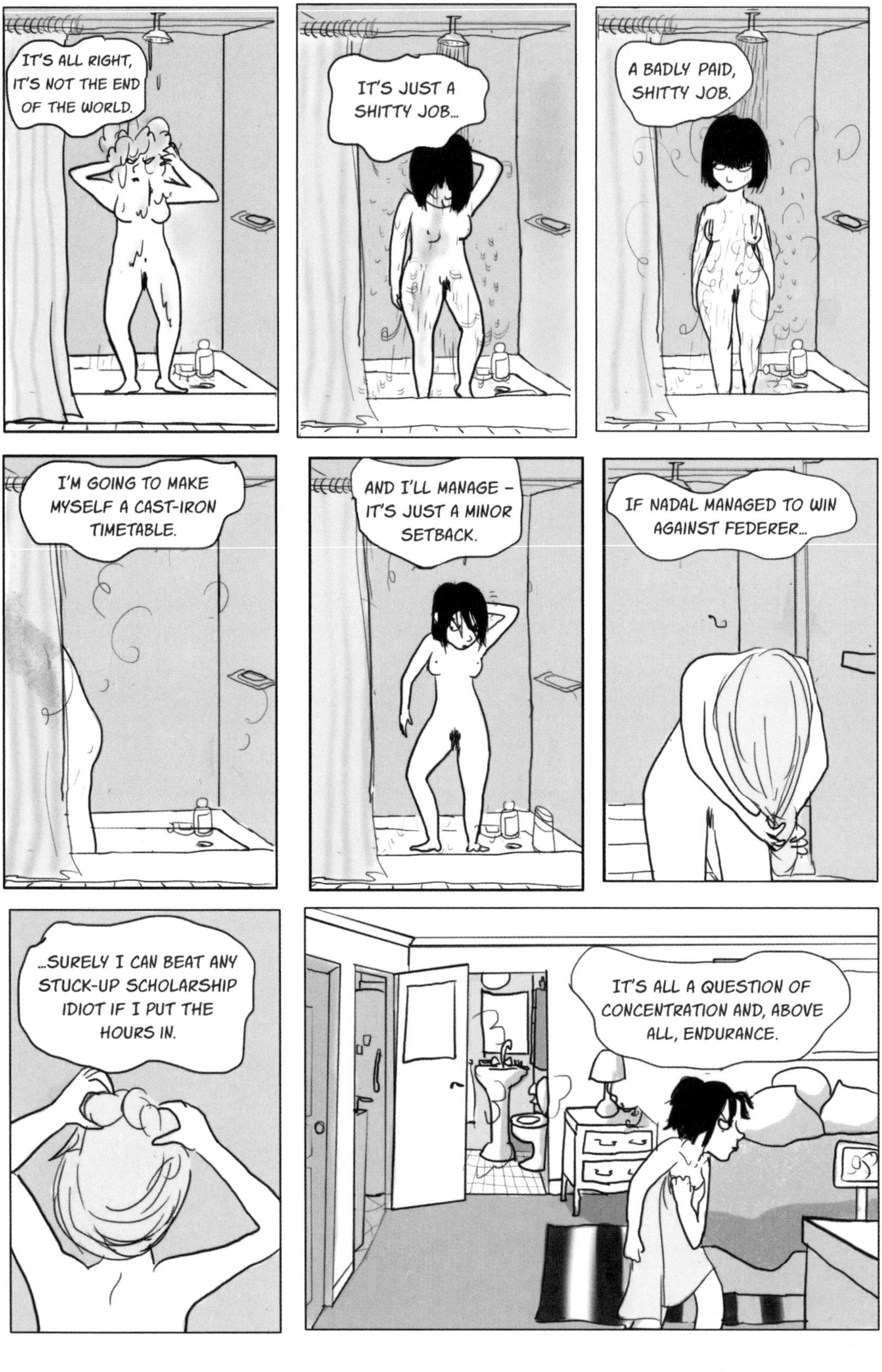
IT'S ALL RIGHT, IT'S NOT THE END OF THE WORLD.
IT'S JUST A SHITTY JOB...
A BADLY PAID, SHITTY JOB.
I'M GOING TO MAKE MYSELF A CAST-IRON TIMETABLE.
AND I'LL MANAGE – IT'S JUST A MINOR SETBACK.
IF NADAL MANAGED TO WIN AGAINST FEDERER...
...SURELY I CAN BEAT ANY STUCK-UP SCHOLARSHIP IDIOT IF I PUT THE HOURS IN.
IT'S ALL A QUESTION OF CONCENTRATION AND, ABOVE ALL, ENDURANCE.

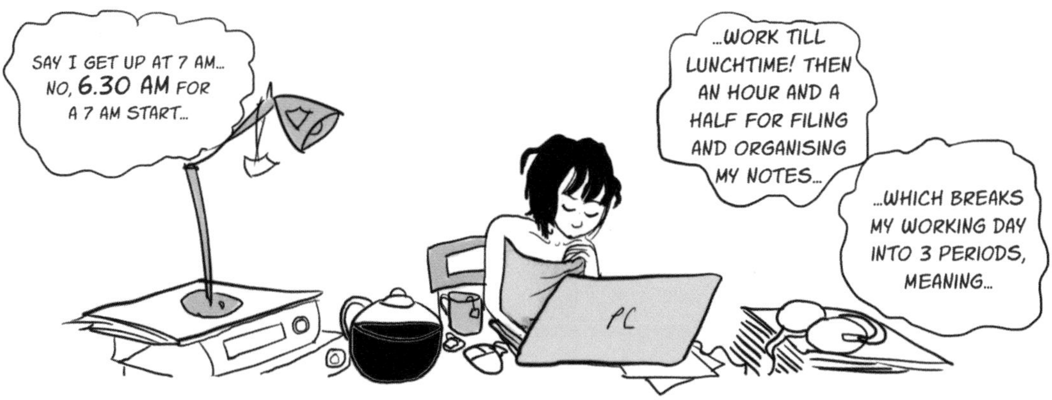
SAY I GET UP AT 7 AM... NO, 6.30 AM FOR A 7 AM START...
...WORK TILL LUNCHTIME! THEN AN HOUR AND A HALF FOR FILING AND ORGANISING MY NOTES...
...WHICH BREAKS MY WORKING DAY INTO 3 PERIODS, MEANING...
PC

	Monday	Tuesday	Wednesday	Thursday	Friday
7	Reading	Reading	Reading	Reading	Reading
8	Reading	Reading	Reading	Reading	Reading
9	Travel	Travel	Travel	Travel	Travel
10	In the office	In the office	In the office	In the office	In the office
11	In the office	In the office	In the office	In the office	In the office
12	In the office	In the office	In the office	In the office	In the office
13	Reading	Reading	Reading	Reading	Reading
14	In the office	In the office	In the office	In the office	In the office
15	In the office	In the office	In the office	Travel	In the office
16	In the office	In the office	In the office	2nd year class	In the office
17	Travel	Travel	Travel	2nd year class	Travel
18	Reading	Reading	Lesson planning	Travel	Reading
19	Reading	Reading	Lesson planning	Reading	Reading
20	Revise notes	Revise notes	Lesson planning	Revise notes	Revise notes
21	PhD planning	PhD planning	Lesson planning	PhD planning	PhD planning
22	PhD planning	PhD planning	Lesson planning	PhD planning	PhD planning
23	PhD planning	PhD planning	Lesson planning	PhD planning	PhD planning

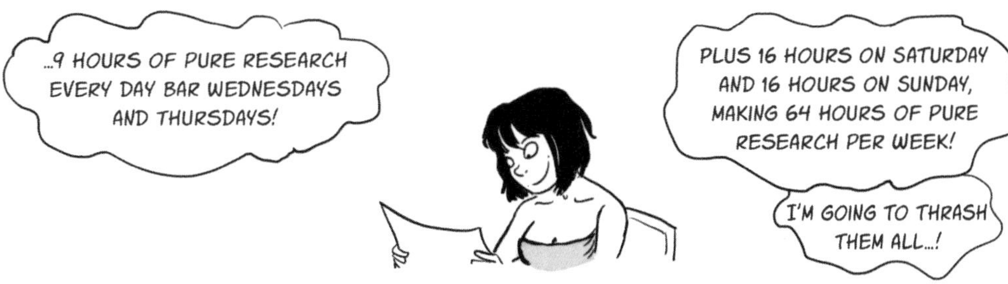
...9 HOURS OF PURE RESEARCH EVERY DAY BAR WEDNESDAYS AND THURSDAYS!
PLUS 16 HOURS ON SATURDAY AND 16 HOURS ON SUNDAY, MAKING 64 HOURS OF PURE RESEARCH PER WEEK!
I'M GOING TO THRASH THEM ALL...!

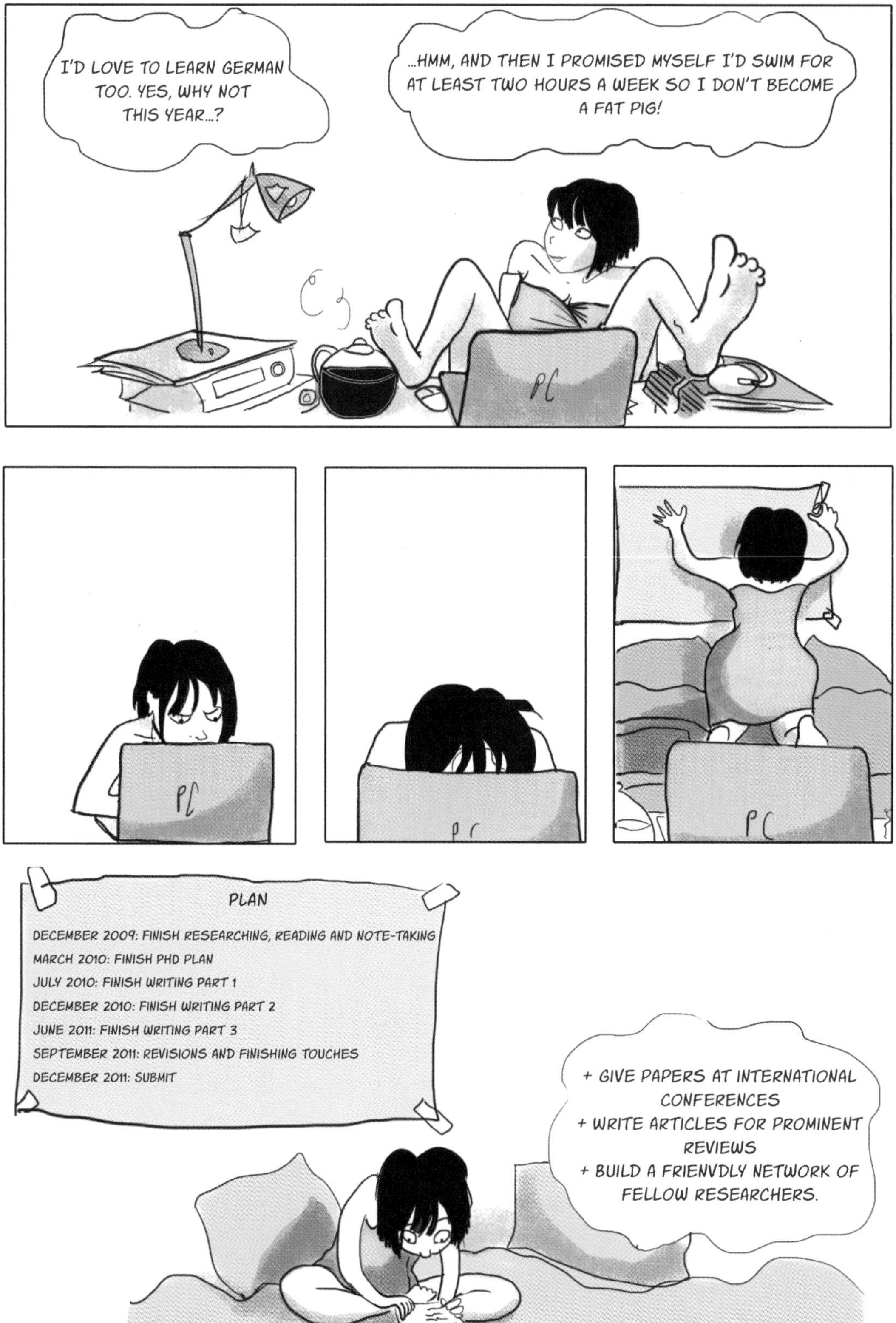
I'D LOVE TO LEARN GERMAN TOO. YES, WHY NOT THIS YEAR...?
...HMM, AND THEN I PROMISED MYSELF I'D SWIM FOR AT LEAST TWO HOURS A WEEK SO I DON'T BECOME A FAT PIG!
PC
PC
PC
PC
PLAN
DECEMBER 2009: FINISH RESEARCHING, READING AND NOTE-TAKING
MARCH 2010: FINISH PHD PLAN
JULY 2010: FINISH WRITING PART 1
DECEMBER 2010: FINISH WRITING PART 2
JUNE 2011: FINISH WRITING PART 3
SEPTEMBER 2011: REVISIONS AND FINISHING TOUCHES
DECEMBER 2011: SUBMIT
+ GIVE PAPERS AT INTERNATIONAL CONFERENCES
+ WRITE ARTICLES FOR PROMINENT REVIEWS
+ BUILD A FRIENVDLY NETWORK OF FELLOW RESEARCHERS.

2 YEARS LATER...

JEANNE DARGAN
2008

Surname: ....DARGAN
First name: ....JEANNE
Enrollment: ....1st YEAR
Supervisor: ....A. KARPOV
Funding source: ....NONE

Thesis Subject: 'The Labyrinthine Motif in the Parable of the Law in Kafka's *The Trial*.'

JEANNE DARGAN
2009

Surname: ....DARGAN
First name: ....JEANNE
Enrollment: ....2nd YEAR
Supervisor: ....A. KARPOV
Funding source: ....NONE

Thesis Subject:......*Revised*.............
'The Concept of the Labyrinth in the Parable of the Law in Kafka's *The Trial*.'

JEANNE DARGAN
2010

Surname: ....DARGAN
First name:..............................JEANNE
Enrollment: ....3rd YEAR
Supervisor: ....A.KARPOV
Funding source:...........................NONE

Thesis Subject: ....*Revised*..........
'The Labyrinthine Concept of a Motif in the Parable of the Law in Kafka's *The Trial*.'

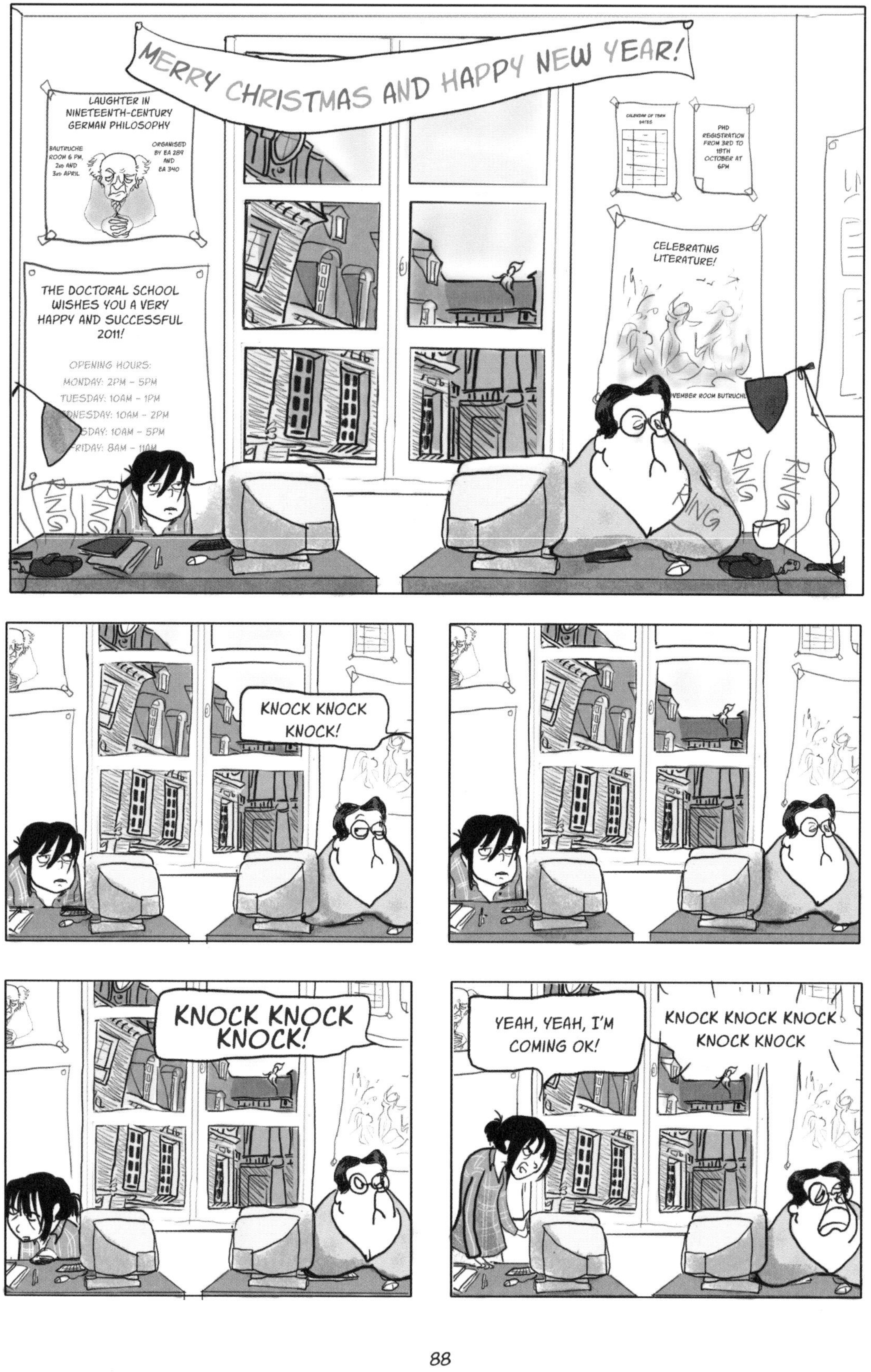
MERRY CHRISTMAS AND HAPPY NEW YEAR!
LAUGHTER IN NINETEENTH-CENTURY GERMAN PHILOSOPHY
BAUTRUCHE ROOM 6 PM, 2ND AND 3RD APRIL
ORGANISED BY EA 289 AND EA 340
THE DOCTORAL SCHOOL WISHES YOU A VERY HAPPY AND SUCCESSFUL 2011!
OPENING HOURS:
MONDAY: 2PM – 5PM
TUESDAY: 10AM – 1PM
PHD REGISTRATION FROM 3RD TO 18TH OCTOBER AT 6PM
CELEBRATING LITERATURE!
RING
RING
RING
RING
RING
KNOCK KNOCK KNOCK!
KNOCK KNOCK KNOCK!
YEAH, YEAH, I'M COMING OK!
KNOCK KNOCK KNOCK KNOCK KNOCK

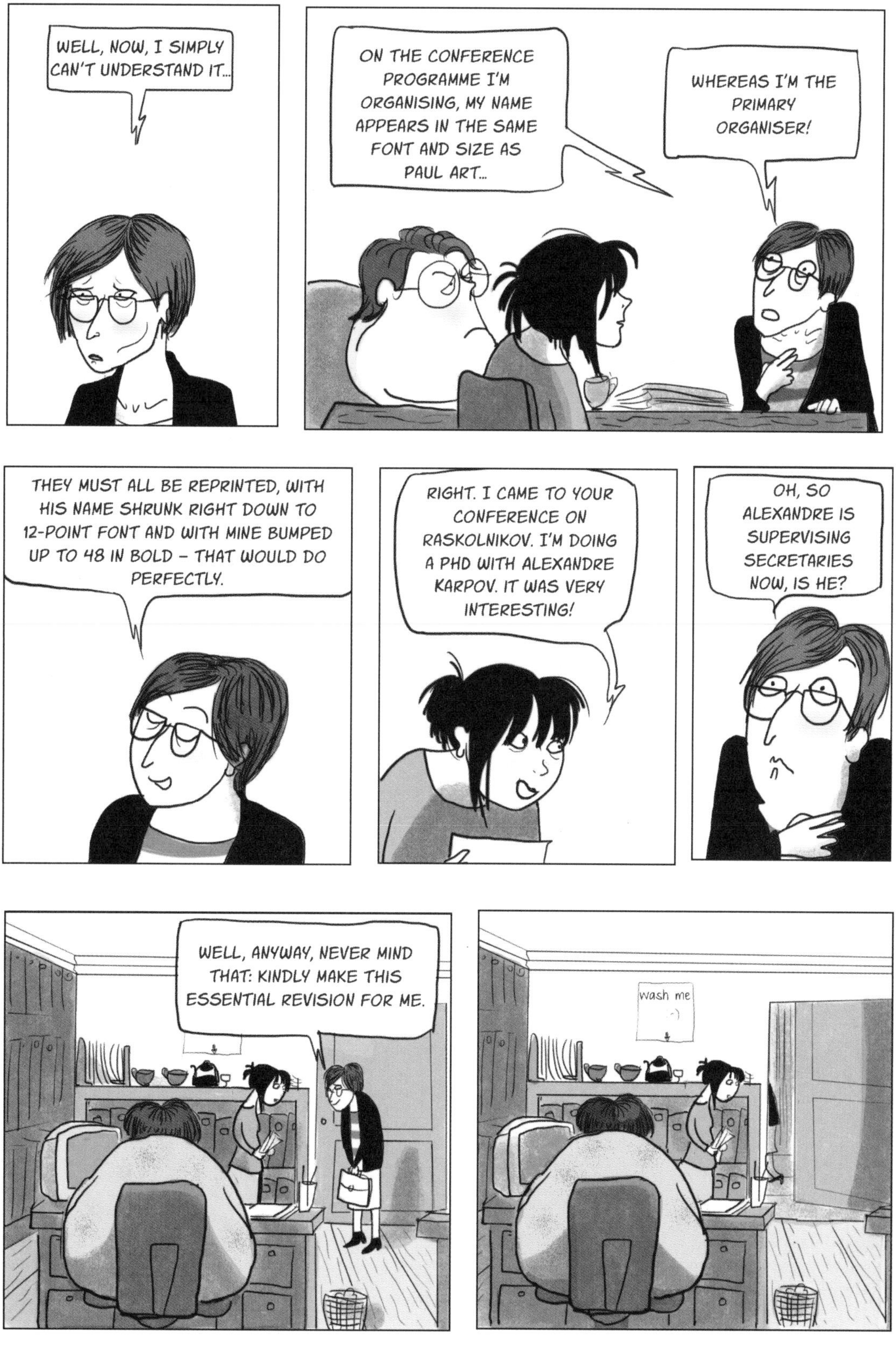
WELL, NOW, I SIMPLY CAN'T UNDERSTAND IT...
ON THE CONFERENCE PROGRAMME I'M ORGANISING, MY NAME APPEARS IN THE SAME FONT AND SIZE AS PAUL ART...
WHEREAS I'M THE PRIMARY ORGANISER!
THEY MUST ALL BE REPRINTED, WITH HIS NAME SHRUNK RIGHT DOWN TO 12-POINT FONT AND WITH MINE BUMPED UP TO 48 IN BOLD – THAT WOULD DO PERFECTLY.
RIGHT. I CAME TO YOUR CONFERENCE ON RASKOLNIKOV. I'M DOING A PHD WITH ALEXANDRE KARPOV. IT WAS VERY INTERESTING!
OH, SO ALEXANDRE IS SUPERVISING SECRETARIES NOW, IS HE?
WELL, ANYWAY, NEVER MIND THAT: KINDLY MAKE THIS ESSENTIAL REVISION FOR ME.
wash me

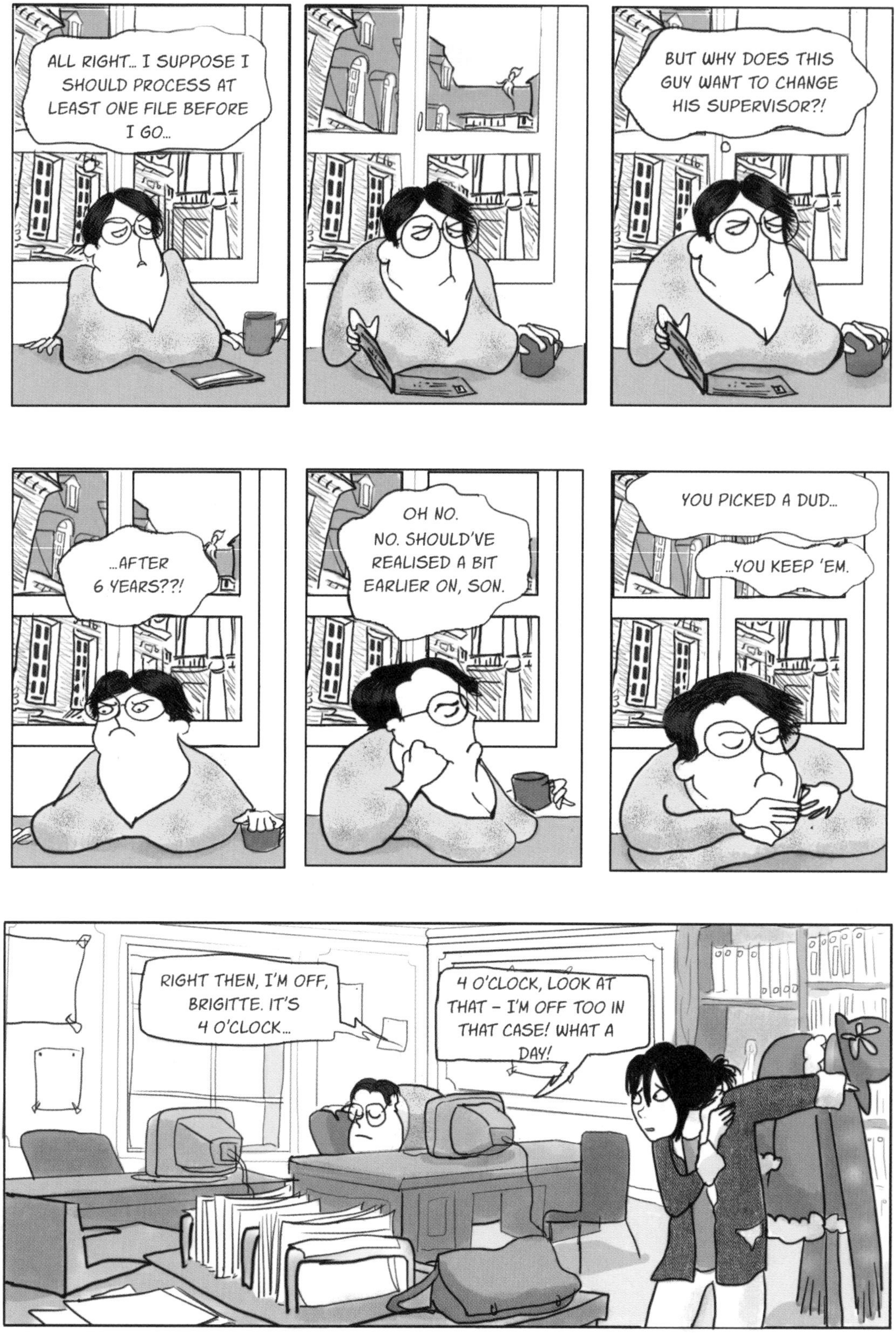
ALL RIGHT... I SUPPOSE I SHOULD PROCESS AT LEAST ONE FILE BEFORE I GO...
BUT WHY DOES THIS GUY WANT TO CHANGE HIS SUPERVISOR?!
...AFTER 6 YEARS??!
OH NO. NO. SHOULD'VE REALISED A BIT EARLIER ON, SON.
YOU PICKED A DUD...
...YOU KEEP 'EM.
RIGHT THEN, I'M OFF, BRIGITTE. IT'S 4 O'CLOCK...
4 O'CLOCK, LOOK AT THAT – I'M OFF TOO IN THAT CASE! WHAT A DAY!

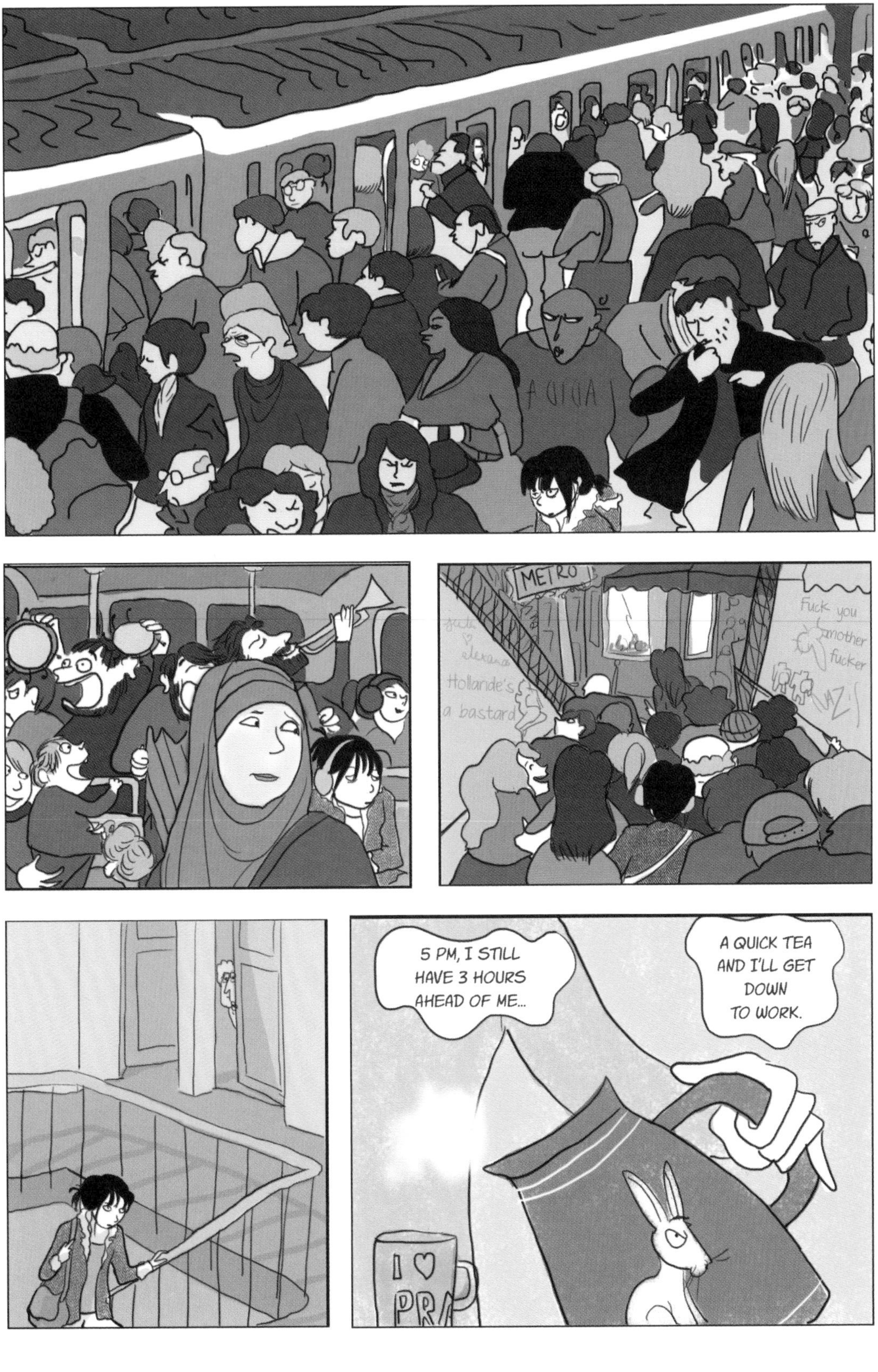
METRO
Hollande's a bastard
Fuck you mother fucker
5 PM, I STILL HAVE 3 HOURS AHEAD OF ME...
A QUICK TEA AND I'LL GET DOWN TO WORK.

IN NEARLY THREE YEARS, JEANNE HAD READ 3,200 WORKS OF LITERARY CRITICISM, WHICH SHE HAD FILED, ARRANGED AND SORTED IN HER SHELVING SYSTEM LABELLED 'PHD RESEARCH'.

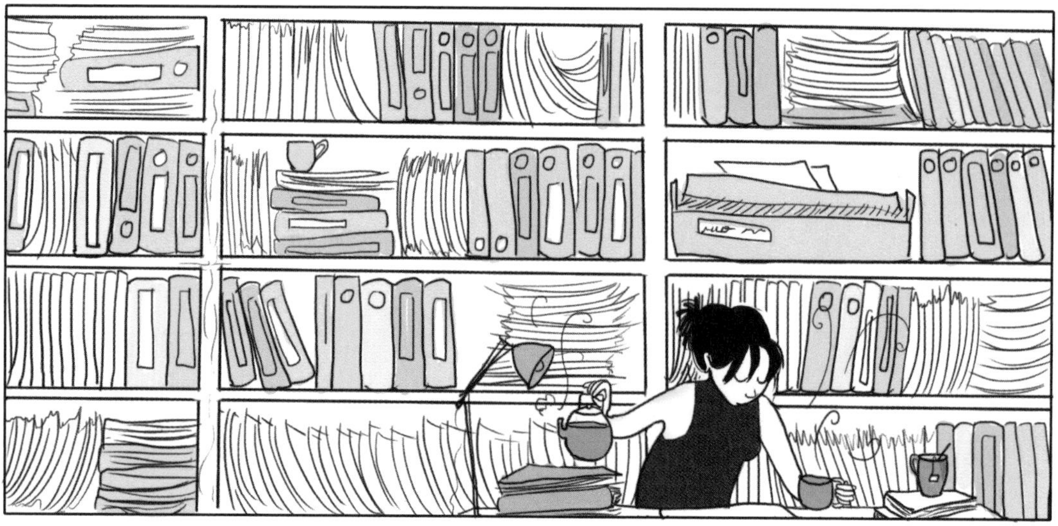

MEANWHILE, SHE HAD DRAWN UP A 69-PAGE PLAN AND THEREFORE HAD A VERY PRECISE IDEA OF THE PHD SHE WANTED TO WRITE.

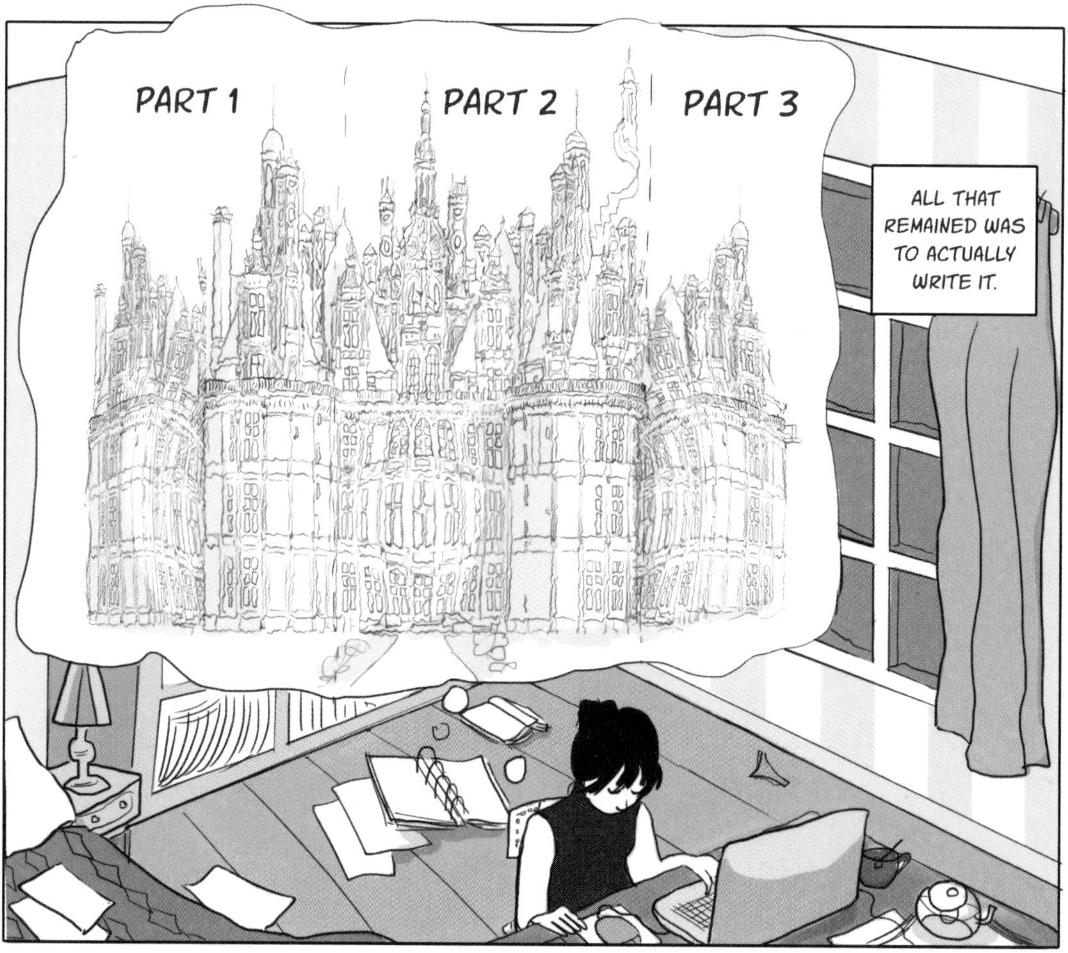
PART 1
PART 2
PART 3
ALL THAT REMAINED WAS TO ACTUALLY WRITE IT.

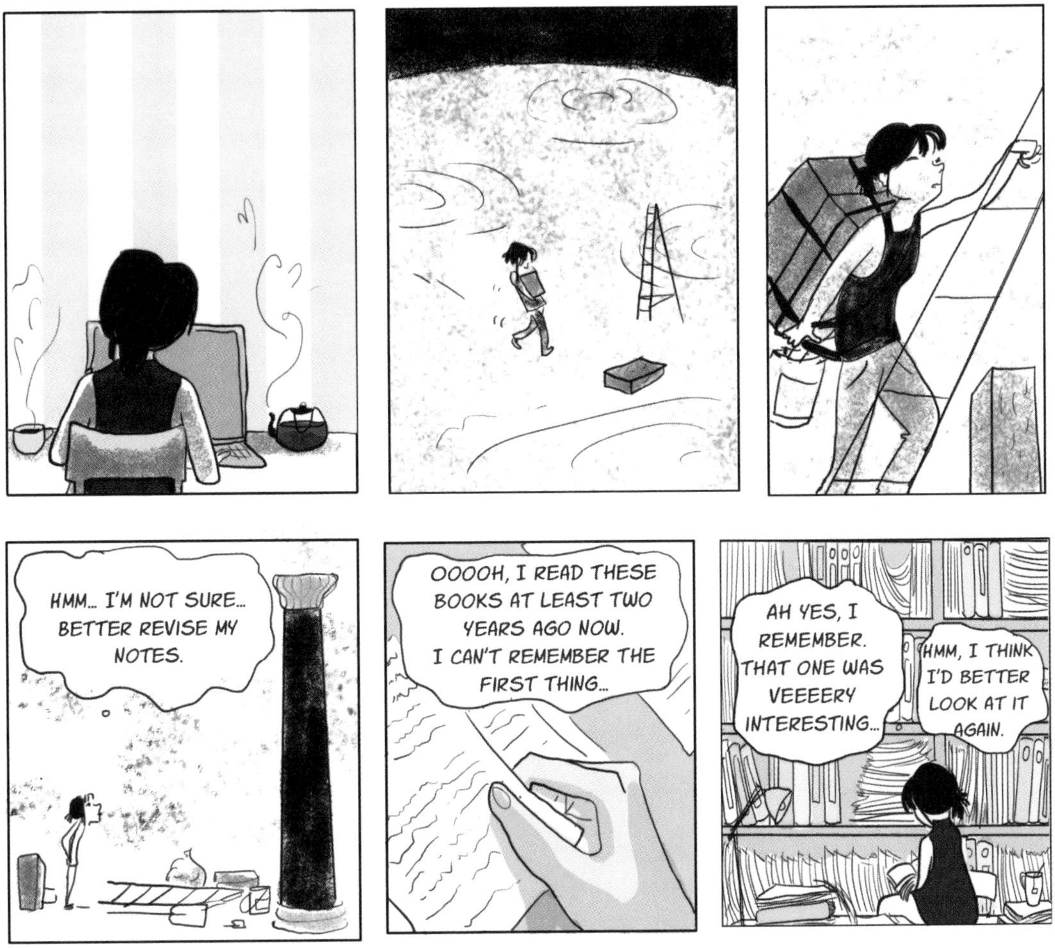
HMM... I'M NOT SURE... BETTER REVISE MY NOTES.
OOOOH, I READ THESE BOOKS AT LEAST TWO YEARS AGO NOW. I CAN'T REMEMBER THE FIRST THING...
AH YES, I REMEMBER. THAT ONE WAS VEEEERY INTERESTING...
HMM, I THINK I'D BETTER LOOK AT IT AGAIN.

FOR THE PAST 8 MONTHS, EVERY TIME JEANNE TRIED TO START WRITING SHE HAD ENDED UP REVISITING BOOKS SHE HAD ALREADY READ.

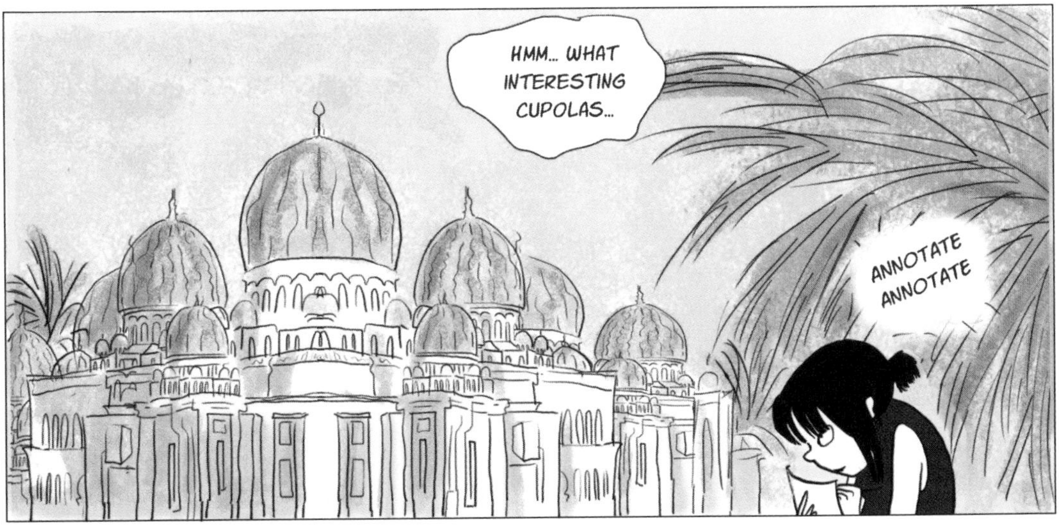
HMM... WHAT INTERESTING CUPOLAS...
ANNOTATE ANNOTATE

EVERY REREADING MEANT REVISIONS TO HER OVERALL PHD PLAN...

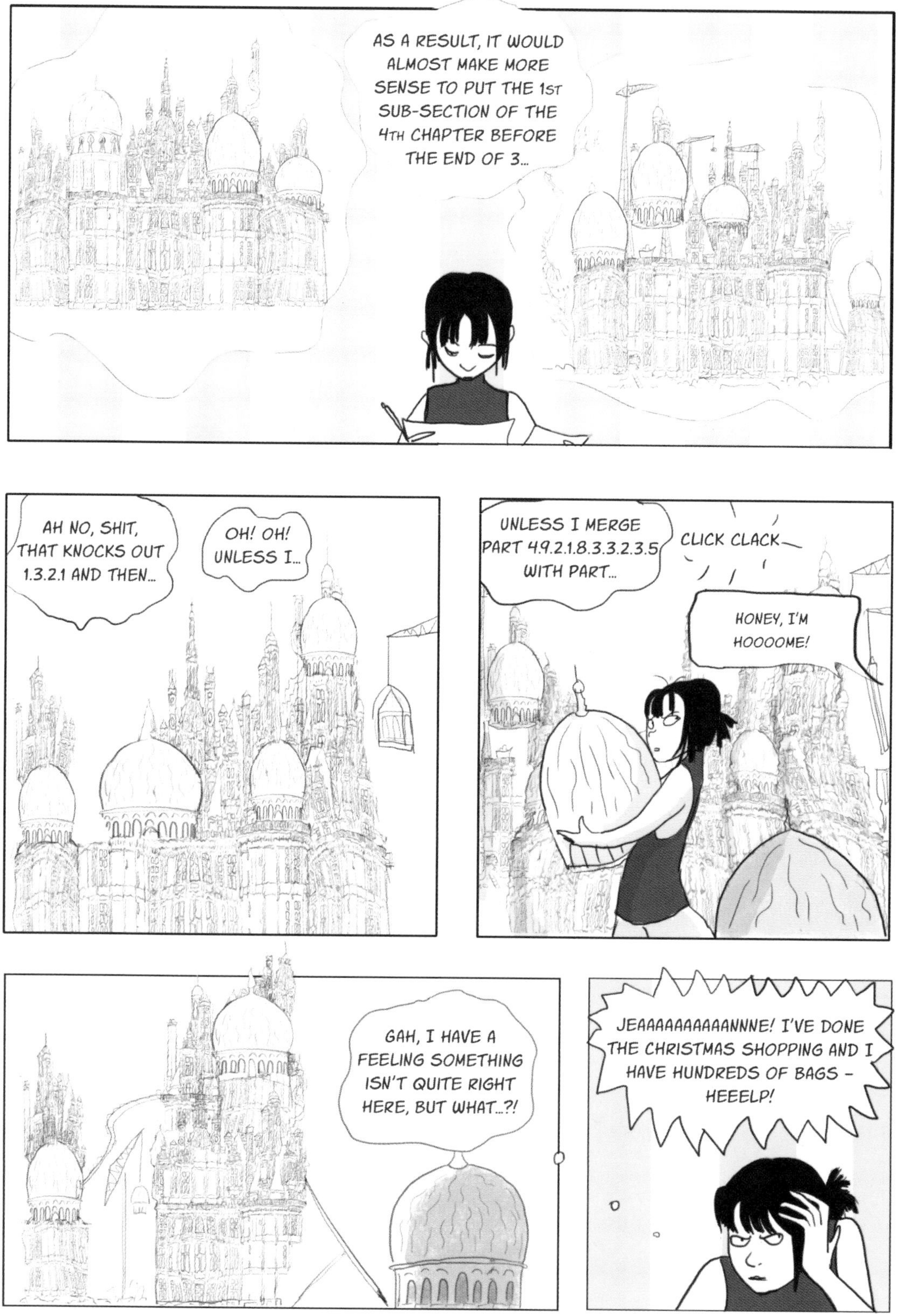
AS A RESULT, IT WOULD ALMOST MAKE MORE SENSE TO PUT THE 1ST SUB-SECTION OF THE 4TH CHAPTER BEFORE THE END OF 3...
AH NO, SHIT, THAT KNOCKS OUT 1.3.2.1 AND THEN...
OH! OH! UNLESS I...
UNLESS I MERGE PART 4.9.2.1.8.3.3.2.3.5 WITH PART...
CLICK CLACK
HONEY, I'M HOOOOME!
GAH, I HAVE A FEELING SOMETHING ISN'T QUITE RIGHT HERE, BUT WHAT...?!
JEAAAAAAAAAANNNE! I'VE DONE THE CHRISTMAS SHOPPING AND I HAVE HUNDREDS OF BAGS - HEEELP!

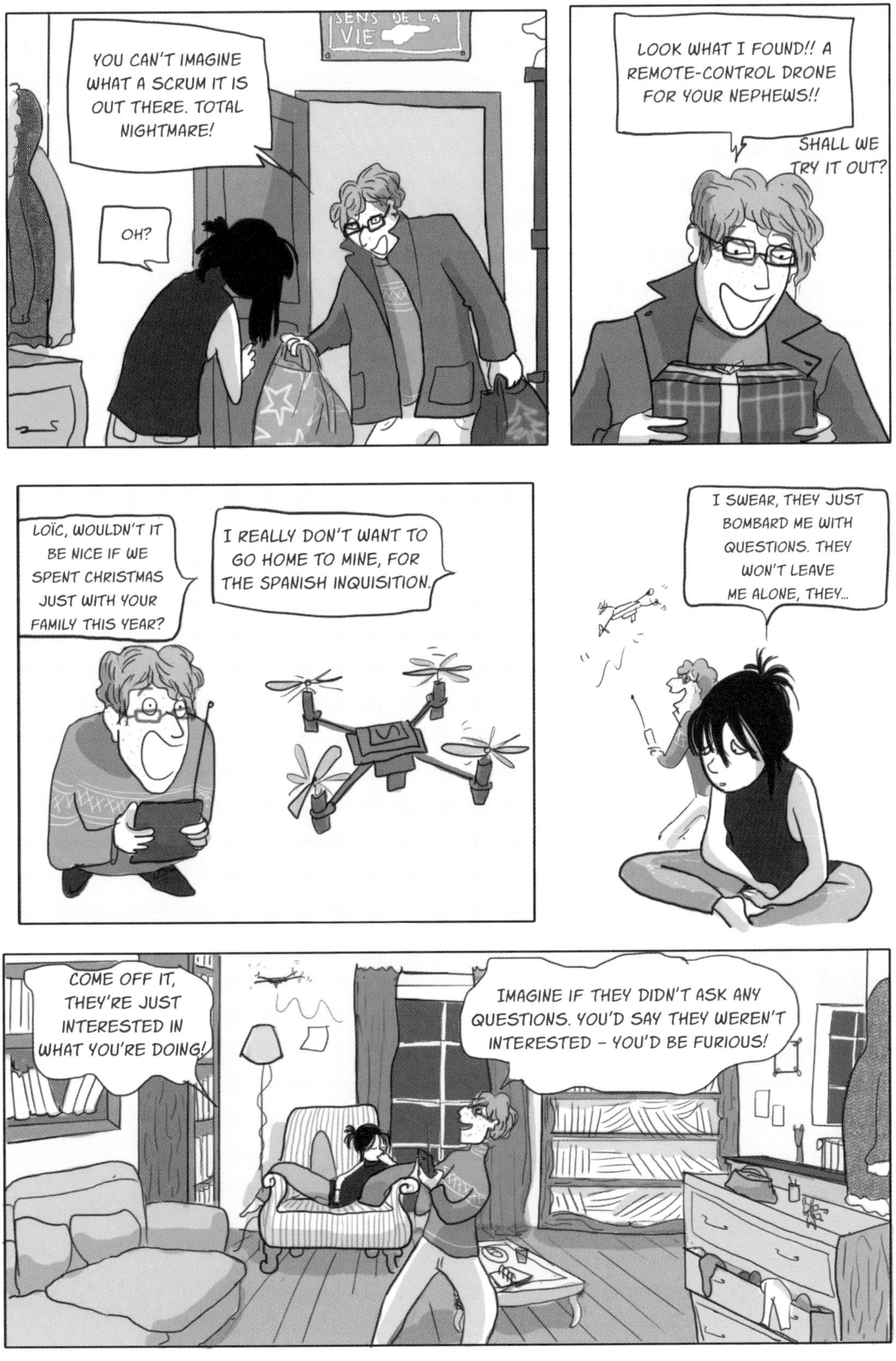
SENS DE LA VIE
YOU CAN'T IMAGINE WHAT A SCRUM IT IS OUT THERE. TOTAL NIGHTMARE!
OH?
LOOK WHAT I FOUND!! A REMOTE-CONTROL DRONE FOR YOUR NEPHEWS!!
SHALL WE TRY IT OUT?
LOÏC, WOULDN'T IT BE NICE IF WE SPENT CHRISTMAS JUST WITH YOUR FAMILY THIS YEAR?
I REALLY DON'T WANT TO GO HOME TO MINE, FOR THE SPANISH INQUISITION.
I SWEAR, THEY JUST BOMBARD ME WITH QUESTIONS. THEY WON'T LEAVE ME ALONE, THEY...
COME OFF IT, THEY'RE JUST INTERESTED IN WHAT YOU'RE DOING!
IMAGINE IF THEY DIDN'T ASK ANY QUESTIONS. YOU'D SAY THEY WEREN'T INTERESTED – YOU'D BE FURIOUS!

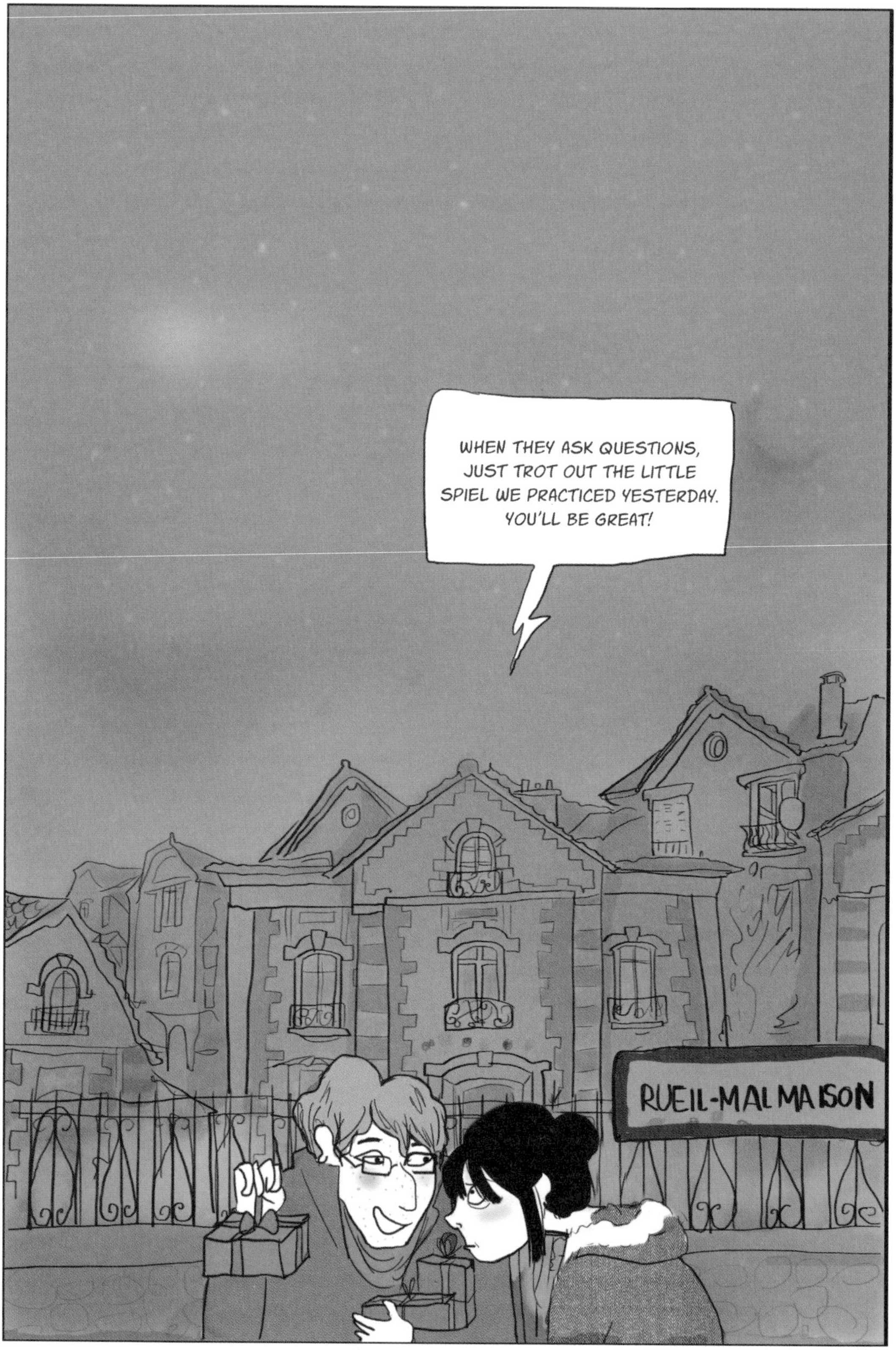
WHEN THEY ASK QUESTIONS, JUST TROT OUT THE LITTLE SPIEL WE PRACTICED YESTERDAY. YOU'LL BE GREAT!
RUEIL-MALMAISON

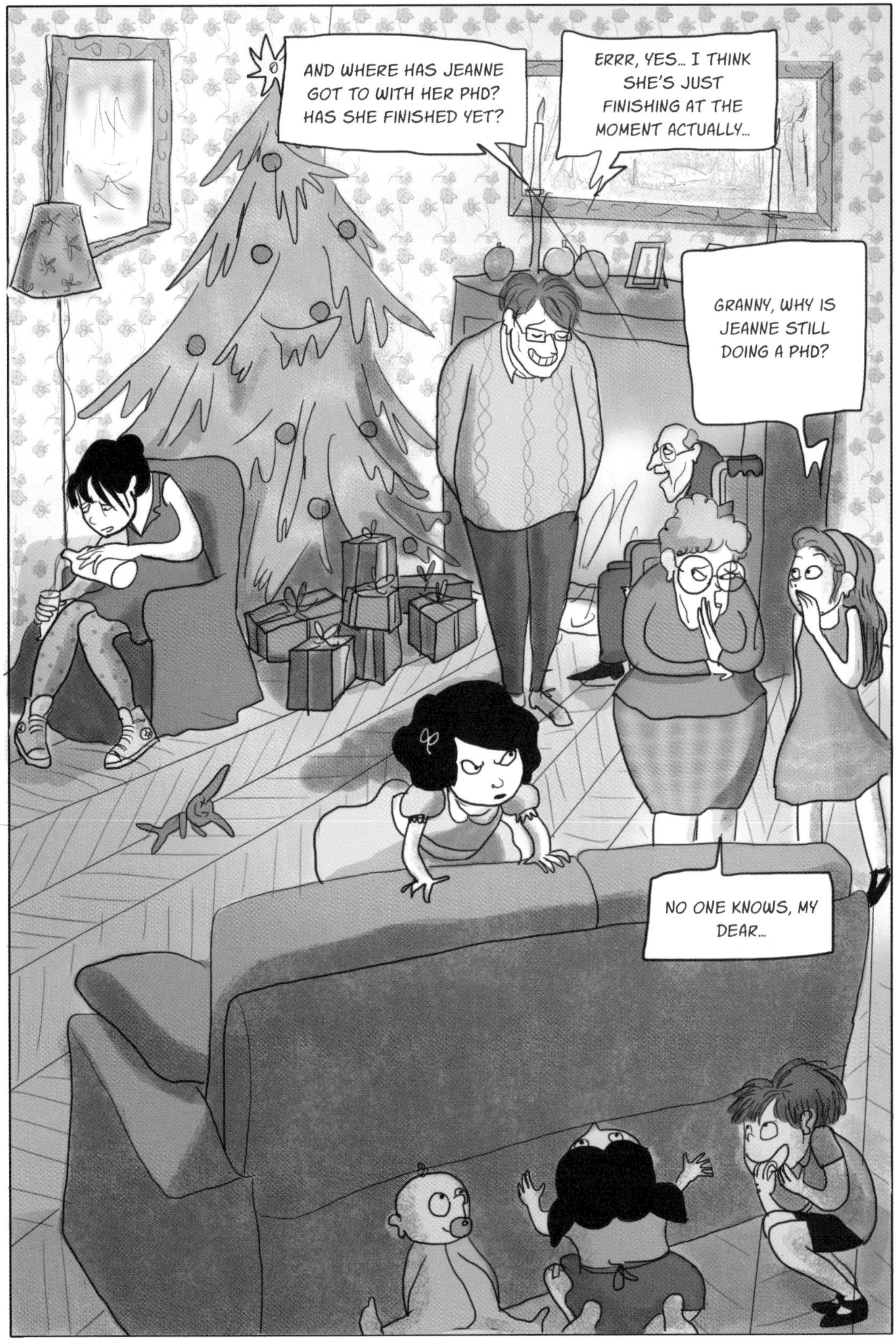
AND WHERE HAS JEANNE GOT TO WITH HER PHD? HAS SHE FINISHED YET?
ERRR, YES... I THINK SHE'S JUST FINISHING AT THE MOMENT ACTUALLY...
GRANNY, WHY IS JEANNE STILL DOING A PHD?
NO ONE KNOWS, MY DEAR...

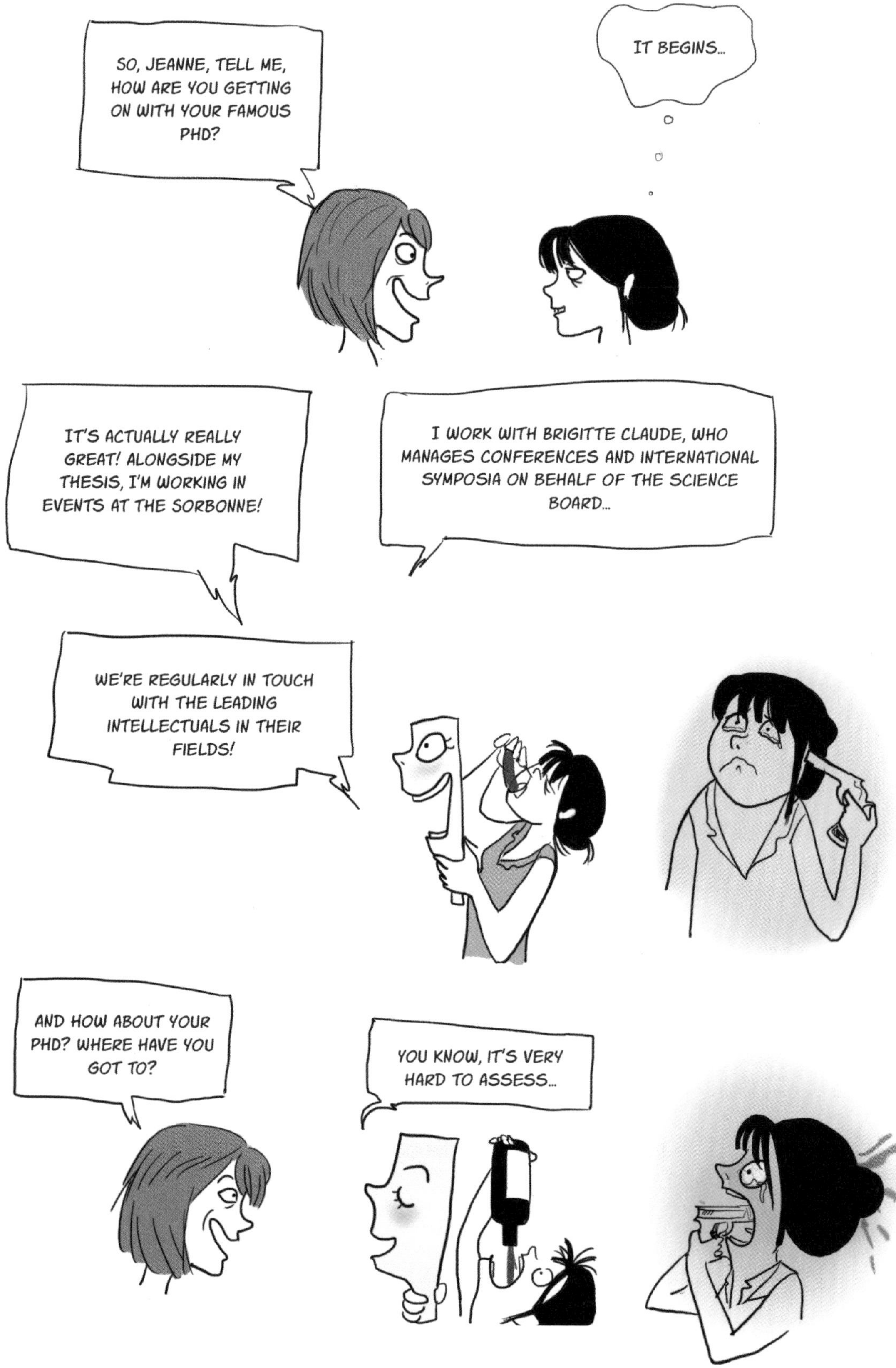
SO, JEANNE, TELL ME, HOW ARE YOU GETTING ON WITH YOUR FAMOUS PHD?
IT BEGINS...
IT'S ACTUALLY REALLY GREAT! ALONGSIDE MY THESIS, I'M WORKING IN EVENTS AT THE SORBONNE!
I WORK WITH BRIGITTE CLAUDE, WHO MANAGES CONFERENCES AND INTERNATIONAL SYMPOSIA ON BEHALF OF THE SCIENCE BOARD...
WE'RE REGULARLY IN TOUCH WITH THE LEADING INTELLECTUALS IN THEIR FIELDS!
AND HOW ABOUT YOUR PHD? WHERE HAVE YOU GOT TO?
YOU KNOW, IT'S VERY HARD TO ASSESS...

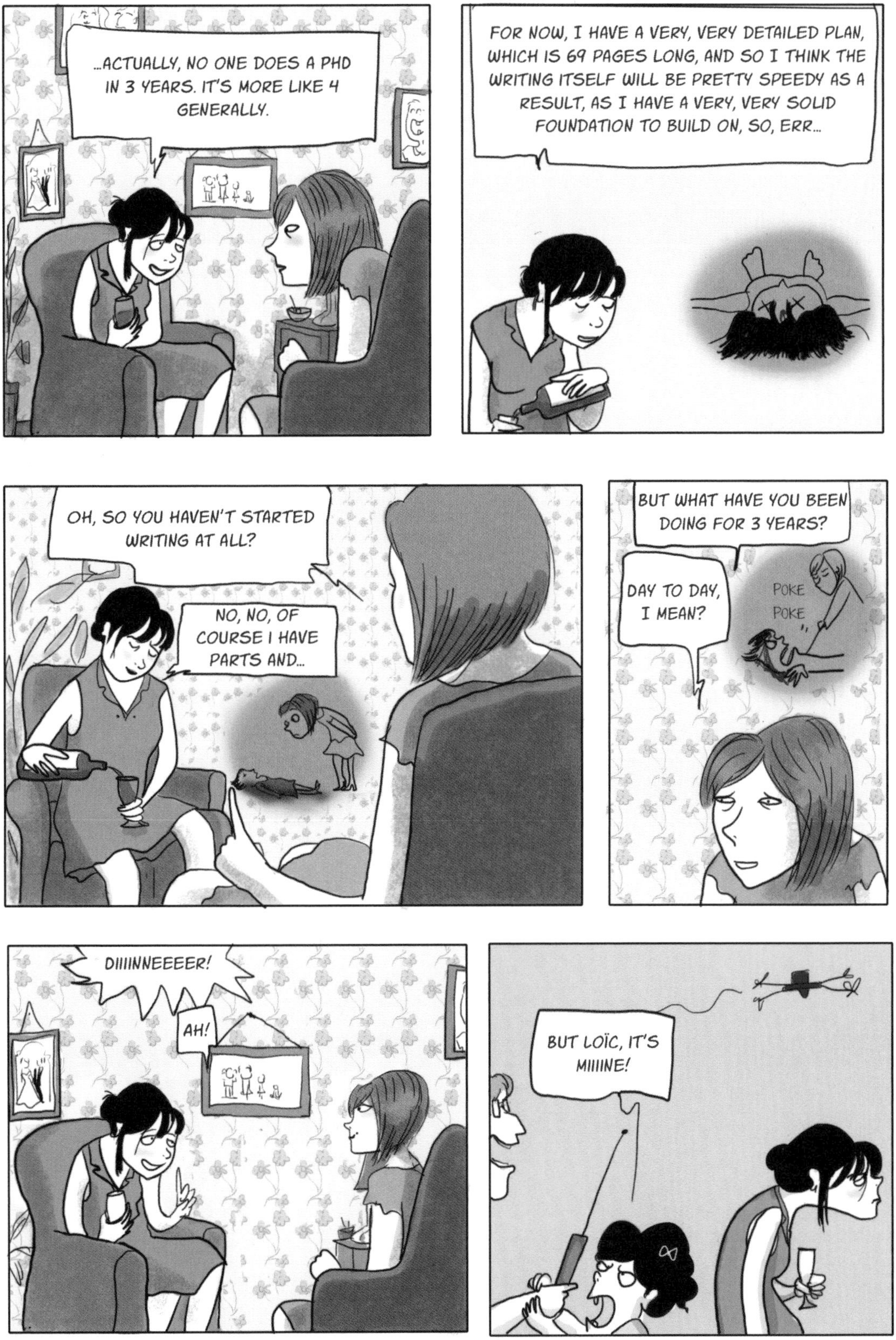
...ACTUALLY, NO ONE DOES A PHD IN 3 YEARS. IT'S MORE LIKE 4 GENERALLY.
FOR NOW, I HAVE A VERY, VERY DETAILED PLAN, WHICH IS 69 PAGES LONG, AND SO I THINK THE WRITING ITSELF WILL BE PRETTY SPEEDY AS A RESULT, AS I HAVE A VERY, VERY SOLID FOUNDATION TO BUILD ON, SO, ERR...
OH, SO YOU HAVEN'T STARTED WRITING AT ALL?
NO, NO, OF COURSE I HAVE PARTS AND...
BUT WHAT HAVE YOU BEEN DOING FOR 3 YEARS?
DAY TO DAY, I MEAN?
POKE
POKE
DIIIINNEEEER!
AH!
BUT LOÏC, IT'S MIIINE!

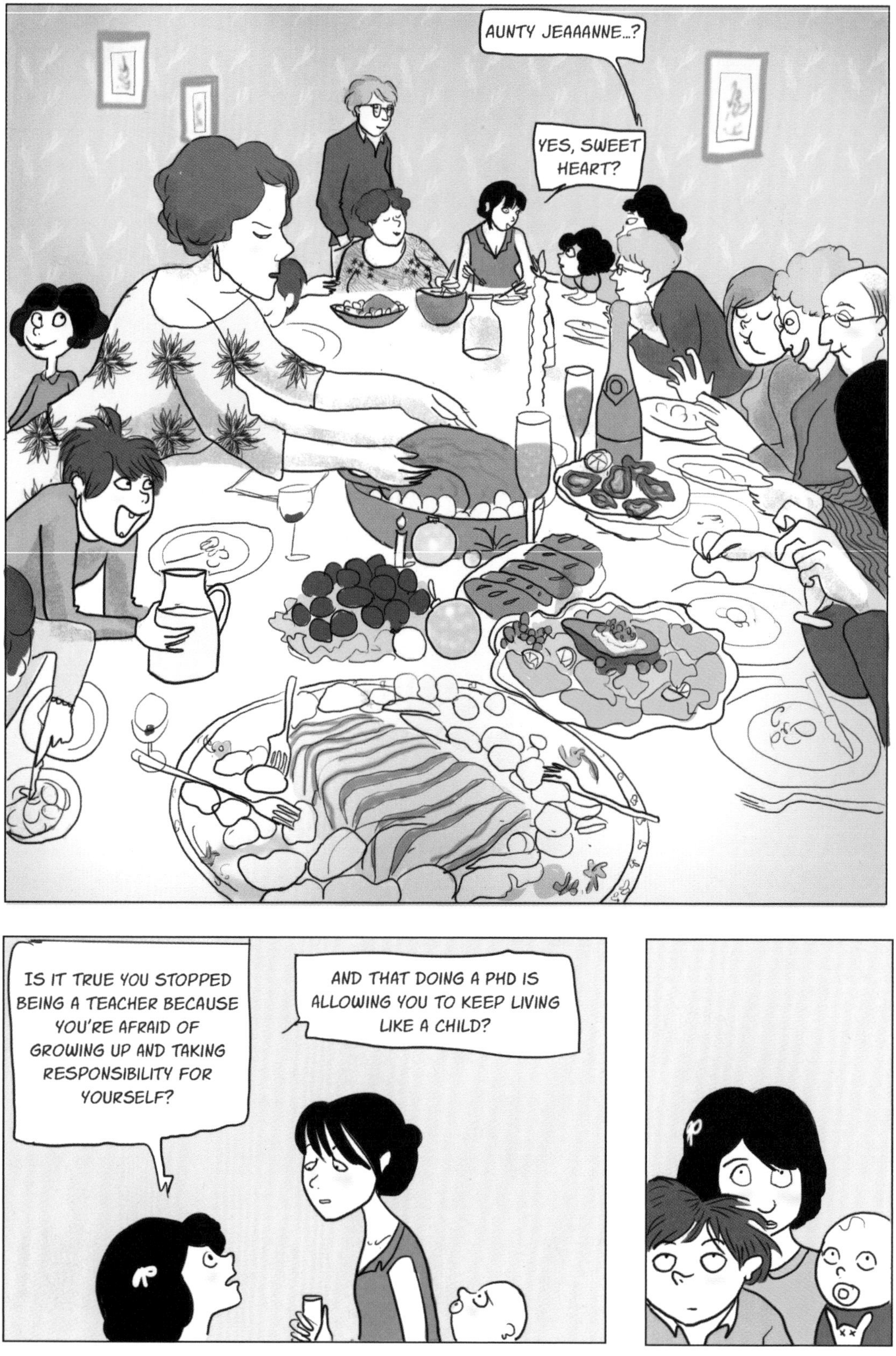
AUNTY JEAAANNE...?
YES, SWEET HEART?
IS IT TRUE YOU STOPPED BEING A TEACHER BECAUSE YOU'RE AFRAID OF GROWING UP AND TAKING RESPONSIBILITY FOR YOURSELF?
AND THAT DOING A PHD IS ALLOWING YOU TO KEEP LIVING LIKE A CHILD?

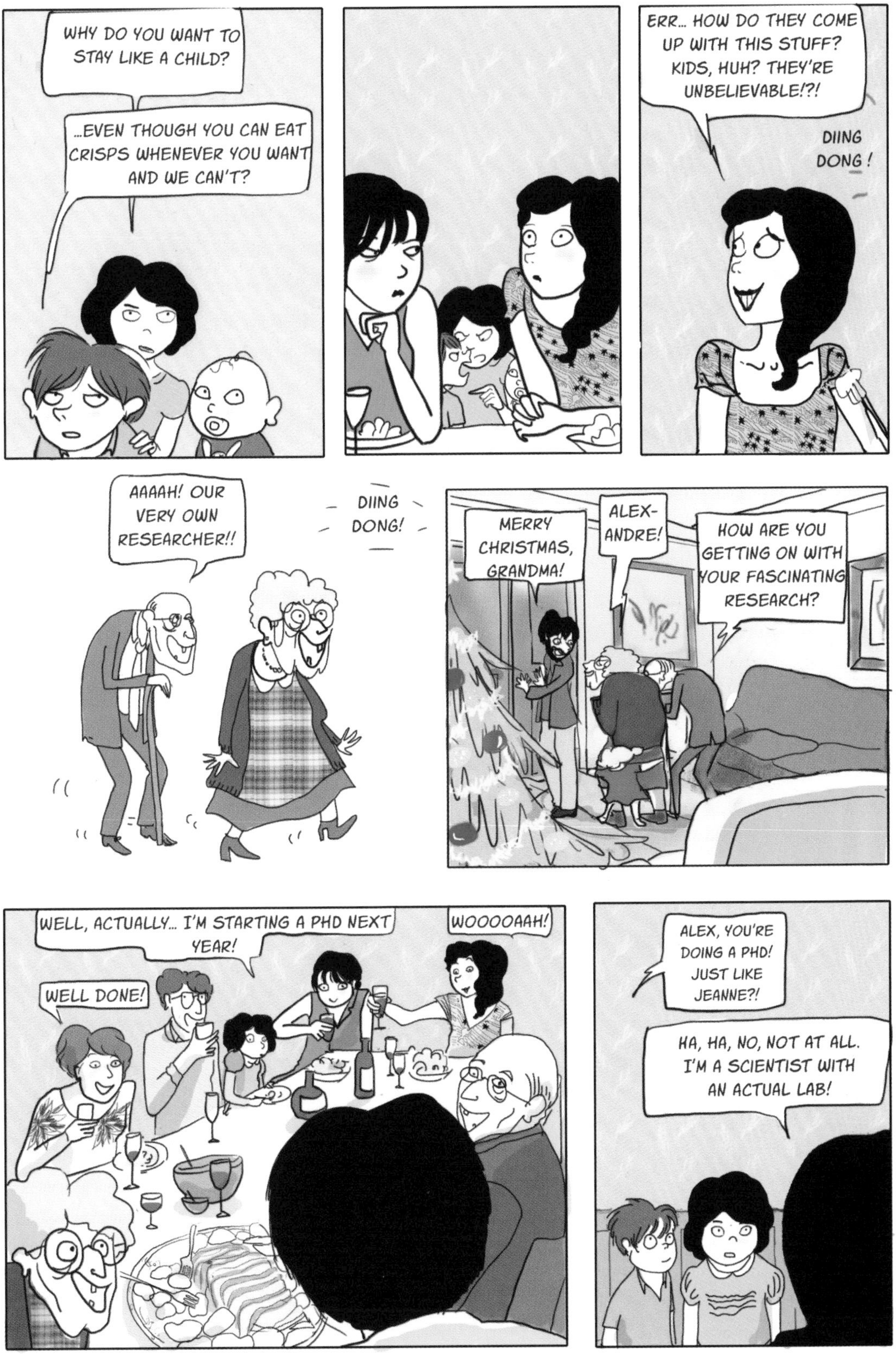
WHY DO YOU WANT TO STAY LIKE A CHILD?
...EVEN THOUGH YOU CAN EAT CRISPS WHENEVER YOU WANT AND WE CAN'T?
ERR... HOW DO THEY COME UP WITH THIS STUFF? KIDS, HUH? THEY'RE UNBELIEVABLE!?!
DIING DONG!
AAAAH! OUR VERY OWN RESEARCHER!!
DIING DONG!
MERRY CHRISTMAS, GRANDMA!
ALEX-ANDRE!
HOW ARE YOU GETTING ON WITH YOUR FASCINATING RESEARCH?
WELL, ACTUALLY... I'M STARTING A PHD NEXT YEAR!
WOOOOAAH!
WELL DONE!
ALEX, YOU'RE DOING A PHD! JUST LIKE JEANNE?!
HA, HA, NO, NOT AT ALL. I'M A SCIENTIST WITH AN ACTUAL LAB!

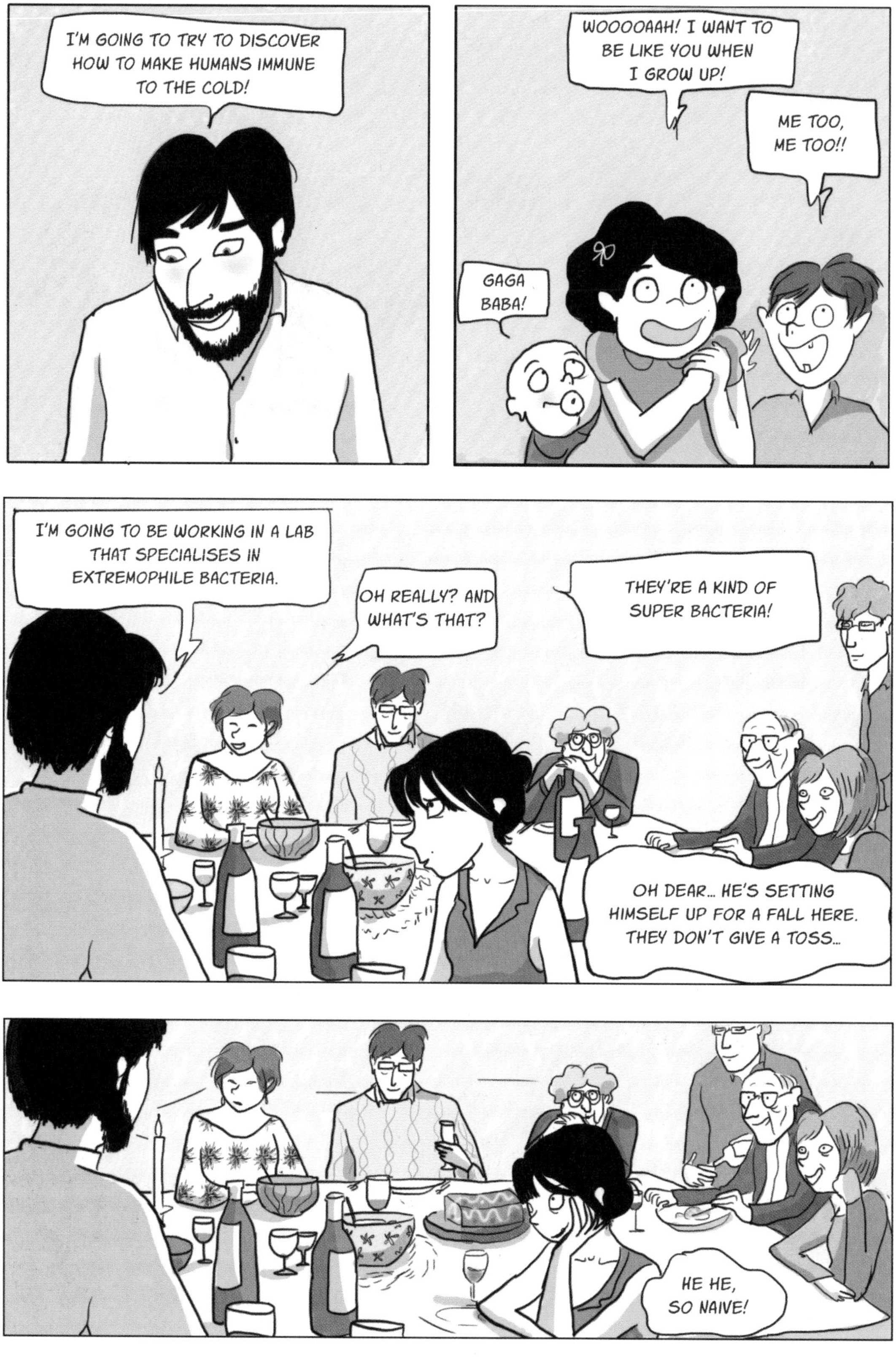
I'M GOING TO TRY TO DISCOVER HOW TO MAKE HUMANS IMMUNE TO THE COLD!
WOOOOAAH! I WANT TO BE LIKE YOU WHEN I GROW UP!
ME TOO, ME TOO!!
GAGA BABA!
I'M GOING TO BE WORKING IN A LAB THAT SPECIALISES IN EXTREMOPHILE BACTERIA.
OH REALLY? AND WHAT'S THAT?
THEY'RE A KIND OF SUPER BACTERIA!
OH DEAR... HE'S SETTING HIMSELF UP FOR A FALL HERE. THEY DON'T GIVE A TOSS...
HE HE, SO NAIVE!

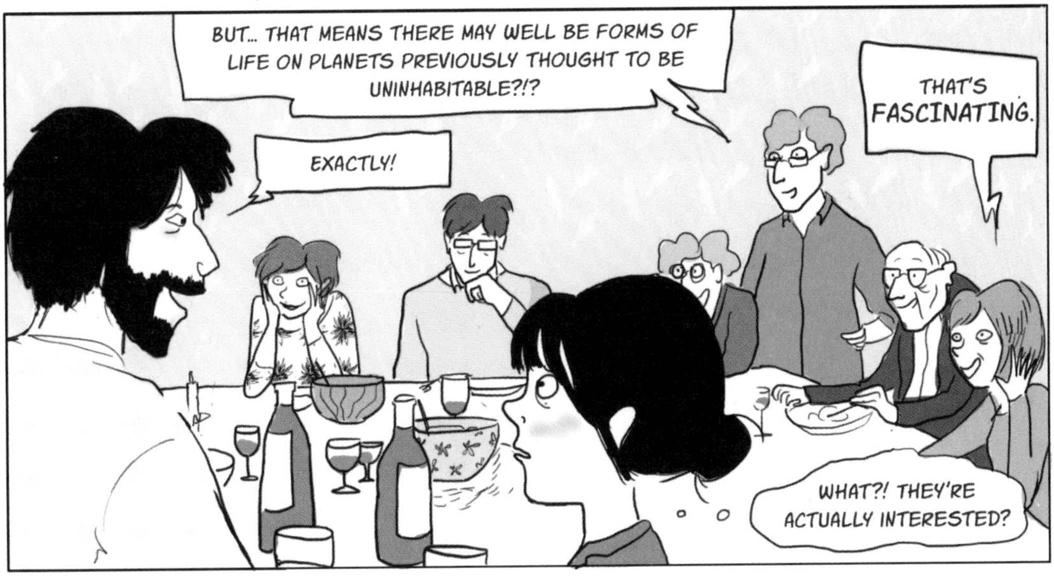
BUT... THAT MEANS THERE MAY WELL BE FORMS OF LIFE ON PLANETS PREVIOUSLY THOUGHT TO BE UNINHABITABLE?!?
EXACTLY!
THAT'S FASCINATING.
WHAT?! THEY'RE ACTUALLY INTERESTED?

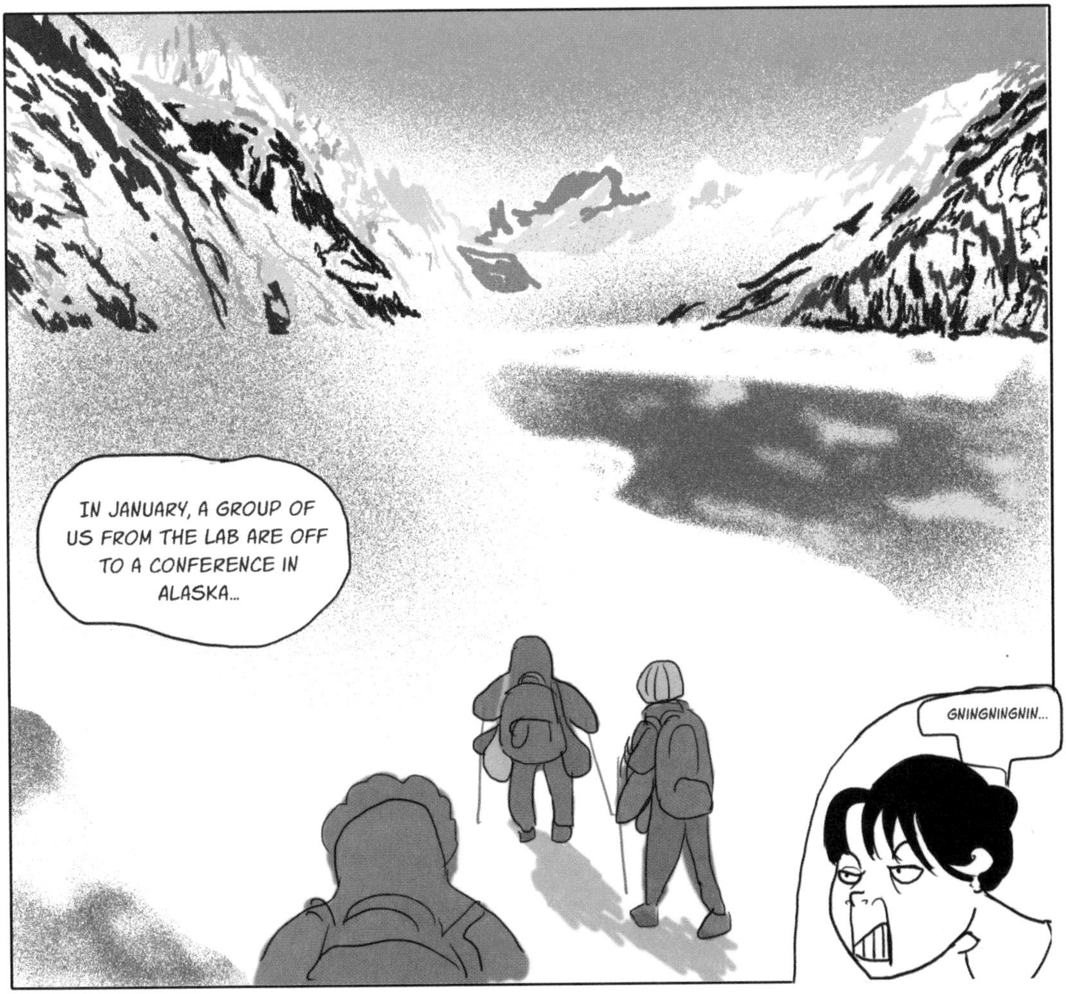
IN JANUARY, A GROUP OF US FROM THE LAB ARE OFF TO A CONFERENCE IN ALASKA...
GNINGNINGNIN...

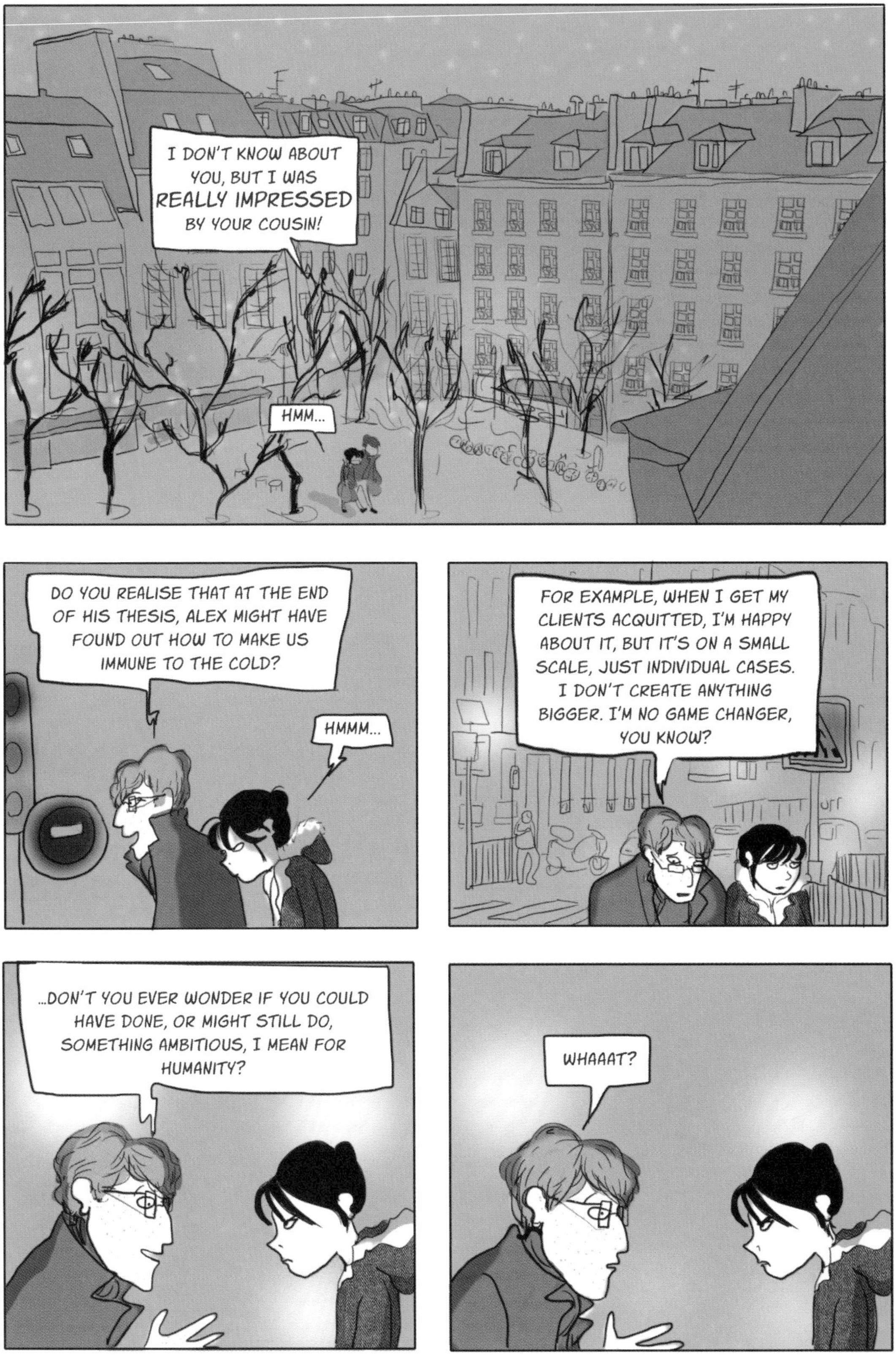

I DON'T KNOW ABOUT YOU, BUT I WAS REALLY IMPRESSED BY YOUR COUSIN!
HMM...
DO YOU REALISE THAT AT THE END OF HIS THESIS, ALEX MIGHT HAVE FOUND OUT HOW TO MAKE US IMMUNE TO THE COLD?
HMMM...
FOR EXAMPLE, WHEN I GET MY CLIENTS ACQUITTED, I'M HAPPY ABOUT IT, BUT IT'S ON A SMALL SCALE, JUST INDIVIDUAL CASES. I DON'T CREATE ANYTHING BIGGER. I'M NO GAME CHANGER, YOU KNOW?
...DON'T YOU EVER WONDER IF YOU COULD HAVE DONE, OR MIGHT STILL DO, SOMETHING AMBITIOUS, I MEAN FOR HUMANITY?
WHAAAT?

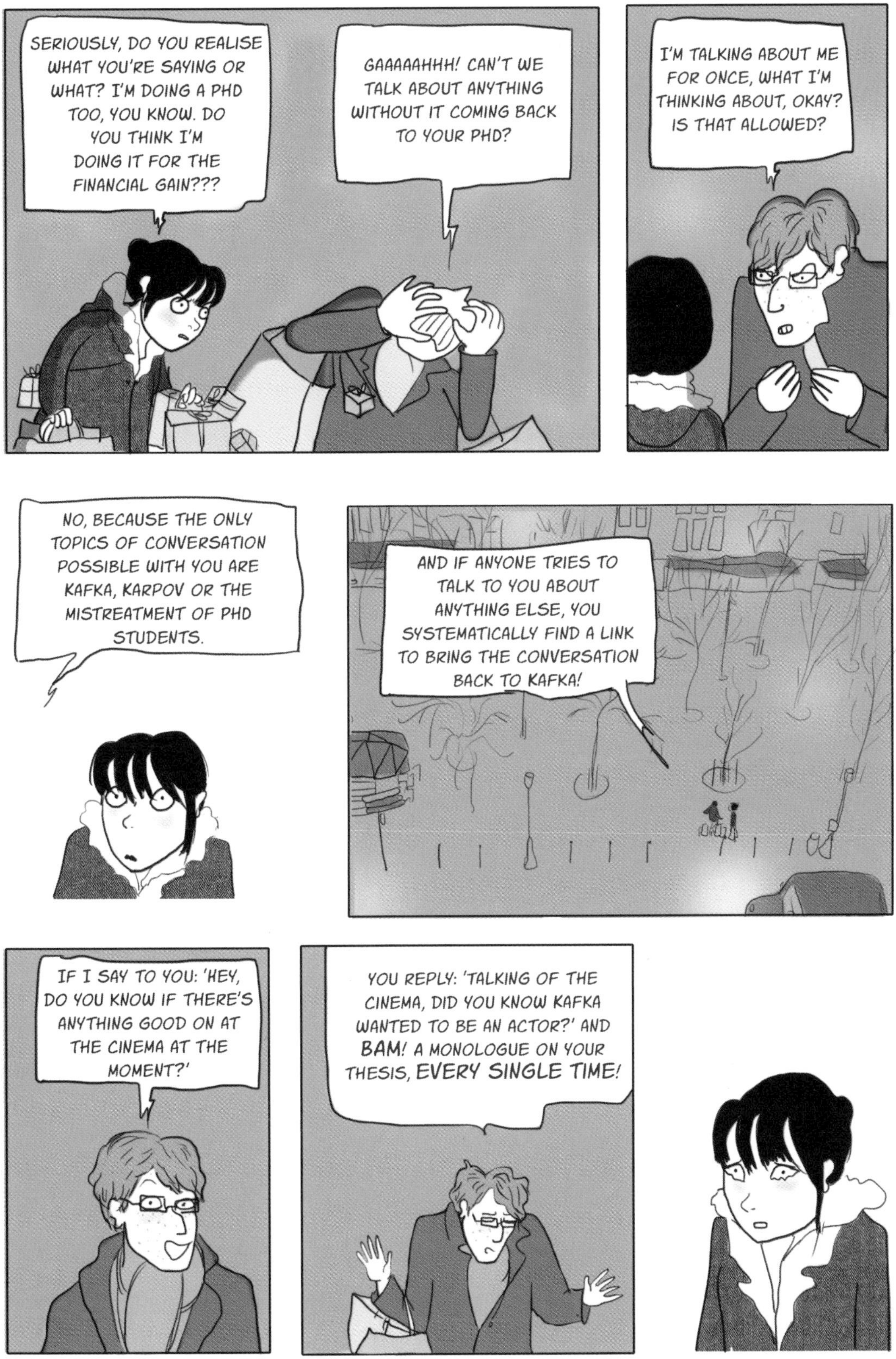
SERIOUSLY, DO YOU REALISE WHAT YOU'RE SAYING OR WHAT? I'M DOING A PHD TOO, YOU KNOW. DO YOU THINK I'M DOING IT FOR THE FINANCIAL GAIN???
GAAAAAHHH! CAN'T WE TALK ABOUT ANYTHING WITHOUT IT COMING BACK TO YOUR PHD?
I'M TALKING ABOUT ME FOR ONCE, WHAT I'M THINKING ABOUT, OKAY? IS THAT ALLOWED?
NO, BECAUSE THE ONLY TOPICS OF CONVERSATION POSSIBLE WITH YOU ARE KAFKA, KARPOV OR THE MISTREATMENT OF PHD STUDENTS.
AND IF ANYONE TRIES TO TALK TO YOU ABOUT ANYTHING ELSE, YOU SYSTEMATICALLY FIND A LINK TO BRING THE CONVERSATION BACK TO KAFKA!
IF I SAY TO YOU: 'HEY, DO YOU KNOW IF THERE'S ANYTHING GOOD ON AT THE CINEMA AT THE MOMENT?'
YOU REPLY: 'TALKING OF THE CINEMA, DID YOU KNOW KAFKA WANTED TO BE AN ACTOR?' AND BAM! A MONOLOGUE ON YOUR THESIS, EVERY SINGLE TIME!

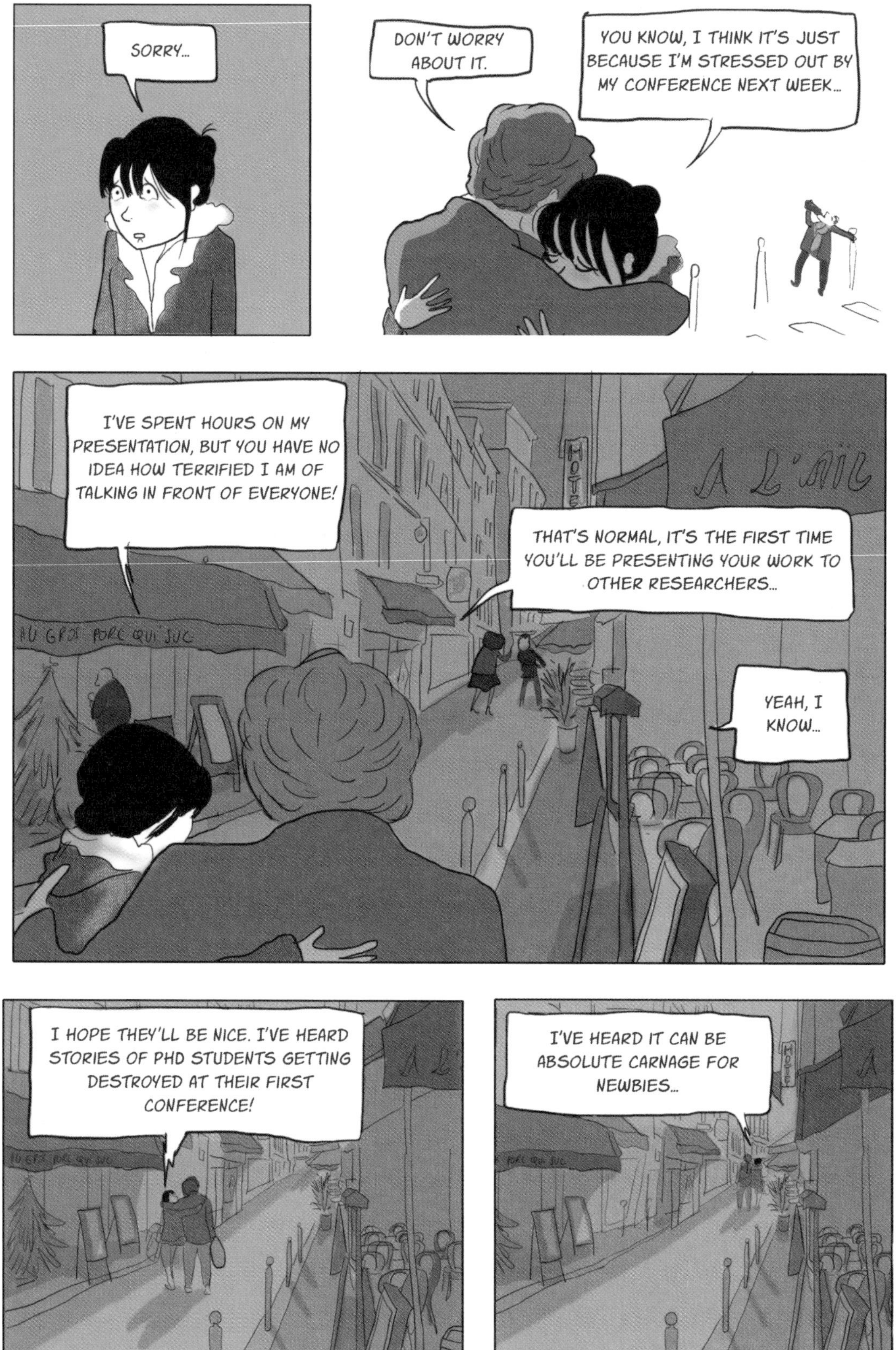
SORRY...
DON'T WORRY ABOUT IT.
YOU KNOW, I THINK IT'S JUST BECAUSE I'M STRESSED OUT BY MY CONFERENCE NEXT WEEK...
I'VE SPENT HOURS ON MY PRESENTATION, BUT YOU HAVE NO IDEA HOW TERRIFIED I AM OF TALKING IN FRONT OF EVERYONE!
THAT'S NORMAL, IT'S THE FIRST TIME YOU'LL BE PRESENTING YOUR WORK TO OTHER RESEARCHERS...
YEAH, I KNOW...
I HOPE THEY'LL BE NICE. I'VE HEARD STORIES OF PHD STUDENTS GETTING DESTROYED AT THEIR FIRST CONFERENCE!
I'VE HEARD IT CAN BE ABSOLUTE CARNAGE FOR NEWBIES...

BREATHE, JEANNE, BREATHE...

REALLY IT'S NO DIFFERENT FROM THE LECTURES I GIVE TO STUDENTS...

JUST IN FRONT OF POTENTIALLY HOSTILE...

...TOP SPECIALISTS.

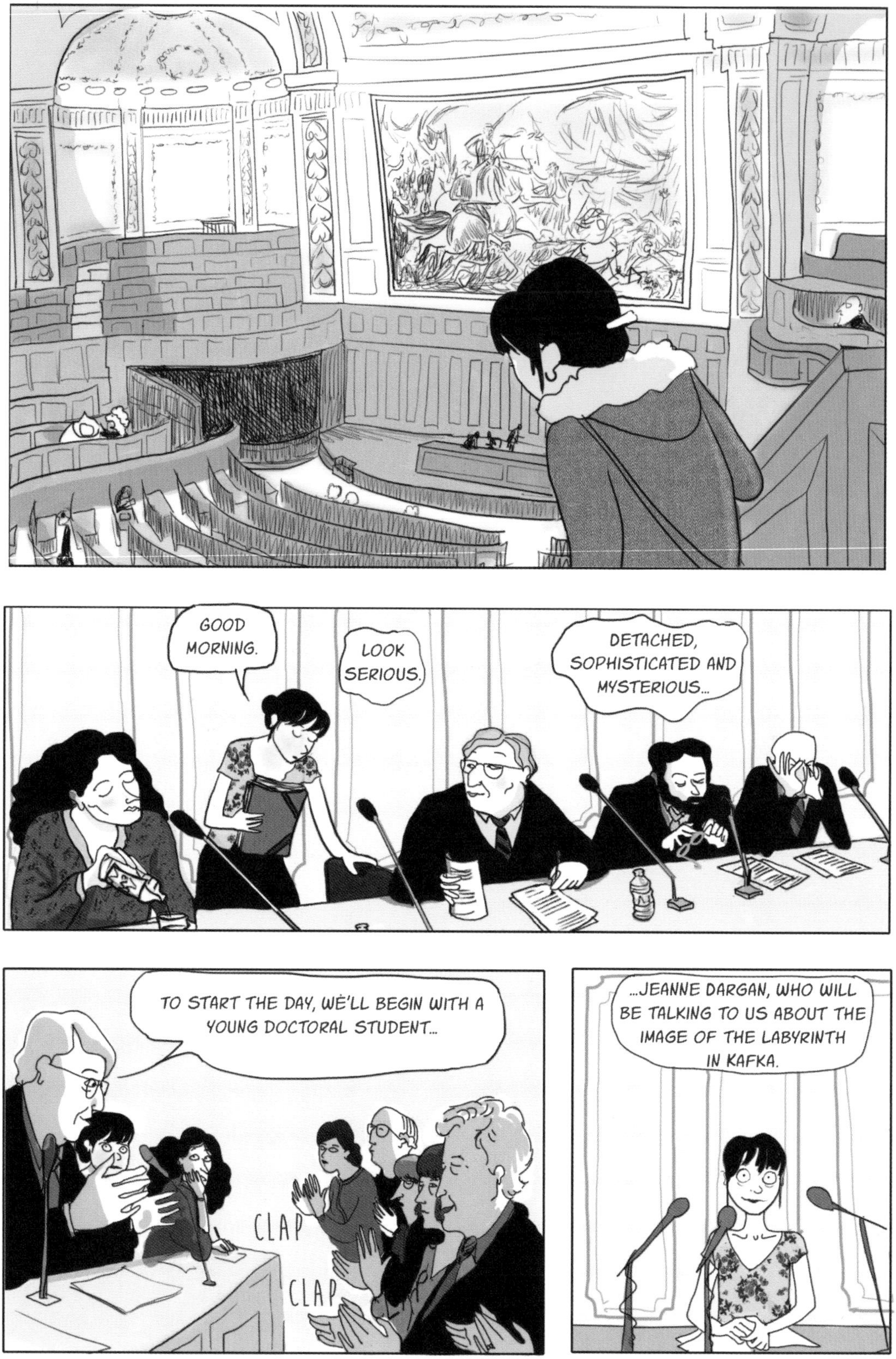
GOOD MORNING.
LOOK SERIOUS.
DETACHED, SOPHISTICATED AND MYSTERIOUS...
TO START THE DAY, WE'LL BEGIN WITH A YOUNG DOCTORAL STUDENT...
CLAP
CLAP
...JEANNE DARGAN, WHO WILL BE TALKING TO US ABOUT THE IMAGE OF THE LABYRINTH IN KAFKA.

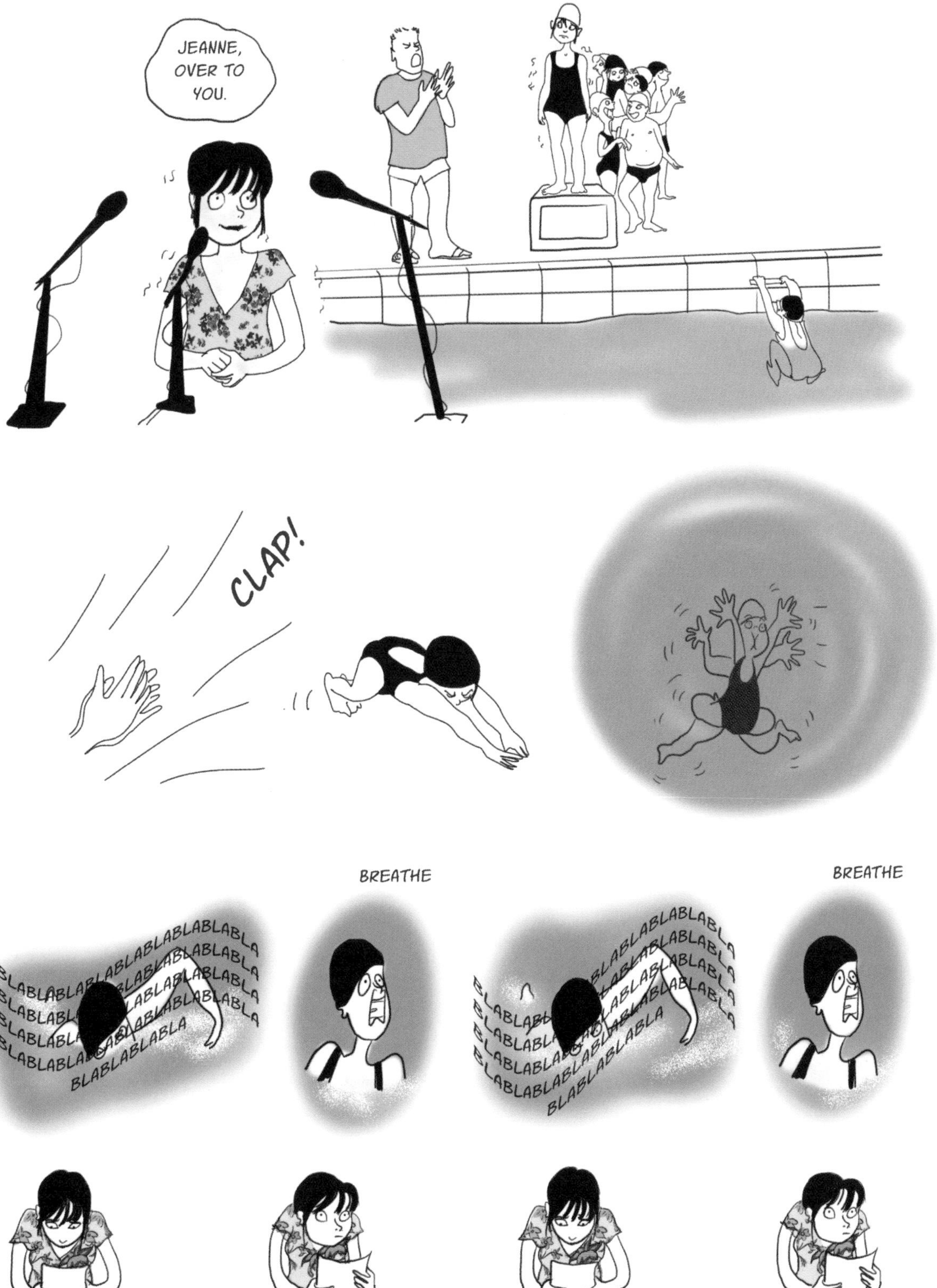
JEANNE, OVER TO YOU.
CLAP!
BLABLABLABLA
BREATHE
BLABLABLABLA
BREATHE

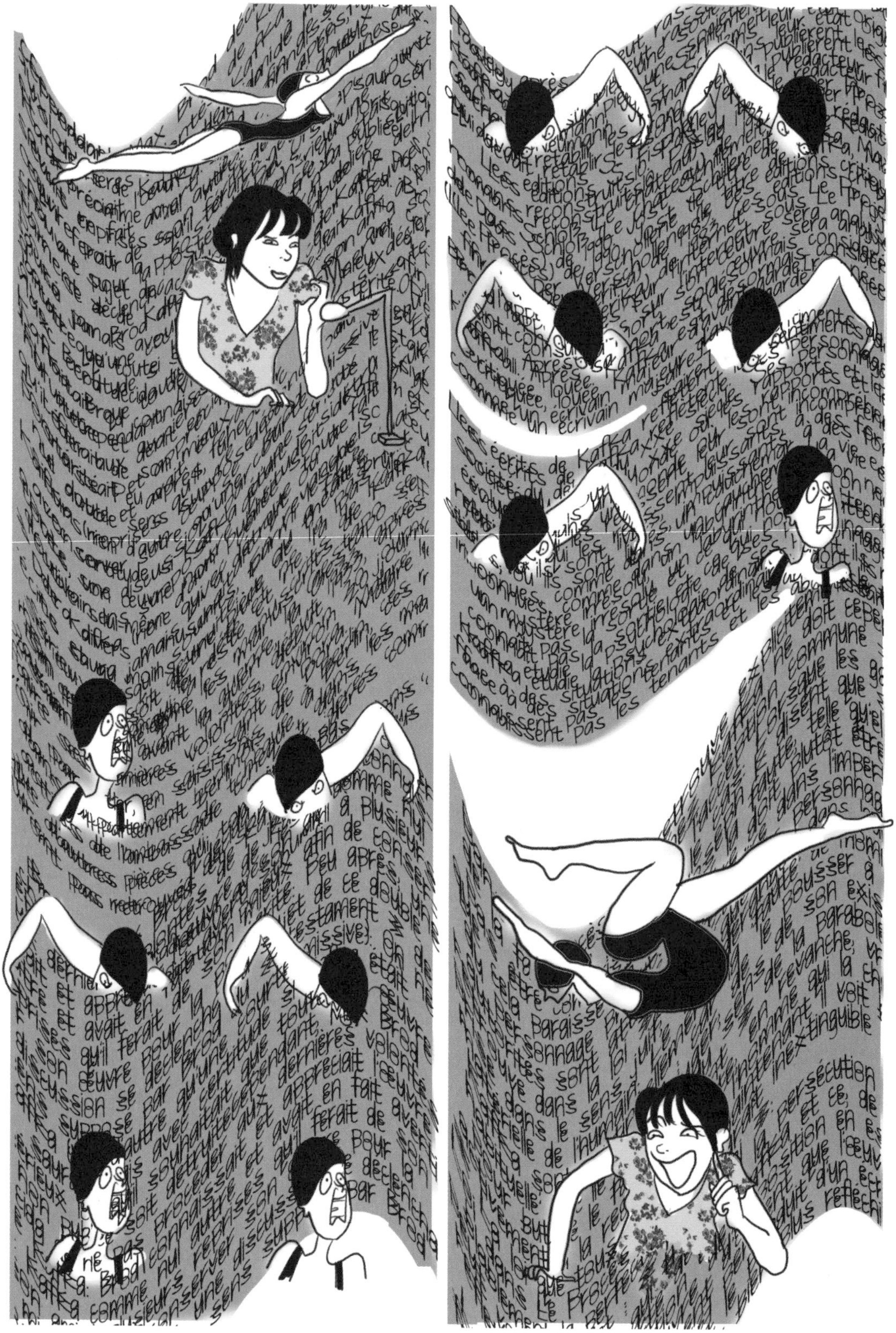

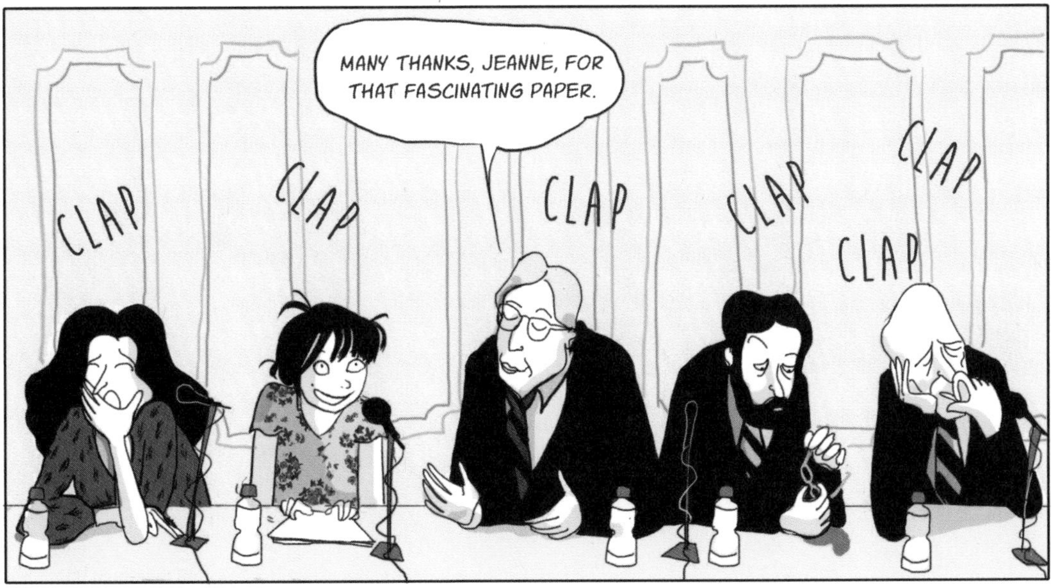
CLAP
CLAP
MANY THANKS, JEANNE, FOR THAT FASCINATING PAPER.
CLAP
CLAP
CLAP
CLAP

AND NOW WE'LL OPEN UP THE FLOOR TO QUESTIONS.

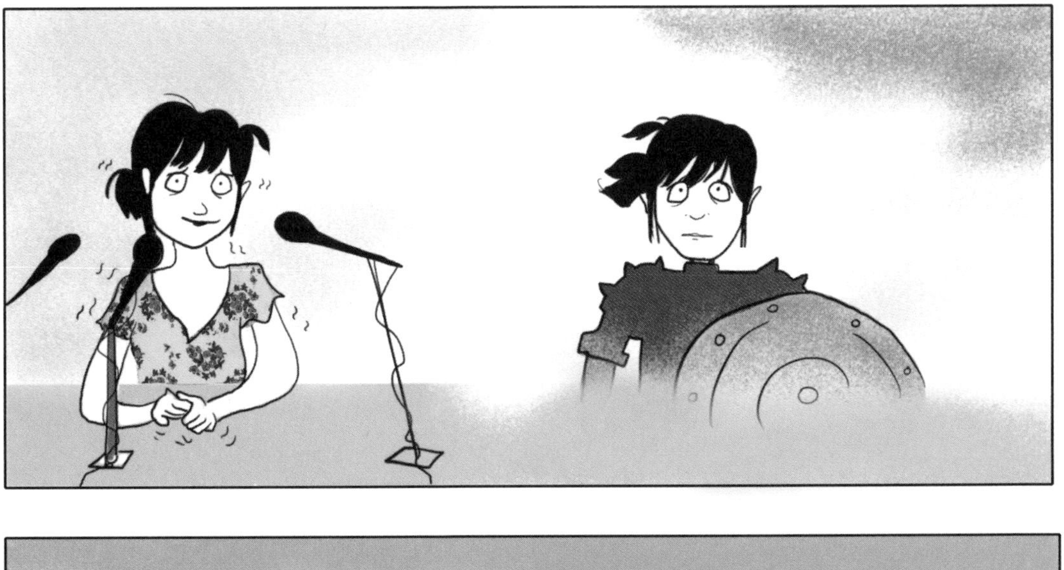

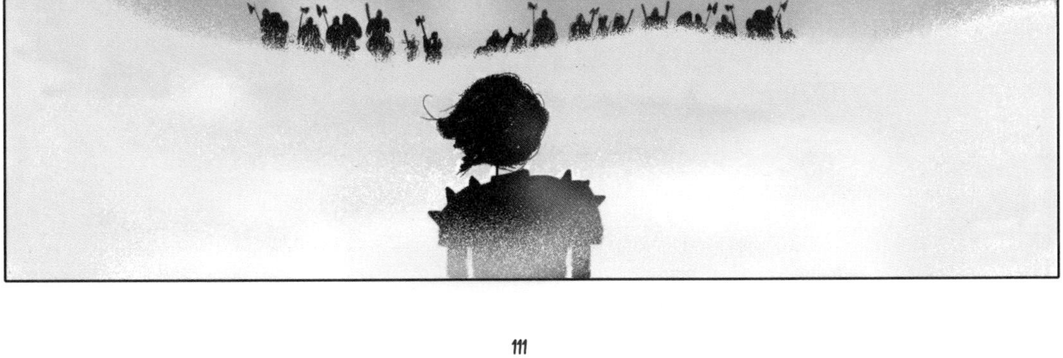

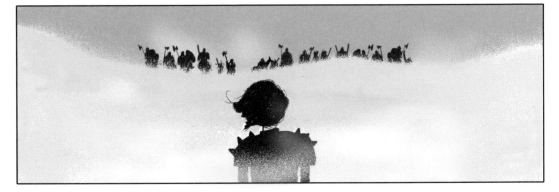

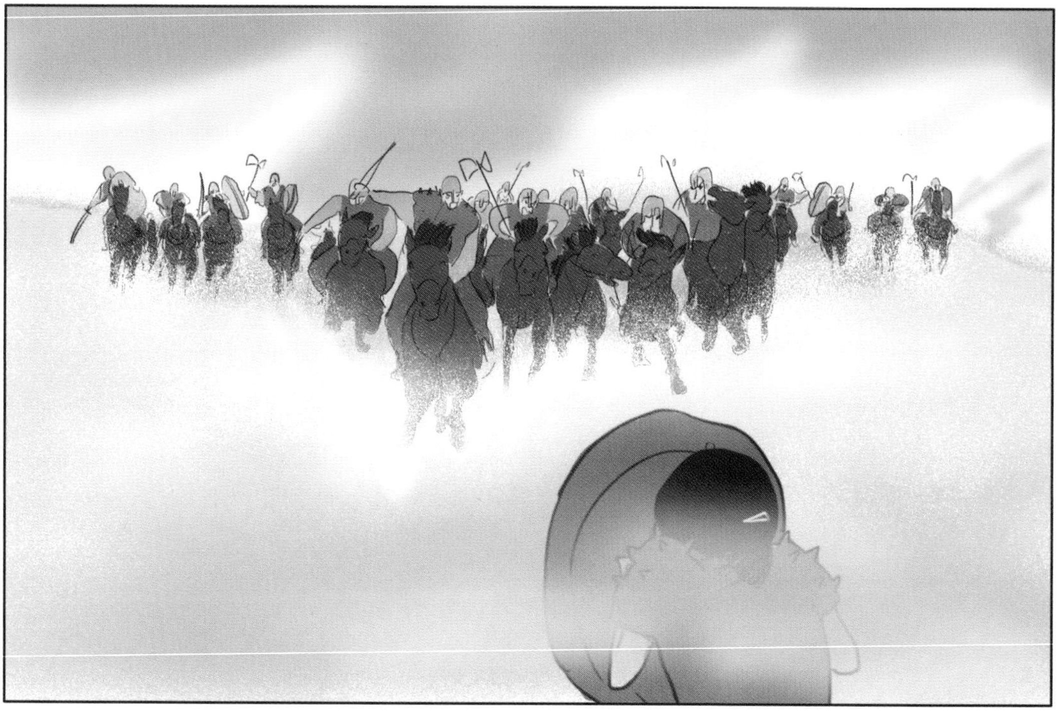

DOES ANYONE HAVE A QUESTION FOR JEANNE DARGAN?

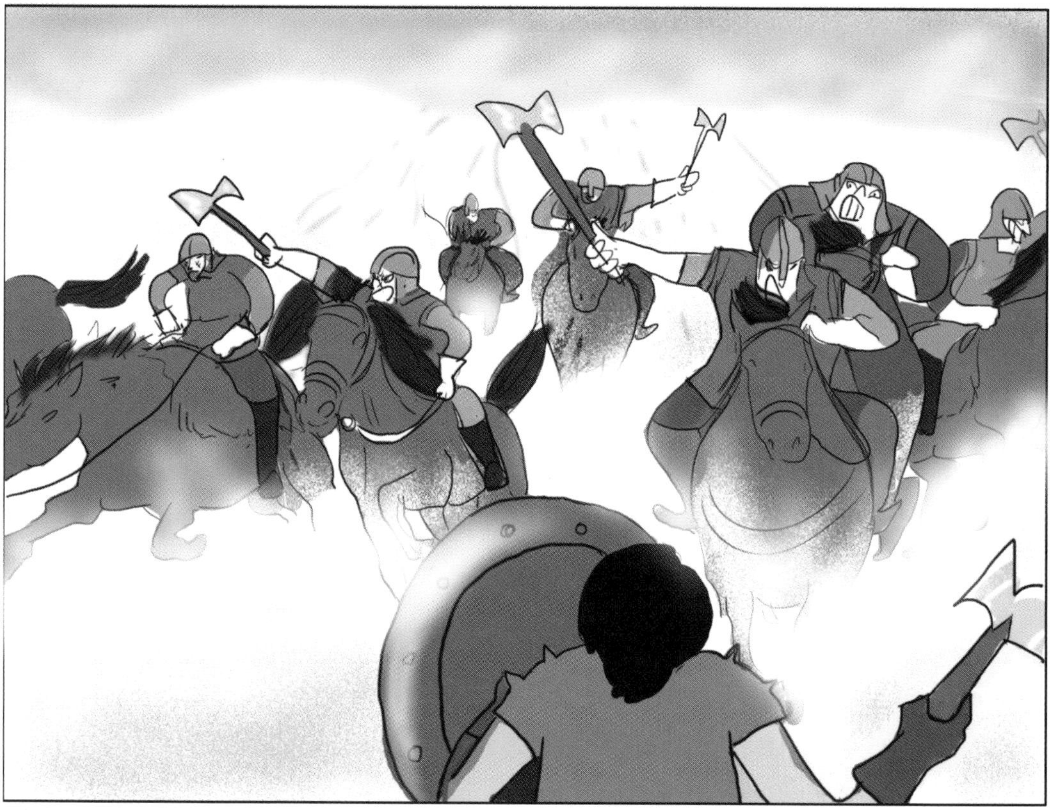

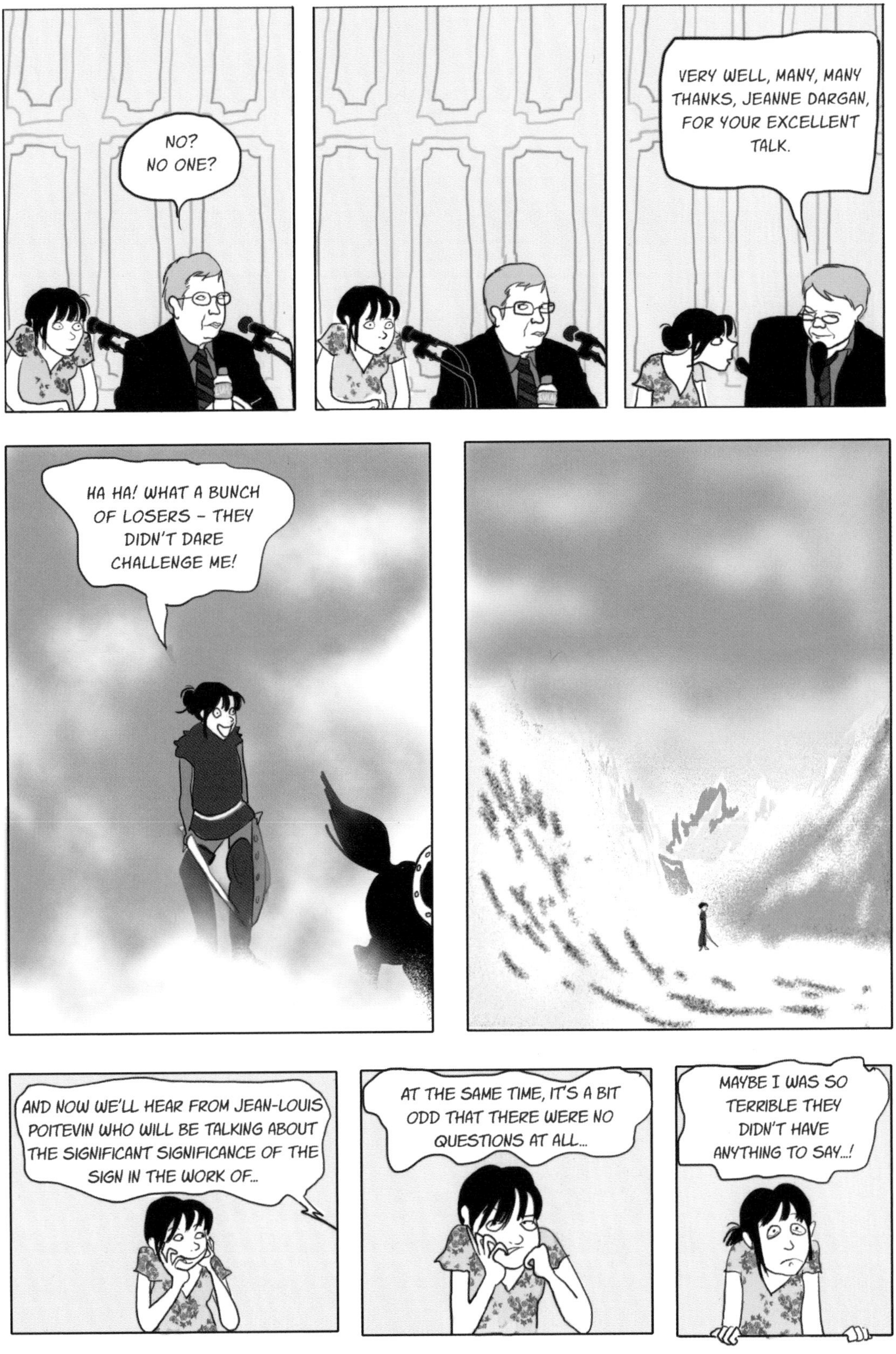
NO? NO ONE?
VERY WELL, MANY, MANY THANKS, JEANNE DARGAN, FOR YOUR EXCELLENT TALK.
HA HA! WHAT A BUNCH OF LOSERS – THEY DIDN'T DARE CHALLENGE ME!
AND NOW WE'LL HEAR FROM JEAN-LOUIS POITEVIN WHO WILL BE TALKING ABOUT THE SIGNIFICANT SIGNIFICANCE OF THE SIGN IN THE WORK OF...
AT THE SAME TIME, IT'S A BIT ODD THAT THERE WERE NO QUESTIONS AT ALL...
MAYBE I WAS SO TERRIBLE THEY DIDN'T HAVE ANYTHING TO SAY...!

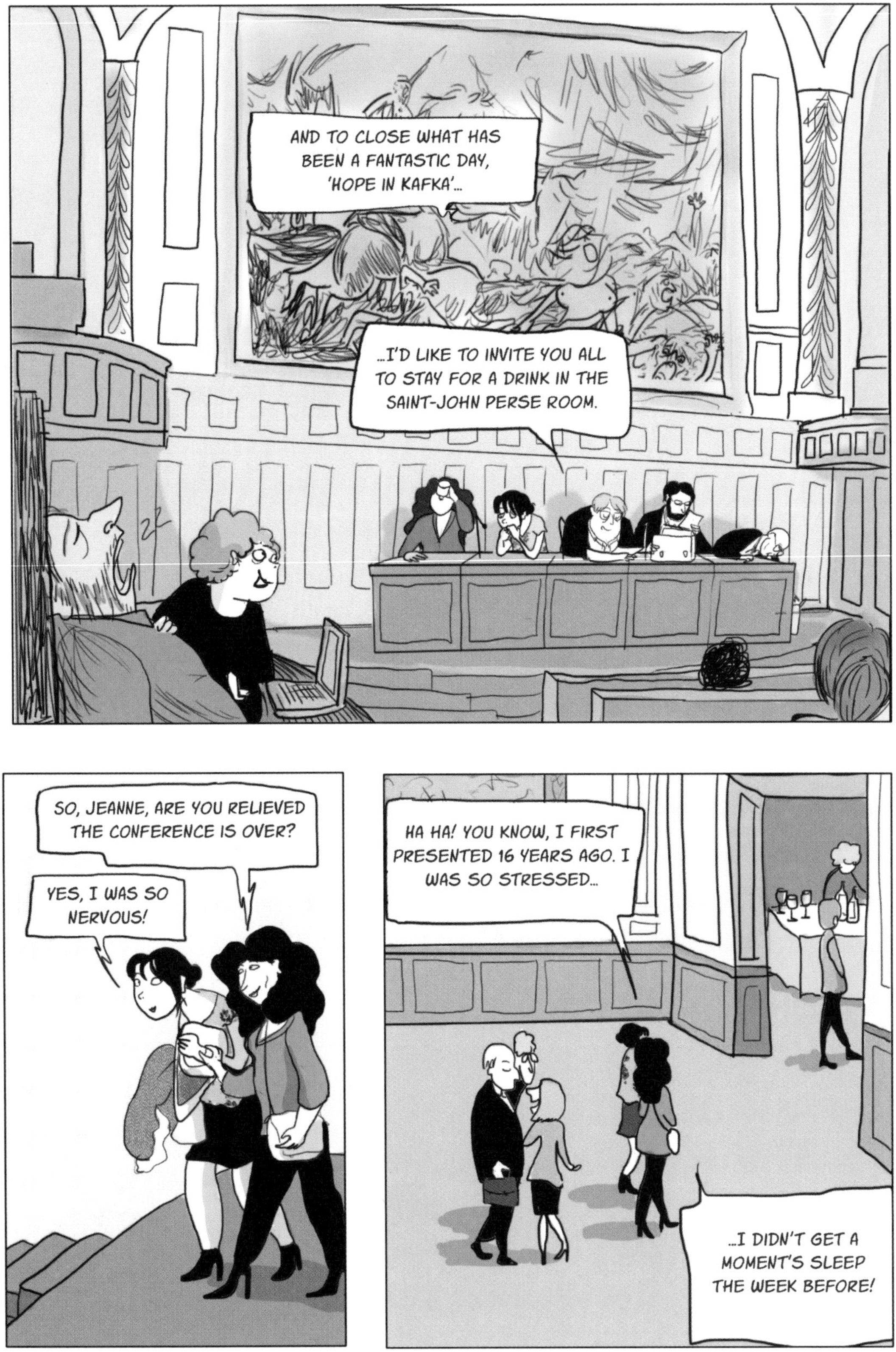
AND TO CLOSE WHAT HAS BEEN A FANTASTIC DAY, 'HOPE IN KAFKA'...
...I'D LIKE TO INVITE YOU ALL TO STAY FOR A DRINK IN THE SAINT-JOHN PERSE ROOM.
SO, JEANNE, ARE YOU RELIEVED THE CONFERENCE IS OVER?
YES, I WAS SO NERVOUS!
HA HA! YOU KNOW, I FIRST PRESENTED 16 YEARS AGO. I WAS SO STRESSED...
...I DIDN'T GET A MOMENT'S SLEEP THE WEEK BEFORE!

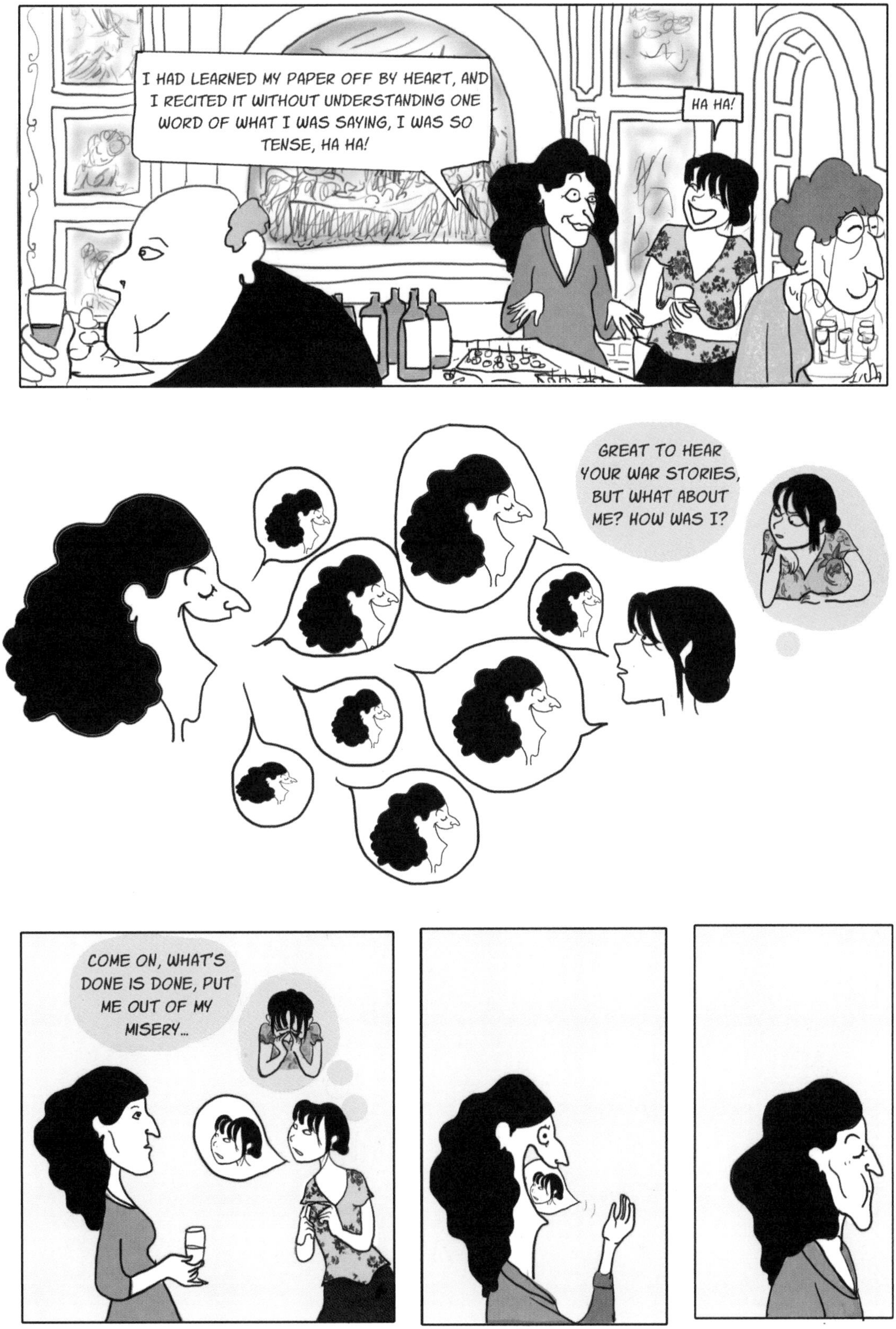
I HAD LEARNED MY PAPER OFF BY HEART, AND I RECITED IT WITHOUT UNDERSTANDING ONE WORD OF WHAT I WAS SAYING, I WAS SO TENSE, HA HA!
HA HA!
GREAT TO HEAR YOUR WAR STORIES, BUT WHAT ABOUT ME? HOW WAS I?
COME ON, WHAT'S DONE IS DONE, PUT ME OUT OF MY MISERY...

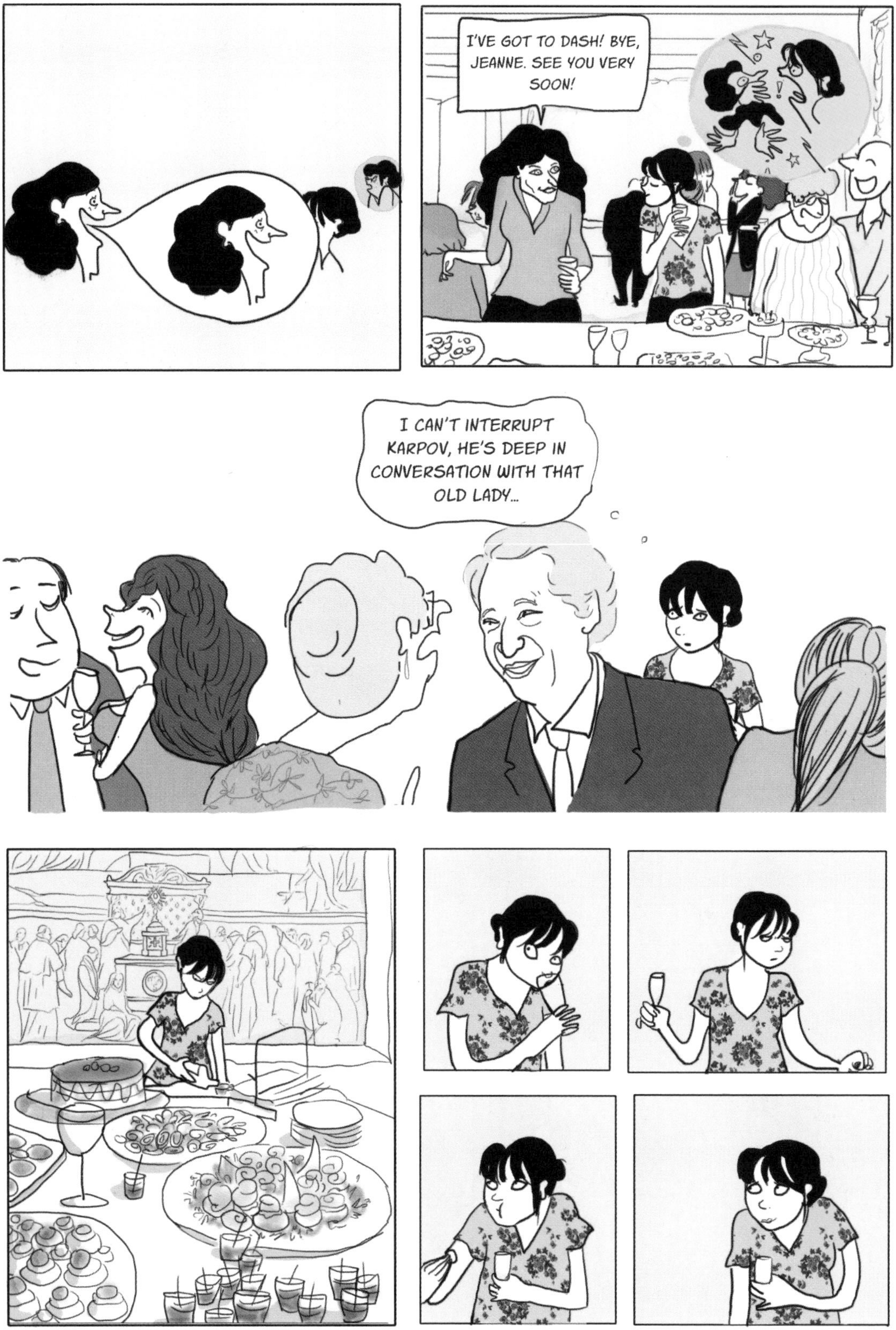
I'VE GOT TO DASH! BYE, JEANNE. SEE YOU VERY SOON!
I CAN'T INTERRUPT KARPOV, HE'S DEEP IN CONVERSATION WITH THAT OLD LADY...

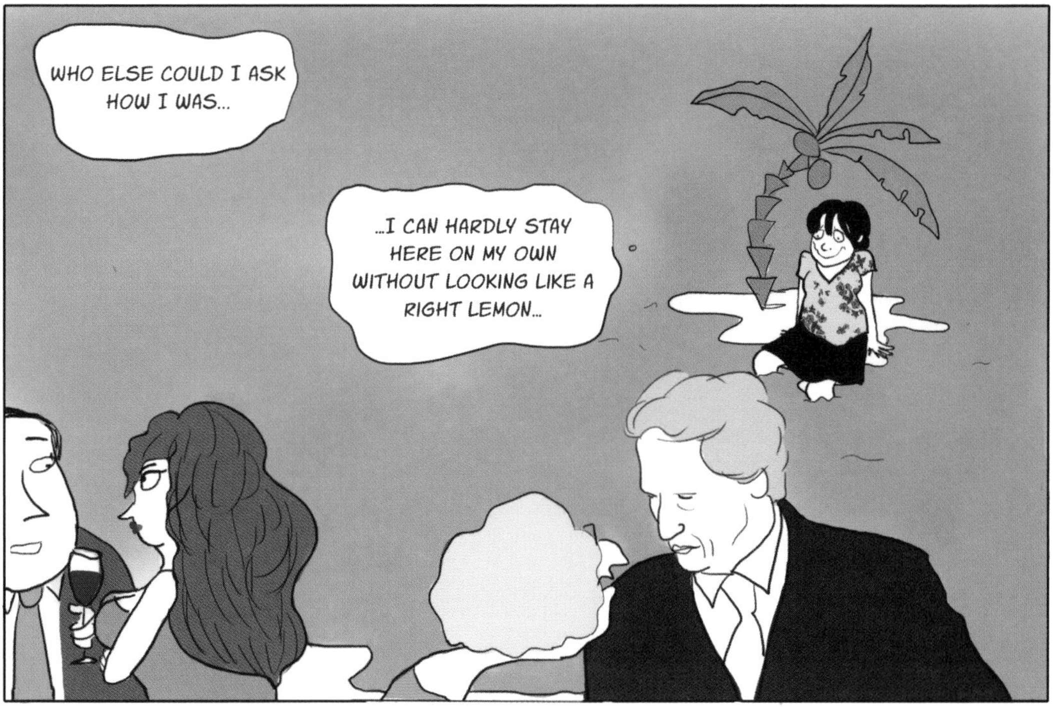
WHO ELSE COULD I ASK HOW I WAS...
...I CAN HARDLY STAY HERE ON MY OWN WITHOUT LOOKING LIKE A RIGHT LEMON...

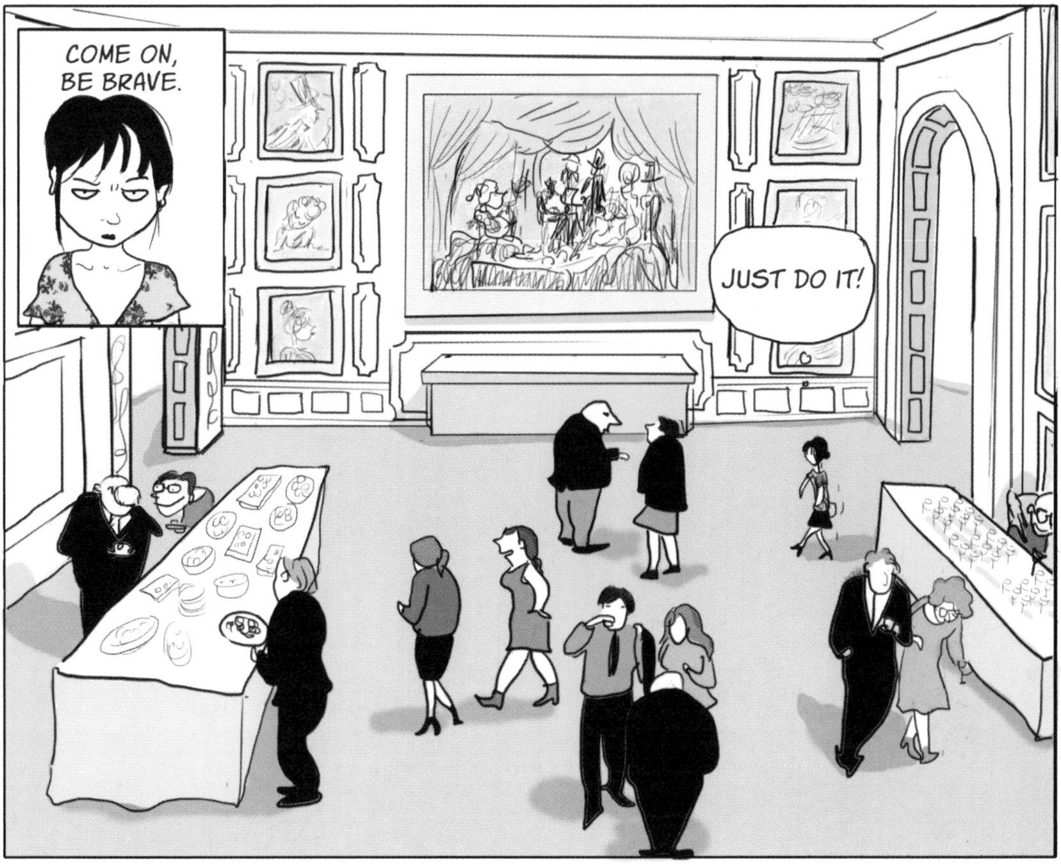
COME ON, BE BRAVE.
JUST DO IT!

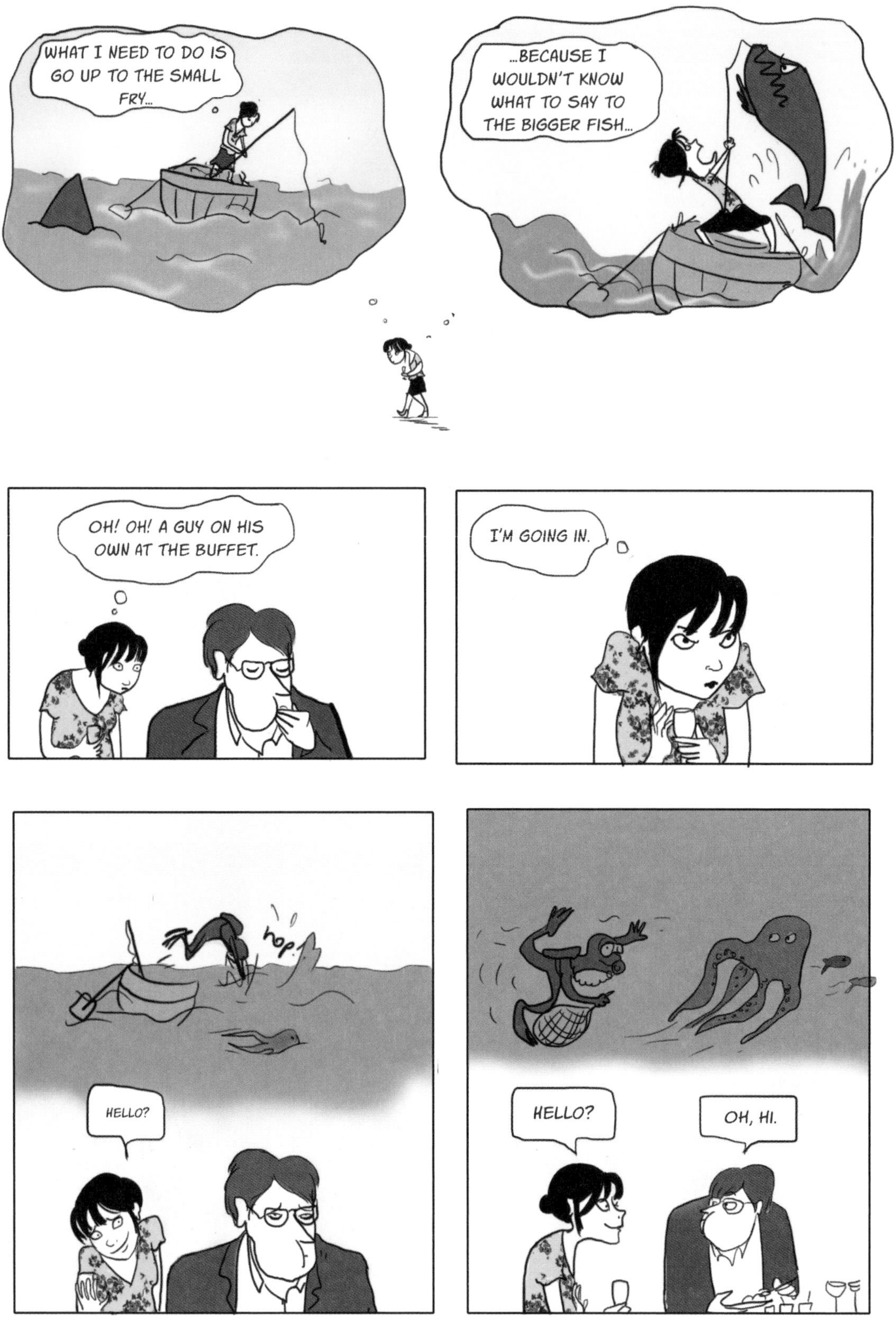
WHAT I NEED TO DO IS GO UP TO THE SMALL FRY...
...BECAUSE I WOULDN'T KNOW WHAT TO SAY TO THE BIGGER FISH...
OH! OH! A GUY ON HIS OWN AT THE BUFFET.
I'M GOING IN.
hop!
HELLO?
HELLO?
OH, HI.

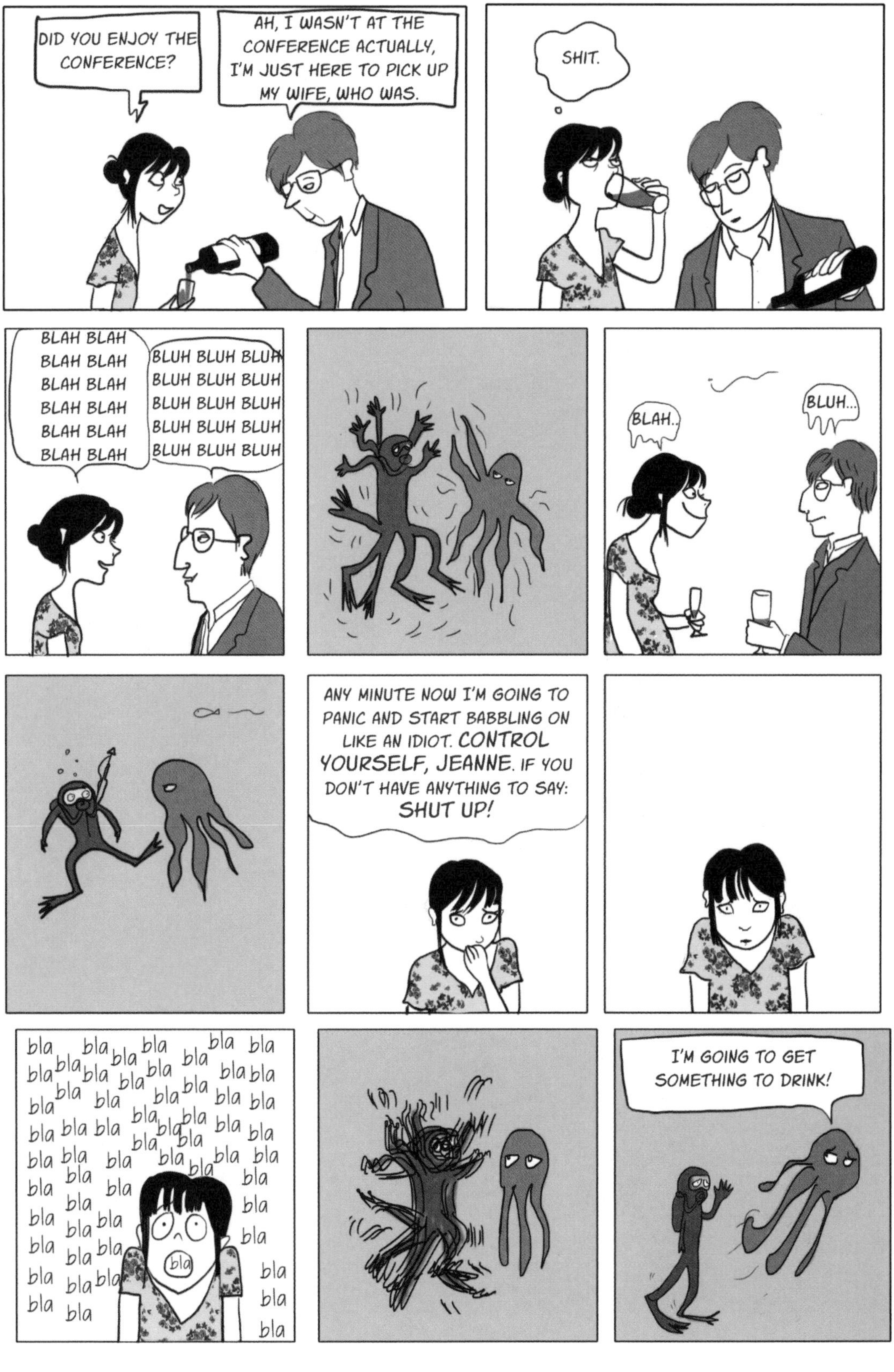

DID YOU ENJOY THE CONFERENCE?
AH, I WASN'T AT THE CONFERENCE ACTUALLY, I'M JUST HERE TO PICK UP MY WIFE, WHO WAS.
SHIT.
BLAH BLAH BLAH BLAH BLAH BLAH BLAH BLAH BLAH BLAH BLAH BLAH
BLUH BLUH BLUH BLUH BLUH BLUH BLUH BLUH BLUH BLUH BLUH BLUH BLUH BLUH BLUH
BLAH...
BLUH...
ANY MINUTE NOW I'M GOING TO PANIC AND START BABBLING ON LIKE AN IDIOT. CONTROL YOURSELF, JEANNE. IF YOU DON'T HAVE ANYTHING TO SAY: SHUT UP!
bla bla bla bla bla bla bla
bla bla bla bla bla bla bla bla
bla bla bla bla bla bla bla
bla bla bla bla bla bla bla bla
bla bla bla bla bla bla bla bla
bla bla bla bla bla bla
bla bla bla bla
bla bla bla bla bla
bla bla bla bla
bla bla bla bla
bla bla bla bla
bla bla bla
I'M GOING TO GET SOMETHING TO DRINK!

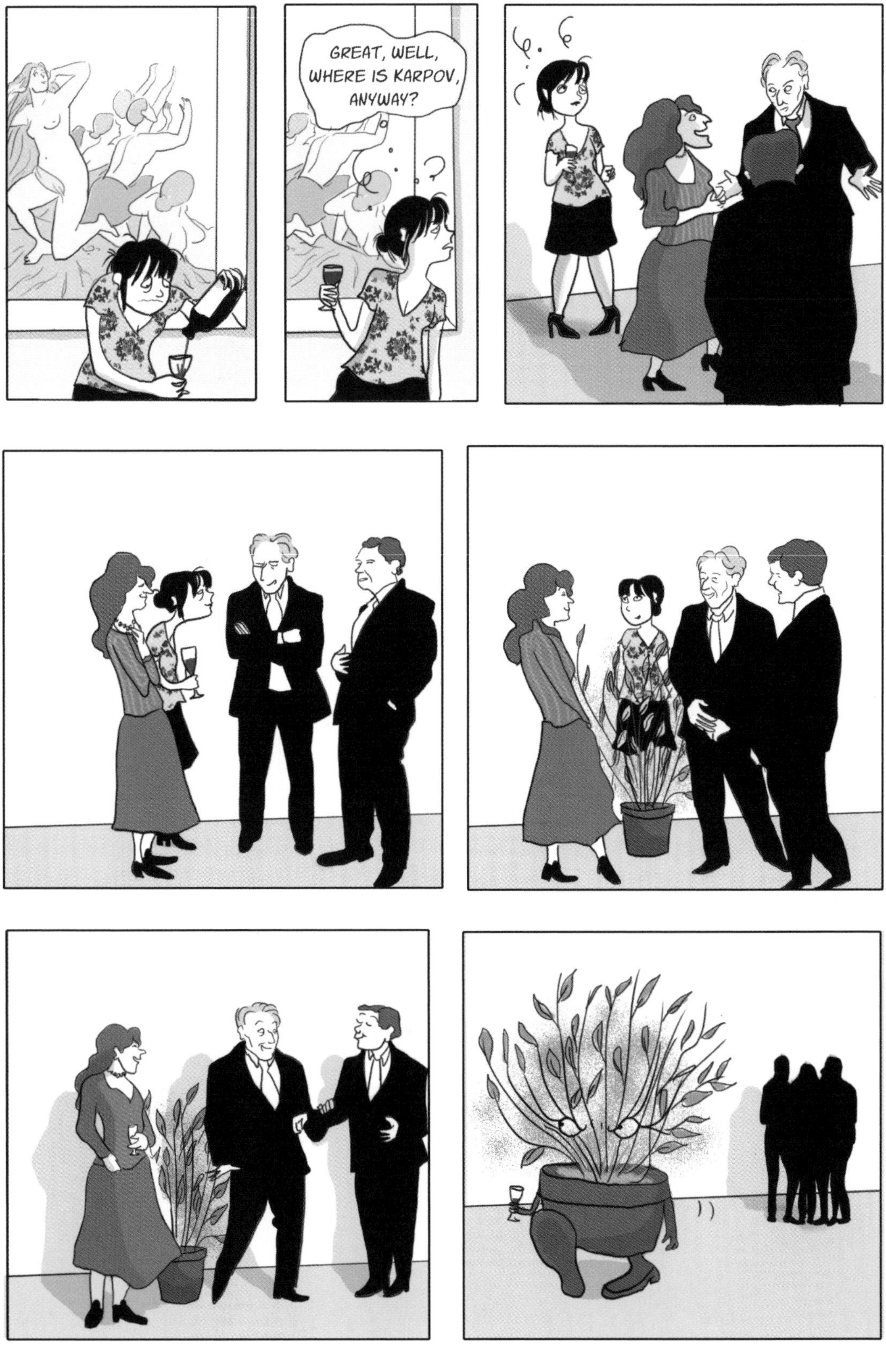
GREAT, WELL, WHERE IS KARPOV, ANYWAY?

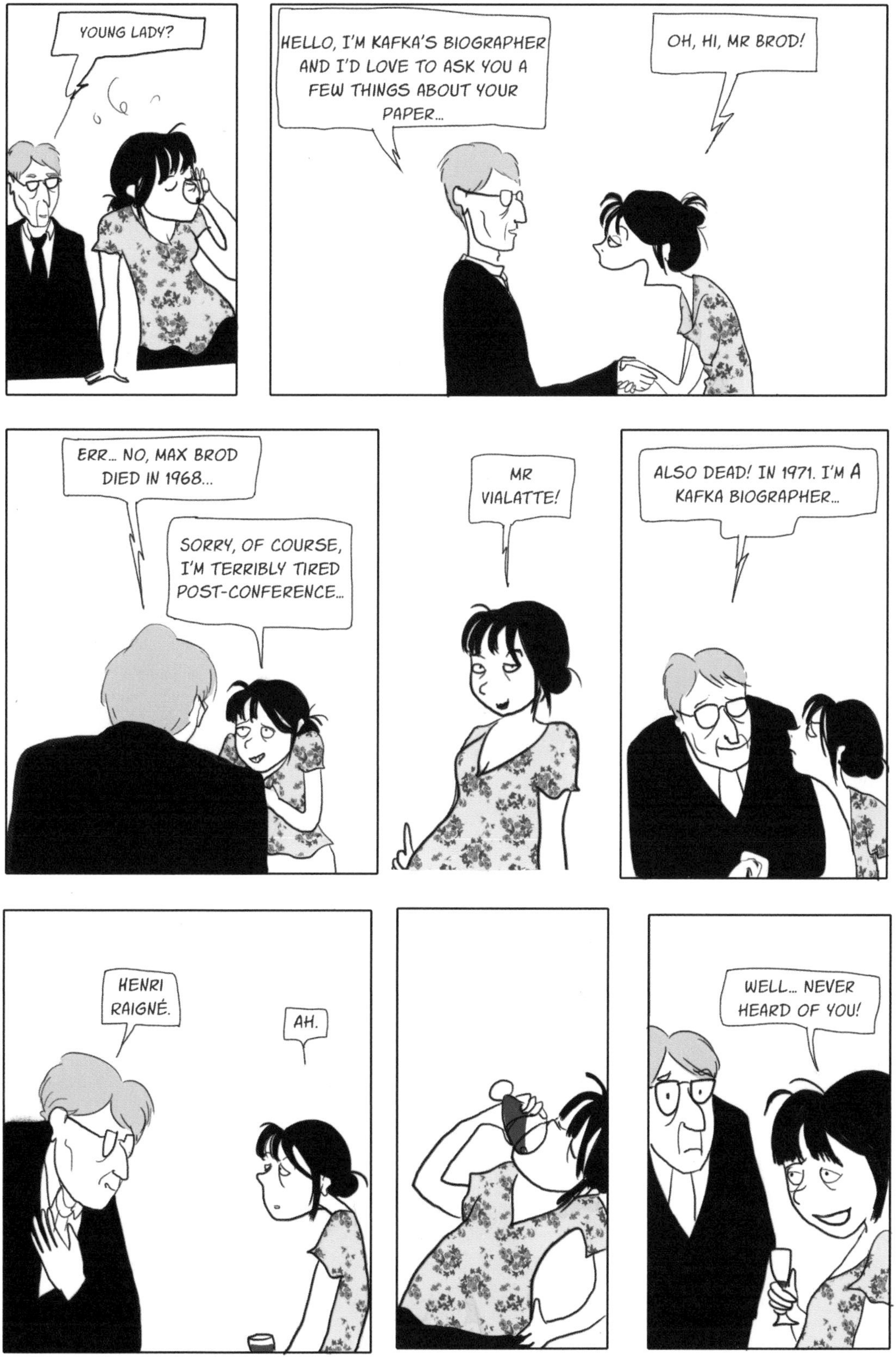
YOUNG LADY?
HELLO, I'M KAFKA'S BIOGRAPHER AND I'D LOVE TO ASK YOU A FEW THINGS ABOUT YOUR PAPER...
OH, HI, MR BROD!
ERR... NO, MAX BROD DIED IN 1968...
SORRY, OF COURSE, I'M TERRIBLY TIRED POST-CONFERENCE...
MR VIALATTE!
ALSO DEAD! IN 1971. I'M A KAFKA BIOGRAPHER...
HENRI RAIGNÉ.
AH.
WELL... NEVER HEARD OF YOU!

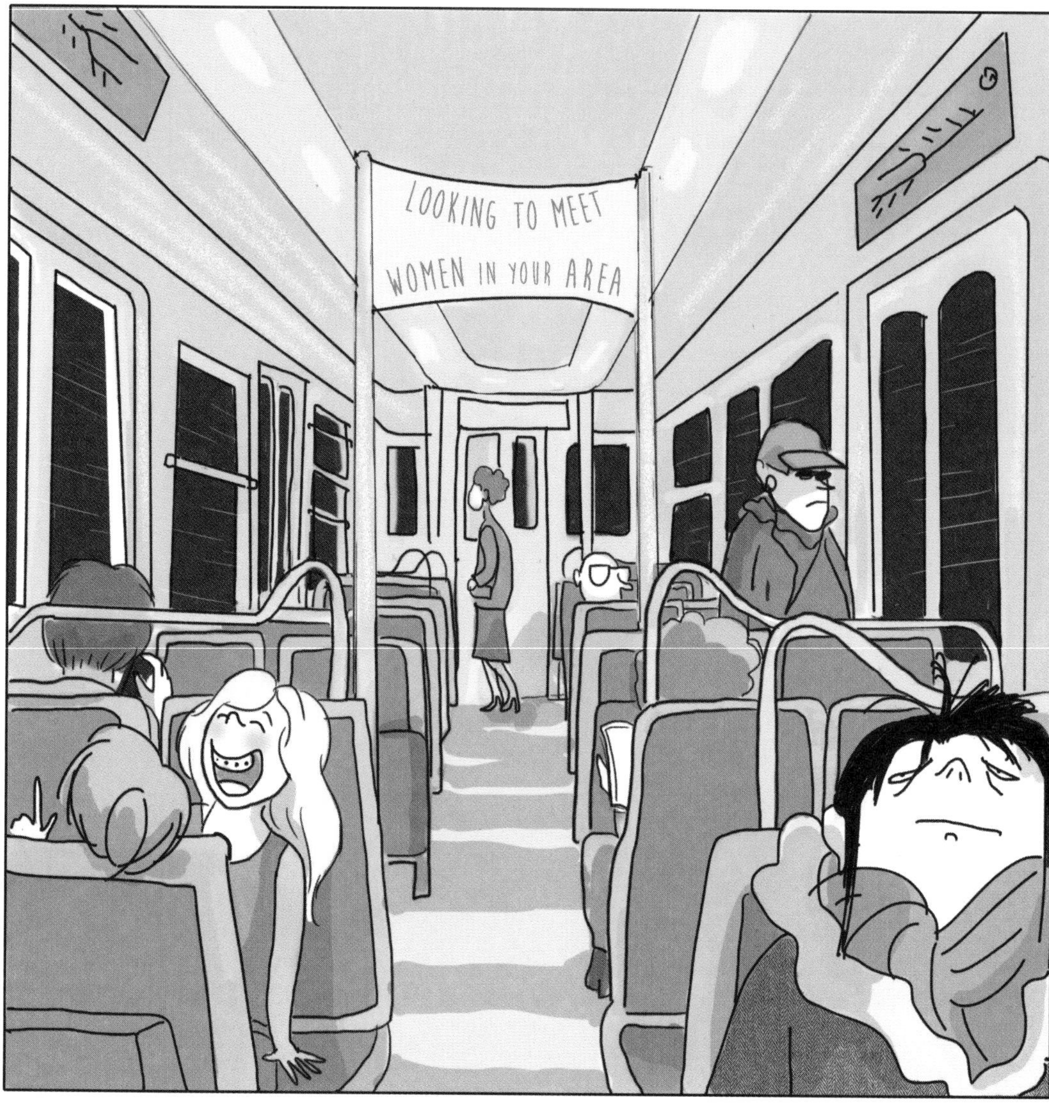
LOOKING TO MEET
WOMEN IN YOUR AREA

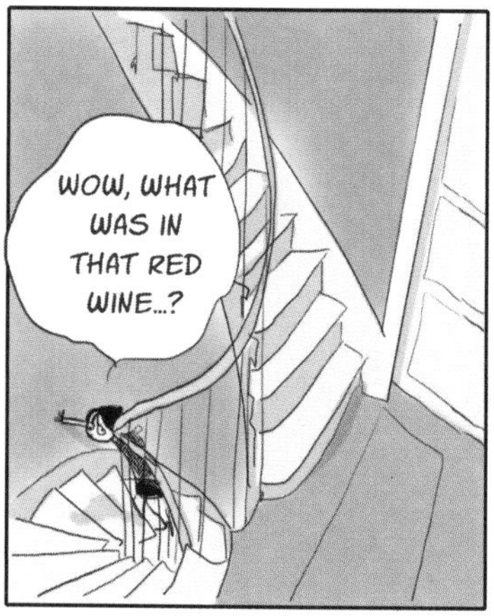
WOW, WHAT WAS IN THAT RED WINE...?

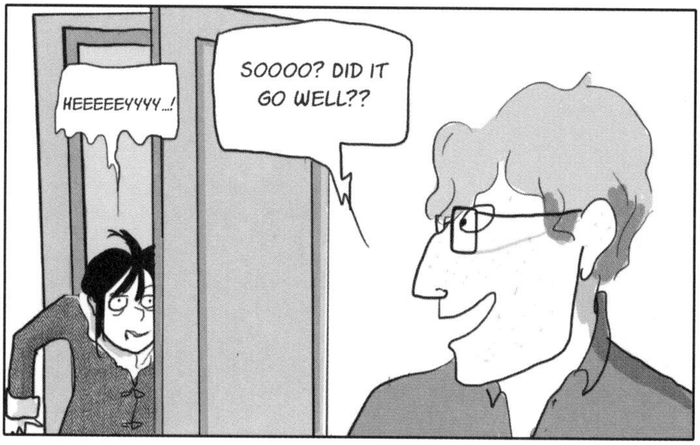
HEEEEEYYYY...!
SOOOO? DID IT GO WELL??

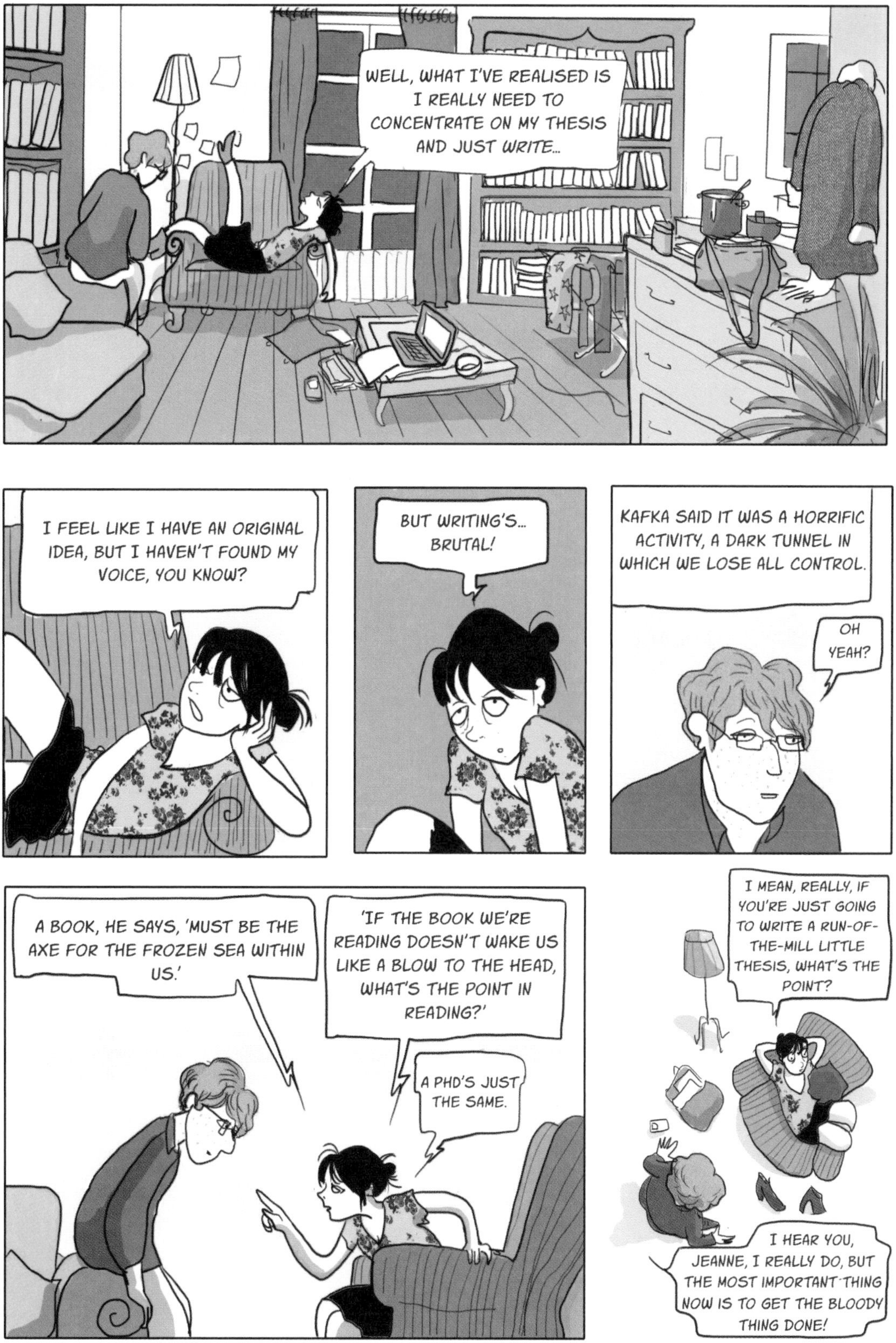
WELL, WHAT I'VE REALISED IS I REALLY NEED TO CONCENTRATE ON MY THESIS AND JUST WRITE...
I FEEL LIKE I HAVE AN ORIGINAL IDEA, BUT I HAVEN'T FOUND MY VOICE, YOU KNOW?
BUT WRITING'S... BRUTAL!
KAFKA SAID IT WAS A HORRIFIC ACTIVITY, A DARK TUNNEL IN WHICH WE LOSE ALL CONTROL.
OH YEAH?
A BOOK, HE SAYS, 'MUST BE THE AXE FOR THE FROZEN SEA WITHIN US.'
'IF THE BOOK WE'RE READING DOESN'T WAKE US LIKE A BLOW TO THE HEAD, WHAT'S THE POINT IN READING?'
A PHD'S JUST THE SAME.
I MEAN, REALLY, IF YOU'RE JUST GOING TO WRITE A RUN-OF-THE-MILL LITTLE THESIS, WHAT'S THE POINT?
I HEAR YOU, JEANNE, I REALLY DO, BUT THE MOST IMPORTANT THING NOW IS TO GET THE BLOODY THING DONE!

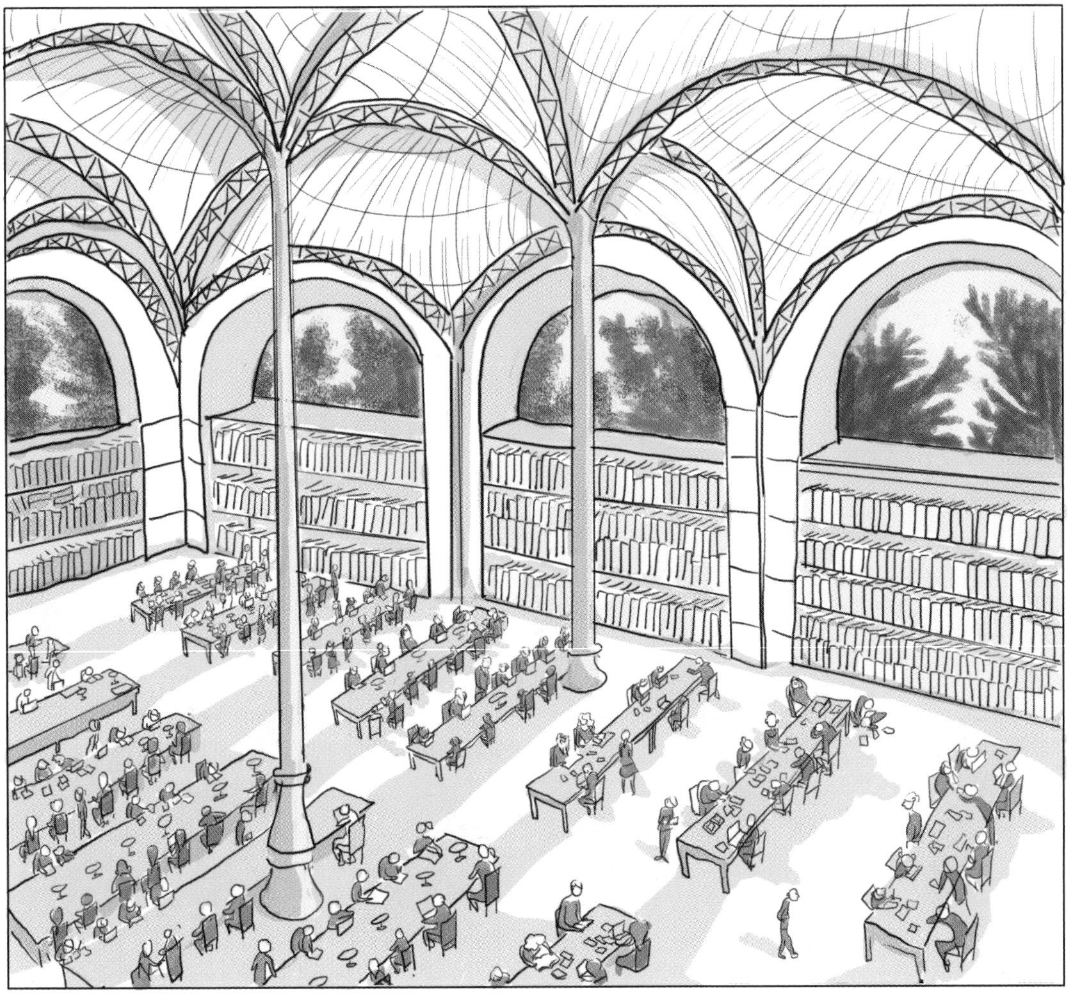

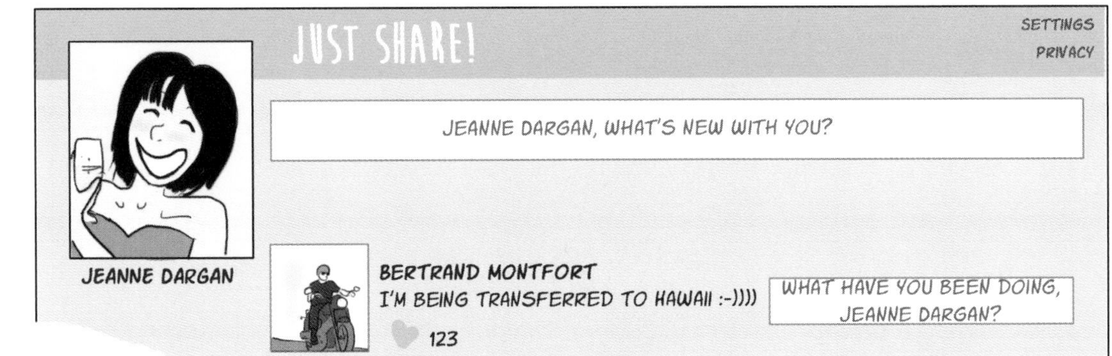
JUST SHARE!
SETTINGS
PRIVACY
JEANNE DARGAN, WHAT'S NEW WITH YOU?
JEANNE DARGAN
BERTRAND MONTFORT
I'M BEING TRANSFERRED TO HAWAII :-))))
123
WHAT HAVE YOU BEEN DOING, JEANNE DARGAN?
JULIE GIRARD
OFFLINE FOR 21 DAYS!
HONEYMOONING IN... BRITISH COLUMBIA!
1022
WHAT HAVE YOU BEEN DOING, JEANNE DARGAN?

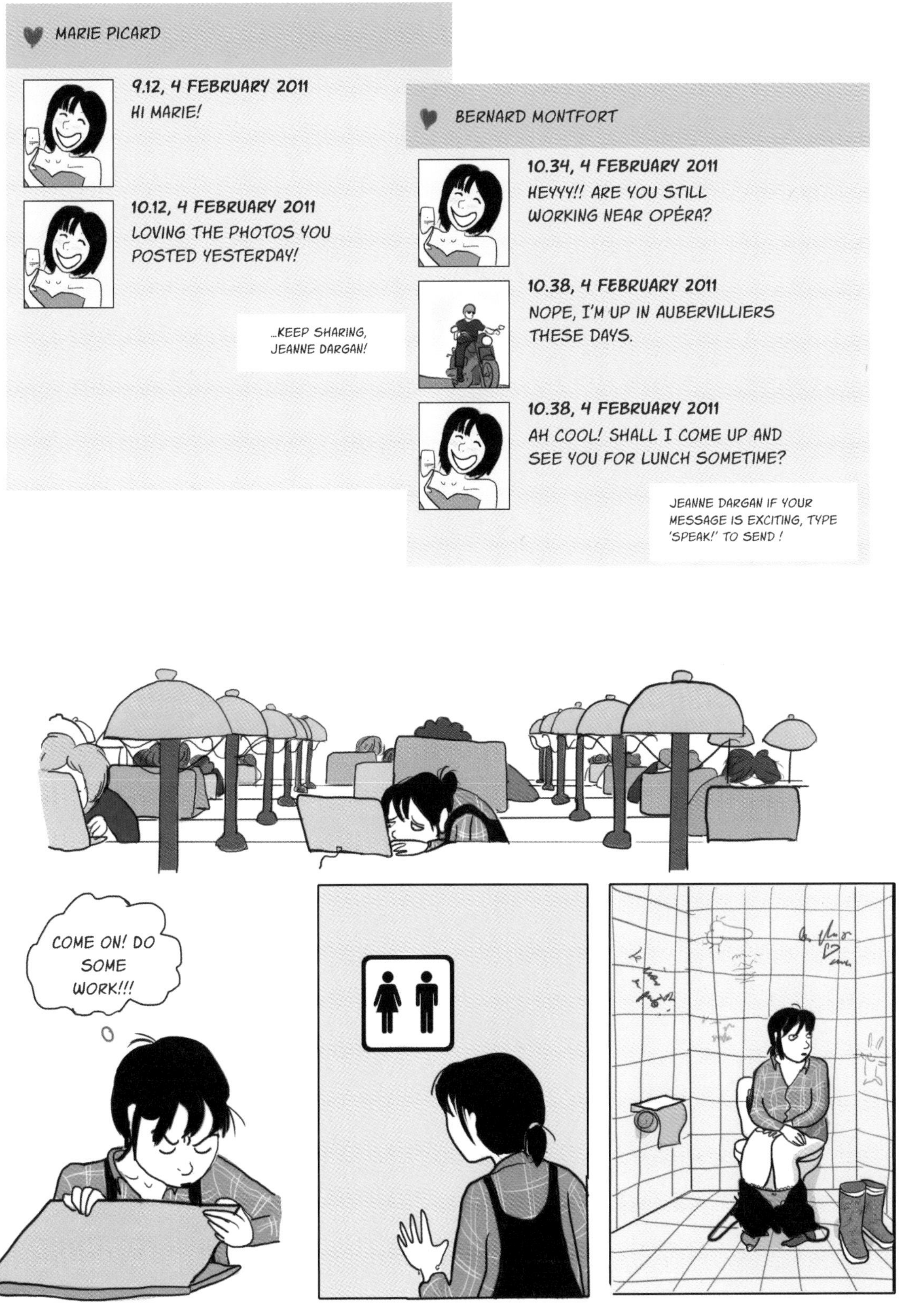
MARIE PICARD
9.12, 4 FEBRUARY 2011
HI MARIE!
10.12, 4 FEBRUARY 2011
LOVING THE PHOTOS YOU POSTED YESTERDAY!
...KEEP SHARING, JEANNE DARGAN!
BERNARD MONTFORT
10.34, 4 FEBRUARY 2011
HEYYY!! ARE YOU STILL WORKING NEAR OPÉRA?
10.38, 4 FEBRUARY 2011
NOPE, I'M UP IN AUBERVILLIERS THESE DAYS.
10.38, 4 FEBRUARY 2011
AH COOL! SHALL I COME UP AND SEE YOU FOR LUNCH SOMETIME?
JEANNE DARGAN IF YOUR MESSAGE IS EXCITING, TYPE 'SPEAK!' TO SEND !
COME ON! DO SOME WORK!!!

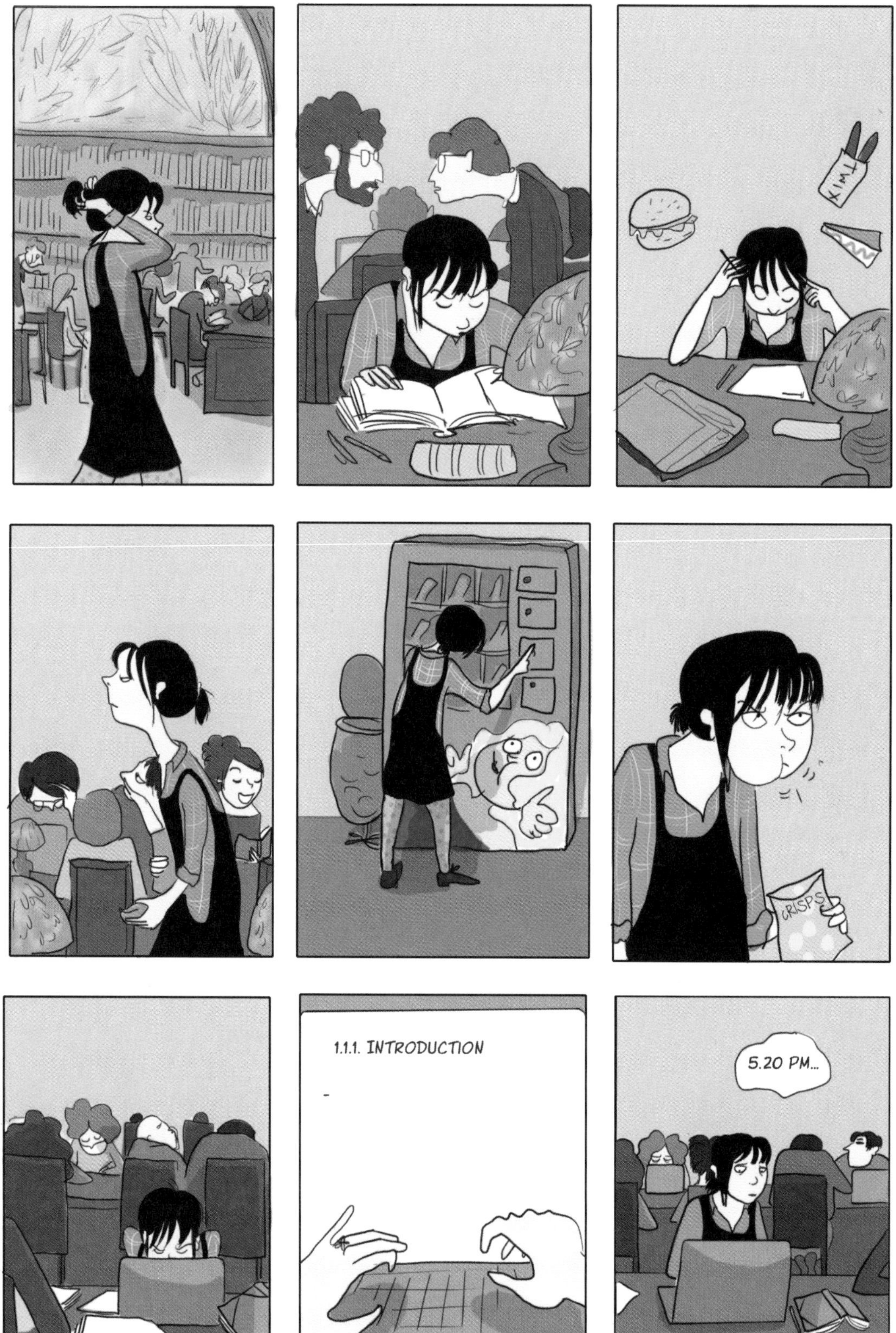
TWIX
CRISPS
1.1.1. INTRODUCTION
5.20 PM...

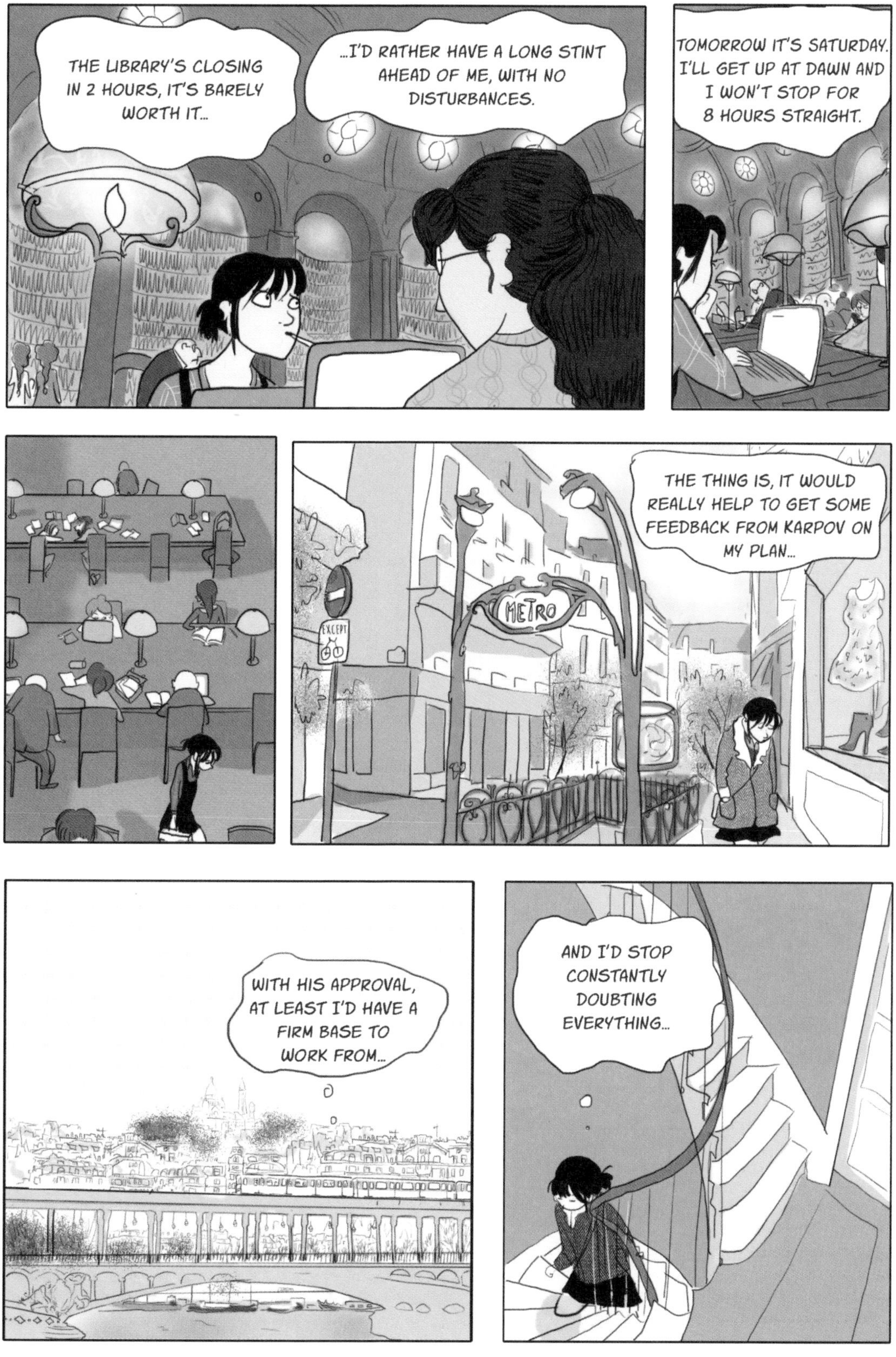
THE LIBRARY'S CLOSING IN 2 HOURS, IT'S BARELY WORTH IT...
...I'D RATHER HAVE A LONG STINT AHEAD OF ME, WITH NO DISTURBANCES.
TOMORROW IT'S SATURDAY. I'LL GET UP AT DAWN AND I WON'T STOP FOR 8 HOURS STRAIGHT.
EXCEPT
METRO
THE THING IS, IT WOULD REALLY HELP TO GET SOME FEEDBACK FROM KARPOV ON MY PLAN...
WITH HIS APPROVAL, AT LEAST I'D HAVE A FIRM BASE TO WORK FROM...
AND I'D STOP CONSTANTLY DOUBTING EVERYTHING...

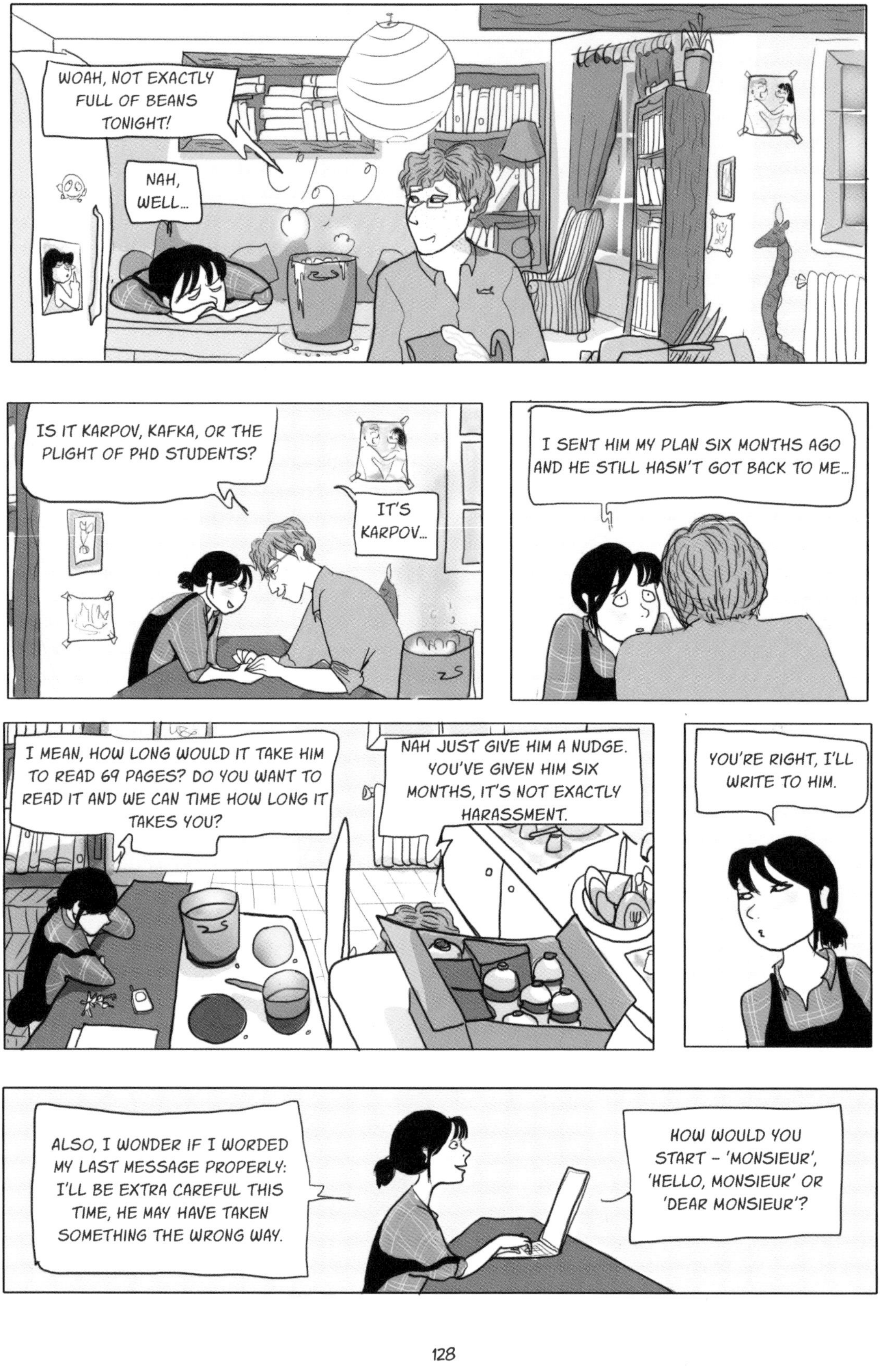
WOAH, NOT EXACTLY FULL OF BEANS TONIGHT!
NAH, WELL...
IS IT KARPOV, KAFKA, OR THE PLIGHT OF PHD STUDENTS?
IT'S KARPOV...
I SENT HIM MY PLAN SIX MONTHS AGO AND HE STILL HASN'T GOT BACK TO ME...
I MEAN, HOW LONG WOULD IT TAKE HIM TO READ 69 PAGES? DO YOU WANT TO READ IT AND WE CAN TIME HOW LONG IT TAKES YOU?
NAH JUST GIVE HIM A NUDGE. YOU'VE GIVEN HIM SIX MONTHS, IT'S NOT EXACTLY HARASSMENT.
YOU'RE RIGHT, I'LL WRITE TO HIM.
ALSO, I WONDER IF I WORDED MY LAST MESSAGE PROPERLY: I'LL BE EXTRA CAREFUL THIS TIME, HE MAY HAVE TAKEN SOMETHING THE WRONG WAY.
HOW WOULD YOU START – 'MONSIEUR', 'HELLO, MONSIEUR' OR 'DEAR MONSIEUR'?

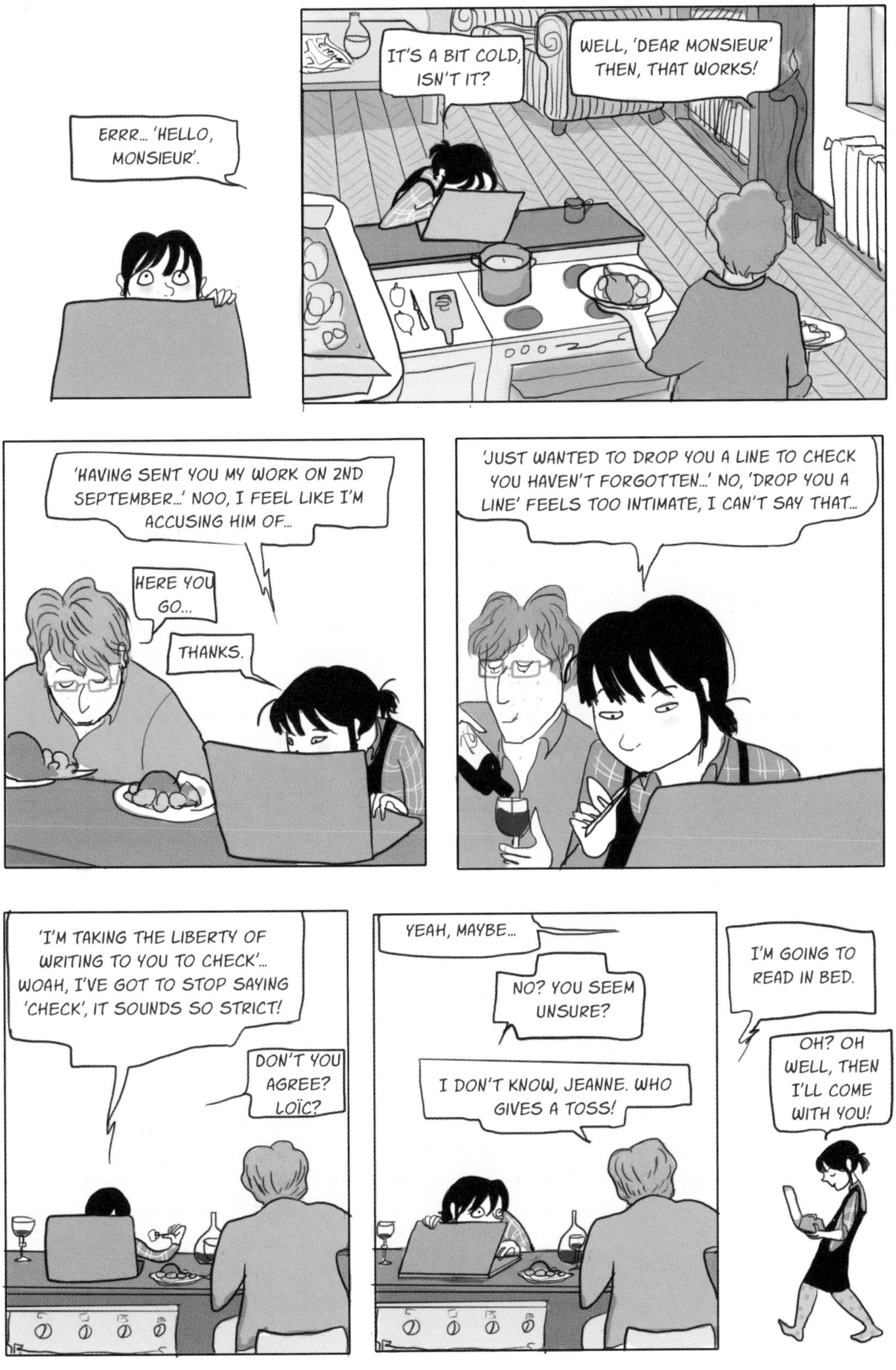
ERRR... 'HELLO, MONSIEUR'.
IT'S A BIT COLD, ISN'T IT?
WELL, 'DEAR MONSIEUR' THEN, THAT WORKS!
'HAVING SENT YOU MY WORK ON 2ND SEPTEMBER...' NOO, I FEEL LIKE I'M ACCUSING HIM OF...
HERE YOU GO...
THANKS.
'JUST WANTED TO DROP YOU A LINE TO CHECK YOU HAVEN'T FORGOTTEN...' NO, 'DROP YOU A LINE' FEELS TOO INTIMATE, I CAN'T SAY THAT...
'I'M TAKING THE LIBERTY OF WRITING TO YOU TO CHECK'... WOAH, I'VE GOT TO STOP SAYING 'CHECK', IT SOUNDS SO STRICT!
DON'T YOU AGREE? LOÏC?
YEAH, MAYBE...
NO? YOU SEEM UNSURE?
I DON'T KNOW, JEANNE. WHO GIVES A TOSS!
I'M GOING TO READ IN BED.
OH? OH WELL, THEN I'LL COME WITH YOU!

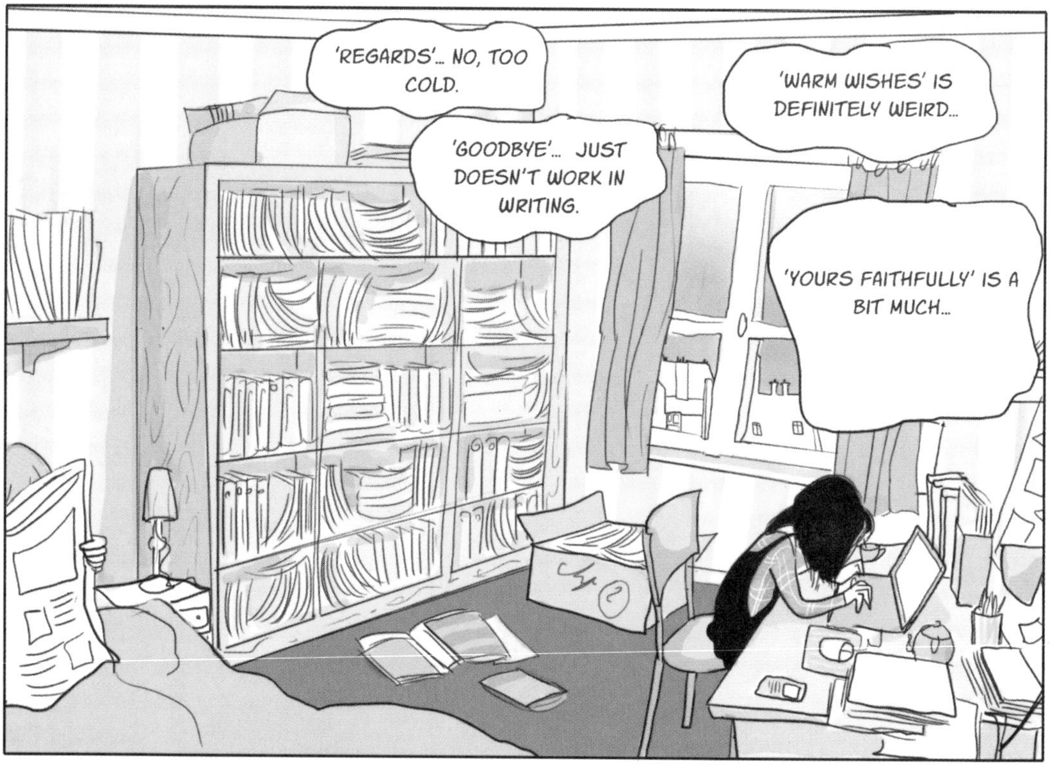
'REGARDS'... NO, TOO COLD.
'GOODBYE'... JUST DOESN'T WORK IN WRITING.
'WARM WISHES' IS DEFINITELY WEIRD...
'YOURS FAITHFULLY' IS A BIT MUCH...

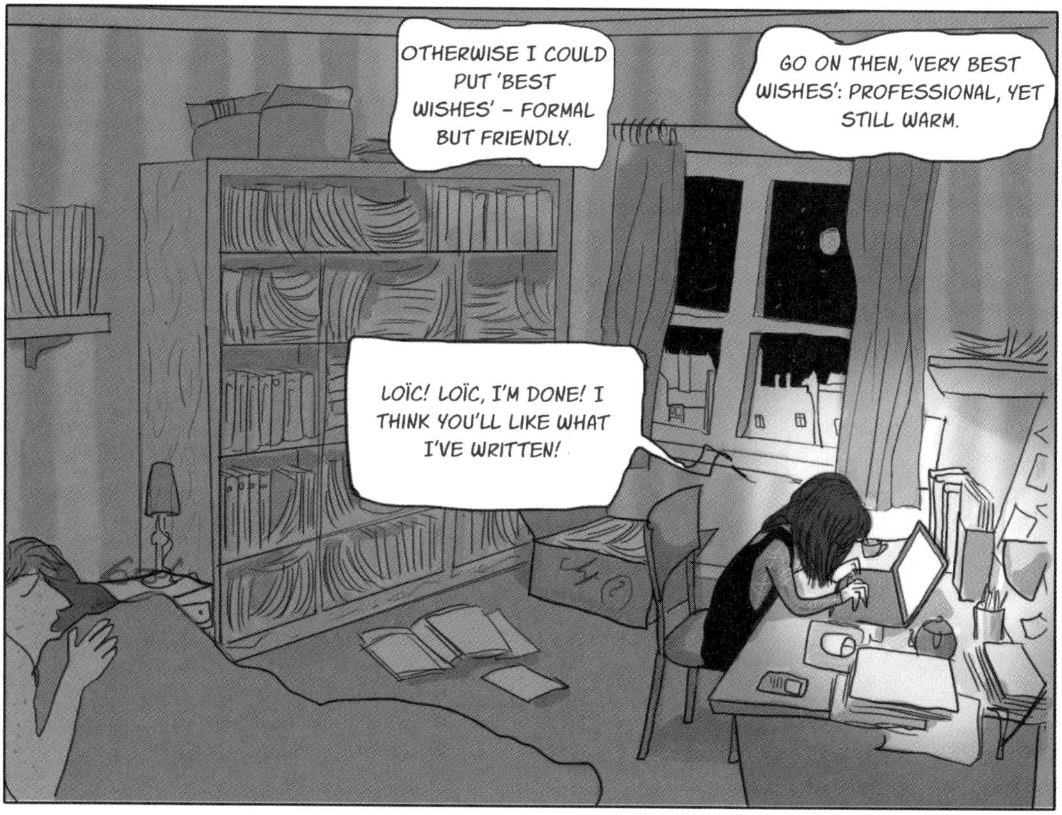
OTHERWISE I COULD PUT 'BEST WISHES' – FORMAL BUT FRIENDLY.
GO ON THEN, 'VERY BEST WISHES': PROFESSIONAL, YET STILL WARM.
LOÏC! LOÏC, I'M DONE! I THINK YOU'LL LIKE WHAT I'VE WRITTEN!

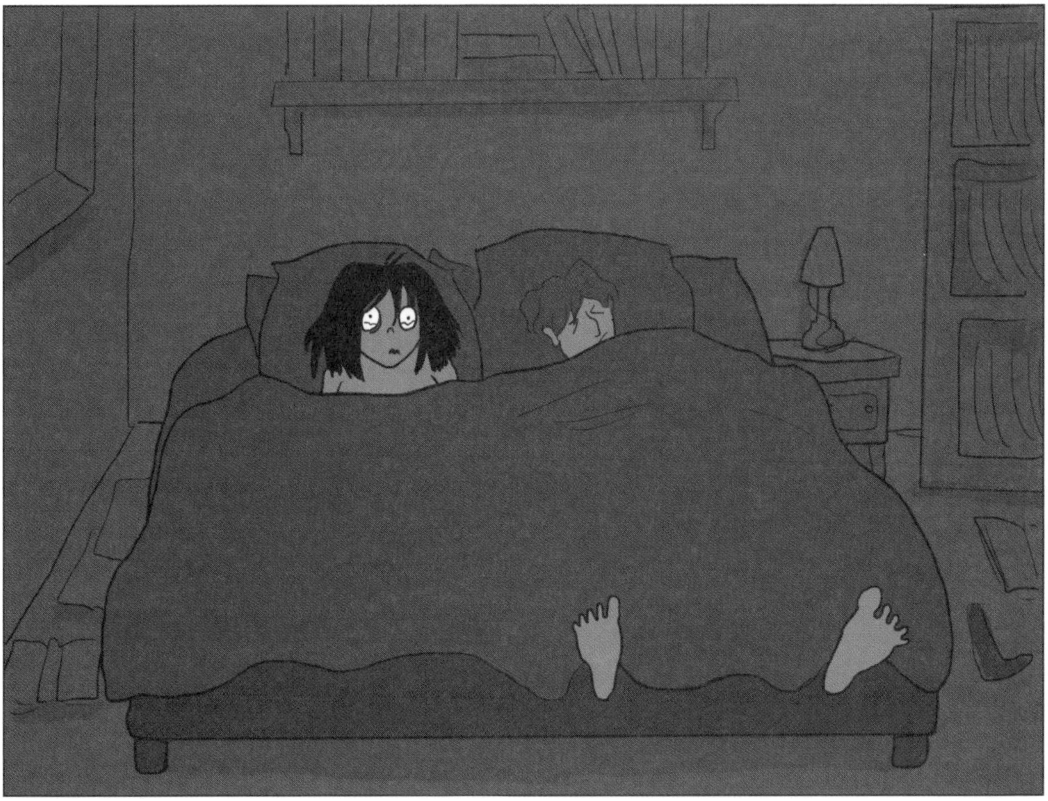

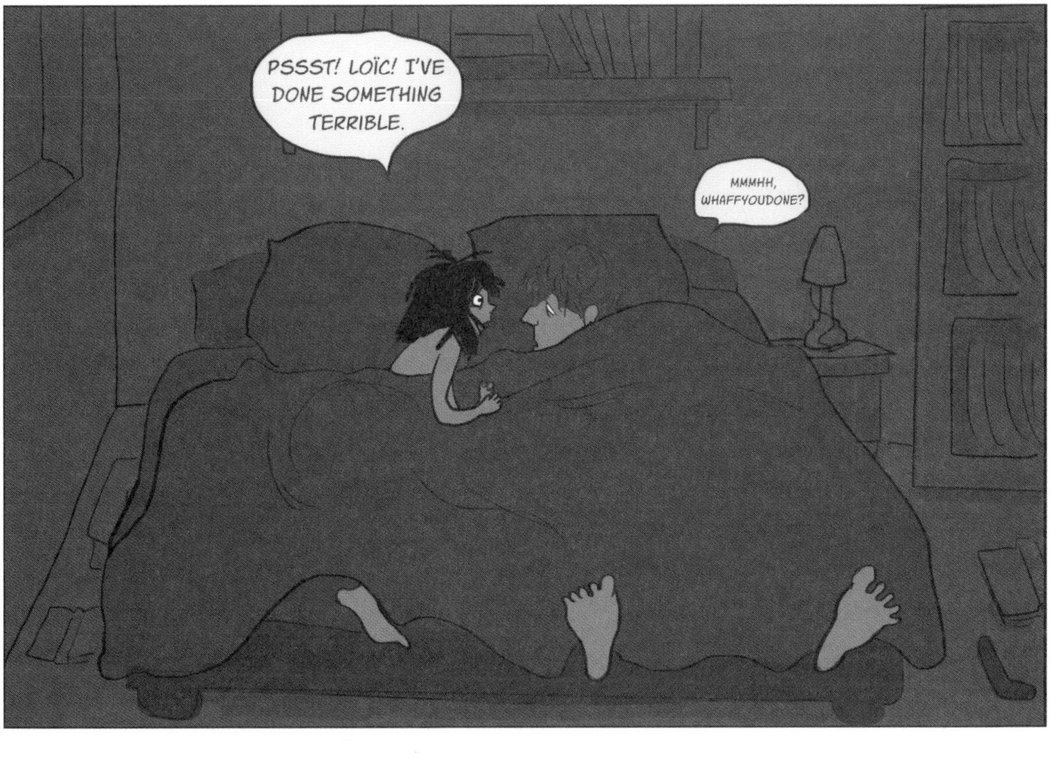
PSSST! LOÏC! I'VE DONE SOMETHING TERRIBLE.
MMMHH, WHAFFYOUDONE?

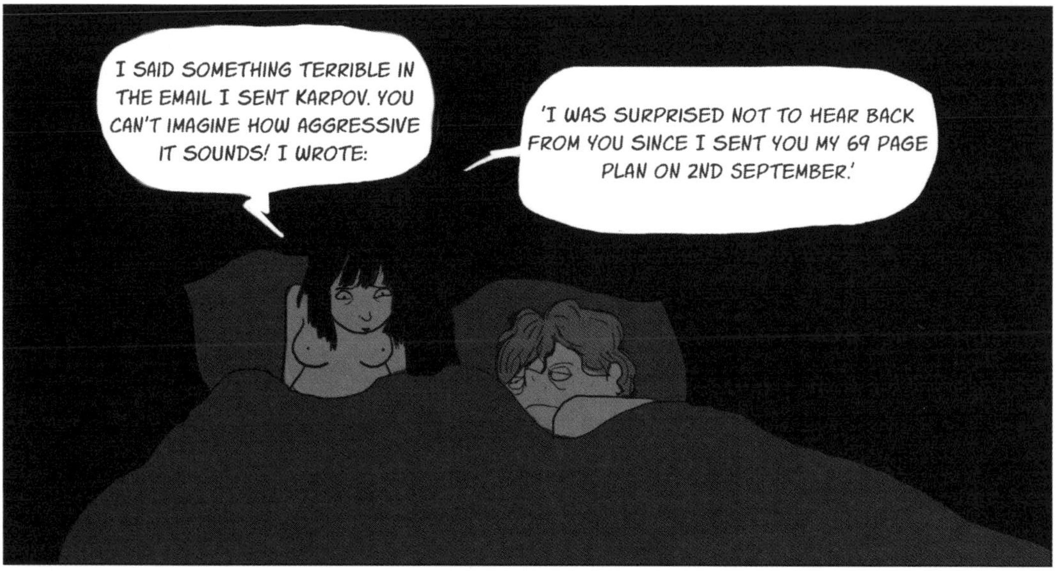
I SAID SOMETHING TERRIBLE IN THE EMAIL I SENT KARPOV. YOU CAN'T IMAGINE HOW AGGRESSIVE IT SOUNDS! I WROTE:
'I WAS SURPRISED NOT TO HEAR BACK FROM YOU SINCE I SENT YOU MY 69 PAGE PLAN ON 2ND SEPTEMBER.'

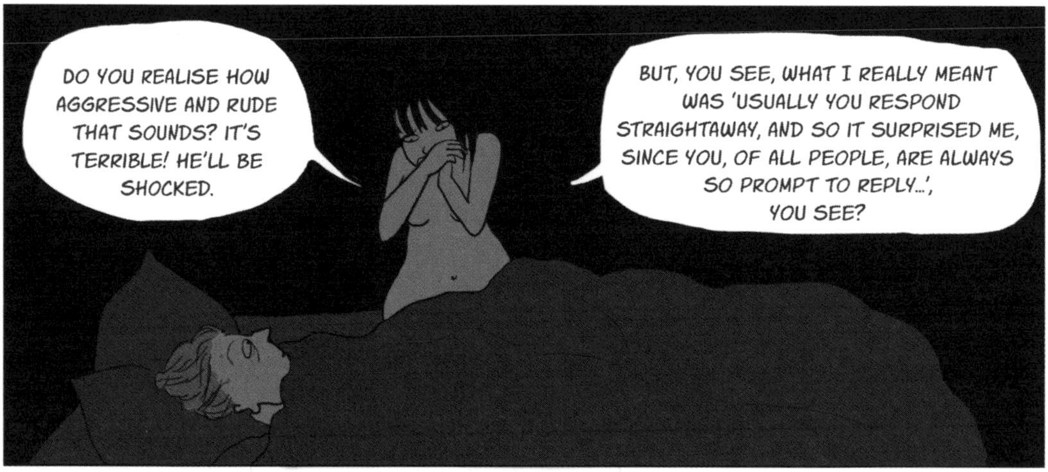
DO YOU REALISE HOW AGGRESSIVE AND RUDE THAT SOUNDS? IT'S TERRIBLE! HE'LL BE SHOCKED.
BUT, YOU SEE, WHAT I REALLY MEANT WAS 'USUALLY YOU RESPOND STRAIGHTAWAY, AND SO IT SURPRISED ME, SINCE YOU, OF ALL PEOPLE, ARE ALWAYS SO PROMPT TO REPLY...', YOU SEE?

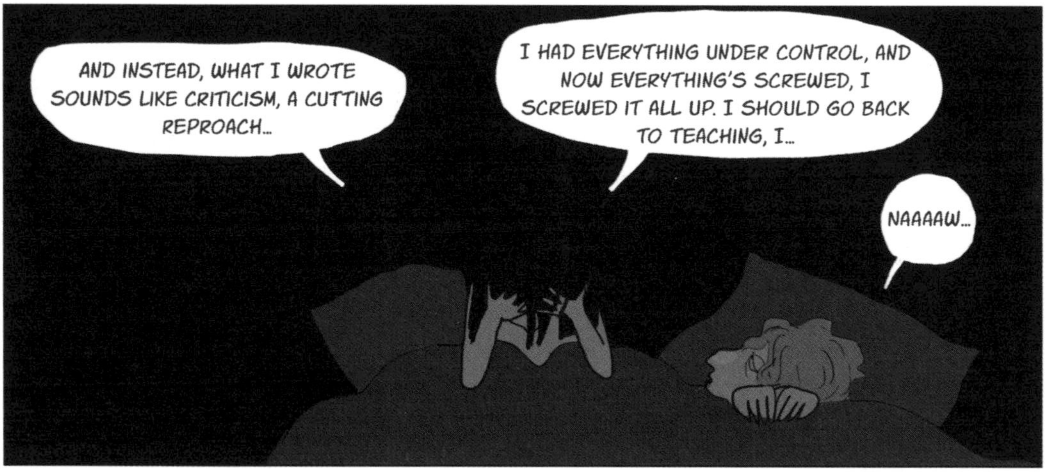
AND INSTEAD, WHAT I WROTE SOUNDS LIKE CRITICISM, A CUTTING REPROACH...
I HAD EVERYTHING UNDER CONTROL, AND NOW EVERYTHING'S SCREWED, I SCREWED IT ALL UP. I SHOULD GO BACK TO TEACHING, I...
NAAAAW...

Dear Monsieur,

I realised on rereading that my previous message could be misinterpreted as a demand to respond swiftly to all my messages. Of course this isn't what I intended and naturally you can read my work whenever it suits you. Please forgive me for being so tactless.

Best wishes,
Jeanne

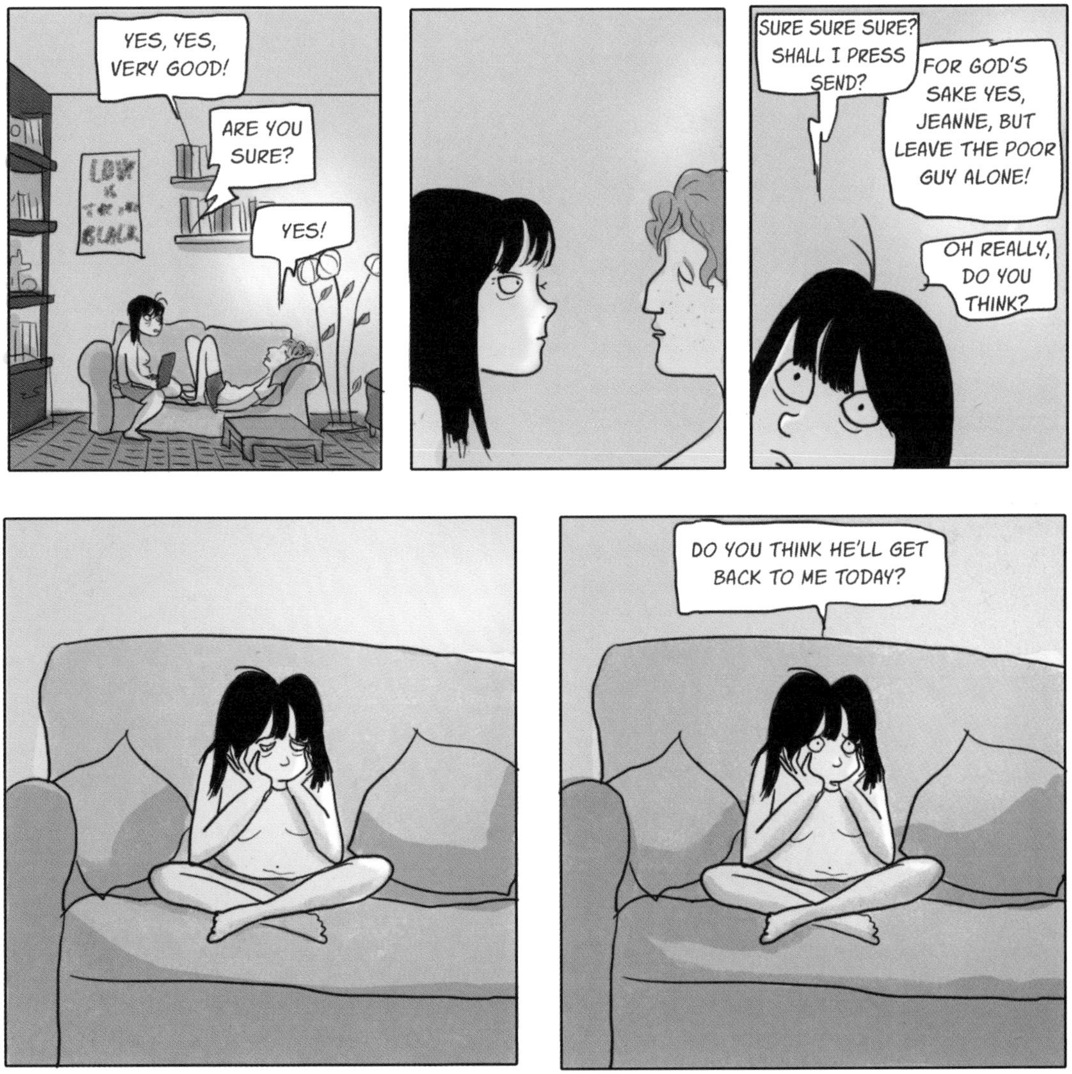

YES, YES, VERY GOOD!
ARE YOU SURE?
YES!
SURE SURE SURE? SHALL I PRESS SEND?
FOR GOD'S SAKE YES, JEANNE, BUT LEAVE THE POOR GUY ALONE!
OH REALLY, DO YOU THINK?
DO YOU THINK HE'LL GET BACK TO ME TODAY?

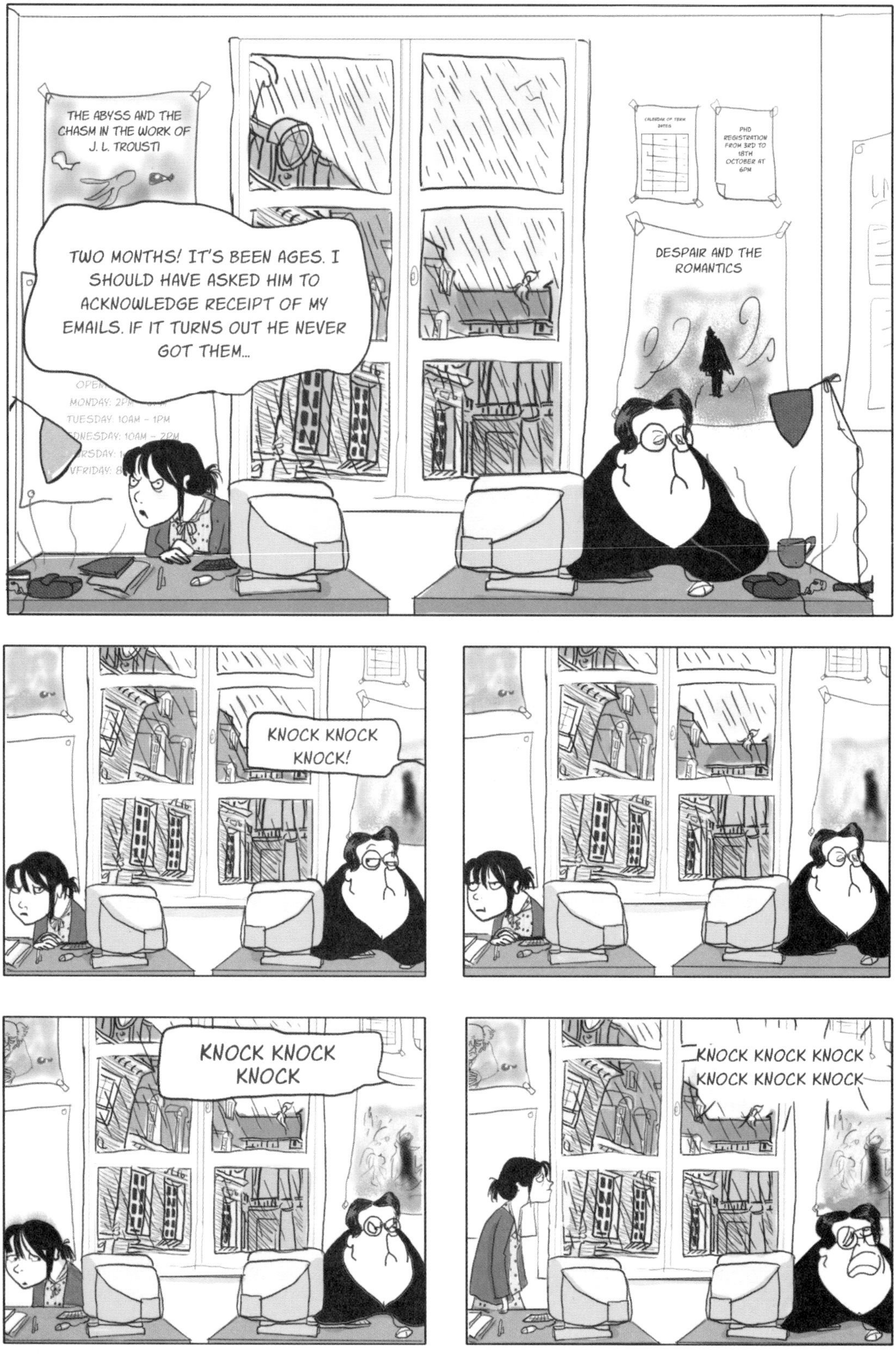
THE ABYSS AND THE CHASM IN THE WORK OF J. L. TROUSTI
CALENDAR OF TERM DATES
PHD REGISTRATION FROM 3RD TO 18TH OCTOBER AT 6PM
DESPAIR AND THE ROMANTICS
TWO MONTHS! IT'S BEEN AGES. I SHOULD HAVE ASKED HIM TO ACKNOWLEDGE RECEIPT OF MY EMAILS. IF IT TURNS OUT HE NEVER GOT THEM...
KNOCK KNOCK KNOCK!
KNOCK KNOCK KNOCK
KNOCK KNOCK KNOCK KNOCK KNOCK KNOCK

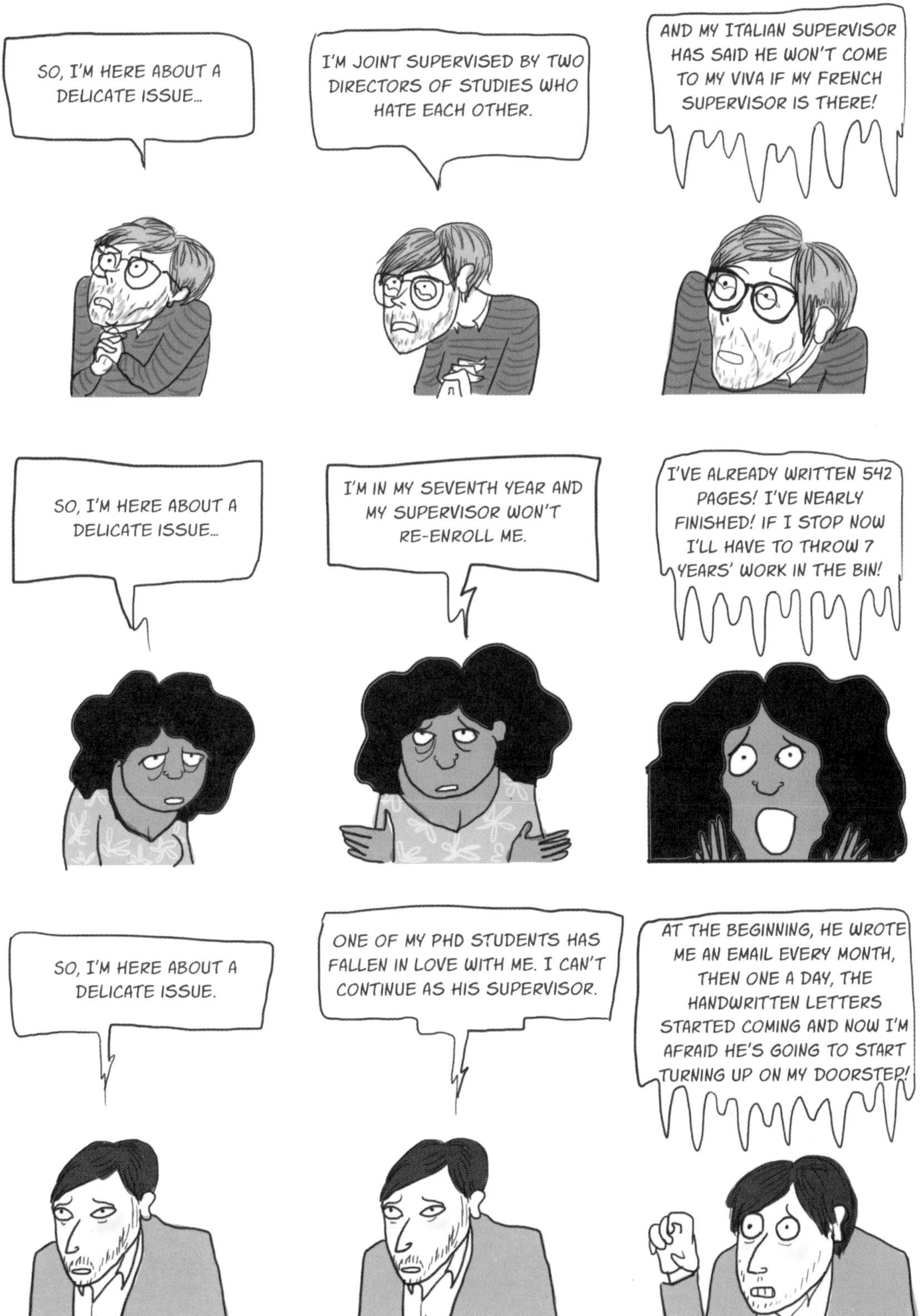
SO, I'M HERE ABOUT A DELICATE ISSUE...
I'M JOINT SUPERVISED BY TWO DIRECTORS OF STUDIES WHO HATE EACH OTHER.
AND MY ITALIAN SUPERVISOR HAS SAID HE WON'T COME TO MY VIVA IF MY FRENCH SUPERVISOR IS THERE!
SO, I'M HERE ABOUT A DELICATE ISSUE...
I'M IN MY SEVENTH YEAR AND MY SUPERVISOR WON'T RE-ENROLL ME.
I'VE ALREADY WRITTEN 542 PAGES! I'VE NEARLY FINISHED! IF I STOP NOW I'LL HAVE TO THROW 7 YEARS' WORK IN THE BIN!
SO, I'M HERE ABOUT A DELICATE ISSUE.
ONE OF MY PHD STUDENTS HAS FALLEN IN LOVE WITH ME. I CAN'T CONTINUE AS HIS SUPERVISOR.
AT THE BEGINNING, HE WROTE ME AN EMAIL EVERY MONTH, THEN ONE A DAY, THE HANDWRITTEN LETTERS STARTED COMING AND NOW I'M AFRAID HE'S GOING TO START TURNING UP ON MY DOORSTEP!

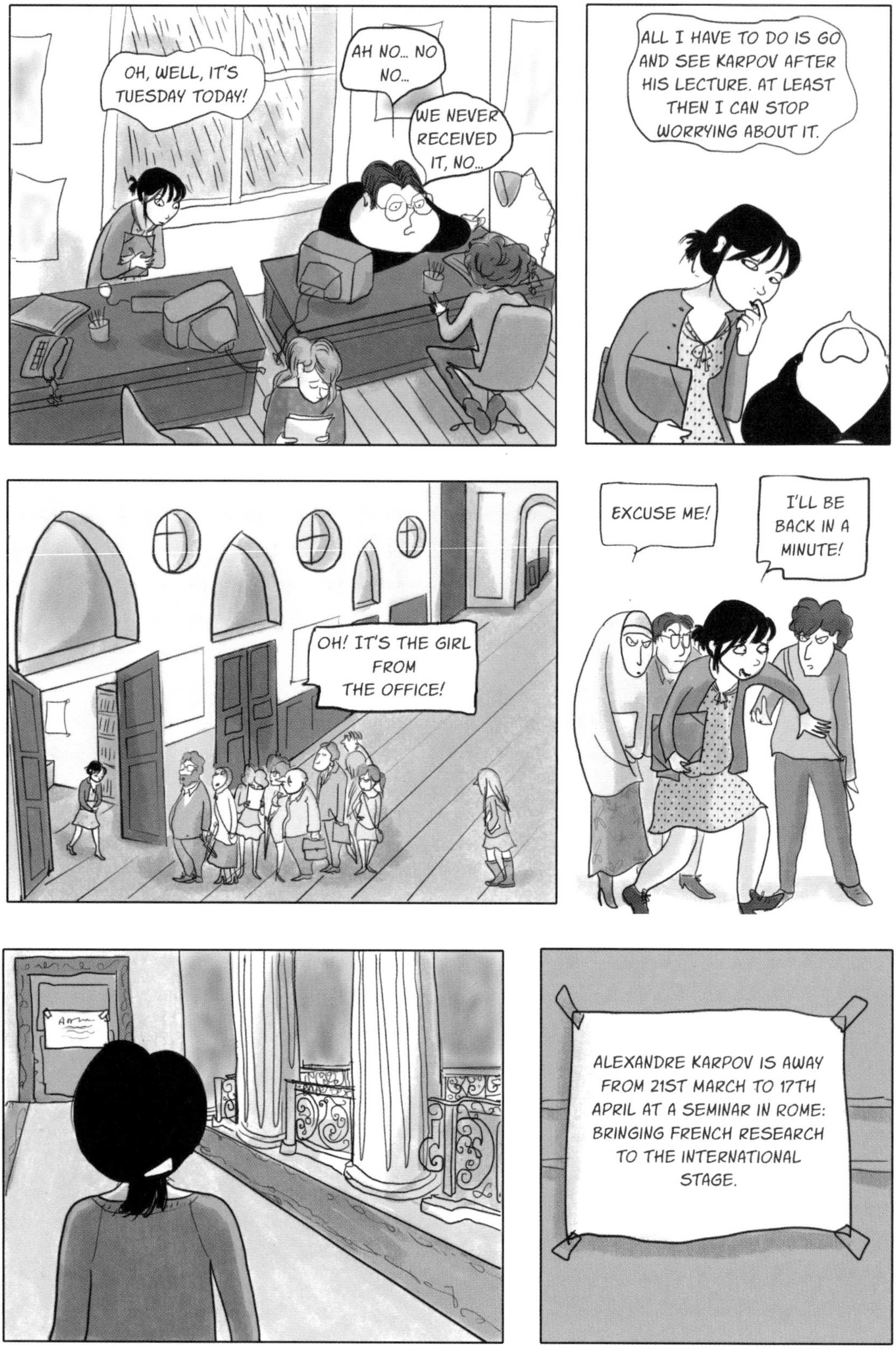
OH, WELL, IT'S TUESDAY TODAY!
AH NO... NO NO...
WE NEVER RECEIVED IT, NO...
ALL I HAVE TO DO IS GO AND SEE KARPOV AFTER HIS LECTURE. AT LEAST THEN I CAN STOP WORRYING ABOUT IT.
OH! IT'S THE GIRL FROM THE OFFICE!
EXCUSE ME!
I'LL BE BACK IN A MINUTE!
ALEXANDRE KARPOV IS AWAY FROM 21ST MARCH TO 17TH APRIL AT A SEMINAR IN ROME: BRINGING FRENCH RESEARCH TO THE INTERNATIONAL STAGE.

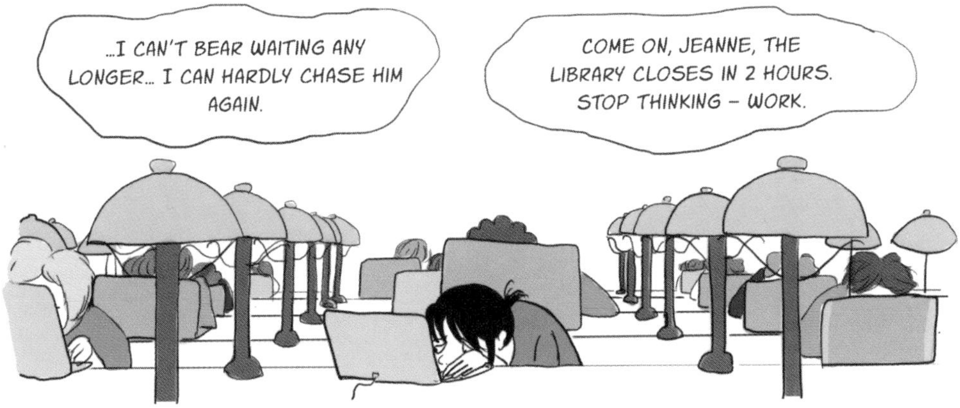
...I CAN'T BEAR WAITING ANY LONGER... I CAN HARDLY CHASE HIM AGAIN.
COME ON, JEANNE, THE LIBRARY CLOSES IN 2 HOURS. STOP THINKING – WORK.

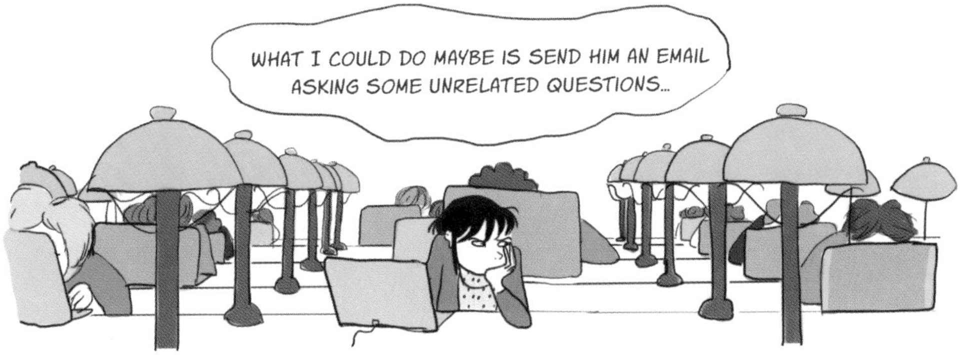
WHAT I COULD DO MAYBE IS SEND HIM AN EMAIL ASKING SOME UNRELATED QUESTIONS...

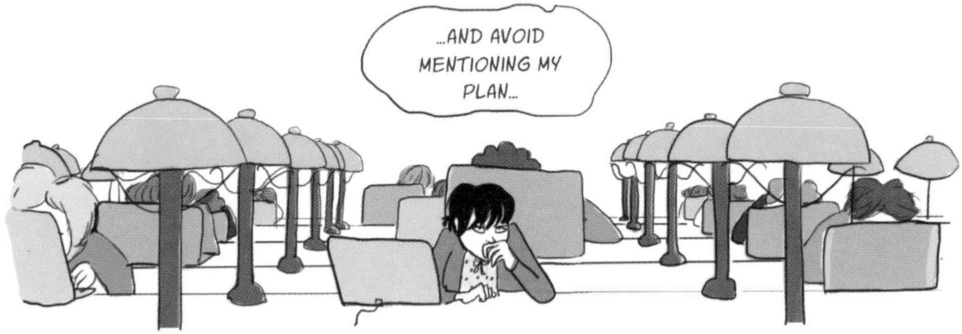
...AND AVOID MENTIONING MY PLAN...

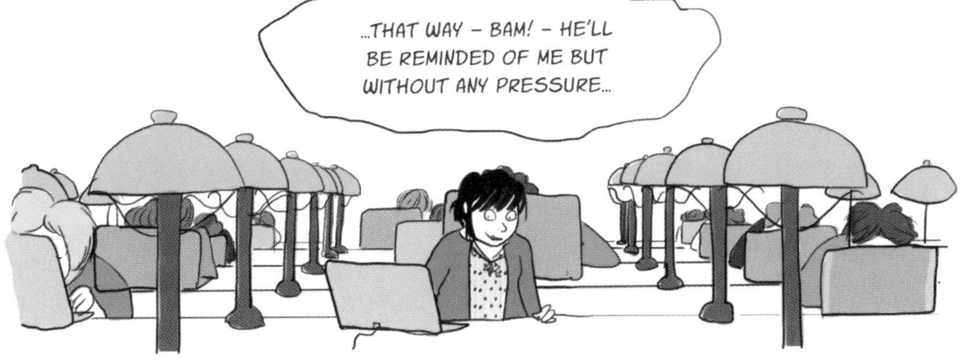
...THAT WAY – BAM! – HE'LL BE REMINDED OF ME BUT WITHOUT ANY PRESSURE...

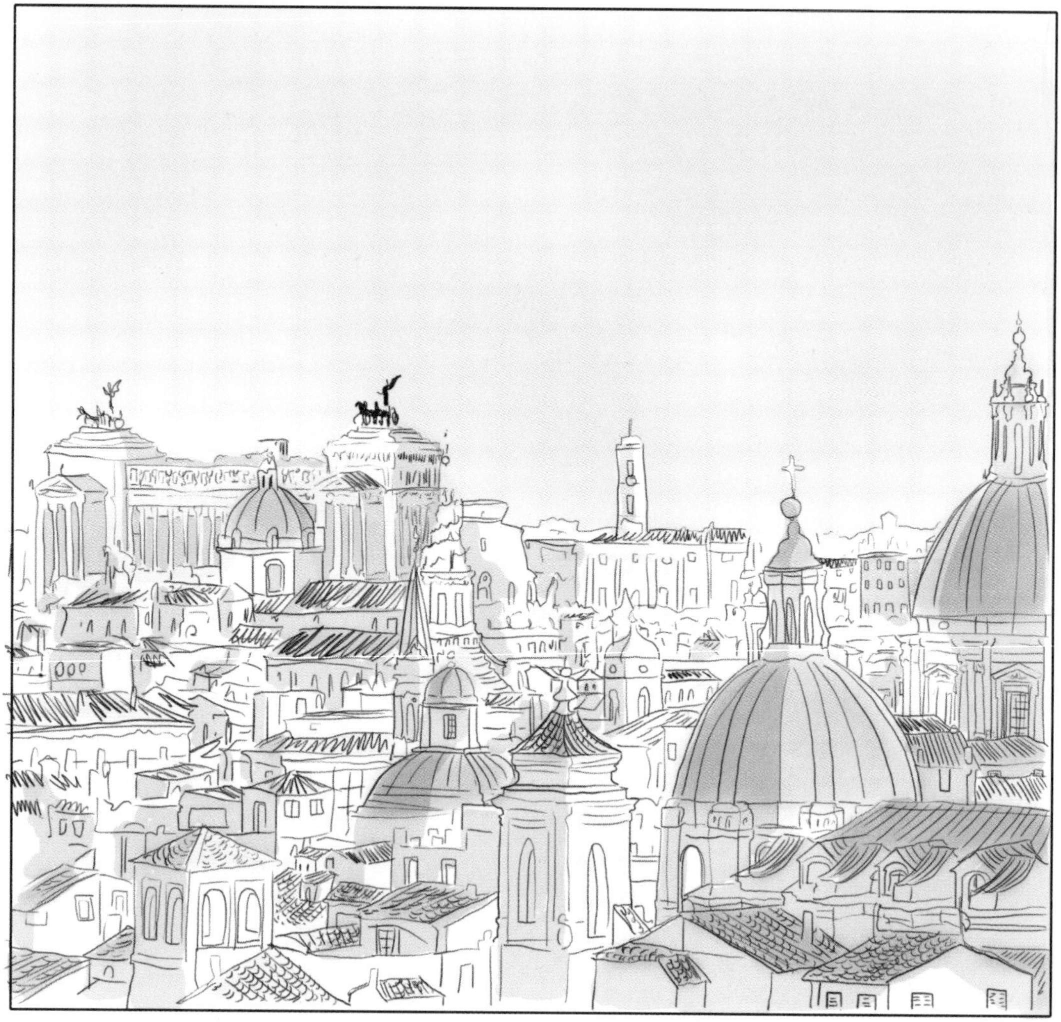

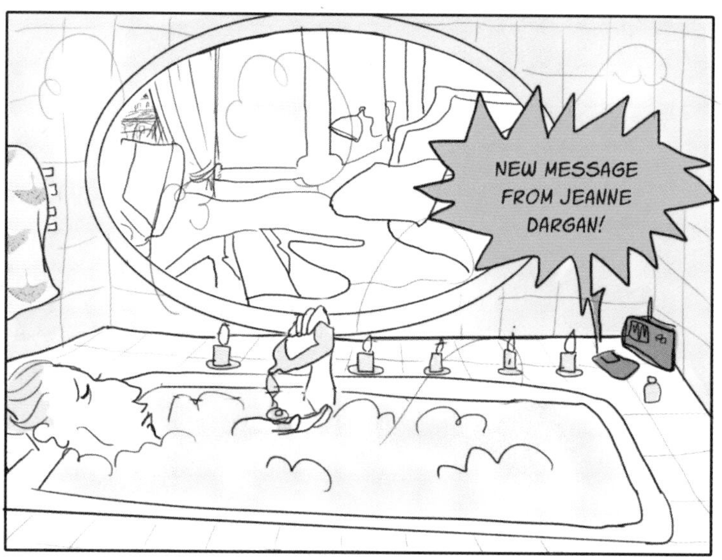
NEW MESSAGE FROM JEANNE DARGAN!

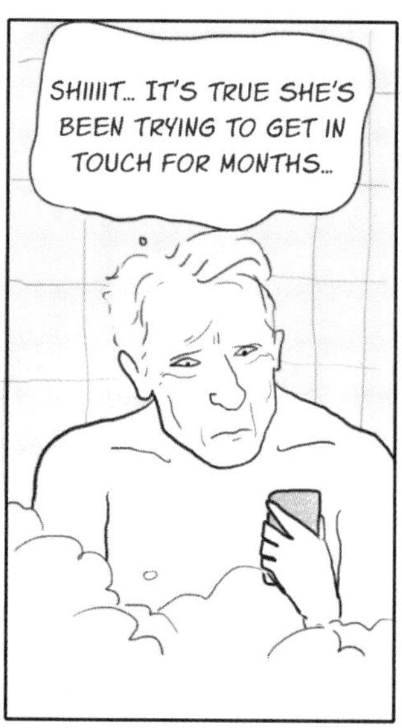
SHIIIIT... IT'S TRUE SHE'S BEEN TRYING TO GET IN TOUCH FOR MONTHS...

DEAR MONSIEUR, GNIGNIGNIGNIN... PERIOD OF DOUBT BLAHBLAHBLAH... WHICH IS WHY I WANTED TO ASK YOU...
THE... 11 FOLLOWING QUESTIONS !??

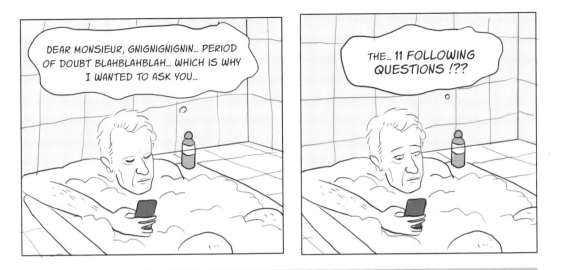

JEANNE DAGAN Jeanne.dargan@gmail.com
Subject: Questions relating to my research
18:16 (10 minutes ago)

ask you the 11 following questions:
1.
In Antigone, Sophocles writes 'Man walks nowhere.' He adds that this doesn't only apply to the present, but to the future and the infinite succession of time. With all possible paths before him, he walks nowhere no matter what happens. Immobility is impossible yet everything is ephemeral and fluctuating.
QUESTION: Do you think that what exists purely through change can only be modified by the very fact that it changes?
2.
For Proust, it was impossible to distinguish between total oblivion and total knowledge. He describes an excess of knowledge as an indistinct vision of all things, compounded by an inability to make sense of anything at all. It brings with it paralysis, an inability to think: the observer is drowned in a flood of memories.
QUESTION: Do you know if Proust talked about the paralysis of thought in *In Search of Lost Time*, and if so, where exactly?
3.
Metaphysics, i.e. everything that one might claim to be knowledge beyond experience, that is to say observed phenomena, or that which is determined by nature in one sense or other, can be considered by Kafka as the expiatory form that

CAN I PLAY DEAD AGAIN WITHOUT SEEMING LIKE A BASTARD...?

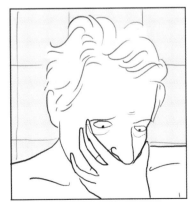

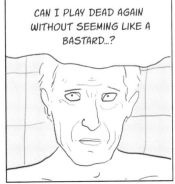

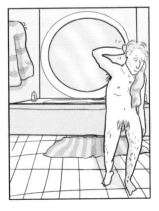

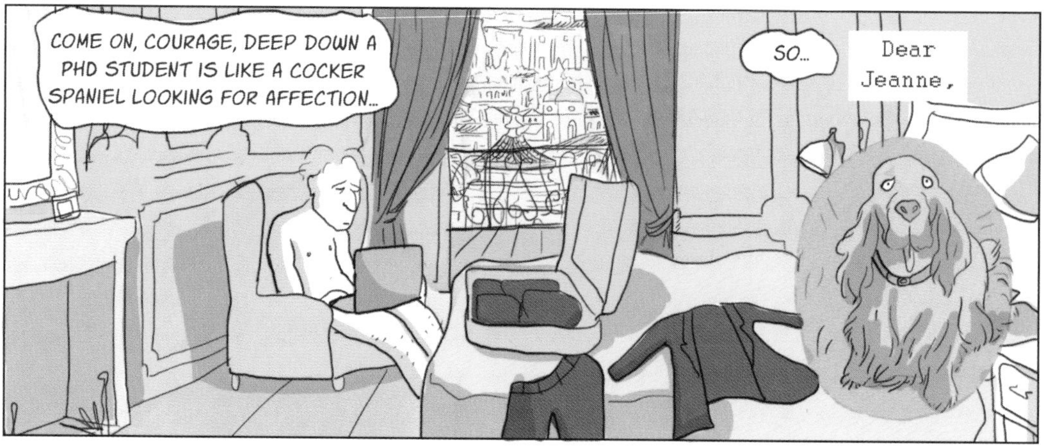
COME ON, COURAGE, DEEP DOWN A PHD STUDENT IS LIKE A COCKER SPANIEL LOOKING FOR AFFECTION...
SO...
Dear Jeanne,

Your questions are highly pertinent and clearly show how far you've come in your thinking

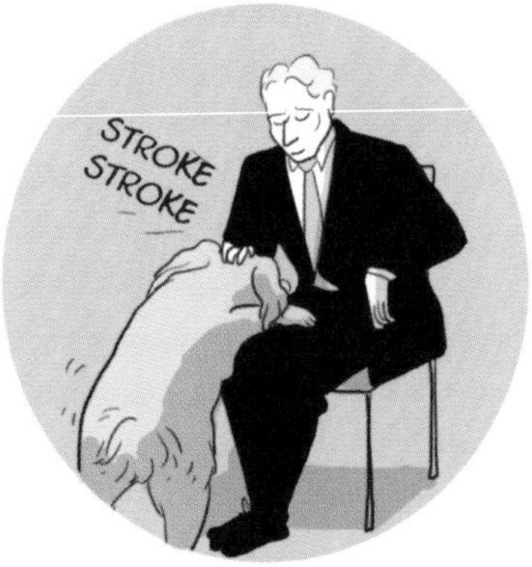
STROKE STROKE

I've been thinking about your research a lot recently.

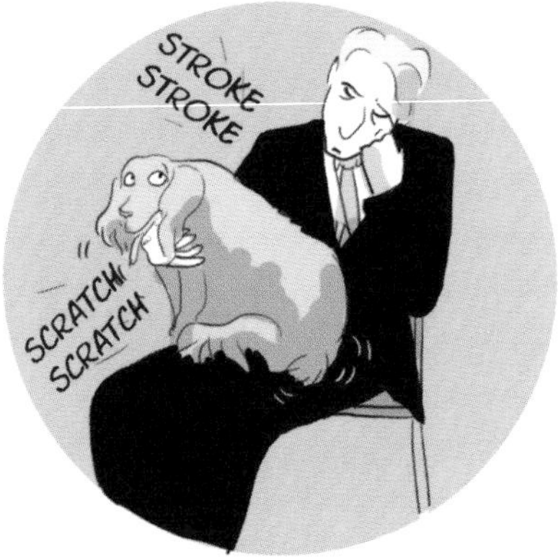
STROKE STROKE
SCRATCH SCRATCH

I think that an exhaustive reading of the work of Schopenhauer and the relevant critical works would more than answer your fascinating questions.

In fact, his approach to questions of JUSTICE and the ABDICATION OF THE WILL would bring a powerful philosophical perspective to your work.

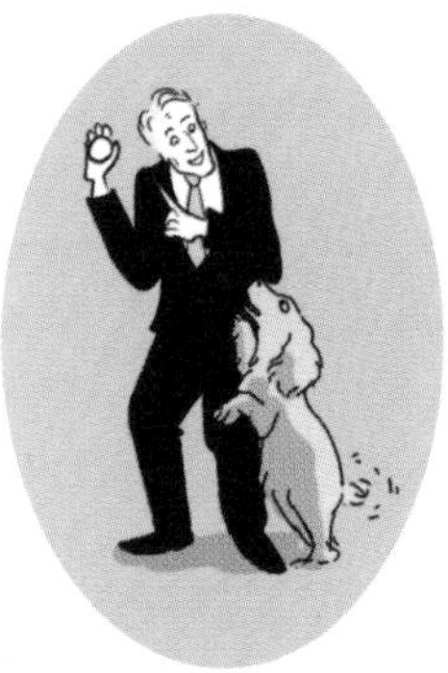

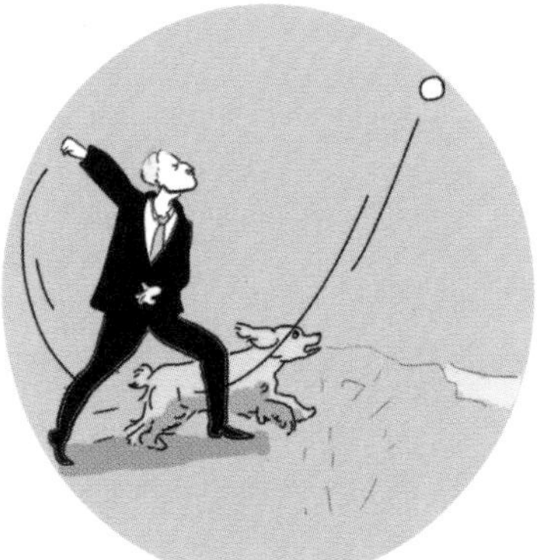

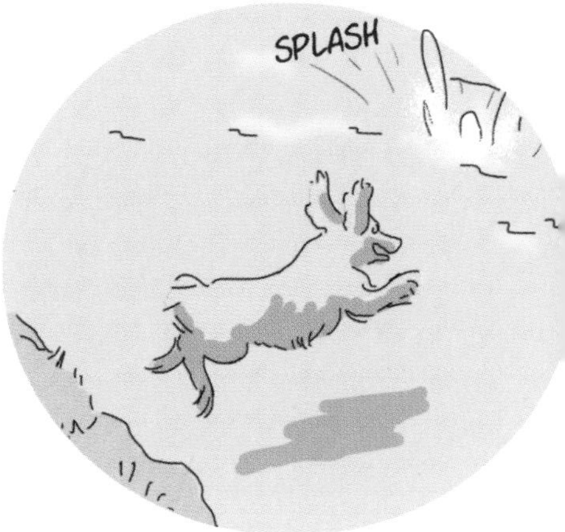
SPLASH

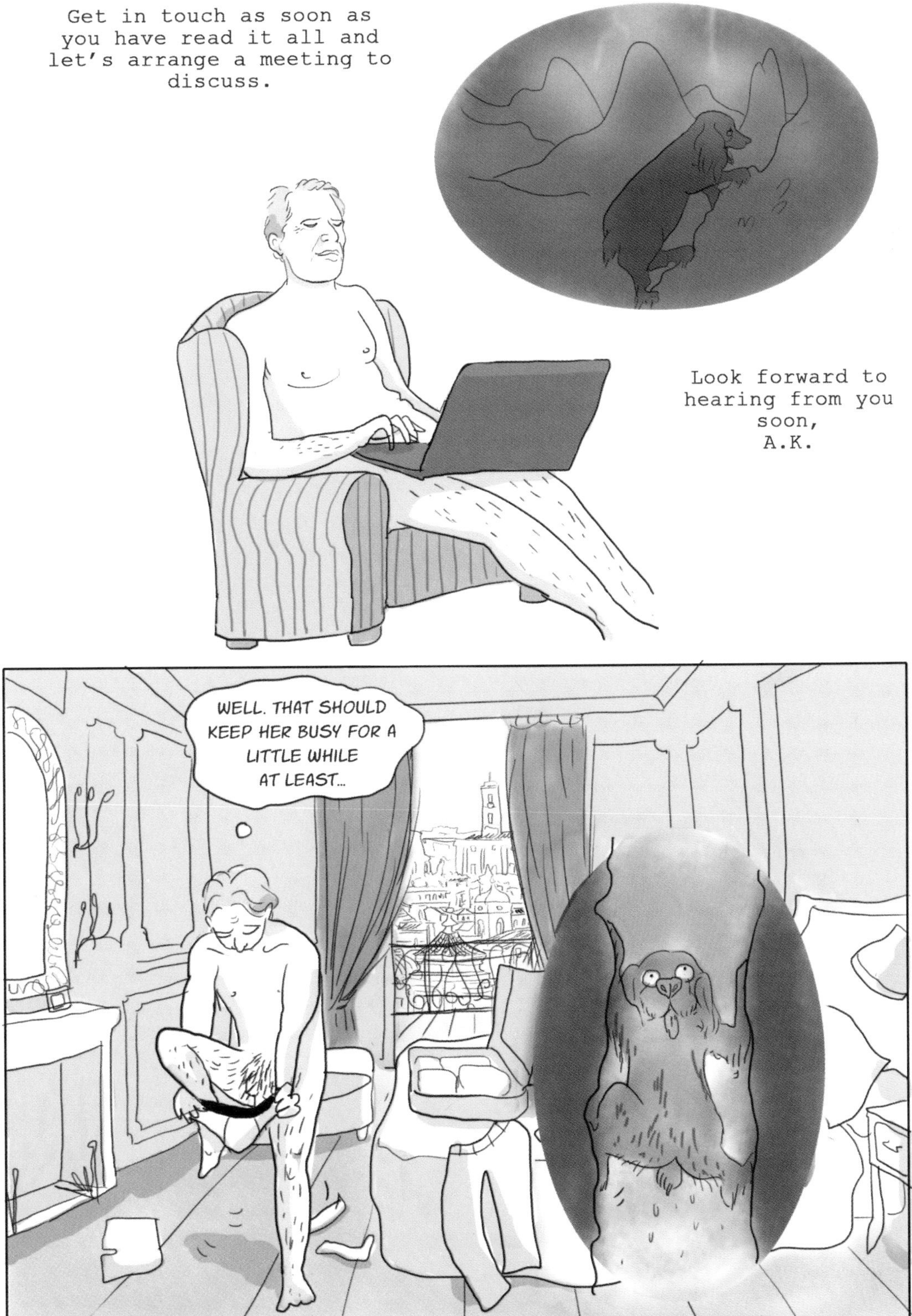
Get in touch as soon as you have read it all and let's arrange a meeting to discuss.
Look forward to hearing from you soon,
A.K.
WELL. THAT SHOULD KEEP HER BUSY FOR A LITTLE WHILE AT LEAST...

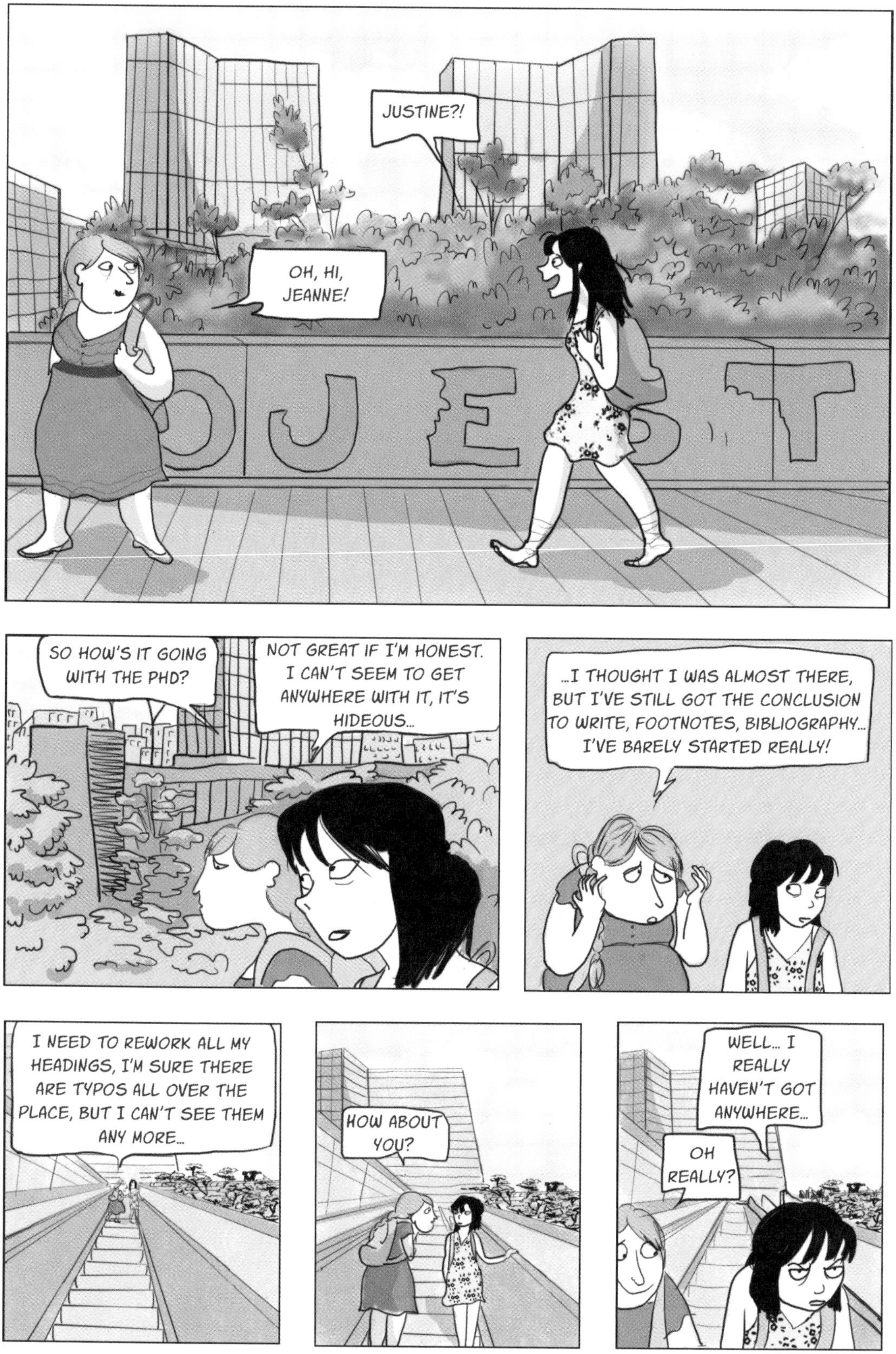

JUSTINE?!
OH, HI, JEANNE!
OJEST
SO HOW'S IT GOING WITH THE PHD?
NOT GREAT IF I'M HONEST. I CAN'T SEEM TO GET ANYWHERE WITH IT, IT'S HIDEOUS...
...I THOUGHT I WAS ALMOST THERE, BUT I'VE STILL GOT THE CONCLUSION TO WRITE, FOOTNOTES, BIBLIOGRAPHY... I'VE BARELY STARTED REALLY!
I NEED TO REWORK ALL MY HEADINGS, I'M SURE THERE ARE TYPOS ALL OVER THE PLACE, BUT I CAN'T SEE THEM ANY MORE...
HOW ABOUT YOU?
WELL... I REALLY HAVEN'T GOT ANYWHERE...
OH REALLY?

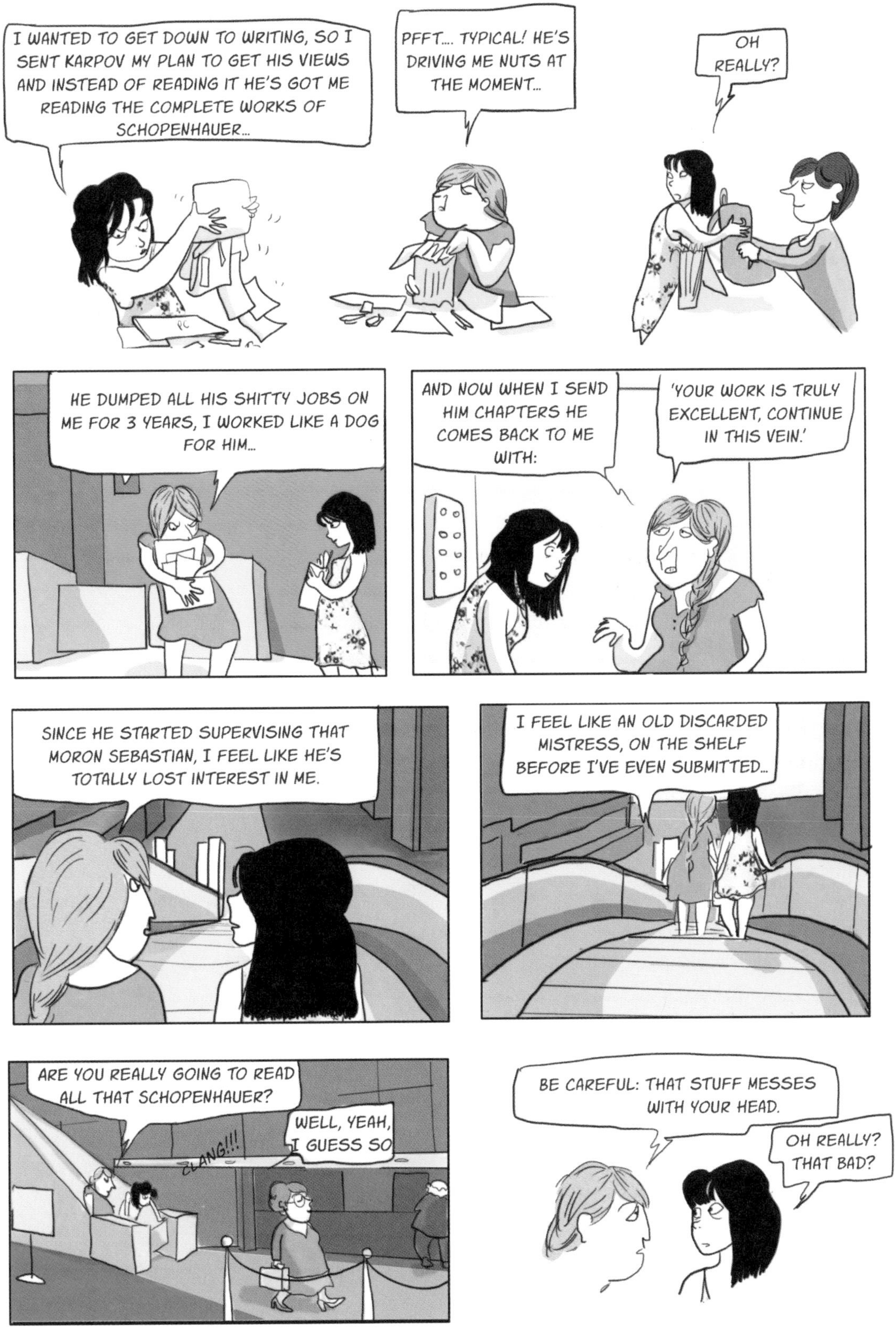

I WANTED TO GET DOWN TO WRITING, SO I SENT KARPOV MY PLAN TO GET HIS VIEWS AND INSTEAD OF READING IT HE'S GOT ME READING THE COMPLETE WORKS OF SCHOPENHAUER...
PFFT.... TYPICAL! HE'S DRIVING ME NUTS AT THE MOMENT...
OH REALLY?
HE DUMPED ALL HIS SHITTY JOBS ON ME FOR 3 YEARS, I WORKED LIKE A DOG FOR HIM...
AND NOW WHEN I SEND HIM CHAPTERS HE COMES BACK TO ME WITH:
'YOUR WORK IS TRULY EXCELLENT, CONTINUE IN THIS VEIN.'
SINCE HE STARTED SUPERVISING THAT MORON SEBASTIAN, I FEEL LIKE HE'S TOTALLY LOST INTEREST IN ME.
I FEEL LIKE AN OLD DISCARDED MISTRESS, ON THE SHELF BEFORE I'VE EVEN SUBMITTED...
ARE YOU REALLY GOING TO READ ALL THAT SCHOPENHAUER?
WELL, YEAH, I GUESS SO
CLANG!!!
BE CAREFUL: THAT STUFF MESSES WITH YOUR HEAD.
OH REALLY? THAT BAD?

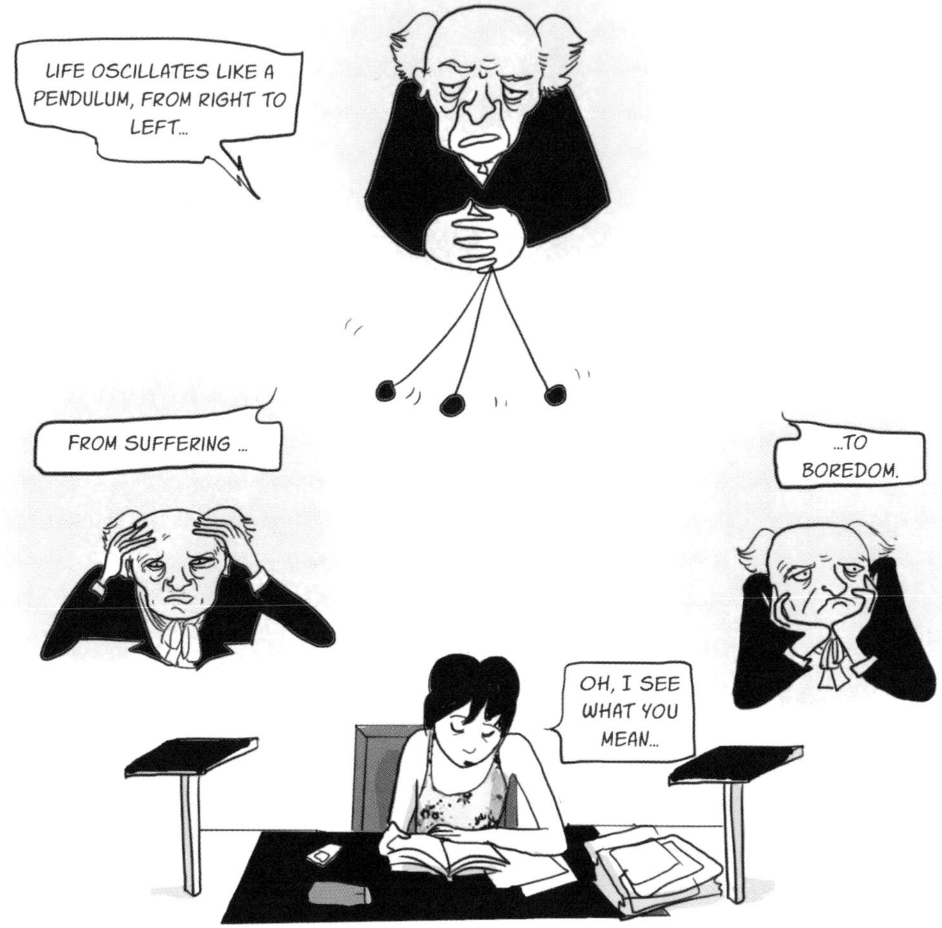
LIFE OSCILLATES LIKE A PENDULUM, FROM RIGHT TO LEFT...
FROM SUFFERING ...
...TO BOREDOM.
OH, I SEE WHAT YOU MEAN...

MAN EXISTS IN A STATE OF PAINFUL DESIRE FOR EVERYTHING HE LACKS...

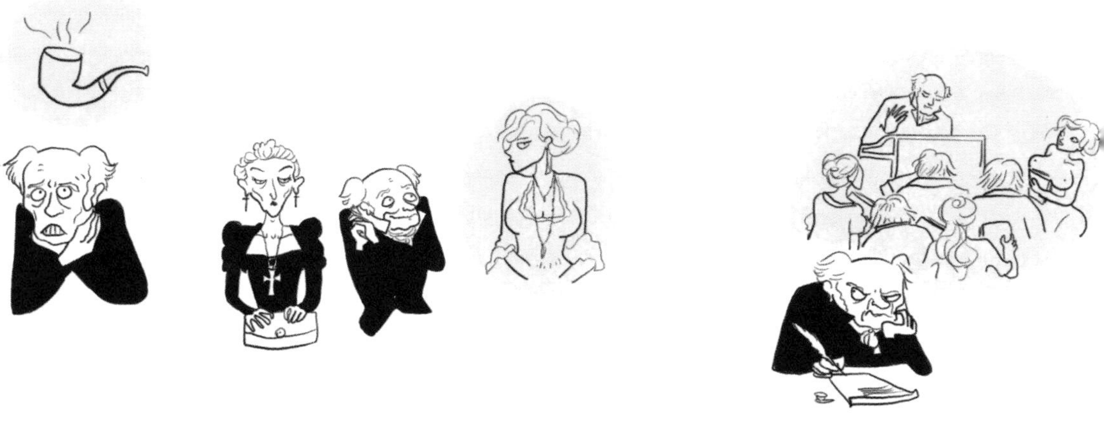

WHEN MAN OBTAINS WHAT ONCE HE DESIRED, THE LACK IS APPEASED, AND SATISFACTION LASTS FOR 3 MINUTES, THE TIME IT TAKES TO BECOME AWARE OF IT.

BUT ONCE THE PAIN OF ABSENCE IS APPEASED...

WE ARE CLUTCHED
BY A VOID...

WE'RE BORED.

JEANNE, YOU REALLY ARE AN EXTRAORDINARY PHD STUDENT.

HUMAN LIFE CONSISTS OF MOVING CONSTANTLY FROM DESIRE BORN OF ABSENCE, AND THE TEDIUM OF SATISFACTION.

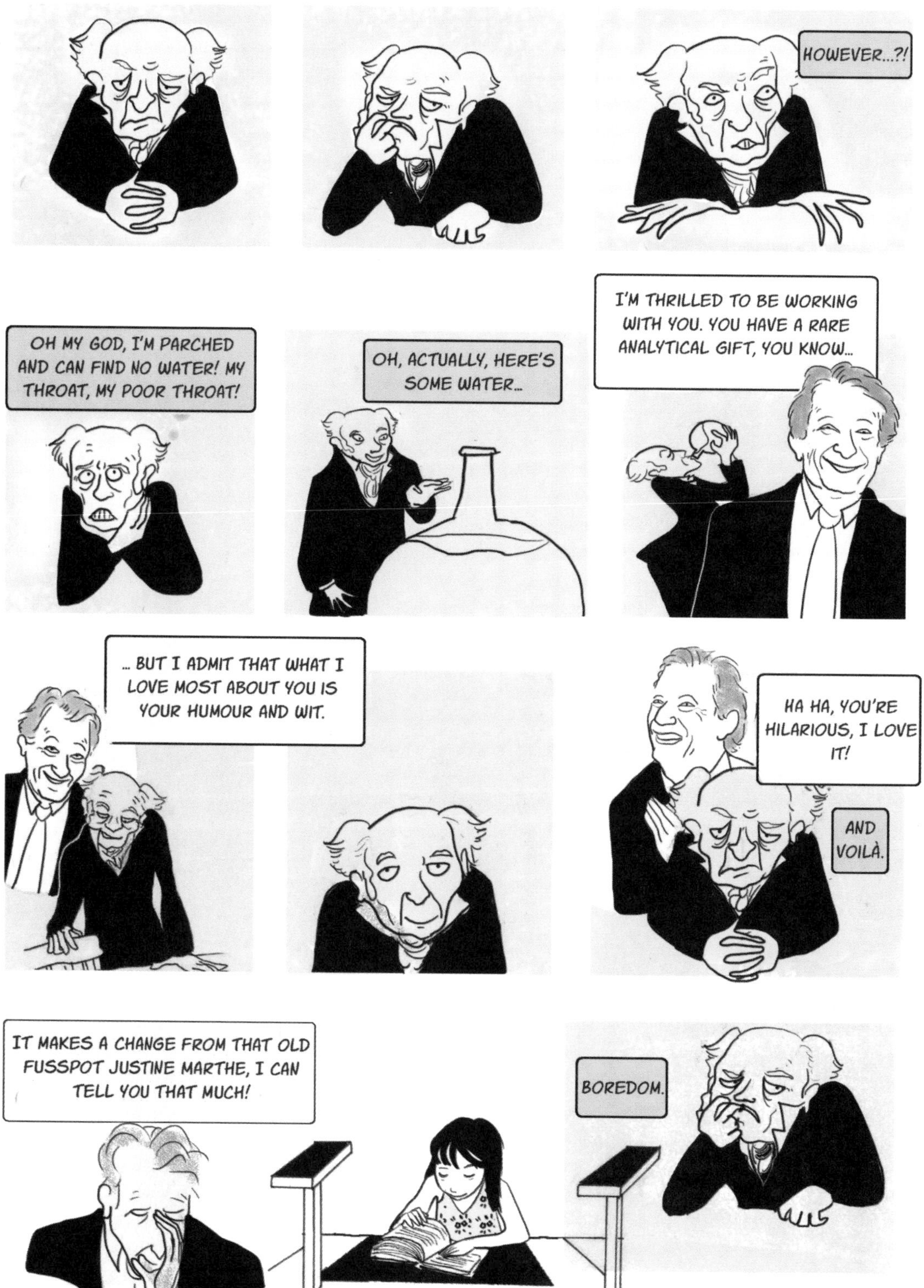
HOWEVER...?!
OH MY GOD, I'M PARCHED AND CAN FIND NO WATER! MY THROAT, MY POOR THROAT!
OH, ACTUALLY, HERE'S SOME WATER...
I'M THRILLED TO BE WORKING WITH YOU. YOU HAVE A RARE ANALYTICAL GIFT, YOU KNOW...
... BUT I ADMIT THAT WHAT I LOVE MOST ABOUT YOU IS YOUR HUMOUR AND WIT.
HA HA, YOU'RE HILARIOUS, I LOVE IT!
AND VOILÀ.
IT MAKES A CHANGE FROM THAT OLD FUSSPOT JUSTINE MARTHE, I CAN TELL YOU THAT MUCH!
BOREDOM.

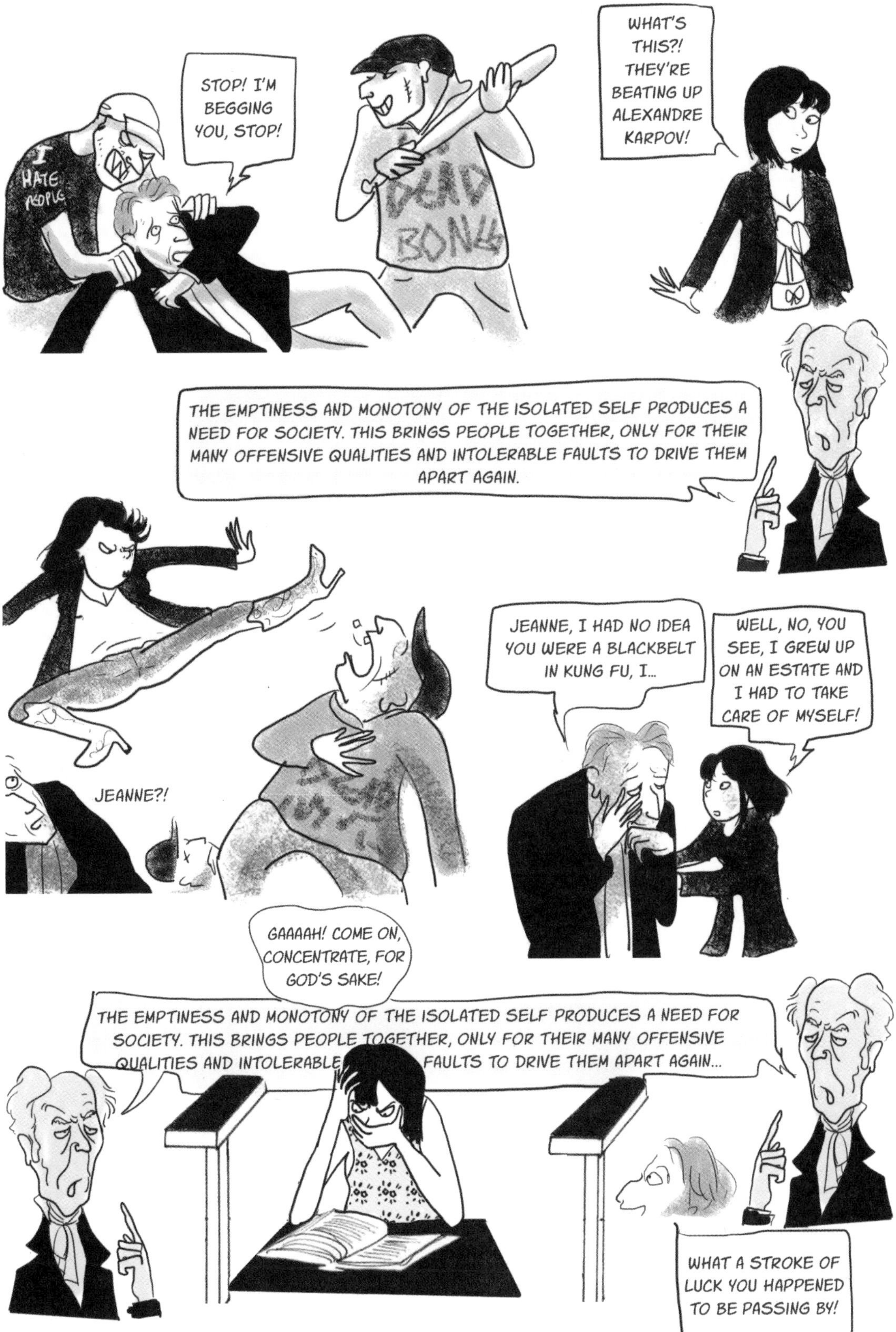
STOP! I'M BEGGING YOU, STOP!
I HATE PEOPLE
DEAD BONG
WHAT'S THIS?! THEY'RE BEATING UP ALEXANDRE KARPOV!
THE EMPTINESS AND MONOTONY OF THE ISOLATED SELF PRODUCES A NEED FOR SOCIETY. THIS BRINGS PEOPLE TOGETHER, ONLY FOR THEIR MANY OFFENSIVE QUALITIES AND INTOLERABLE FAULTS TO DRIVE THEM APART AGAIN.
JEANNE?!
JEANNE, I HAD NO IDEA YOU WERE A BLACKBELT IN KUNG FU, I...
WELL, NO, YOU SEE, I GREW UP ON AN ESTATE AND I HAD TO TAKE CARE OF MYSELF!
GAAAAH! COME ON, CONCENTRATE, FOR GOD'S SAKE!
THE EMPTINESS AND MONOTONY OF THE ISOLATED SELF PRODUCES A NEED FOR SOCIETY. THIS BRINGS PEOPLE TOGETHER, ONLY FOR THEIR MANY OFFENSIVE QUALITIES AND INTOLERABLE FAULTS TO DRIVE THEM APART AGAIN...
WHAT A STROKE OF LUCK YOU HAPPENED TO BE PASSING BY!

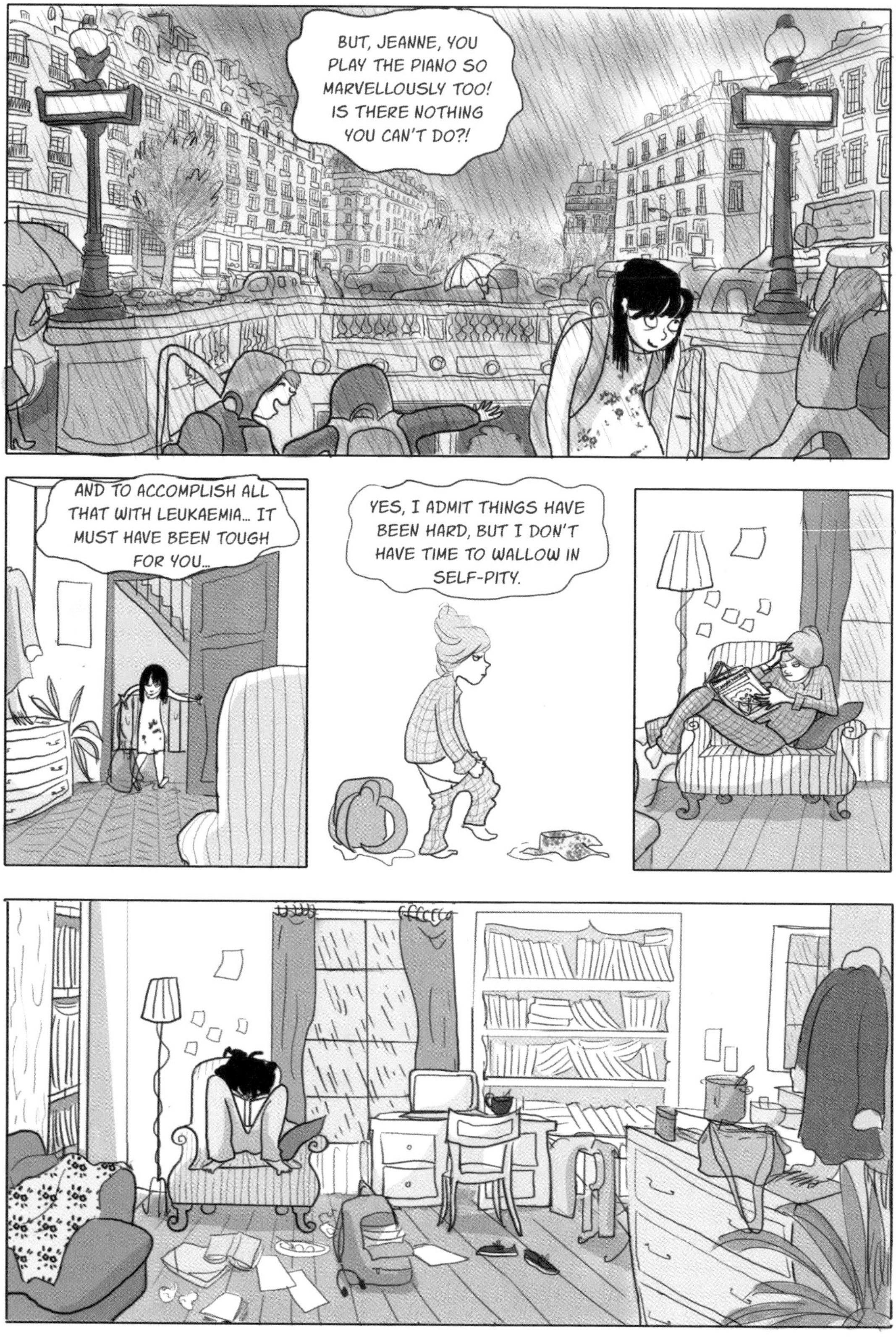
BUT, JEANNE, YOU PLAY THE PIANO SO MARVELLOUSLY TOO! IS THERE NOTHING YOU CAN'T DO?!
AND TO ACCOMPLISH ALL THAT WITH LEUKAEMIA... IT MUST HAVE BEEN TOUGH FOR YOU...
YES, I ADMIT THINGS HAVE BEEN HARD, BUT I DON'T HAVE TIME TO WALLOW IN SELF-PITY.

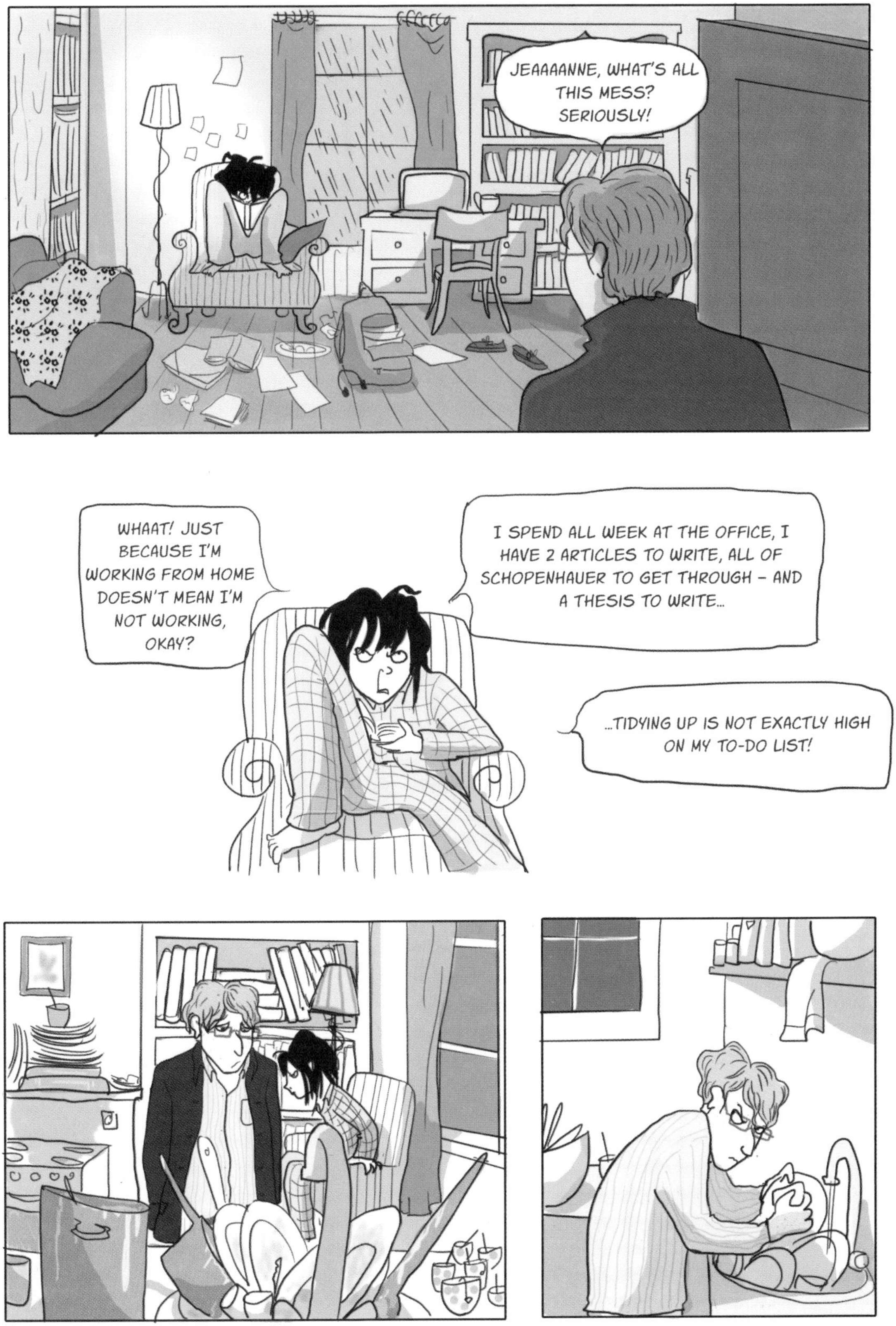
JEAAAANNE, WHAT'S ALL THIS MESS? SERIOUSLY!
WHAAT! JUST BECAUSE I'M WORKING FROM HOME DOESN'T MEAN I'M NOT WORKING, OKAY?
I SPEND ALL WEEK AT THE OFFICE, I HAVE 2 ARTICLES TO WRITE, ALL OF SCHOPENHAUER TO GET THROUGH – AND A THESIS TO WRITE...
...TIDYING UP IS NOT EXACTLY HIGH ON MY TO-DO LIST!

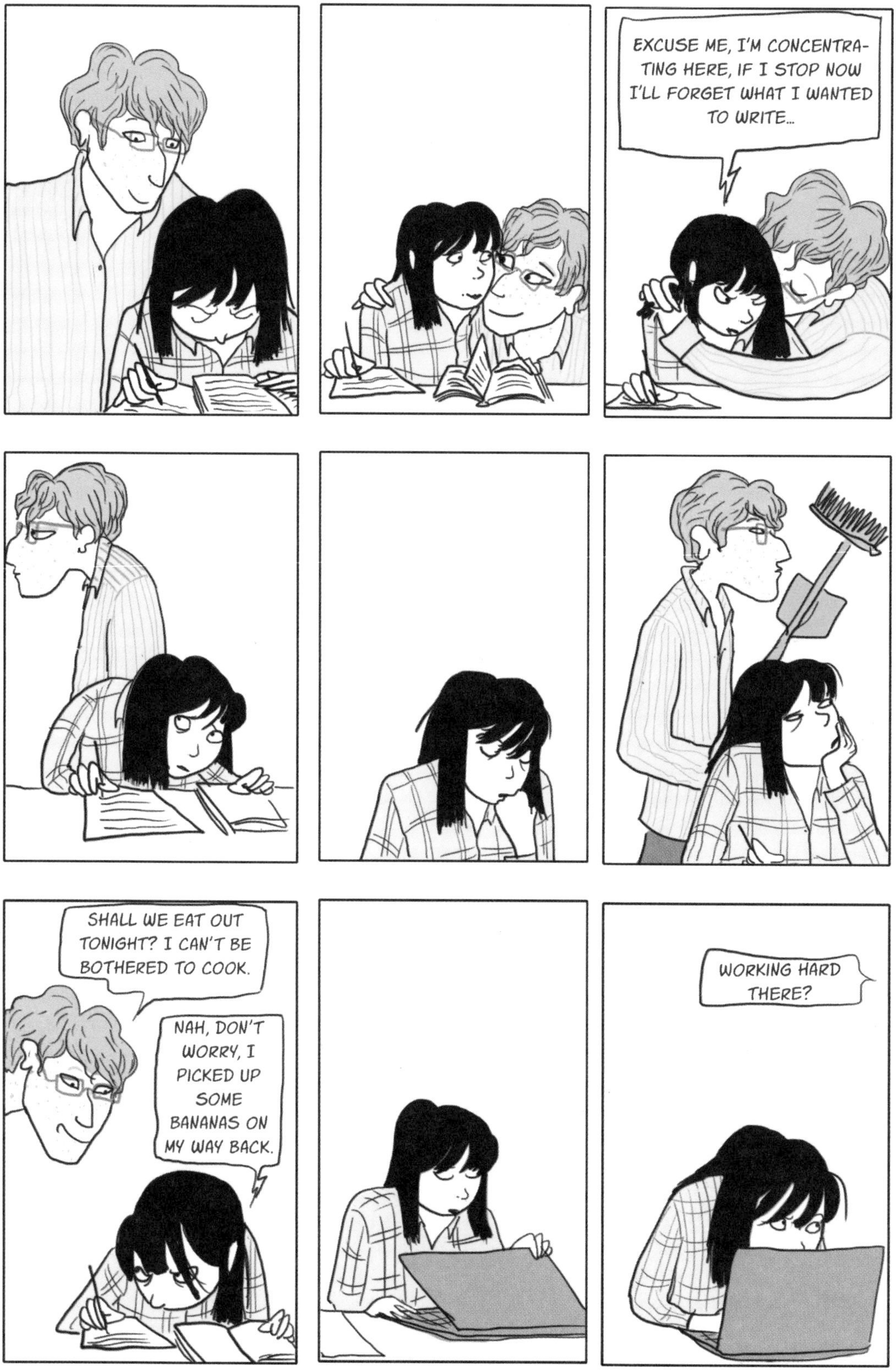
EXCUSE ME, I'M CONCENTRATING HERE, IF I STOP NOW I'LL FORGET WHAT I WANTED TO WRITE...
SHALL WE EAT OUT TONIGHT? I CAN'T BE BOTHERED TO COOK.
NAH, DON'T WORRY, I PICKED UP SOME BANANAS ON MY WAY BACK.
WORKING HARD THERE?

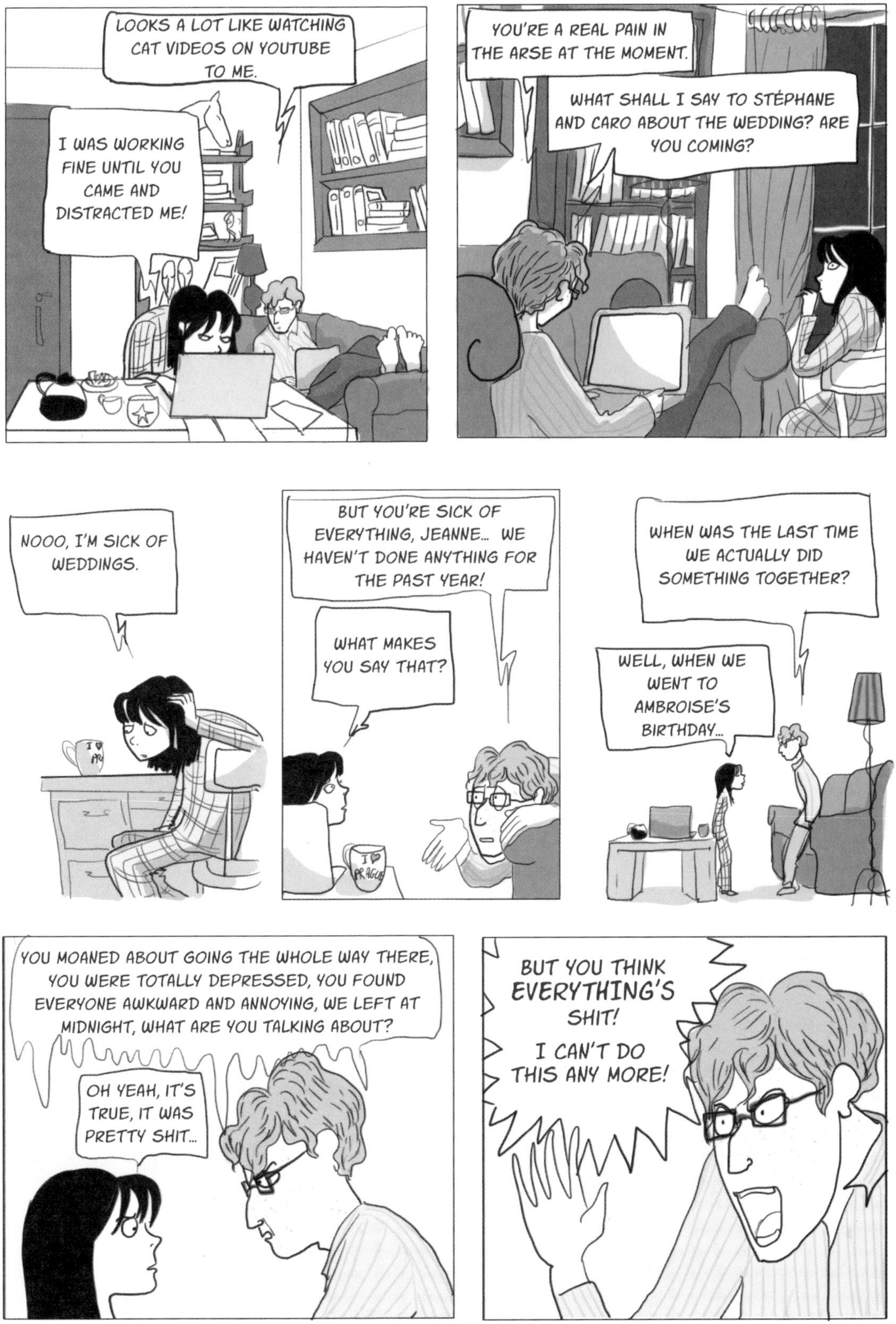
LOOKS A LOT LIKE WATCHING CAT VIDEOS ON YOUTUBE TO ME.
I WAS WORKING FINE UNTIL YOU CAME AND DISTRACTED ME!
YOU'RE A REAL PAIN IN THE ARSE AT THE MOMENT.
WHAT SHALL I SAY TO STÉPHANE AND CARO ABOUT THE WEDDING? ARE YOU COMING?
NOOO, I'M SICK OF WEDDINGS.
BUT YOU'RE SICK OF EVERYTHING, JEANNE... WE HAVEN'T DONE ANYTHING FOR THE PAST YEAR!
WHAT MAKES YOU SAY THAT?
WHEN WAS THE LAST TIME WE ACTUALLY DID SOMETHING TOGETHER?
WELL, WHEN WE WENT TO AMBROISE'S BIRTHDAY...
YOU MOANED ABOUT GOING THE WHOLE WAY THERE, YOU WERE TOTALLY DEPRESSED, YOU FOUND EVERYONE AWKWARD AND ANNOYING, WE LEFT AT MIDNIGHT, WHAT ARE YOU TALKING ABOUT?
OH YEAH, IT'S TRUE, IT WAS PRETTY SHIT...
BUT YOU THINK EVERYTHING'S SHIT!
I CAN'T DO THIS ANY MORE!

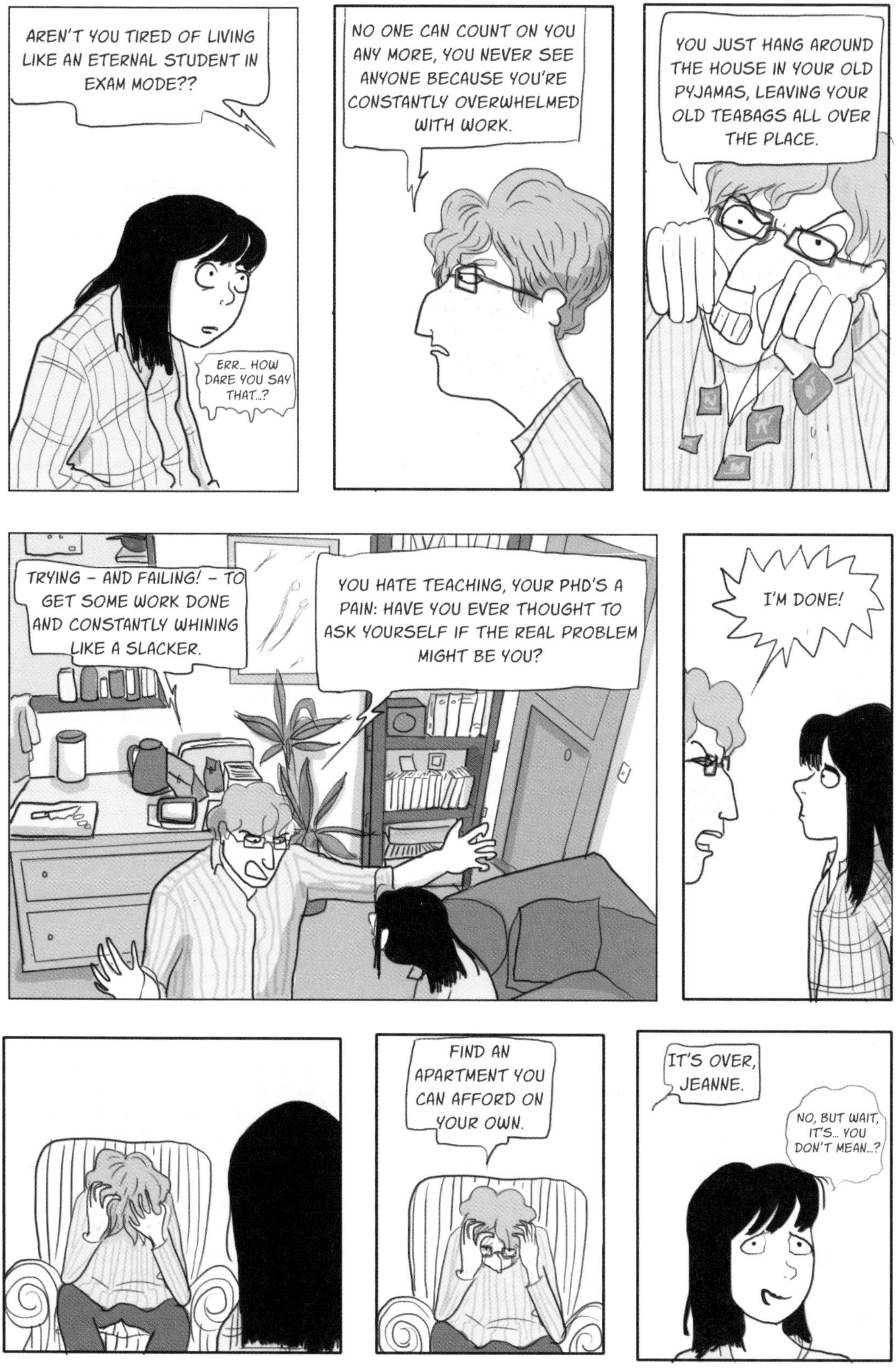
AREN'T YOU TIRED OF LIVING LIKE AN ETERNAL STUDENT IN EXAM MODE??
ERR... HOW DARE YOU SAY THAT...?
NO ONE CAN COUNT ON YOU ANY MORE, YOU NEVER SEE ANYONE BECAUSE YOU'RE CONSTANTLY OVERWHELMED WITH WORK.
YOU JUST HANG AROUND THE HOUSE IN YOUR OLD PYJAMAS, LEAVING YOUR OLD TEABAGS ALL OVER THE PLACE.
TRYING – AND FAILING! – TO GET SOME WORK DONE AND CONSTANTLY WHINING LIKE A SLACKER.
YOU HATE TEACHING, YOUR PHD'S A PAIN: HAVE YOU EVER THOUGHT TO ASK YOURSELF IF THE REAL PROBLEM MIGHT BE YOU?
I'M DONE!
FIND AN APARTMENT YOU CAN AFFORD ON YOUR OWN.
IT'S OVER, JEANNE.
NO, BUT WAIT, IT'S... YOU DON'T MEAN...?

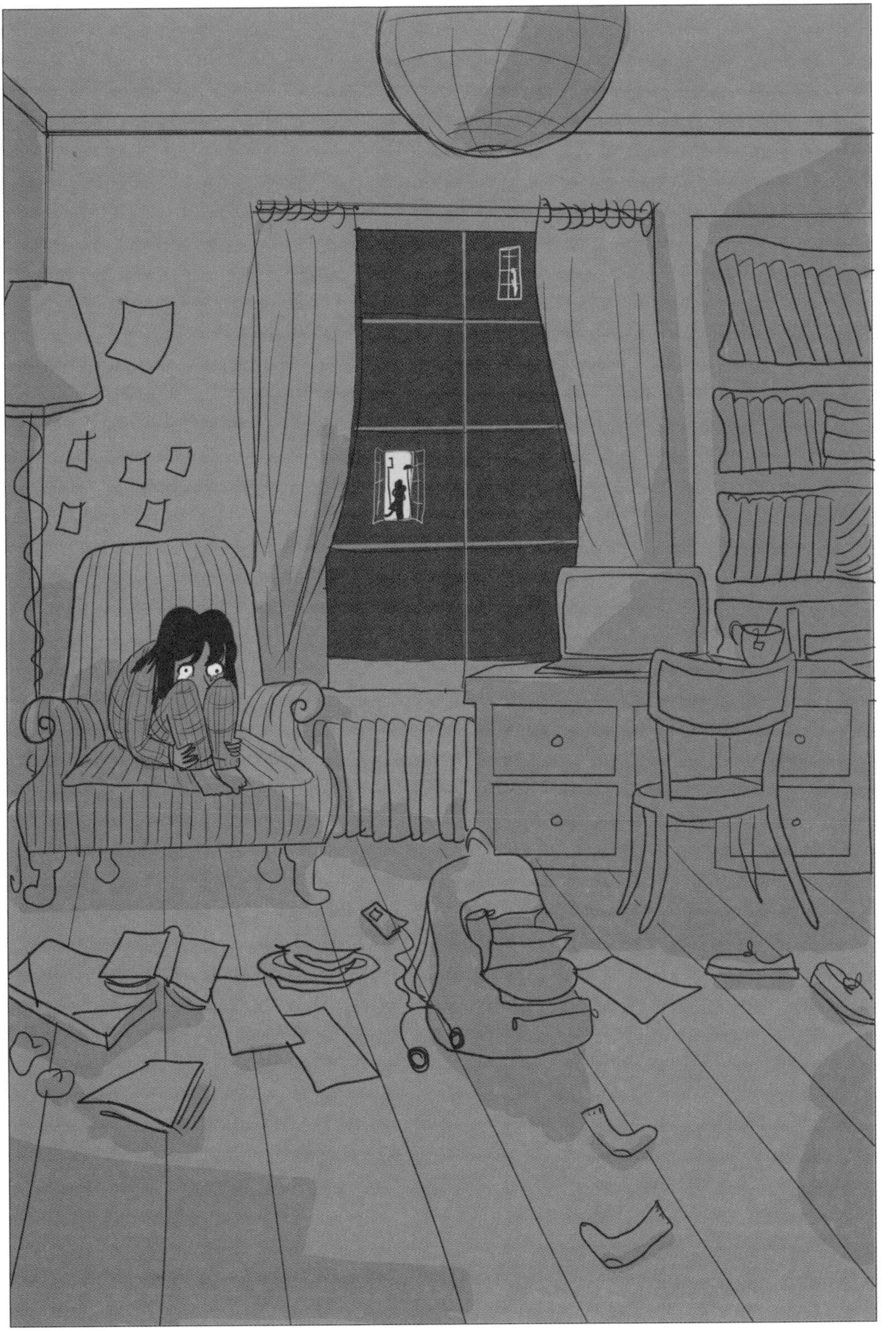

2 YEARS LATER...

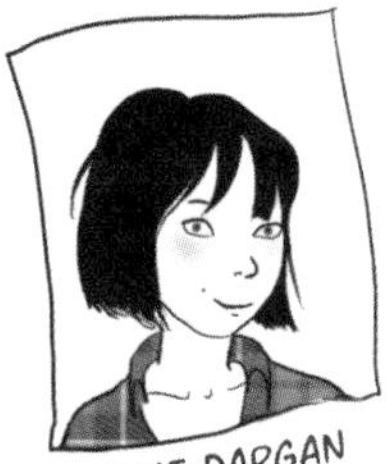

JEANNE DARGAN
2008

Surname: .... DARGAN
First name: .... JEANNE
Enrollment: .... 1st YEAR
Supervisor: .... A. KARPOV
Funding source: .... NONE

Thesis Subject: 'The Labyrinthine Motif in the Parable of the Law in Kafka's *The Trial*.'

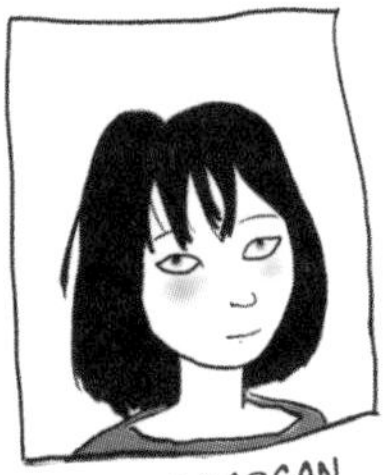

JEANNE DARGAN
2009

Surname: .... DARGAN
First name: .... JEANNE
Enrollment: .... 2nd YEAR
Supervisor: .... A. KARPOV
Funding source: .... NONE

Thesis Subject: .... Revised ....

'The Concept of the Labyrinth in the Parable of the Law in Kafka's *The Trial*.'

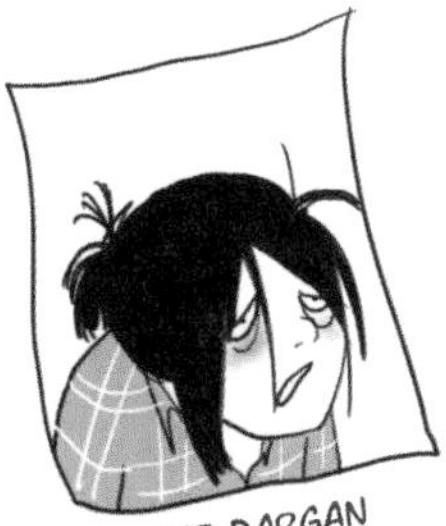

JEANNE DARGAN
2010

Surname: .... DARGAN
First name: .... JEANNE
Enrollment: .... 3rd YEAR
Supervisor: .... A. KARPOV
Funding source: .... NONE

Thesis Subject: .... Revised ....

'The Labyrinthine Concept of a Motif in the Parable of the Law in Kafka's *The Trial*'.

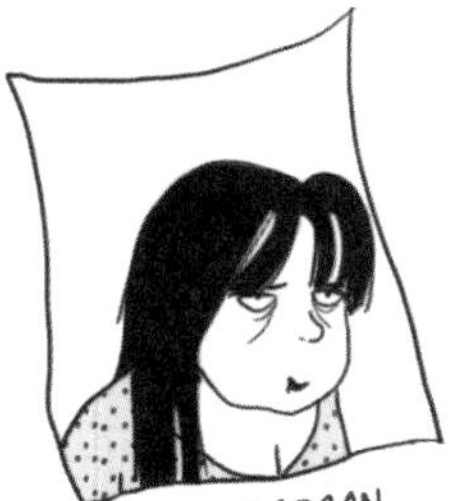

JEANNE DARGAN
2011

Surname: .... DARGAN
First name: .... JEANNE
Enrollment: .... 4th YEAR
Supervisor: .... A. KARPOV
Funding source: .... NONE

Thesis Subject: ... Reverted to original subject ...

'The Labyrinthine Motif in the Parable of the Law in Kafka's *The Trial*.'

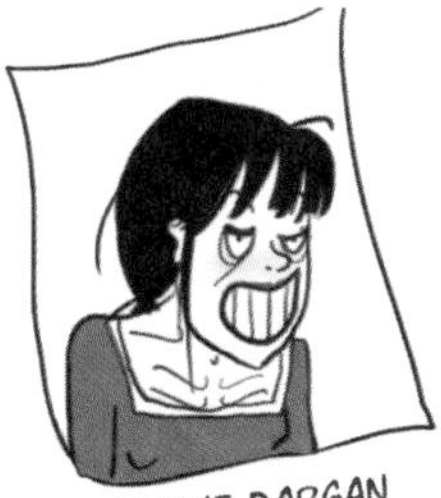

JEANNE DARGAN
2012

Surname: .... DARGAN
First name: .... JEANNE
Enrollment: .... 5th YEAR
Supervisor: .... A. KARPOV
Funding source: .... NONE

Thesis Subject: .... Revised ....

'Disorientation, Solitude and Depression: Going Nowhere in the Works of Kafka.'

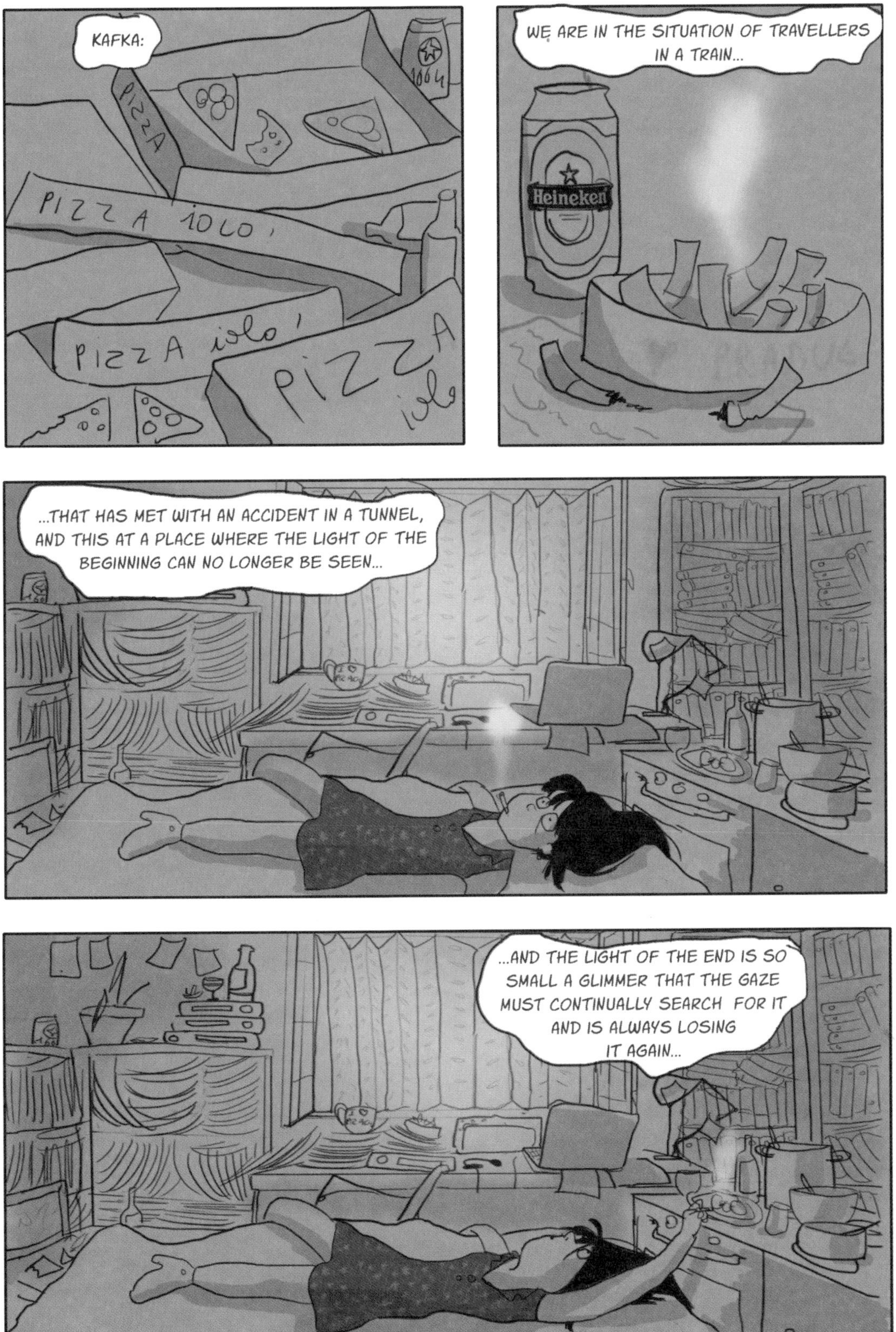
KAFKA:
WE ARE IN THE SITUATION OF TRAVELLERS IN A TRAIN...
Heineken
...THAT HAS MET WITH AN ACCIDENT IN A TUNNEL, AND THIS AT A PLACE WHERE THE LIGHT OF THE BEGINNING CAN NO LONGER BE SEEN...
...AND THE LIGHT OF THE END IS SO SMALL A GLIMMER THAT THE GAZE MUST CONTINUALLY SEARCH FOR IT AND IS ALWAYS LOSING IT AGAIN...

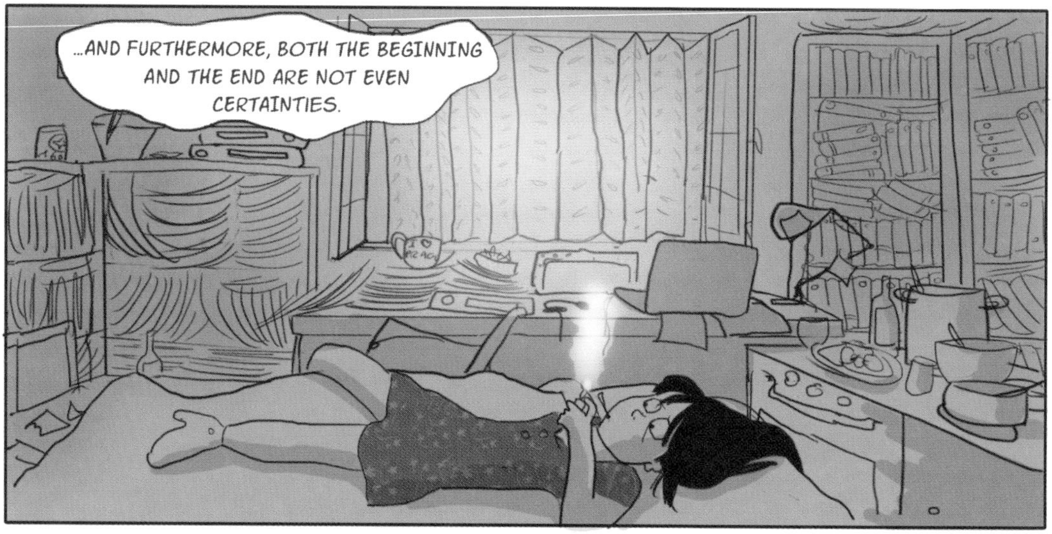
...AND FURTHERMORE, BOTH THE BEGINNING AND THE END ARE NOT EVEN CERTAINTIES.

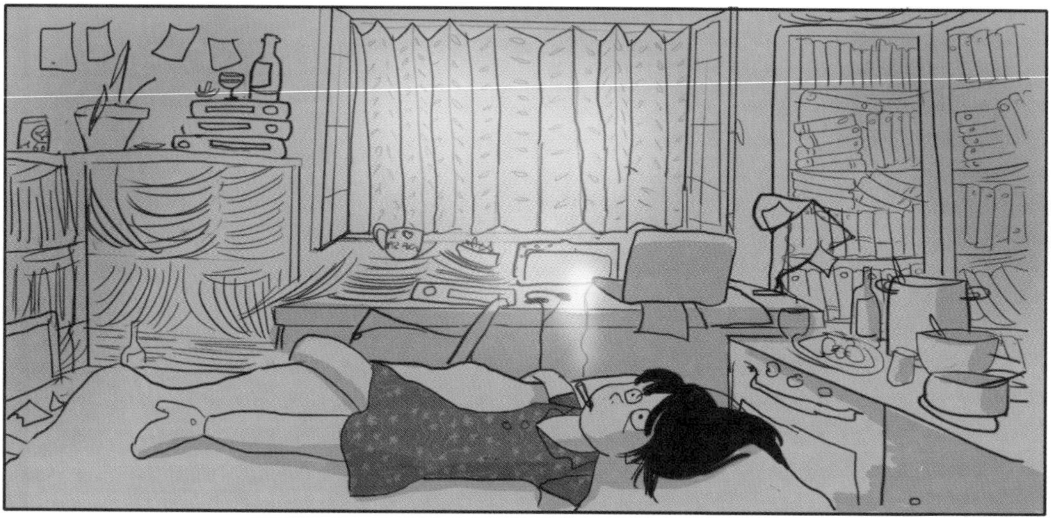

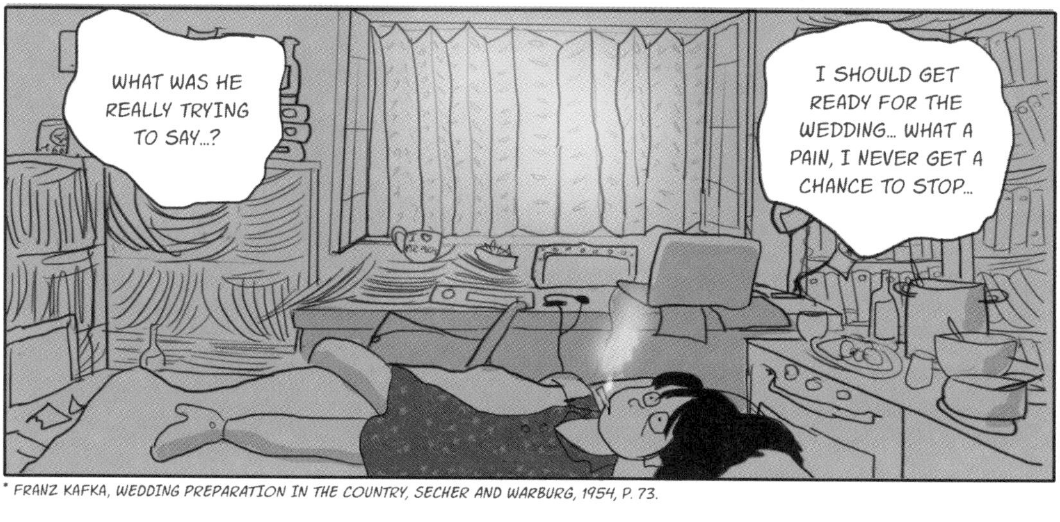
WHAT WAS HE REALLY TRYING TO SAY...?
I SHOULD GET READY FOR THE WEDDING... WHAT A PAIN, I NEVER GET A CHANCE TO STOP...

* FRANZ KAFKA, WEDDING PREPARATION IN THE COUNTRY, SECHER AND WARBURG, 1954, P. 73.

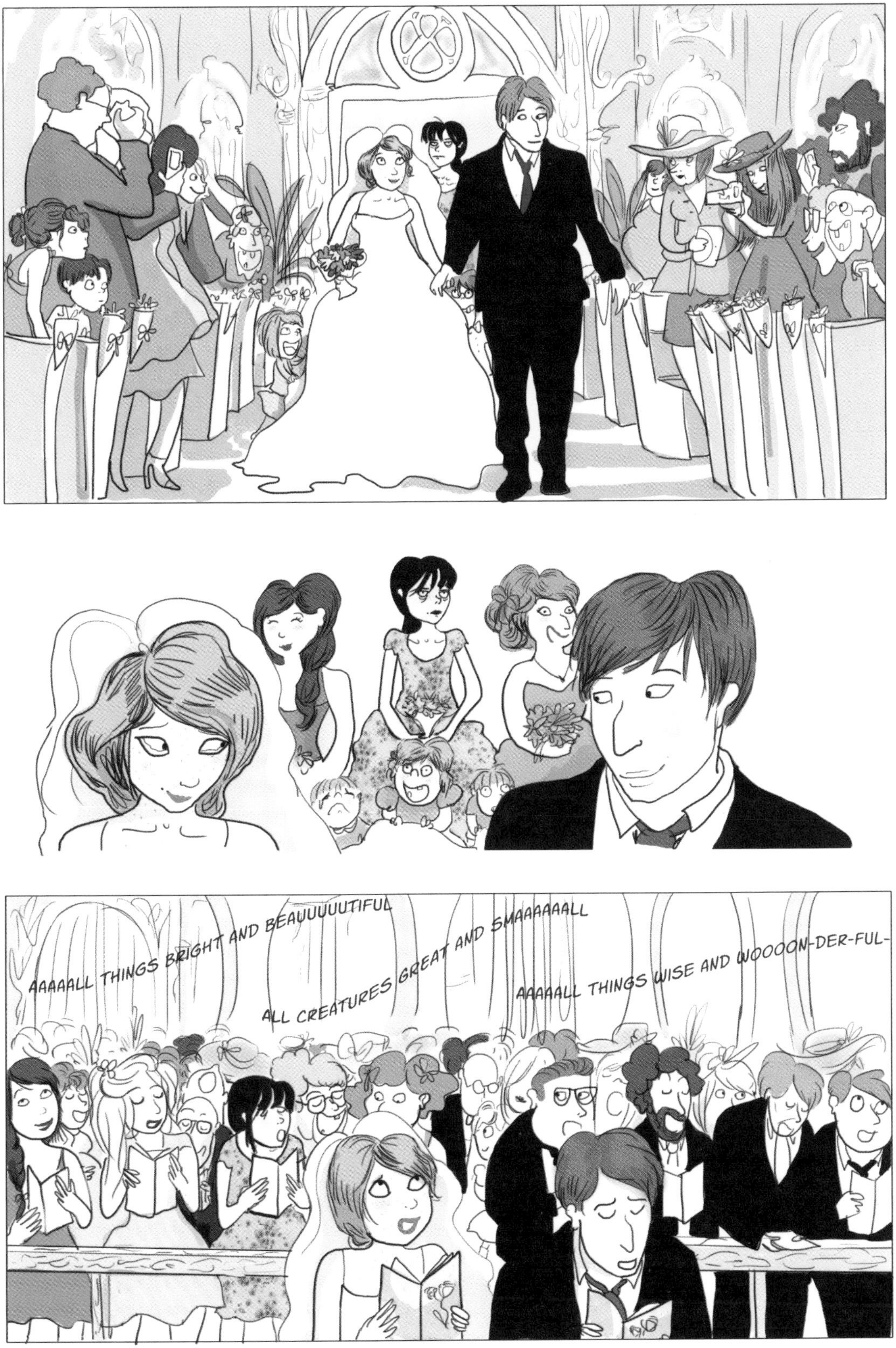
AAAAALL THINGS BRIGHT AND BEAUUUUUTIFUL
ALL CREATURES GREAT AND SMAAAAAALL
AAAAALL THINGS WISE AND WOOOON-DER-FUL-

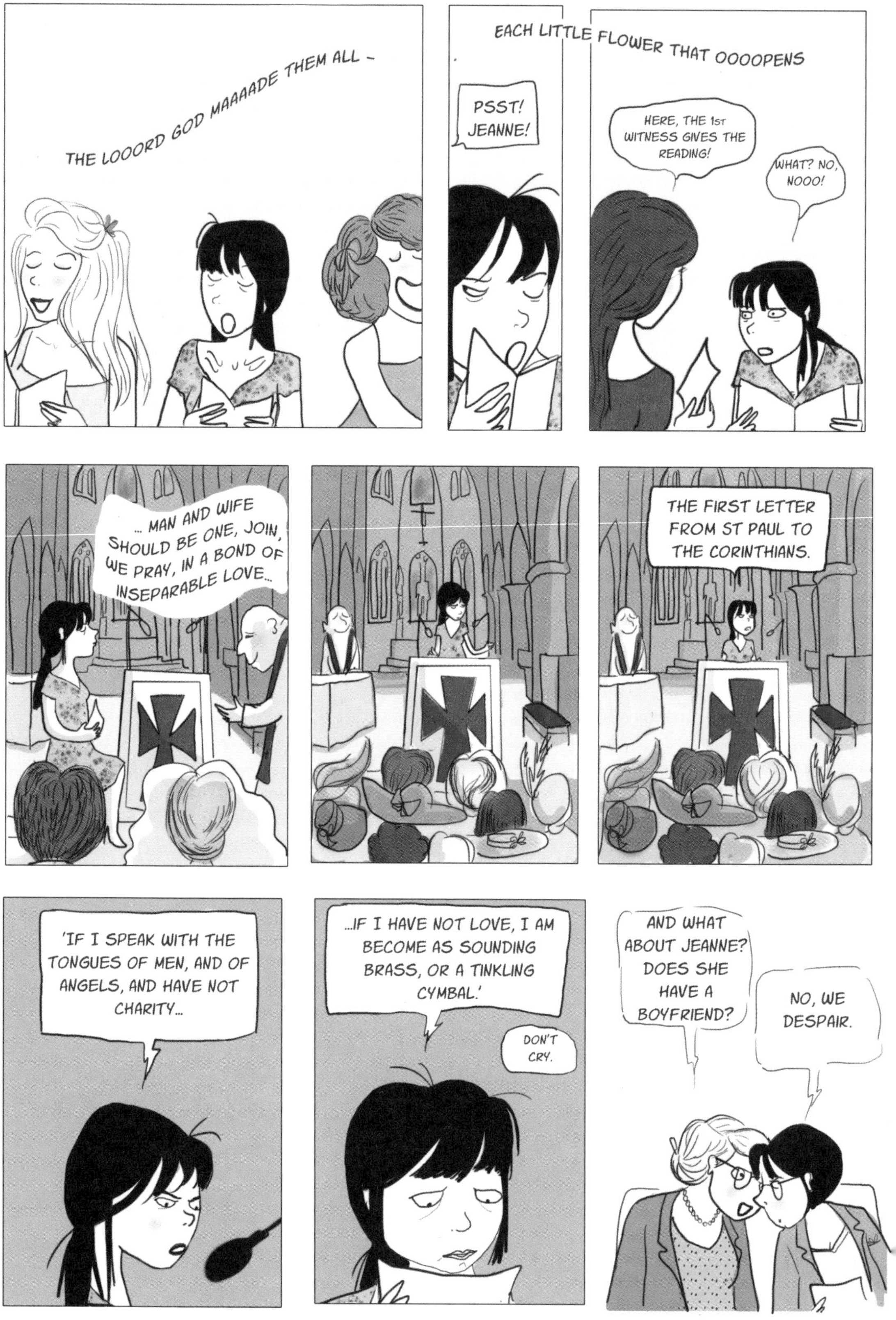
THE LOOORD GOD MAAAADE THEM ALL –
EACH LITTLE FLOWER THAT OOOOPENS
PSST! JEANNE!
HERE, THE 1ST WITNESS GIVES THE READING!
WHAT? NO, NOOO!
... MAN AND WIFE SHOULD BE ONE, JOIN, WE PRAY, IN A BOND OF INSEPARABLE LOVE...
THE FIRST LETTER FROM ST PAUL TO THE CORINTHIANS.
'IF I SPEAK WITH THE TONGUES OF MEN, AND OF ANGELS, AND HAVE NOT CHARITY...
...IF I HAVE NOT LOVE, I AM BECOME AS SOUNDING BRASS, OR A TINKLING CYMBAL.'
DON'T CRY.
AND WHAT ABOUT JEANNE? DOES SHE HAVE A BOYFRIEND?
NO, WE DESPAIR.

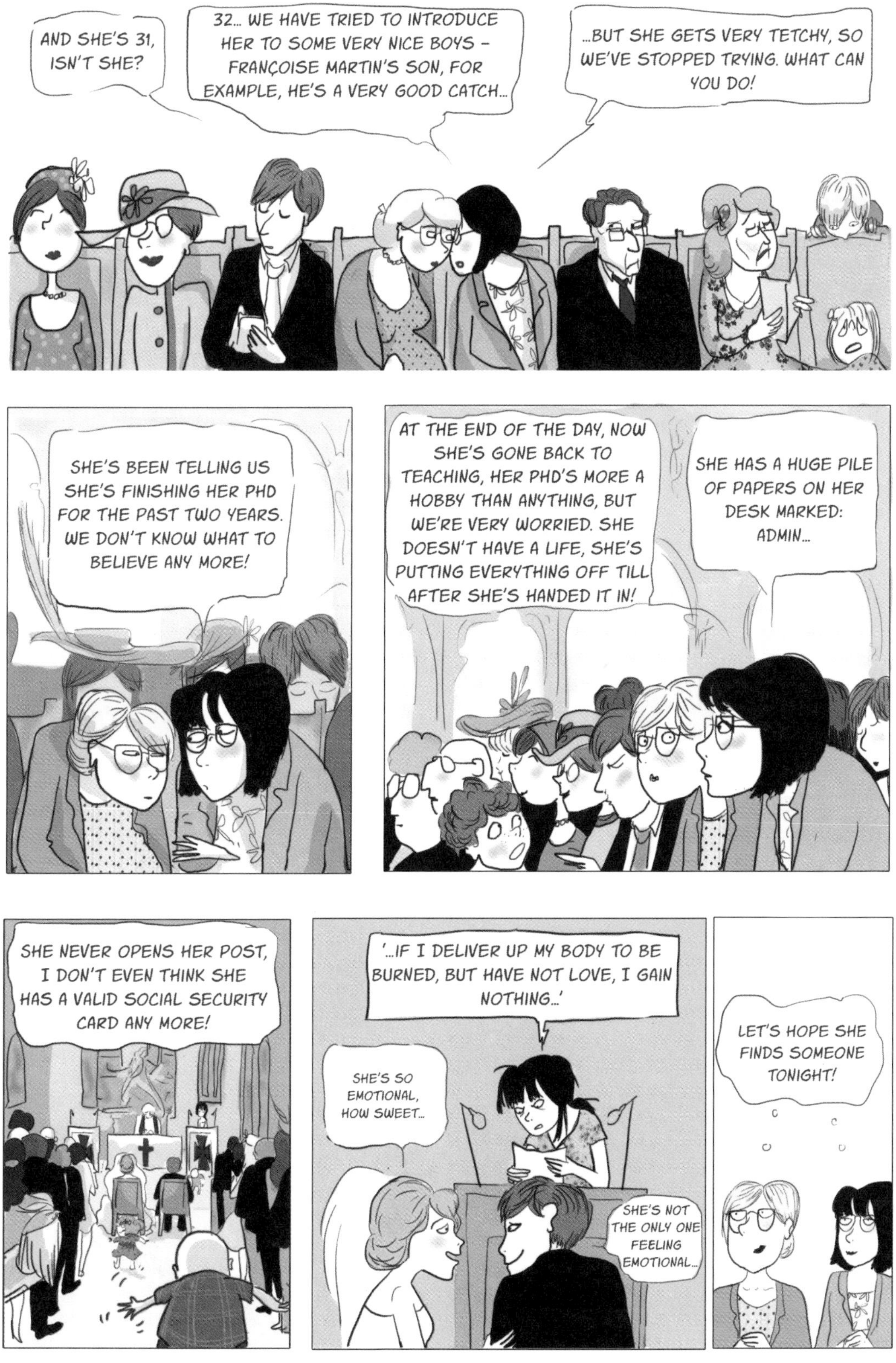
AND SHE'S 31, ISN'T SHE?
32... WE HAVE TRIED TO INTRODUCE HER TO SOME VERY NICE BOYS – FRANÇOISE MARTIN'S SON, FOR EXAMPLE, HE'S A VERY GOOD CATCH...
...BUT SHE GETS VERY TETCHY, SO WE'VE STOPPED TRYING. WHAT CAN YOU DO!
SHE'S BEEN TELLING US SHE'S FINISHING HER PHD FOR THE PAST TWO YEARS. WE DON'T KNOW WHAT TO BELIEVE ANY MORE!
AT THE END OF THE DAY, NOW SHE'S GONE BACK TO TEACHING, HER PHD'S MORE A HOBBY THAN ANYTHING, BUT WE'RE VERY WORRIED. SHE DOESN'T HAVE A LIFE, SHE'S PUTTING EVERYTHING OFF TILL AFTER SHE'S HANDED IT IN!
SHE HAS A HUGE PILE OF PAPERS ON HER DESK MARKED: ADMIN...
SHE NEVER OPENS HER POST, I DON'T EVEN THINK SHE HAS A VALID SOCIAL SECURITY CARD ANY MORE!
'...IF I DELIVER UP MY BODY TO BE BURNED, BUT HAVE NOT LOVE, I GAIN NOTHING...'
SHE'S SO EMOTIONAL, HOW SWEET...
SHE'S NOT THE ONLY ONE FEELING EMOTIONAL...
LET'S HOPE SHE FINDS SOMEONE TONIGHT!

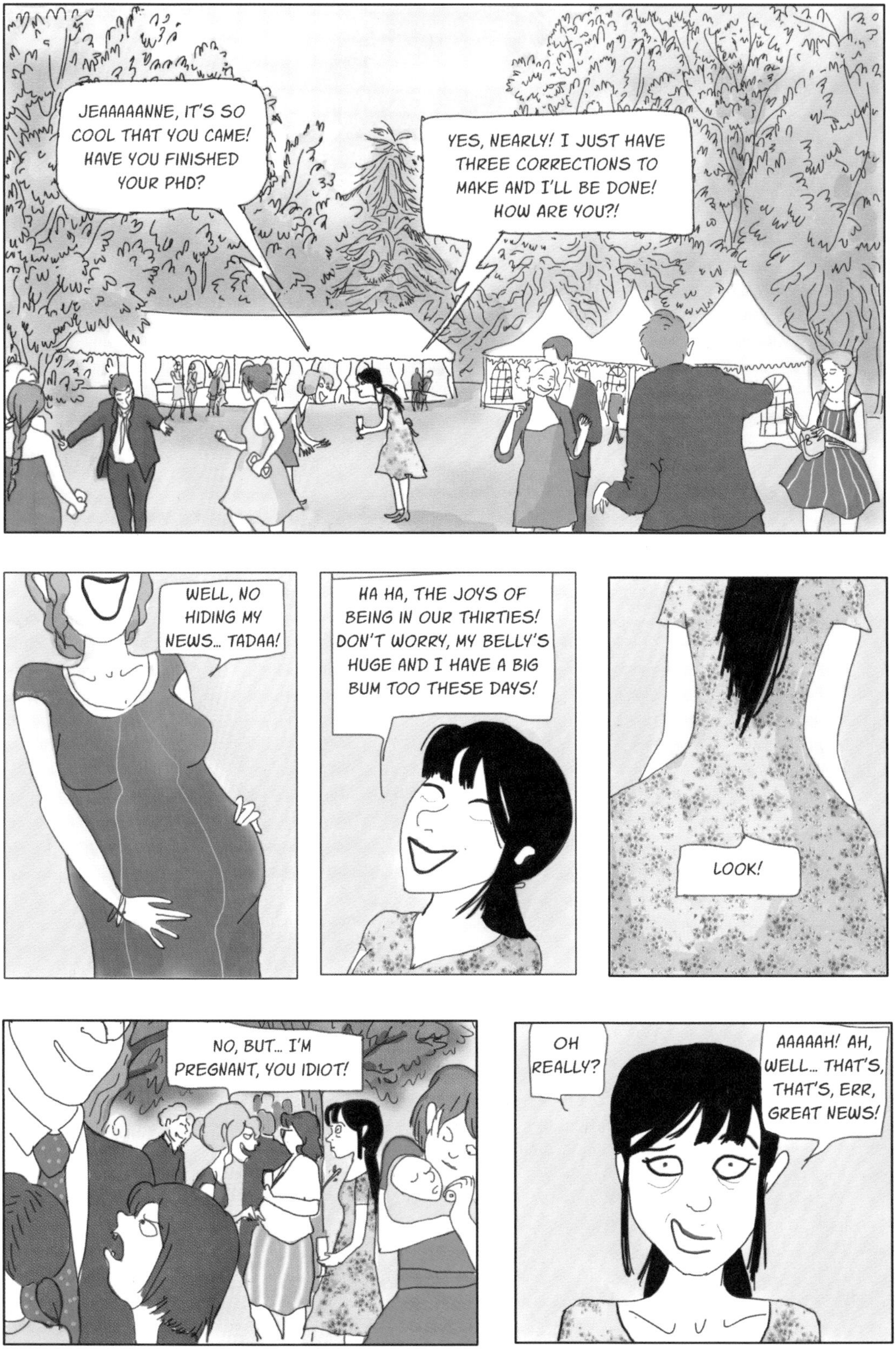

JEAAAAAANNE, IT'S SO COOL THAT YOU CAME! HAVE YOU FINISHED YOUR PHD?
YES, NEARLY! I JUST HAVE THREE CORRECTIONS TO MAKE AND I'LL BE DONE! HOW ARE YOU?!
WELL, NO HIDING MY NEWS... TADAA!
HA HA, THE JOYS OF BEING IN OUR THIRTIES! DON'T WORRY, MY BELLY'S HUGE AND I HAVE A BIG BUM TOO THESE DAYS!
LOOK!
NO, BUT... I'M PREGNANT, YOU IDIOT!
OH REALLY?
AAAAAH! AH, WELL... THAT'S, THAT'S, ERR, GREAT NEWS!

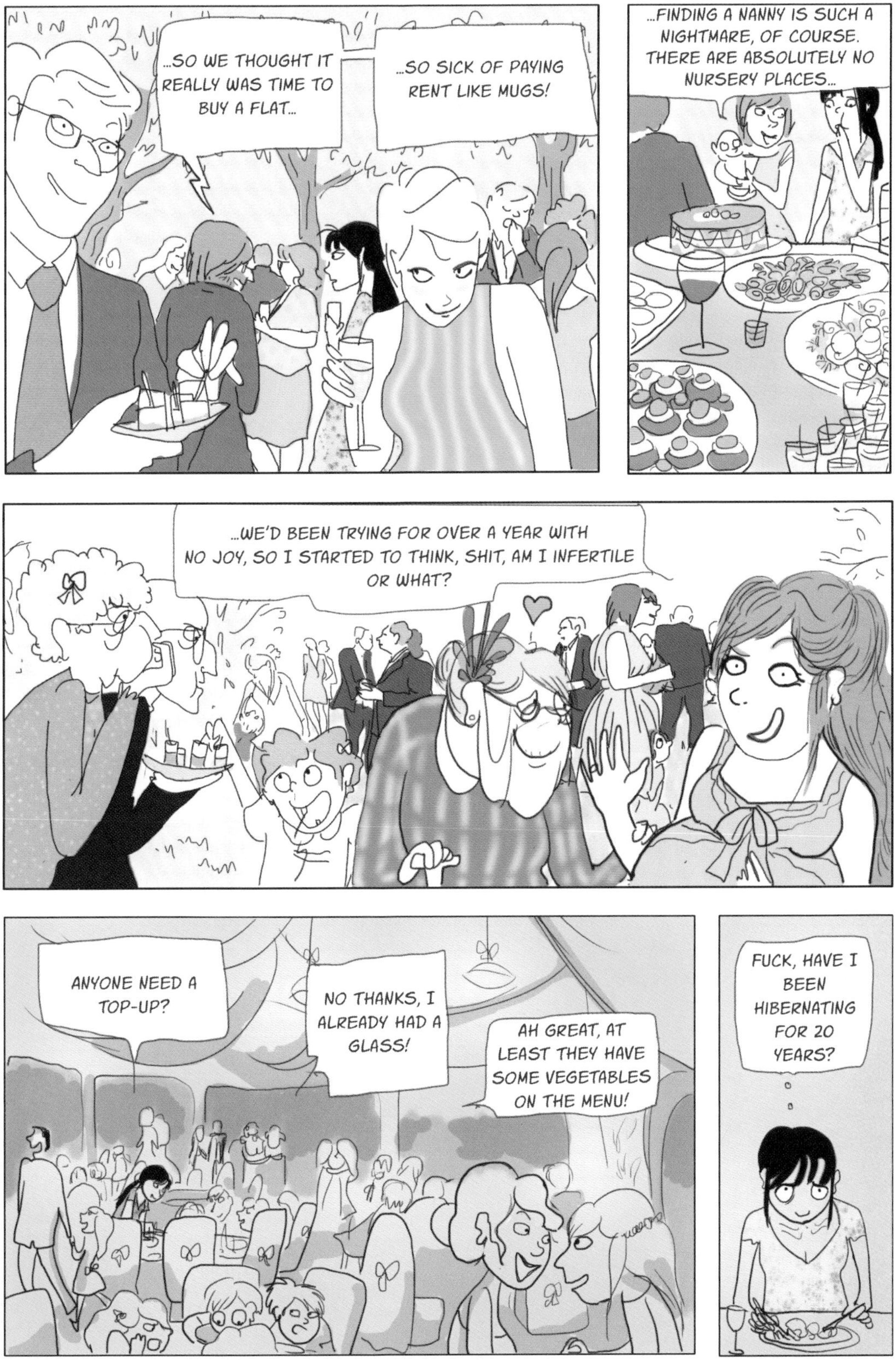
...SO WE THOUGHT IT REALLY WAS TIME TO BUY A FLAT...
...SO SICK OF PAYING RENT LIKE MUGS!
...FINDING A NANNY IS SUCH A NIGHTMARE, OF COURSE. THERE ARE ABSOLUTELY NO NURSERY PLACES...
...WE'D BEEN TRYING FOR OVER A YEAR WITH NO JOY, SO I STARTED TO THINK, SHIT, AM I INFERTILE OR WHAT?
ANYONE NEED A TOP-UP?
NO THANKS, I ALREADY HAD A GLASS!
AH GREAT, AT LEAST THEY HAVE SOME VEGETABLES ON THE MENU!
FUCK, HAVE I BEEN HIBERNATING FOR 20 YEARS?

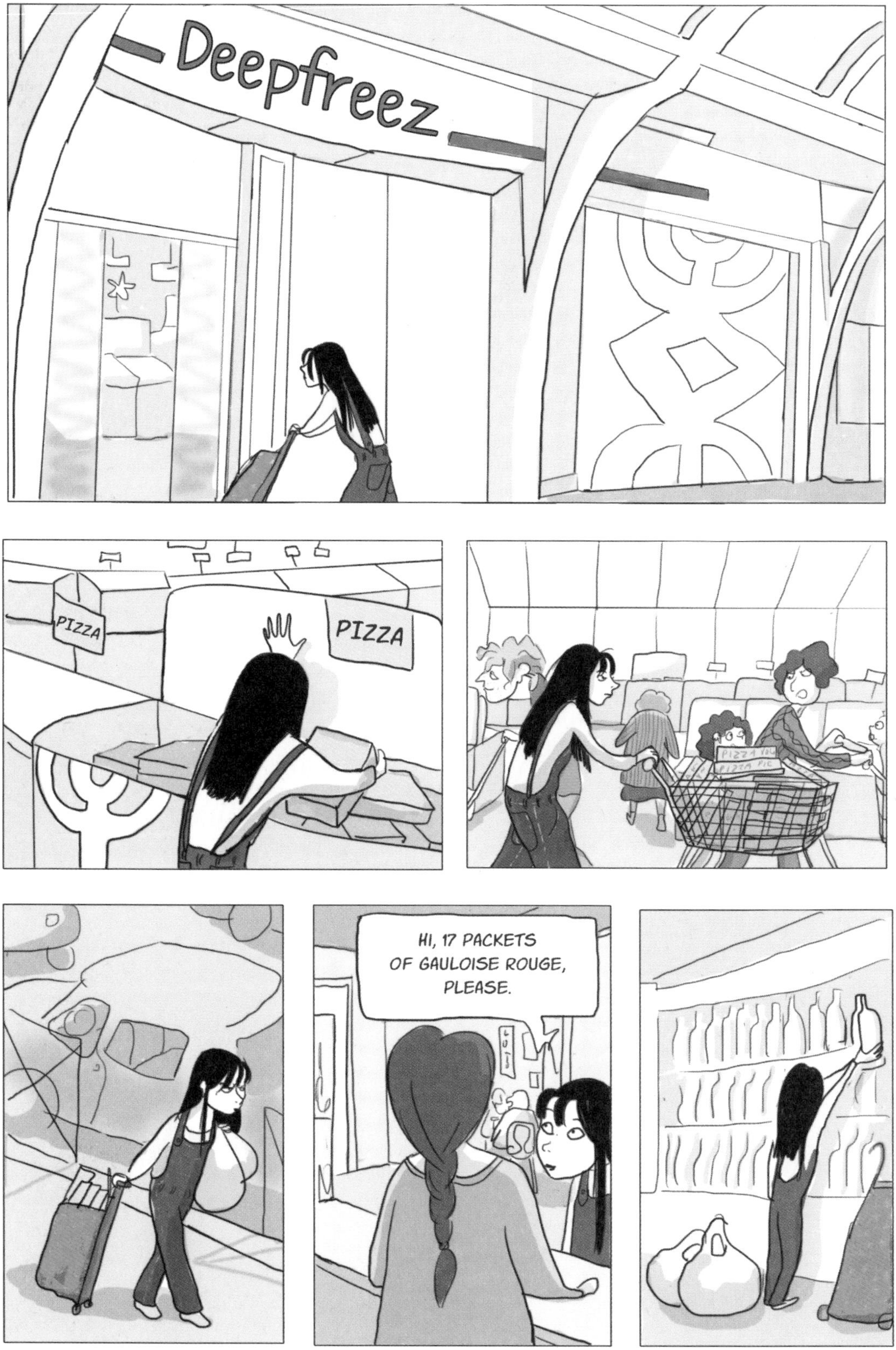
Deepfreez
PIZZA
PIZZA
HI, 17 PACKETS OF GAULOISE ROUGE, PLEASE.

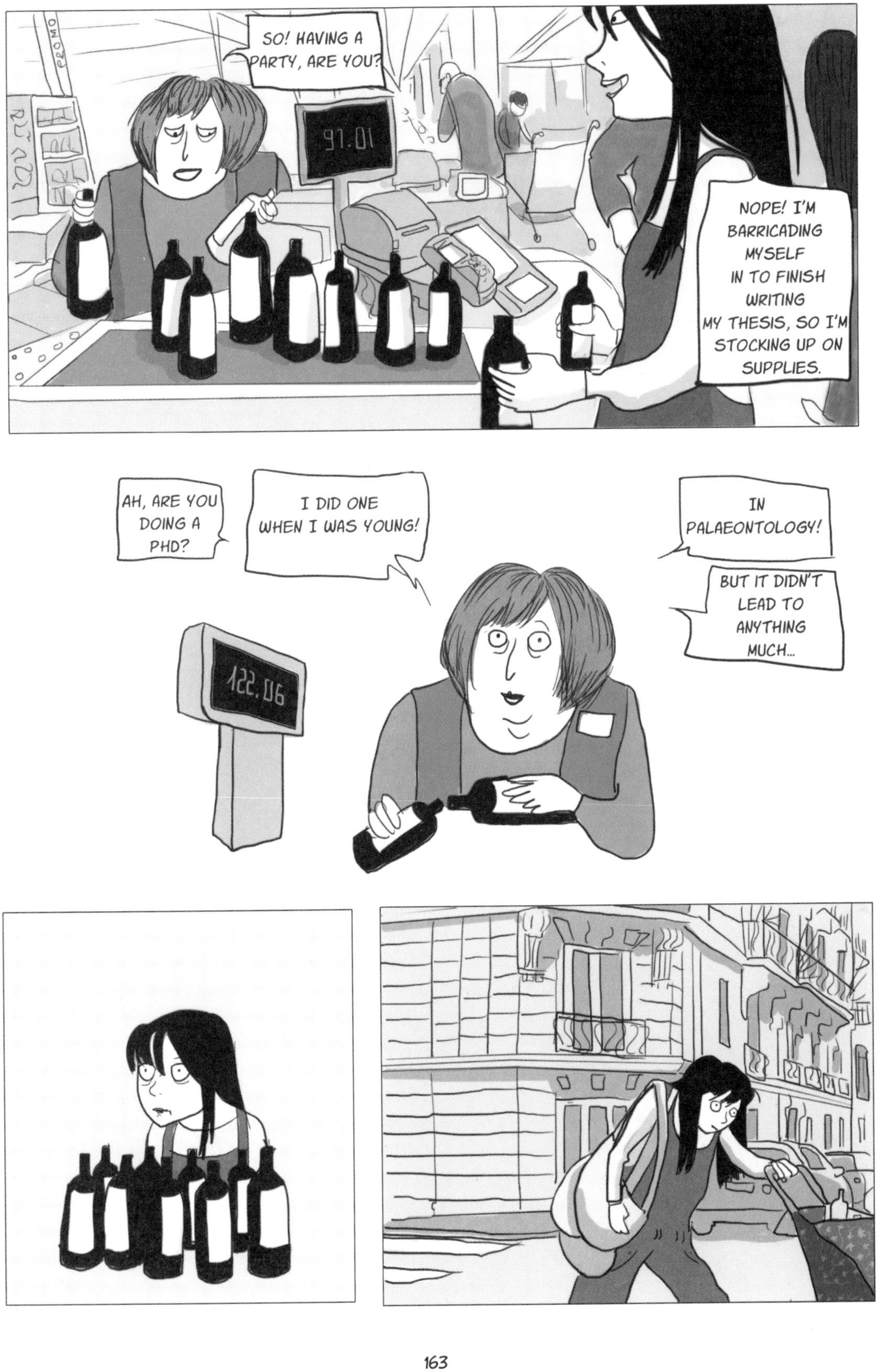
PROMO
SO! HAVING A PARTY, ARE YOU?
NOPE! I'M BARRICADING MYSELF IN TO FINISH WRITING MY THESIS, SO I'M STOCKING UP ON SUPPLIES.
AH, ARE YOU DOING A PHD?
I DID ONE WHEN I WAS YOUNG!
IN PALAEONTOLOGY!
BUT IT DIDN'T LEAD TO ANYTHING MUCH...
122.06

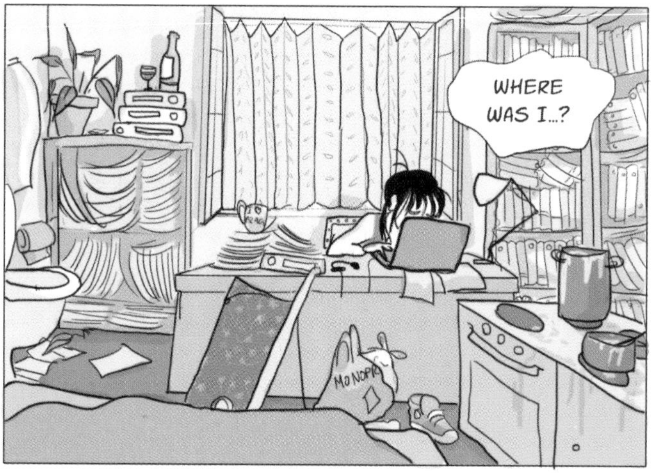
WHERE WAS I...?

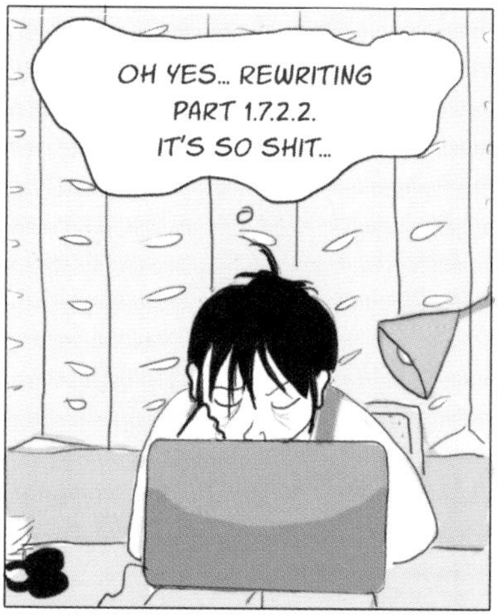
OH YES... REWRITING PART 1.7.2.2. IT'S SO SHIT...

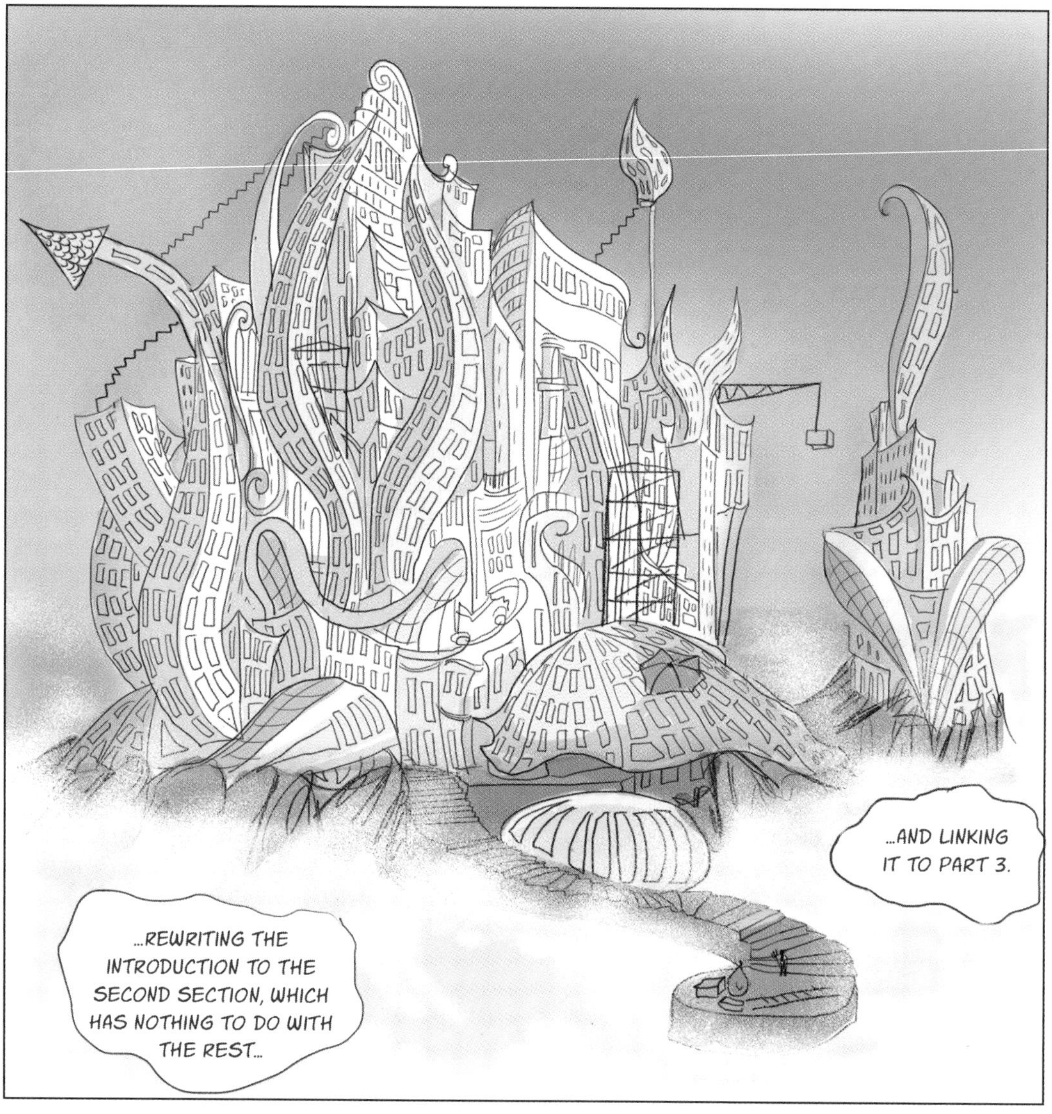
...REWRITING THE INTRODUCTION TO THE SECOND SECTION, WHICH HAS NOTHING TO DO WITH THE REST...
...AND LINKING IT TO PART 3.

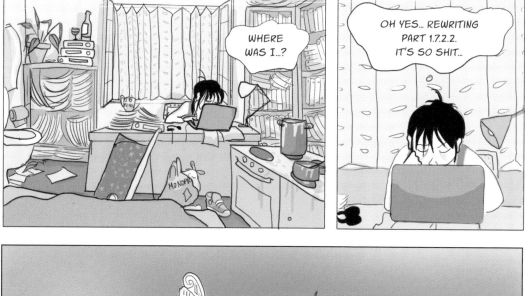

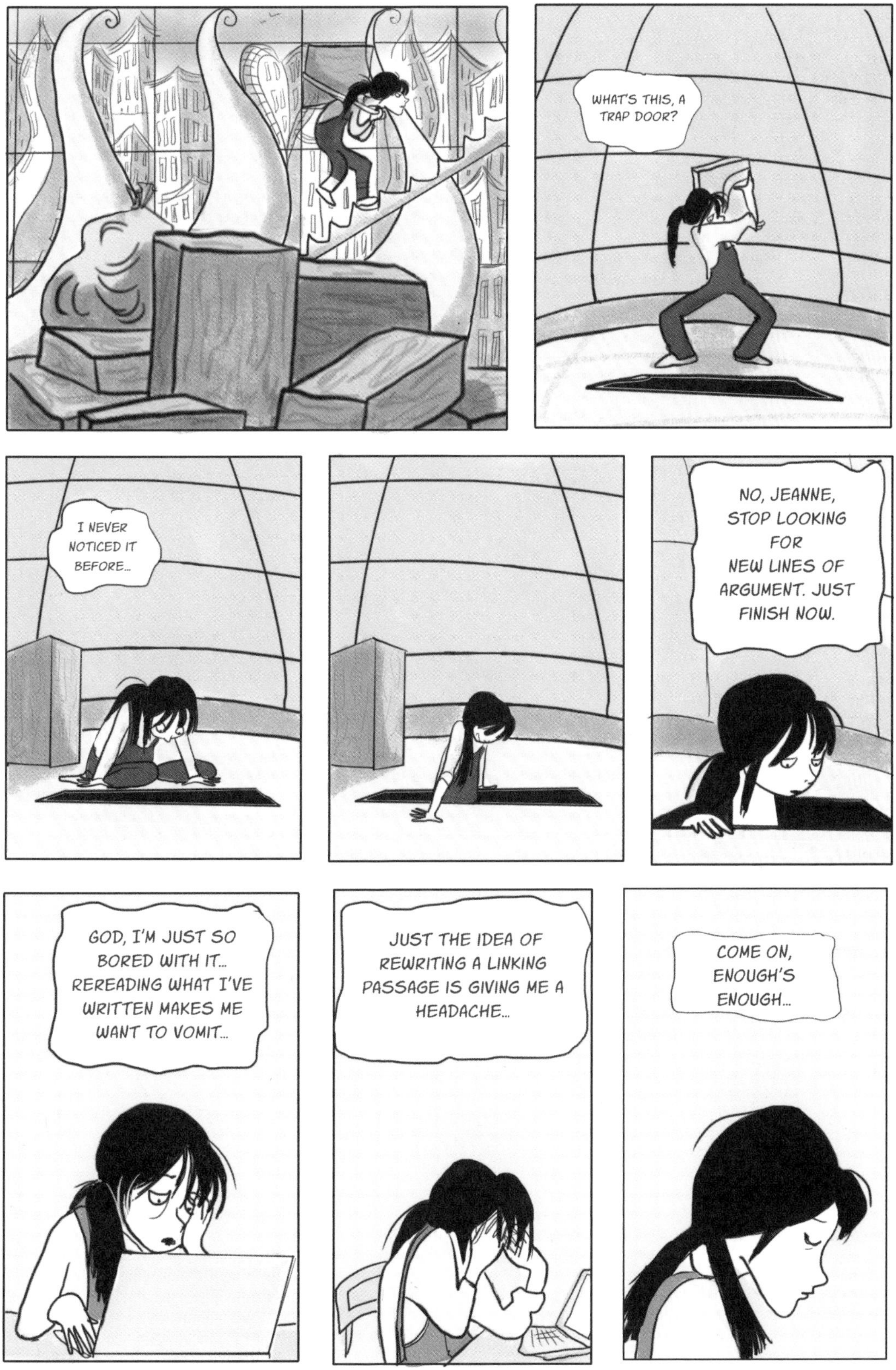
WHAT'S THIS, A TRAP DOOR?
I NEVER NOTICED IT BEFORE...
NO, JEANNE, STOP LOOKING FOR NEW LINES OF ARGUMENT. JUST FINISH NOW.
GOD, I'M JUST SO BORED WITH IT... REREADING WHAT I'VE WRITTEN MAKES ME WANT TO VOMIT...
JUST THE IDEA OF REWRITING A LINKING PASSAGE IS GIVING ME A HEADACHE...
COME ON, ENOUGH'S ENOUGH...

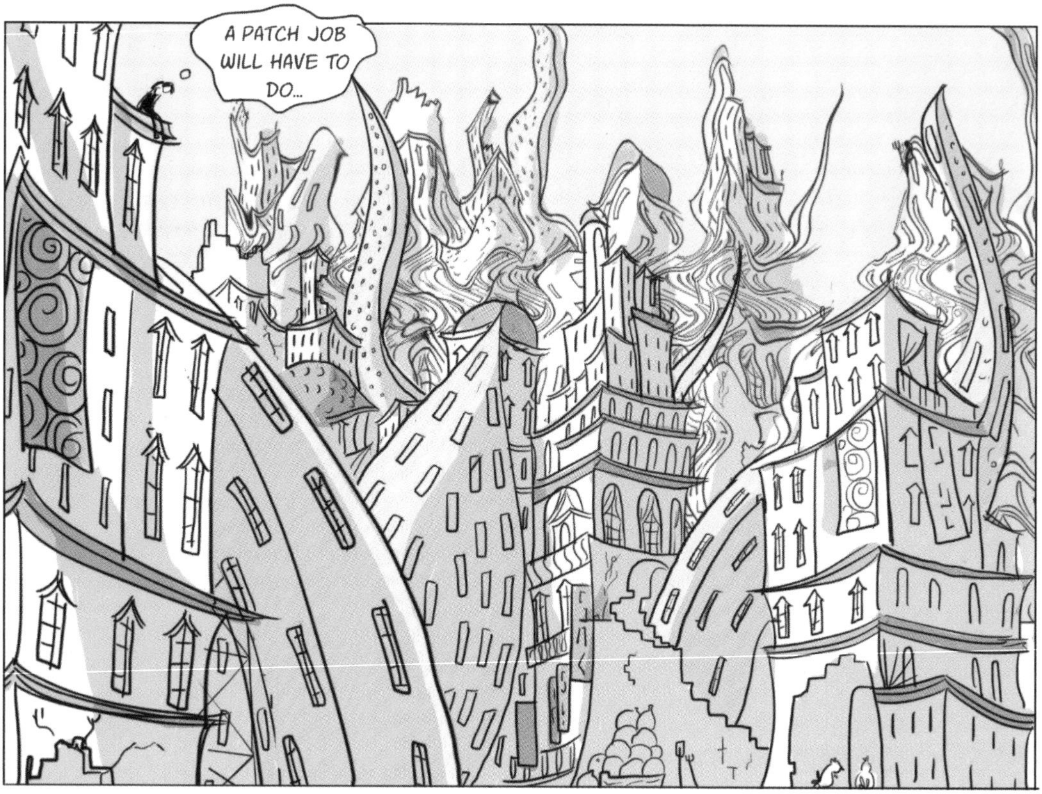
A PATCH JOB
WILL HAVE TO
DO...

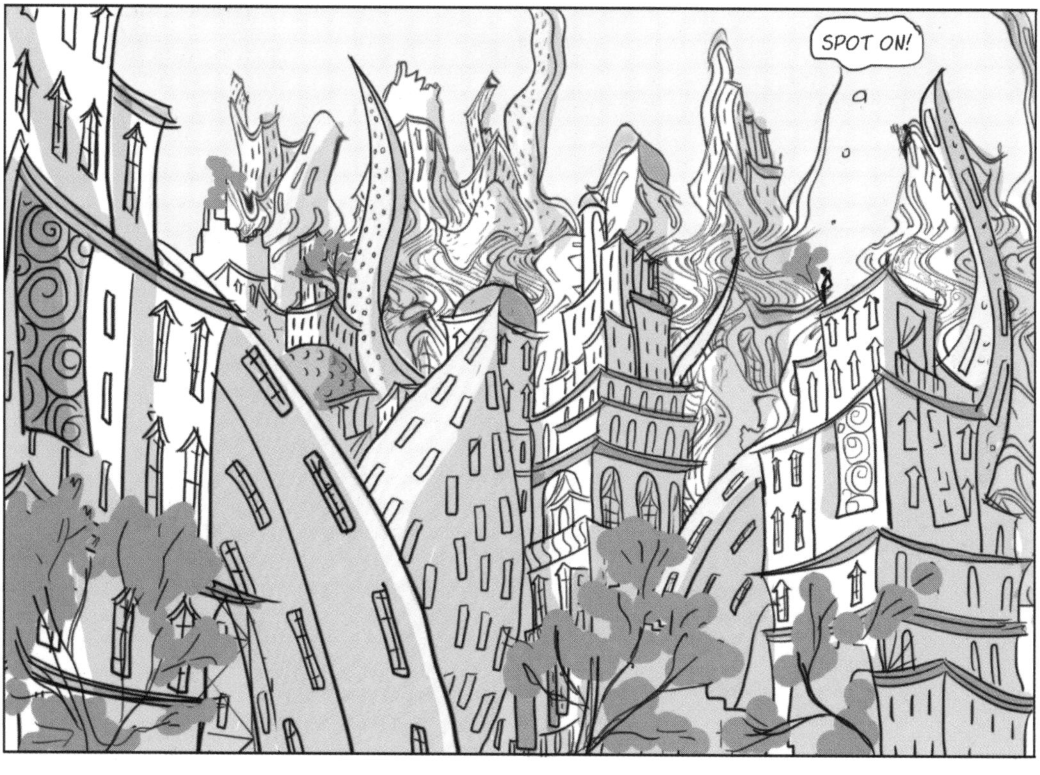
SPOT ON!

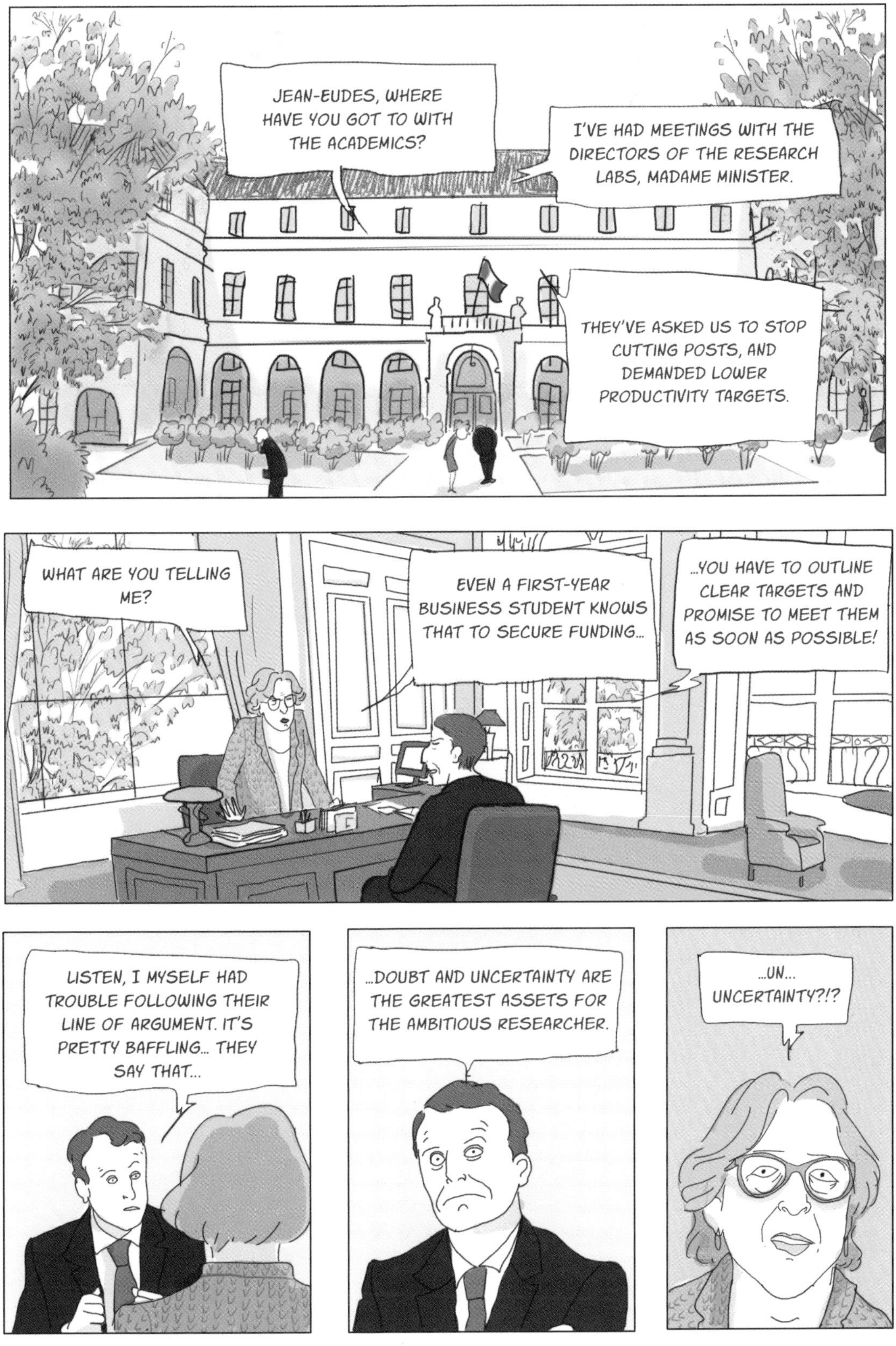
JEAN-EUDES, WHERE HAVE YOU GOT TO WITH THE ACADEMICS?
I'VE HAD MEETINGS WITH THE DIRECTORS OF THE RESEARCH LABS, MADAME MINISTER.
THEY'VE ASKED US TO STOP CUTTING POSTS, AND DEMANDED LOWER PRODUCTIVITY TARGETS.
WHAT ARE YOU TELLING ME?
EVEN A FIRST-YEAR BUSINESS STUDENT KNOWS THAT TO SECURE FUNDING...
...YOU HAVE TO OUTLINE CLEAR TARGETS AND PROMISE TO MEET THEM AS SOON AS POSSIBLE!
LISTEN, I MYSELF HAD TROUBLE FOLLOWING THEIR LINE OF ARGUMENT. IT'S PRETTY BAFFLING... THEY SAY THAT...
...DOUBT AND UNCERTAINTY ARE THE GREATEST ASSETS FOR THE AMBITIOUS RESEARCHER.
...UN... UNCERTAINTY?!?

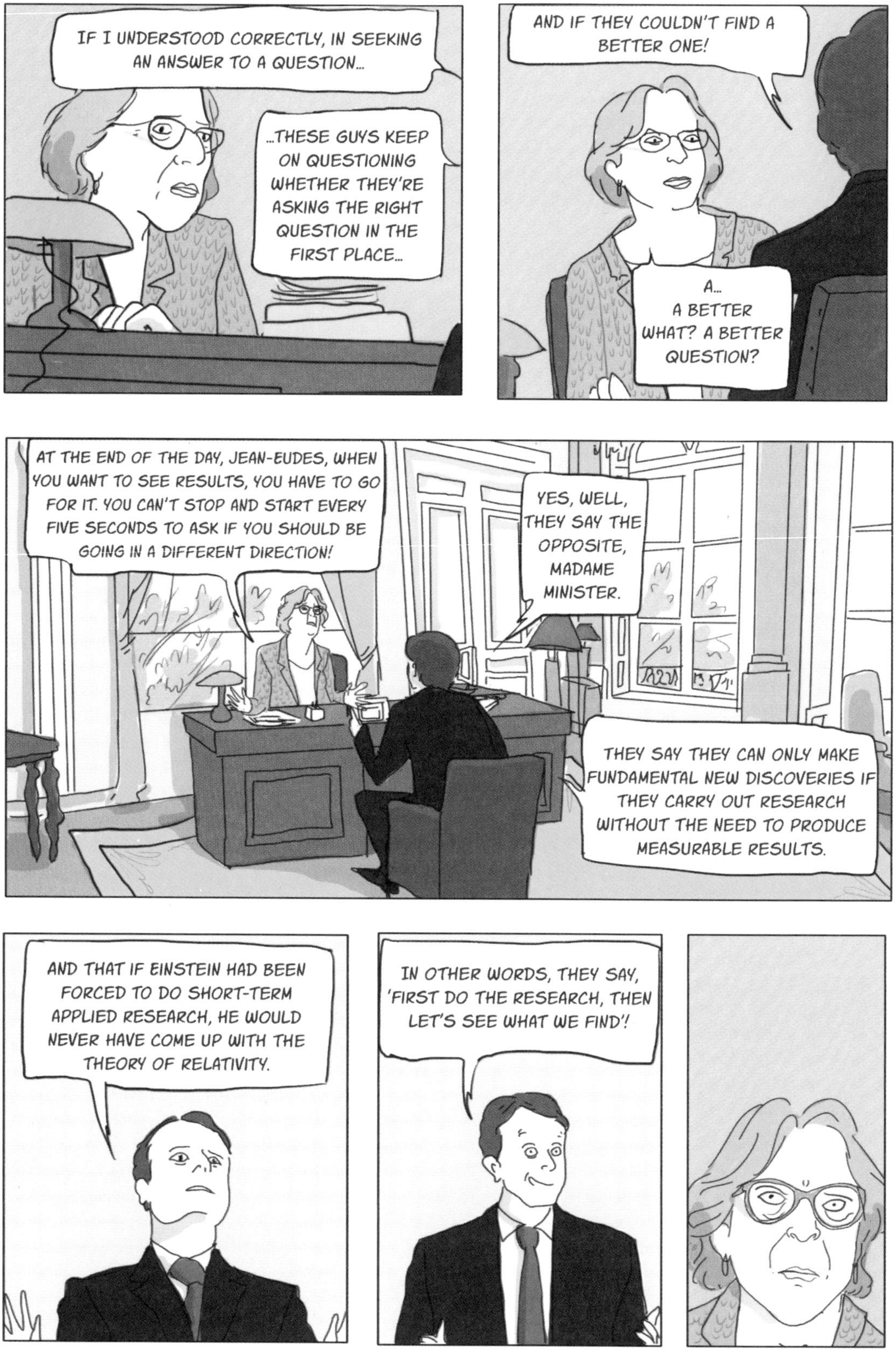
IF I UNDERSTOOD CORRECTLY, IN SEEKING AN ANSWER TO A QUESTION...
...THESE GUYS KEEP ON QUESTIONING WHETHER THEY'RE ASKING THE RIGHT QUESTION IN THE FIRST PLACE...
AND IF THEY COULDN'T FIND A BETTER ONE!
A... A BETTER WHAT? A BETTER QUESTION?
AT THE END OF THE DAY, JEAN-EUDES, WHEN YOU WANT TO SEE RESULTS, YOU HAVE TO GO FOR IT. YOU CAN'T STOP AND START EVERY FIVE SECONDS TO ASK IF YOU SHOULD BE GOING IN A DIFFERENT DIRECTION!
YES, WELL, THEY SAY THE OPPOSITE, MADAME MINISTER.
THEY SAY THEY CAN ONLY MAKE FUNDAMENTAL NEW DISCOVERIES IF THEY CARRY OUT RESEARCH WITHOUT THE NEED TO PRODUCE MEASURABLE RESULTS.
AND THAT IF EINSTEIN HAD BEEN FORCED TO DO SHORT-TERM APPLIED RESEARCH, HE WOULD NEVER HAVE COME UP WITH THE THEORY OF RELATIVITY.
IN OTHER WORDS, THEY SAY, 'FIRST DO THE RESEARCH, THEN LET'S SEE WHAT WE FIND'!

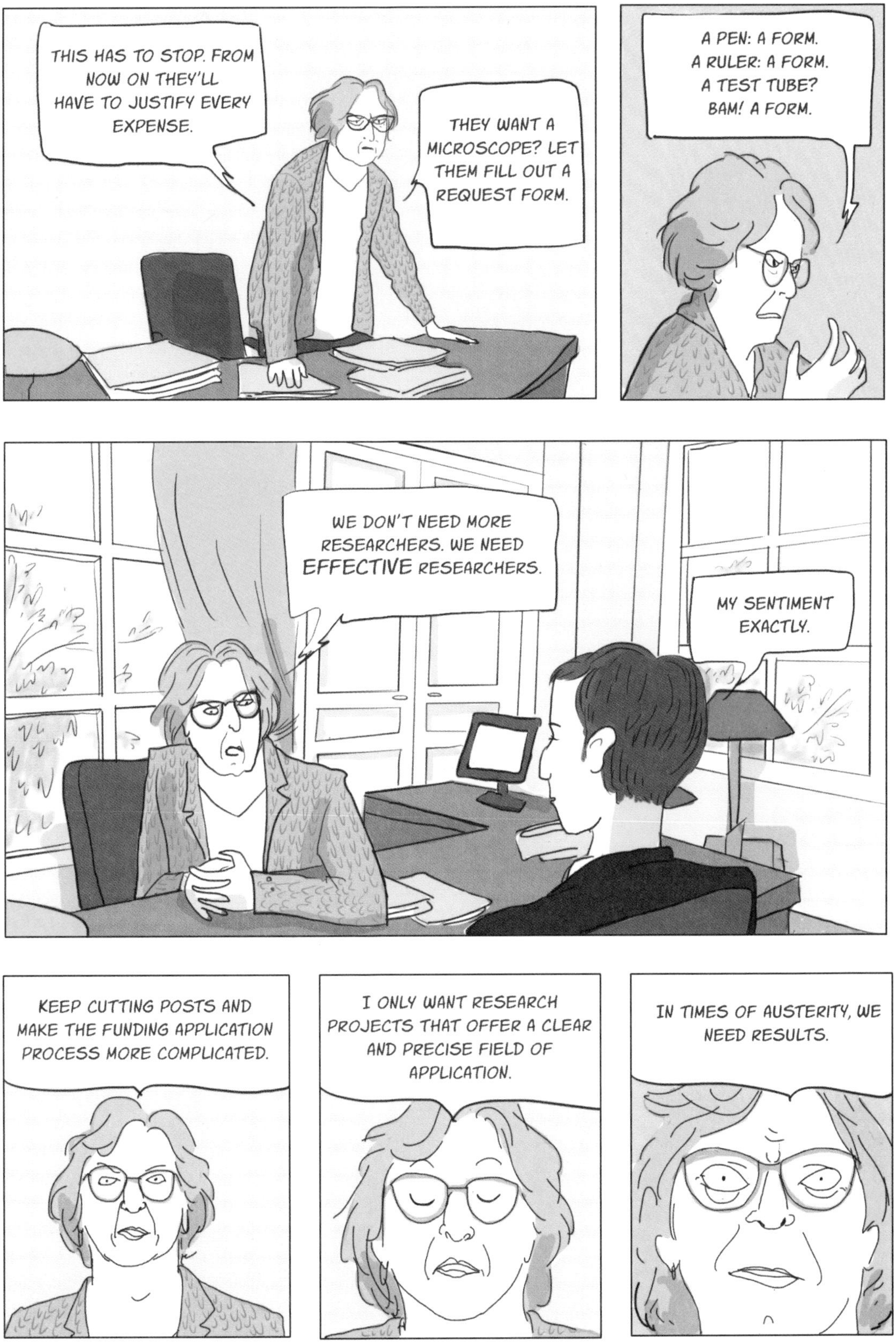
THIS HAS TO STOP. FROM NOW ON THEY'LL HAVE TO JUSTIFY EVERY EXPENSE.
THEY WANT A MICROSCOPE? LET THEM FILL OUT A REQUEST FORM.
A PEN: A FORM. A RULER: A FORM. A TEST TUBE? BAM! A FORM.
WE DON'T NEED MORE RESEARCHERS. WE NEED EFFECTIVE RESEARCHERS.
MY SENTIMENT EXACTLY.
KEEP CUTTING POSTS AND MAKE THE FUNDING APPLICATION PROCESS MORE COMPLICATED.
I ONLY WANT RESEARCH PROJECTS THAT OFFER A CLEAR AND PRECISE FIELD OF APPLICATION.
IN TIMES OF AUSTERITY, WE NEED RESULTS.

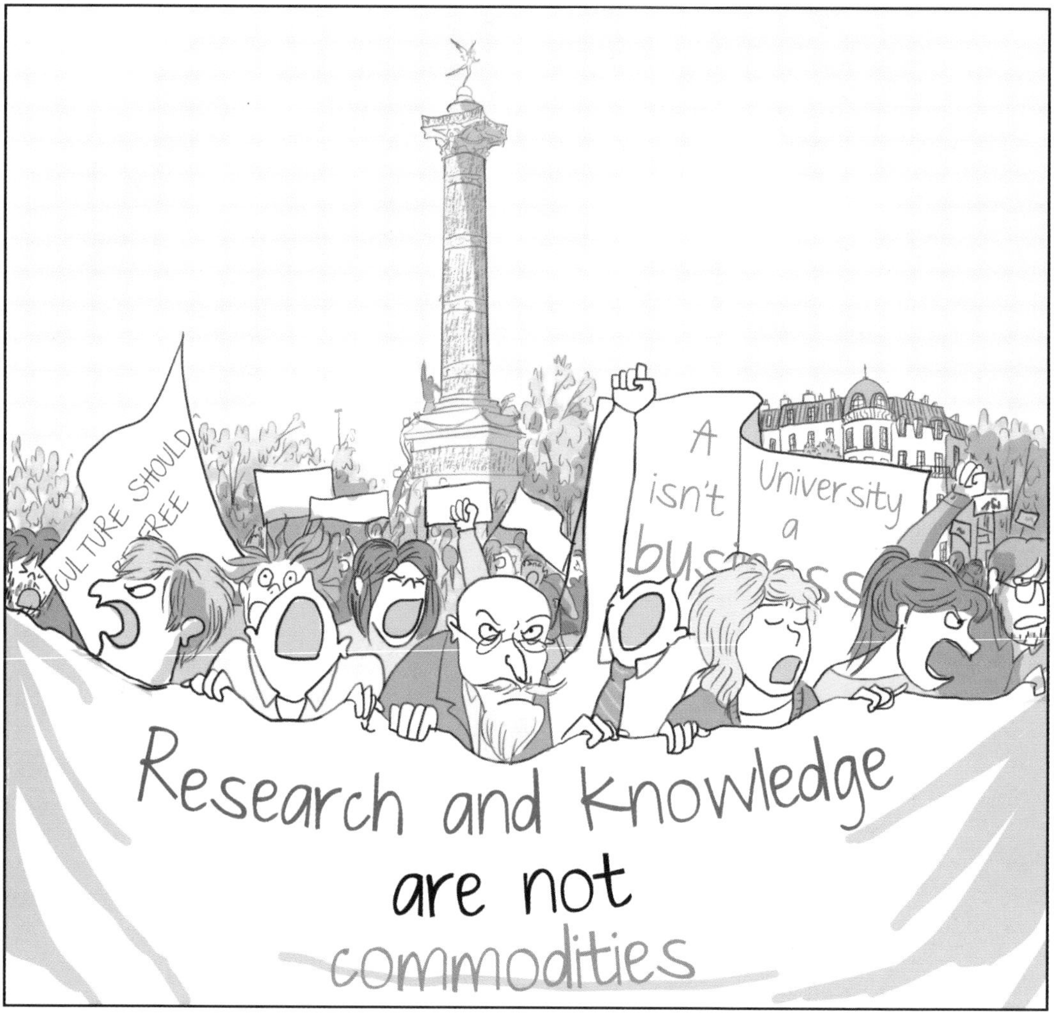
CULTURE SHOULD
FREE
A
isn't
University
a
bus ss
Research and Knowledge
are not
commodities

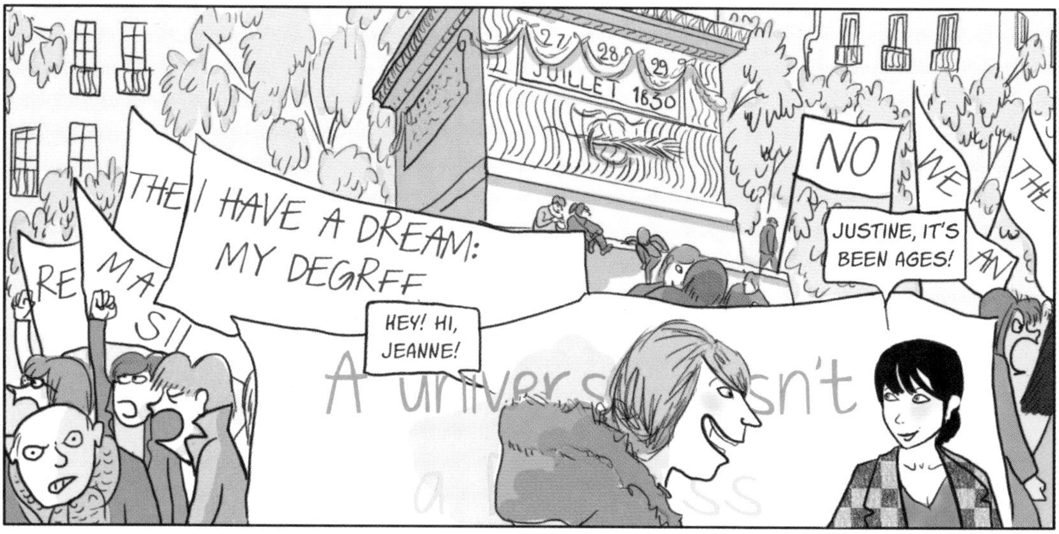
27 28 29
JUILLET 1830
THE
I HAVE A DREAM:
MY DEGREE
RE
MA
SI
NO
WE
AN
THE
HEY! HI, JEANNE!
JUSTINE, IT'S BEEN AGES!
A univers sn't
a ss

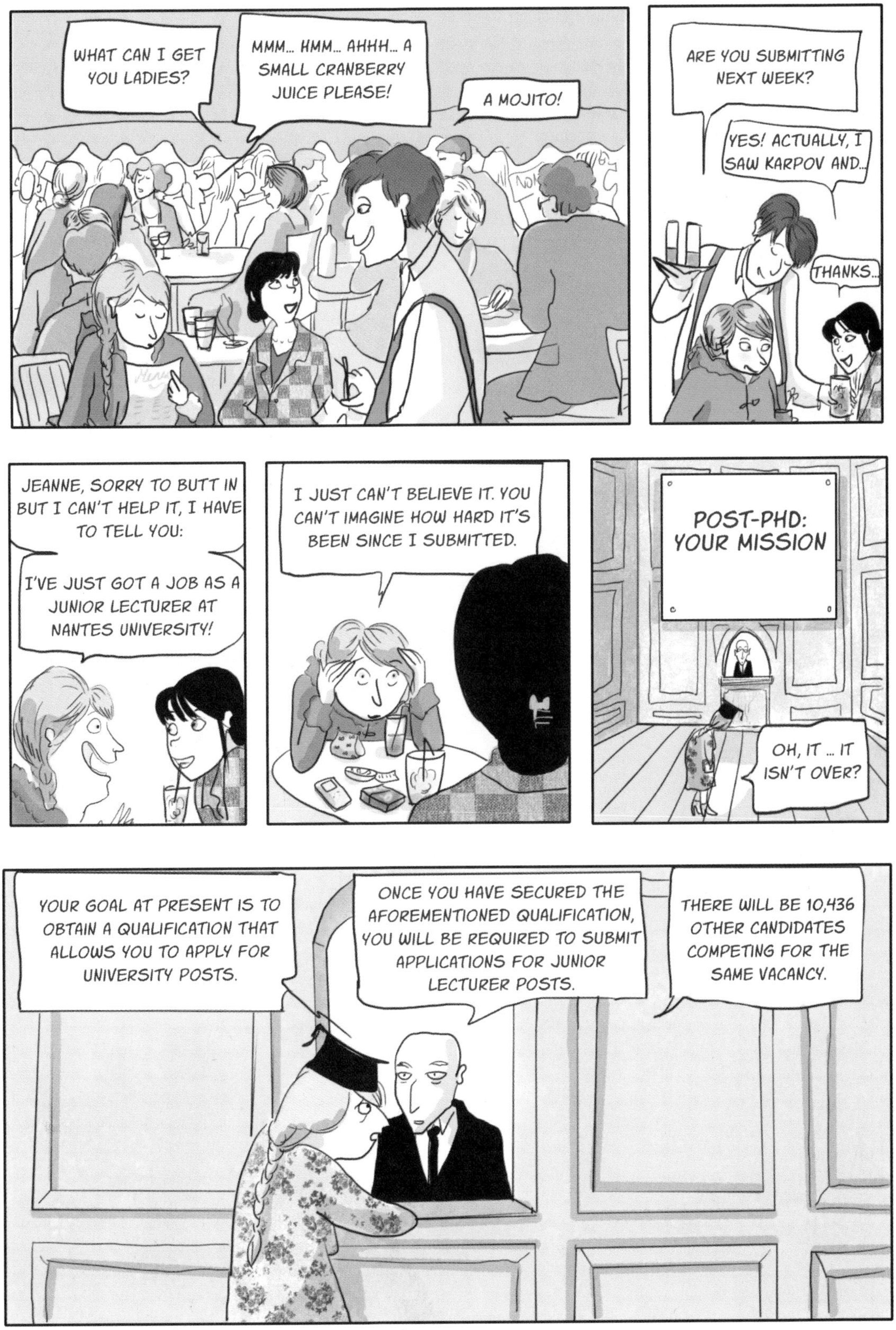
WHAT CAN I GET YOU LADIES?
MMM... HMM... AHHH... A SMALL CRANBERRY JUICE PLEASE!
A MOJITO!
ARE YOU SUBMITTING NEXT WEEK?
YES! ACTUALLY, I SAW KARPOV AND...
THANKS...
JEANNE, SORRY TO BUTT IN BUT I CAN'T HELP IT, I HAVE TO TELL YOU:
I'VE JUST GOT A JOB AS A JUNIOR LECTURER AT NANTES UNIVERSITY!
I JUST CAN'T BELIEVE IT. YOU CAN'T IMAGINE HOW HARD IT'S BEEN SINCE I SUBMITTED.
POST-PHD: YOUR MISSION
OH, IT ... IT ISN'T OVER?
YOUR GOAL AT PRESENT IS TO OBTAIN A QUALIFICATION THAT ALLOWS YOU TO APPLY FOR UNIVERSITY POSTS.
ONCE YOU HAVE SECURED THE AFOREMENTIONED QUALIFICATION, YOU WILL BE REQUIRED TO SUBMIT APPLICATIONS FOR JUNIOR LECTURER POSTS.
THERE WILL BE 10,436 OTHER CANDIDATES COMPETING FOR THE SAME VACANCY.

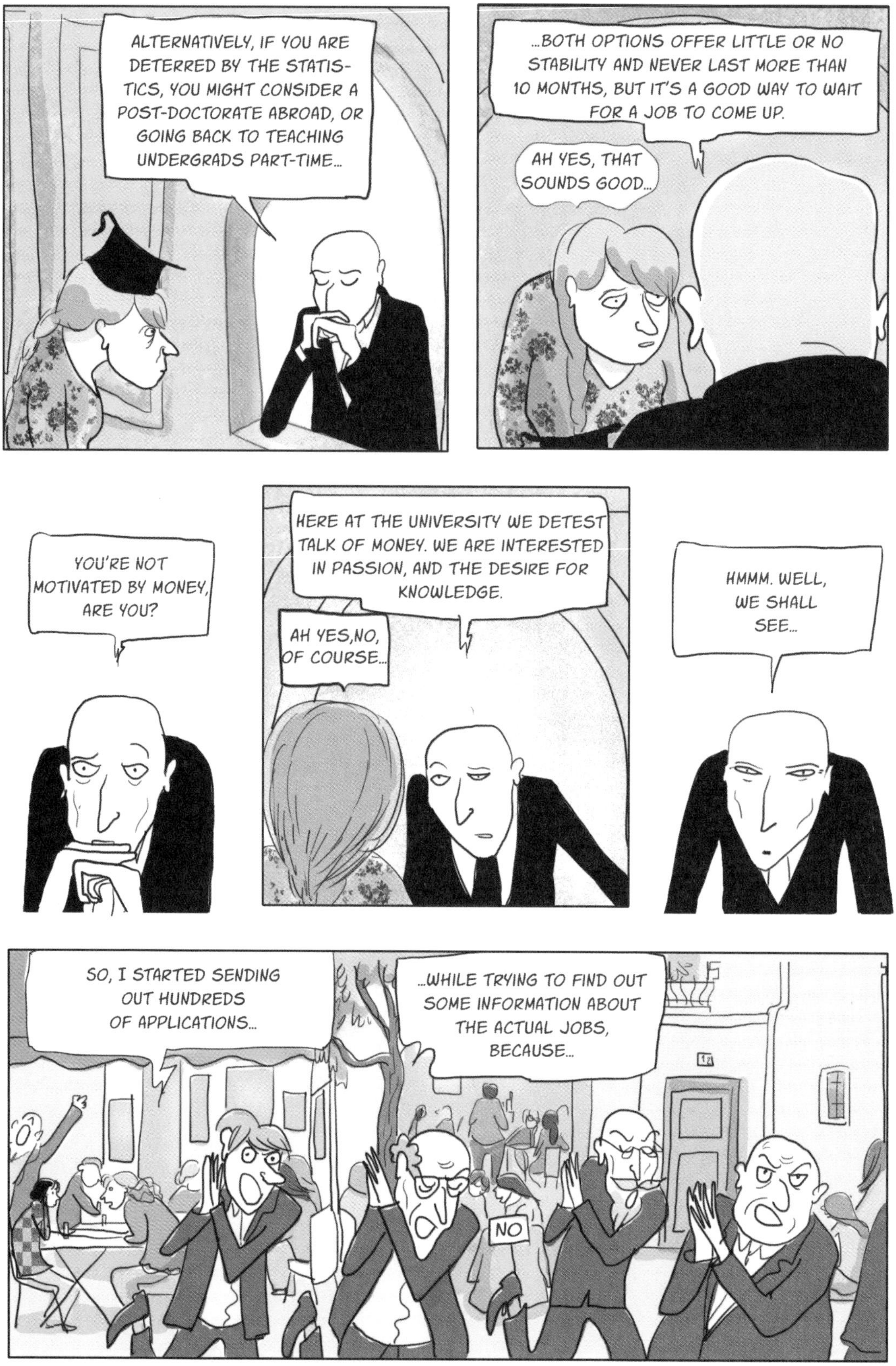
ALTERNATIVELY, IF YOU ARE DETERRED BY THE STATISTICS, YOU MIGHT CONSIDER A POST-DOCTORATE ABROAD, OR GOING BACK TO TEACHING UNDERGRADS PART-TIME...
...BOTH OPTIONS OFFER LITTLE OR NO STABILITY AND NEVER LAST MORE THAN 10 MONTHS, BUT IT'S A GOOD WAY TO WAIT FOR A JOB TO COME UP.
AH YES, THAT SOUNDS GOOD...
YOU'RE NOT MOTIVATED BY MONEY, ARE YOU?
HERE AT THE UNIVERSITY WE DETEST TALK OF MONEY. WE ARE INTERESTED IN PASSION, AND THE DESIRE FOR KNOWLEDGE.
AH YES,NO, OF COURSE...
HMMM. WELL, WE SHALL SEE...
SO, I STARTED SENDING OUT HUNDREDS OF APPLICATIONS...
...WHILE TRYING TO FIND OUT SOME INFORMATION ABOUT THE ACTUAL JOBS, BECAUSE...
NO

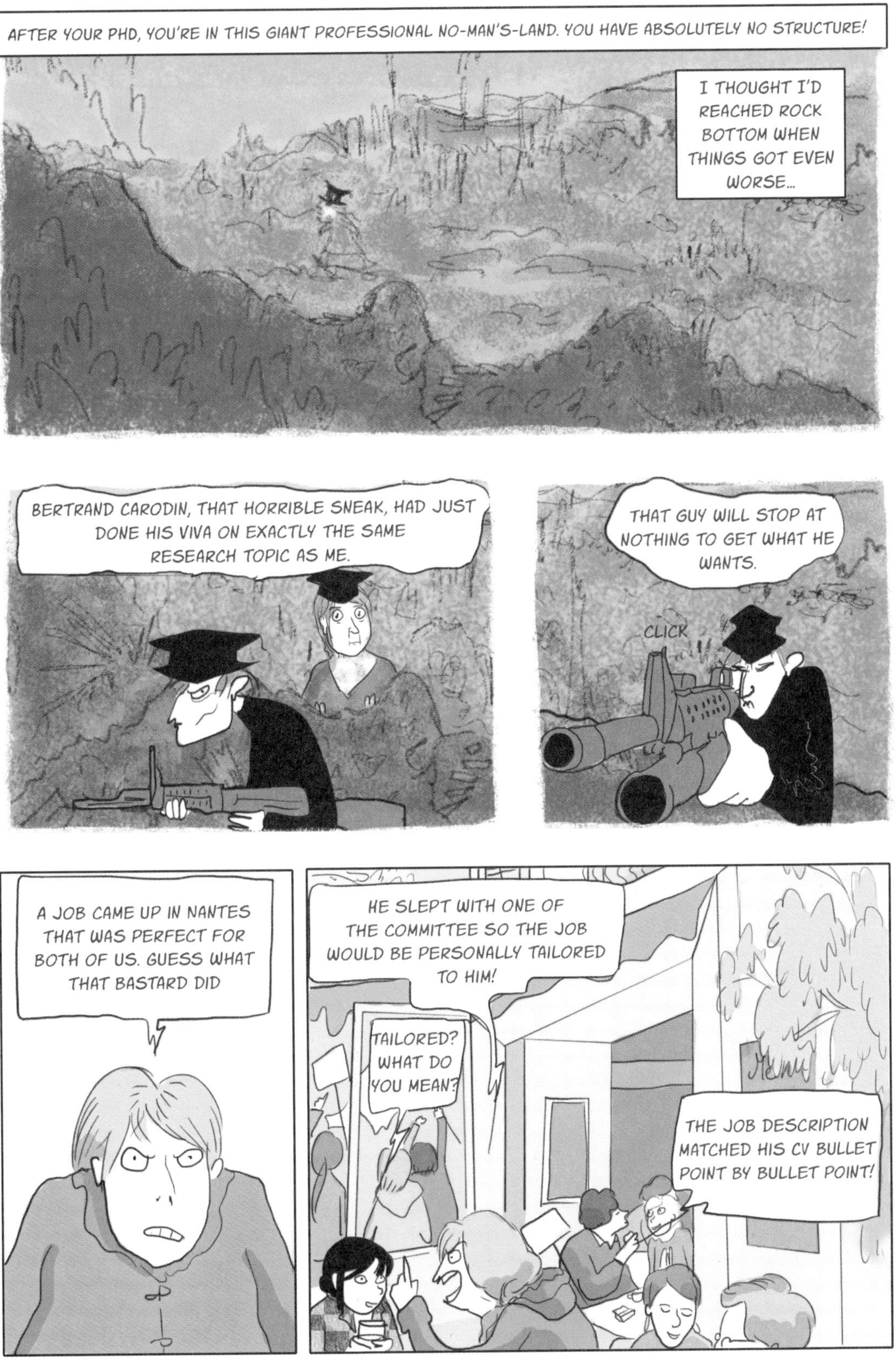
AFTER YOUR PHD, YOU'RE IN THIS GIANT PROFESSIONAL NO-MAN'S-LAND. YOU HAVE ABSOLUTELY NO STRUCTURE!
I THOUGHT I'D REACHED ROCK BOTTOM WHEN THINGS GOT EVEN WORSE...
BERTRAND CARODIN, THAT HORRIBLE SNEAK, HAD JUST DONE HIS VIVA ON EXACTLY THE SAME RESEARCH TOPIC AS ME.
THAT GUY WILL STOP AT NOTHING TO GET WHAT HE WANTS.
CLICK
A JOB CAME UP IN NANTES THAT WAS PERFECT FOR BOTH OF US. GUESS WHAT THAT BASTARD DID
HE SLEPT WITH ONE OF THE COMMITTEE SO THE JOB WOULD BE PERSONALLY TAILORED TO HIM!
TAILORED? WHAT DO YOU MEAN?
THE JOB DESCRIPTION MATCHED HIS CV BULLET POINT BY BULLET POINT!

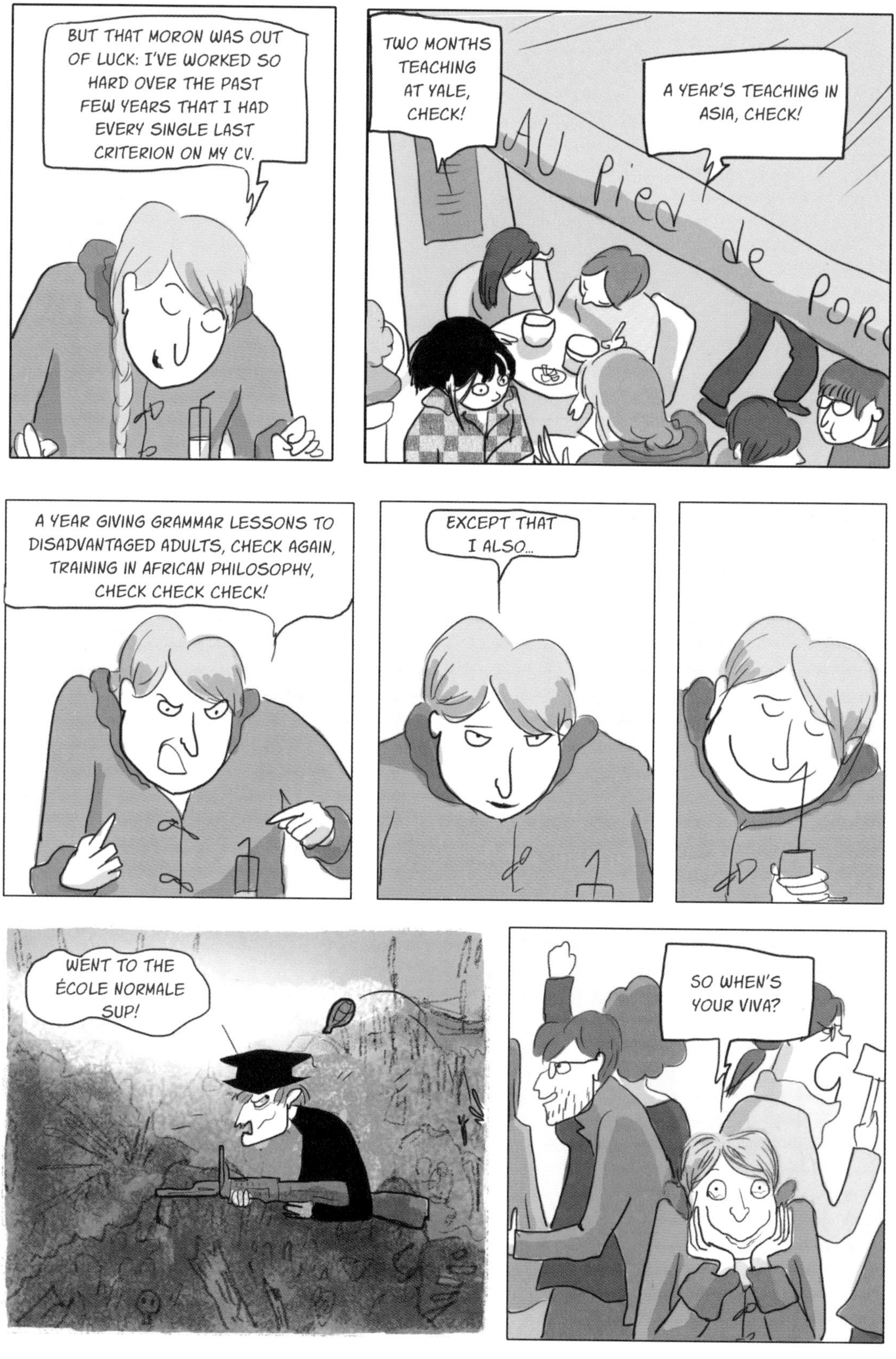
BUT THAT MORON WAS OUT OF LUCK: I'VE WORKED SO HARD OVER THE PAST FEW YEARS THAT I HAD EVERY SINGLE LAST CRITERION ON MY CV.
TWO MONTHS TEACHING AT YALE, CHECK!
A YEAR'S TEACHING IN ASIA, CHECK!
AU Pied de Por
A YEAR GIVING GRAMMAR LESSONS TO DISADVANTAGED ADULTS, CHECK AGAIN, TRAINING IN AFRICAN PHILOSOPHY, CHECK CHECK CHECK!
EXCEPT THAT I ALSO...
WENT TO THE ÉCOLE NORMALE SUP!
SO WHEN'S YOUR VIVA?

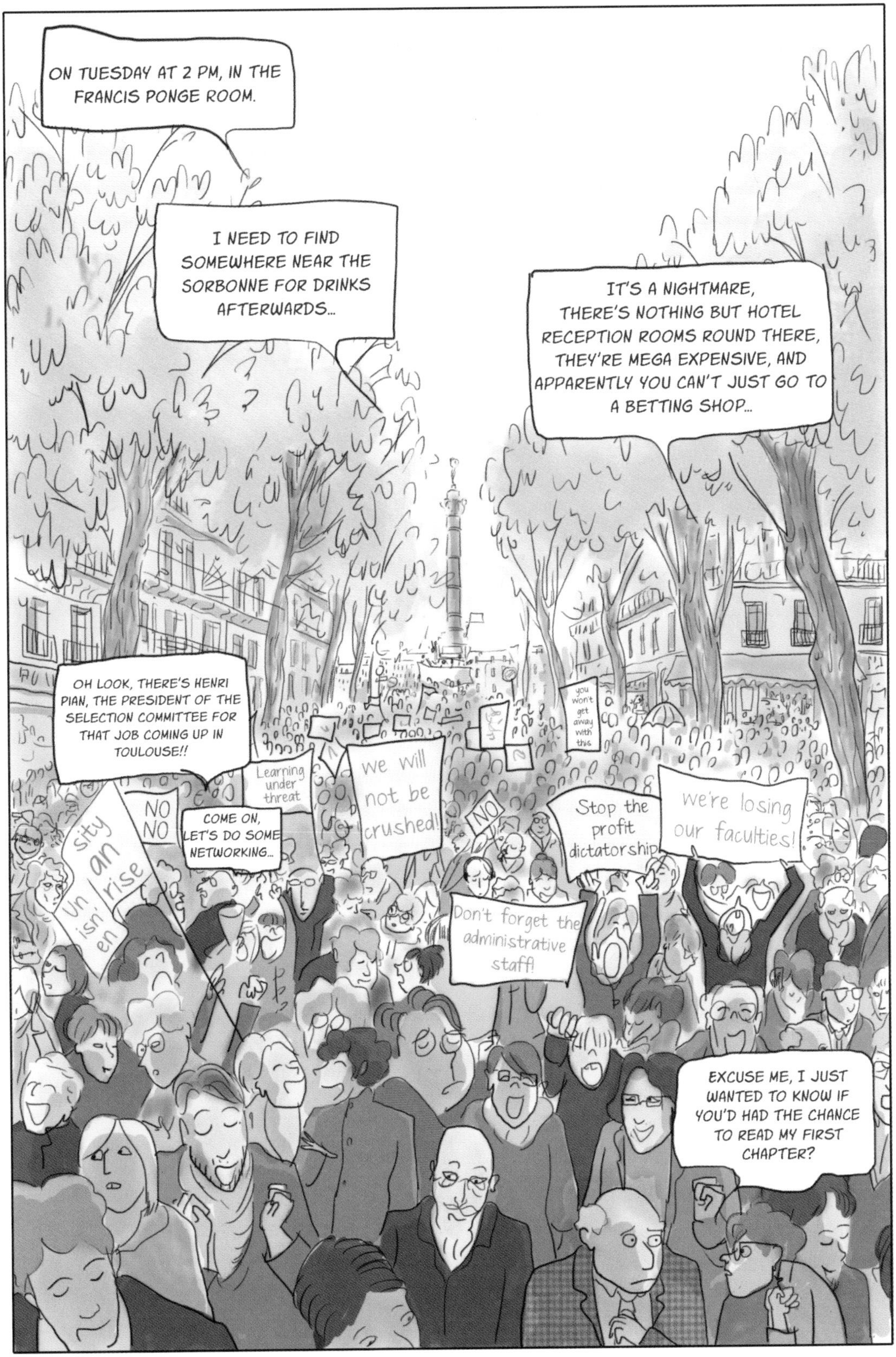
ON TUESDAY AT 2 PM, IN THE FRANCIS PONGE ROOM.
I NEED TO FIND SOMEWHERE NEAR THE SORBONNE FOR DRINKS AFTERWARDS...
IT'S A NIGHTMARE, THERE'S NOTHING BUT HOTEL RECEPTION ROOMS ROUND THERE, THEY'RE MEGA EXPENSIVE, AND APPARENTLY YOU CAN'T JUST GO TO A BETTING SHOP...
OH LOOK, THERE'S HENRI PIAN, THE PRESIDENT OF THE SELECTION COMMITTEE FOR THAT JOB COMING UP IN TOULOUSE!!
COME ON, LET'S DO SOME NETWORKING...
you won't get away with this
Learning under threat
we will not be crushed!
NO NO
NO
Stop the profit dictatorship
we're losing our faculties!
Don't forget the administrative staff!
EXCUSE ME, I JUST WANTED TO KNOW IF YOU'D HAD THE CHANCE TO READ MY FIRST CHAPTER?

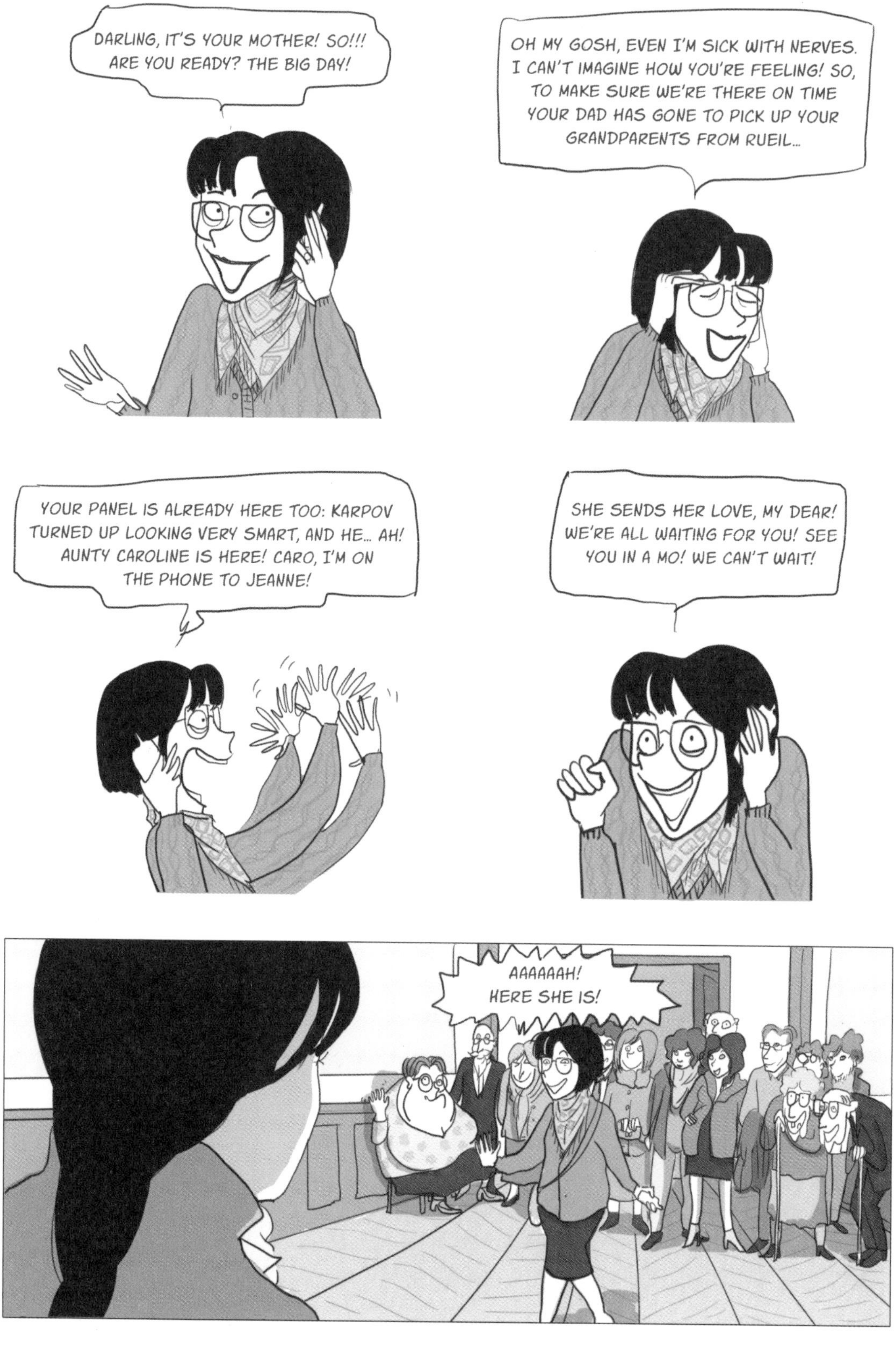
DARLING, IT'S YOUR MOTHER! SO!!! ARE YOU READY? THE BIG DAY!
OH MY GOSH, EVEN I'M SICK WITH NERVES. I CAN'T IMAGINE HOW YOU'RE FEELING! SO, TO MAKE SURE WE'RE THERE ON TIME YOUR DAD HAS GONE TO PICK UP YOUR GRANDPARENTS FROM RUEIL...
YOUR PANEL IS ALREADY HERE TOO: KARPOV TURNED UP LOOKING VERY SMART, AND HE... AH! AUNTY CAROLINE IS HERE! CARO, I'M ON THE PHONE TO JEANNE!
SHE SENDS HER LOVE, MY DEAR! WE'RE ALL WAITING FOR YOU! SEE YOU IN A MO! WE CAN'T WAIT!
AAAAAAH! HERE SHE IS!

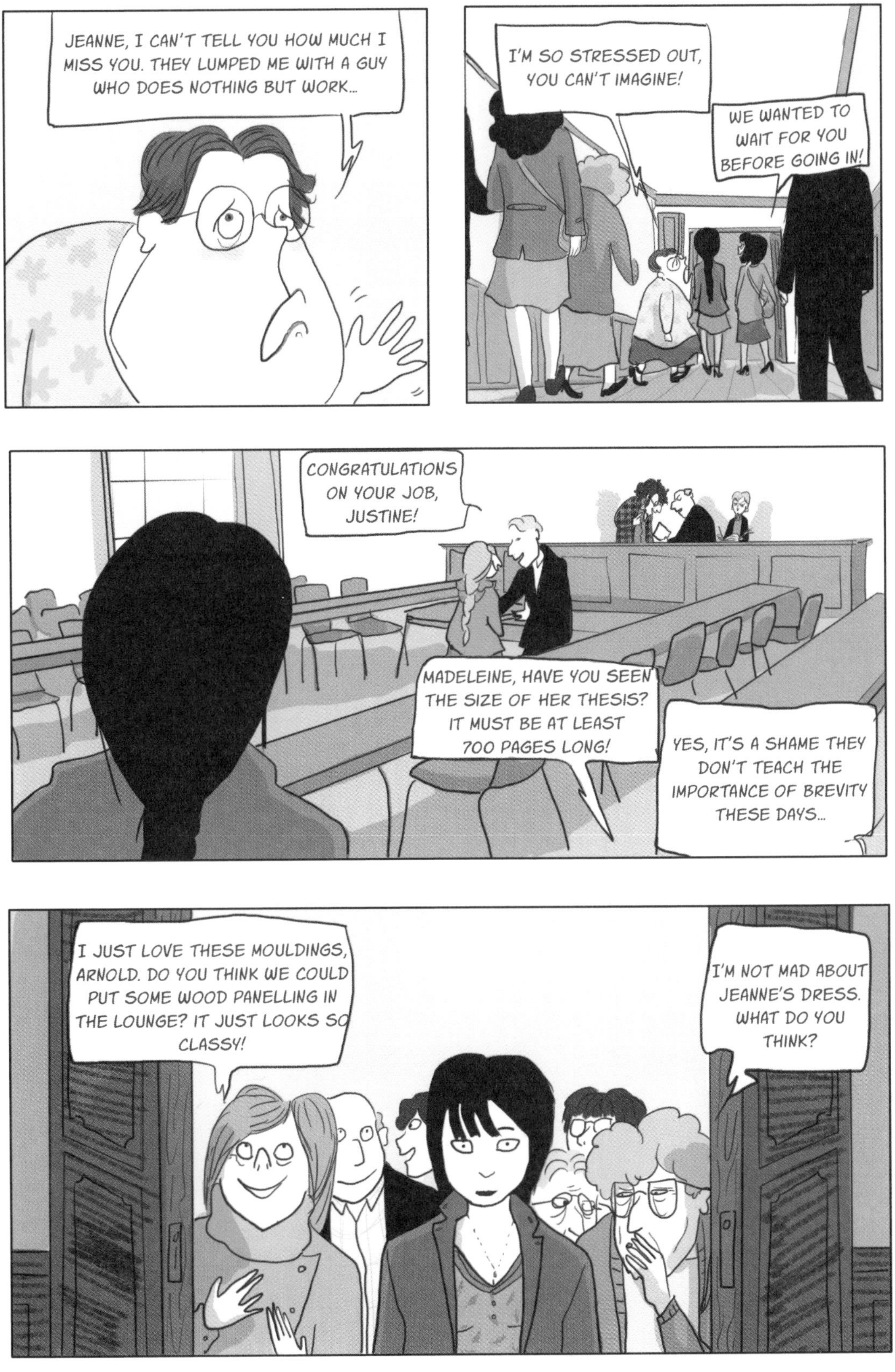
JEANNE, I CAN'T TELL YOU HOW MUCH I MISS YOU. THEY LUMPED ME WITH A GUY WHO DOES NOTHING BUT WORK...
I'M SO STRESSED OUT, YOU CAN'T IMAGINE!
WE WANTED TO WAIT FOR YOU BEFORE GOING IN!
CONGRATULATIONS ON YOUR JOB, JUSTINE!
MADELEINE, HAVE YOU SEEN THE SIZE OF HER THESIS? IT MUST BE AT LEAST 700 PAGES LONG!
YES, IT'S A SHAME THEY DON'T TEACH THE IMPORTANCE OF BREVITY THESE DAYS...
I JUST LOVE THESE MOULDINGS, ARNOLD. DO YOU THINK WE COULD PUT SOME WOOD PANELLING IN THE LOUNGE? IT JUST LOOKS SO CLASSY!
I'M NOT MAD ABOUT JEANNE'S DRESS. WHAT DO YOU THINK?

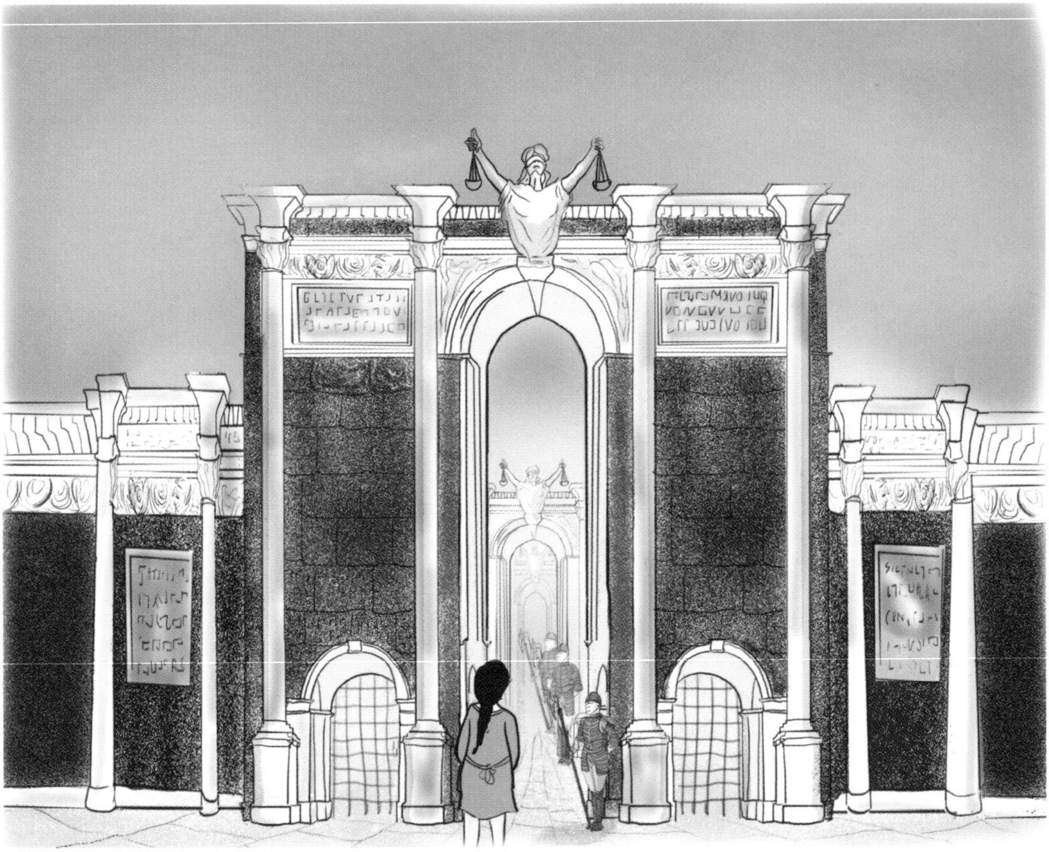

'HOW, IN THIS SHORT LIFE, SO SWIFTLY OVER, ACCOMPANIED BY AN ENDLESS, IMPATIENT WHIRRING, CAN YOU POSSIBLY GO DOWN A STAIRCASE? IT'S IMPOSSIBLE! THE TIME YOU HAVE BEEN GRANTED IS SO BRIEF...

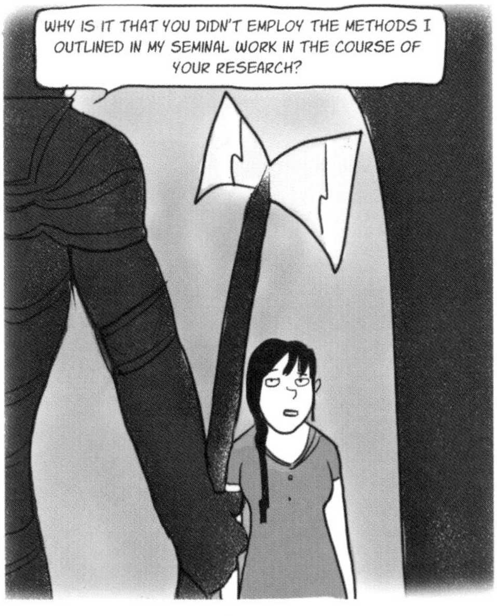
WHY IS IT THAT YOU DIDN'T EMPLOY THE METHODS I OUTLINED IN MY SEMINAL WORK IN THE COURSE OF YOUR RESEARCH?

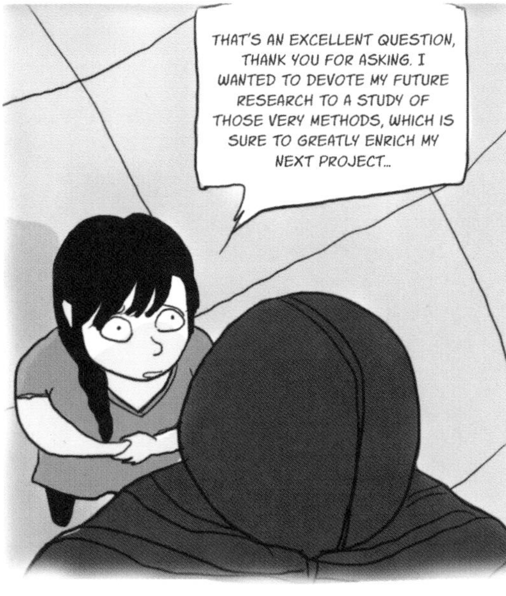
THAT'S AN EXCELLENT QUESTION, THANK YOU FOR ASKING. I WANTED TO DEVOTE MY FUTURE RESEARCH TO A STUDY OF THOSE VERY METHODS, WHICH IS SURE TO GREATLY ENRICH MY NEXT PROJECT...

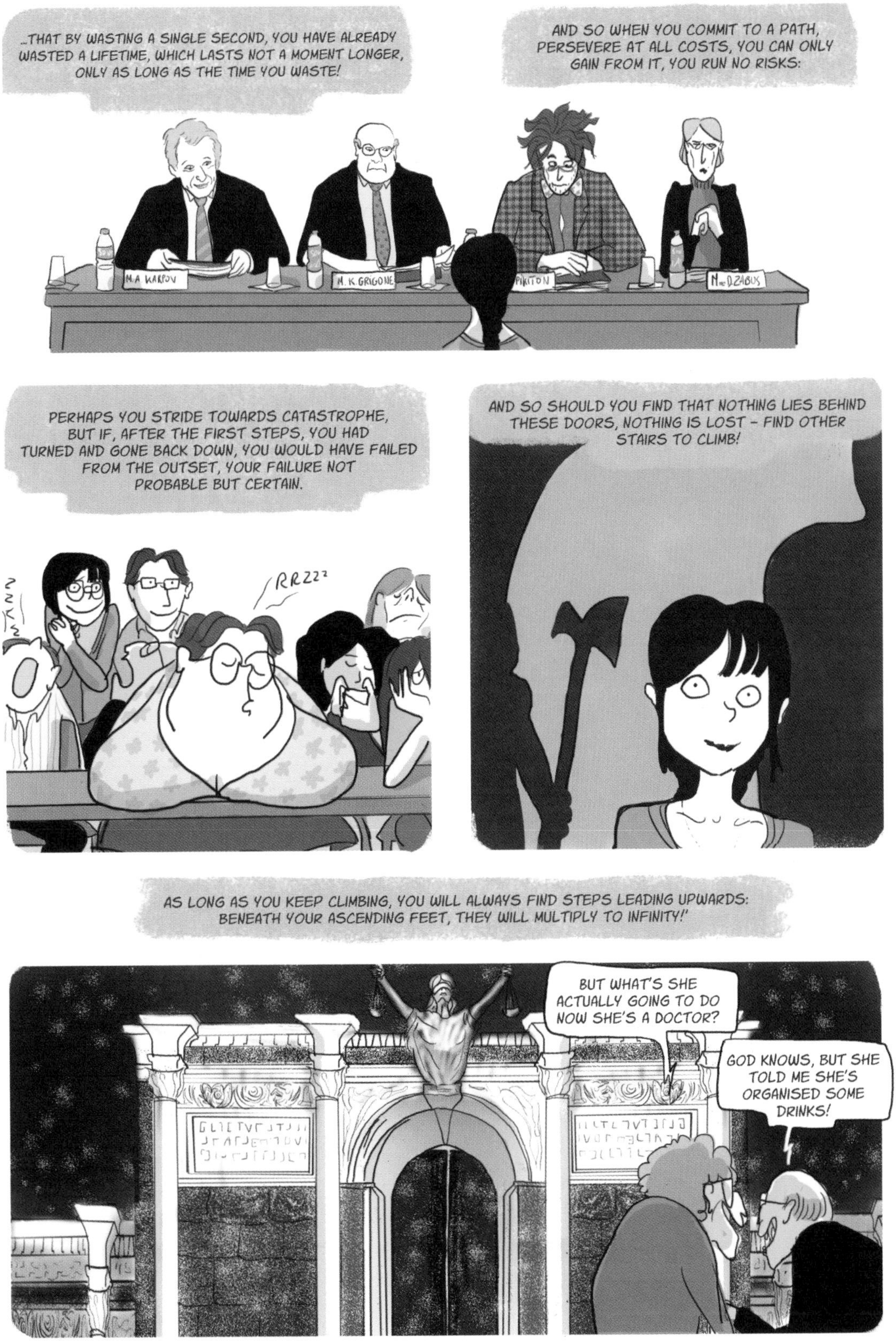
..THAT BY WASTING A SINGLE SECOND, YOU HAVE ALREADY WASTED A LIFETIME, WHICH LASTS NOT A MOMENT LONGER, ONLY AS LONG AS THE TIME YOU WASTE!
AND SO WHEN YOU COMMIT TO A PATH, PERSEVERE AT ALL COSTS, YOU CAN ONLY GAIN FROM IT, YOU RUN NO RISKS:
M.A KARPOV
M. K. GRIGONE
PIKITON
PERHAPS YOU STRIDE TOWARDS CATASTROPHE, BUT IF, AFTER THE FIRST STEPS, YOU HAD TURNED AND GONE BACK DOWN, YOU WOULD HAVE FAILED FROM THE OUTSET, YOUR FAILURE NOT PROBABLE BUT CERTAIN.
RRZZZ
AND SO SHOULD YOU FIND THAT NOTHING LIES BEHIND THESE DOORS, NOTHING IS LOST – FIND OTHER STAIRS TO CLIMB!
AS LONG AS YOU KEEP CLIMBING, YOU WILL ALWAYS FIND STEPS LEADING UPWARDS: BENEATH YOUR ASCENDING FEET, THEY WILL MULTIPLY TO INFINITY!'
BUT WHAT'S SHE ACTUALLY GOING TO DO NOW SHE'S A DOCTOR?
GOD KNOWS, BUT SHE TOLD ME SHE'S ORGANISED SOME DRINKS!